Brendan DuBois is the author of *Resurrection Day*, the Lewis Cole mysteries and numerous short stories, which have earned him a Shamus Award and three Edgar Award nominations. He lives in Exeter, New Hampshire.

You can visit the author's webiste at:
www.brendandubois.com

D0860619

Also by Brendan DuBois

RESURRECTION DAY
SIX DAYS
BETRAYED
DEAD OF NIGHT

Final Winter

Brendan DuBois

sphere

SPHERE

First published in Great Britain by Time Warner Books in 2006
This paperback edition published by Sphere in 2012

Copyright © 2006 by Brendan DuBois

The moral right of the author has been asserted.

*All characters and events in this publication, other than those
clearly in the public domain, are fictitious and any resemblance
to real persons, living or dead, is purely coincidental.*

All rights reserved.
No part of this publication may be reproduced, stored in a
retrieval system, or transmitted, in any form or by any means, without
the prior permission in writing of the publisher, nor be otherwise circulated
in any form of binding or cover other than that in which it is published
and without a similar condition including this condition being
imposed on the subsequent purchaser.

A CIP catalogue record for this book
is available from the British Library.

ISBN 978-0-7515-4801-3

Typeset in Goudy by M Rules
Printed and bound by in Great Britain by
Clays Ltd, St Ives plc

Papers used by Sphere are from well-managed forests
and other responsible sources.

MIX
Paper from
responsible sources
FSC® C104740

Sphere
An imprint of
Little, Brown Book Group
100 Victoria Embankment
London EC4Y 0DY

An Hachette UK Company
www.hachette.co.uk

www.littlebrown.co.uk

For Hilary Hale, with much thanks and affection

Acknowledgements

This novel literally could not have been written without the technical knowledge, advice and suggestions from David Barnes, neighbor, friend, pilot and veteran Navy aviator. He and his family have my deep thanks and appreciation. I would also like to express my appreciation to Steve Shular, Public Affairs Officer of the Shelby (Tennessee) County Sheriff's Department. Any errors contained within this work are those of the author alone. Thanks, also, to my agent Liza Dawson, and my British agent, Antony Topping. Hilary Hale and Louise Davies of Time Warner UK made publishing this novel a joy, and I would like to acknowledge the superb copyediting job performed by Nick Austin. My wife Mona also made this novel possible through her constant encouragement and sharp editorial eye. And a special thanks to the volunteers of the New England English Springer Spaniel Rescue League (www.essrescue.org) for the added joy of Tucker to our household.

'Quis custodiet ipsos custodes?'

> – Roman satirist Juvenal
> (Decimus Junius Juvenalis) circa AD 100

'We have met the enemy and he is us!'

> – American philosopher Pogo circa AD 1970

PART ONE

CHAPTER ONE

The meeting took place at a time when the wreckage of the World Trade Center was still being doused with water, portions of the Pentagon's south wall were still collapsing, and bits of metal from what had once been a Boeing 767 passenger jet were being dug out of the ground in a rural area of Pennsylvania. It was held in a small, carpeted room with wood paneling, a badly polished conference-room table, and framed Audubon Society bird prints on the wall. The dull-colored furniture and decorations announced that the room had last been serviced during the Johnson Administration; the smell and general dampness in its interior also announced that, despite its looks, the room was in a concrete cube, one hundred feet beneath the ground. The air smelled of soot and sweat and defeat.

Three men were at the meeting. In front of each of them was a fresh yellow legal pad, sharpened pencils, and uncapped black-ink Bic pens. The CIA man who had called the meeting looked at the other two participants: a heavyset man from the FBI who had not shaved in at least two days, and a taller, thinner man, whose blue Oxford shirt had one collar flap unbuttoned and who worked for the National Security Agency. Both men's eyes were red-rimmed and watery, unfocused a bit with exhaustion and fear, and the CIA man knew he looked just as distressed.

He said, 'There's going to be lots of time later for investigations, for recriminations. This isn't going to be that time.'

The NSA man said, 'Then why the hell are we here? Look, none of us have the time to fuck around with—'

The FBI man held up a hand. 'There's a point. Always has to be a point. Let him finish.'

He nodded in appreciation. 'We all know what's going to happen. After the initial shock, in a week, maybe a month, the headhunters will be out there, hunting for us. And we all know that we're going to have the information and the evidence they need to bloody us and our people.'

The other two men sat silently. Not one of them had picked up a pencil or a pen. The CIA man said, 'Let's be honest. Once we start walking back the dog, once we start going through all those terabytes of information and e-mail intercepts and cellphone recordings, we're going to find the bits and pieces of what had been going on during the past year or so. Something this elaborate, this well planned, didn't happen without us getting the hints that something was up. And that will come out, and we're going to take major grief before it's over.'

The FBI man opened his hands in apparent despair. 'You know what we're up against. We didn't have the people, the resources, hell, we don't even have enough Arabic translators on hand to . . .'

The voice dribbled off, like he knew he had been preaching to the converted. The FBI man wiped at his eyes. 'Go on.'

The CIA man said, 'There will be changes ahead. Shifts in agencies, budgets. Rumsfeld will get everything he wants and more. We'll probably get what we want, though we'll have to sacrifice some bodies to make Capitol Hill and the *Post* and the *Times* happy. Everybody will think that an intelligence failure this huge has been corrected. There's even talk about setting up some damn homeland-security department. But it's not going to work. You know it, I know it. It's not going to work. We're just too damn big and complex. Things get missed all the goddam time.'

The NSA man said, 'NASA.'

'Excuse me?'

'NASA,' he repeated, his fingers wiggling slightly, from energy fueled by lots of caffeine and not much sleep. 'In the late 1950s is when it was organized. We were getting our asses kicked by the Soviets in the space program. Our rockets kept on blowing up. So the brightest young pups were hired, were stuck in a swamp in Florida, and were told to get the job done. They built their rockets, their capsules, and you know what they did if they found out they needed a special wrench or tool? They drove to the nearest fucking hardware store and bought it, that's what. No contract bidding. No purchase orders. No reviews of parts-procurement that could eat up six or eight months. No required diversity training for their contractors. No, they bought the tools they needed and got the job done. And less than ten years later, we were walking on the moon.'

The CIA man could see he was making progress. He pressed on. 'Yeah, they got the job done. And then they got fat, slow, cautious. They became experts on filling out paperwork. Not experts on buying the right wrenches. We should have the stars-and-stripes flying on Mars right now. And we're not going to do that, not in our lifetimes.'

The FBI man said, 'What are you suggesting?'

The CIA man shifted in the seat, felt the ache in his hips. 'We have a chance now, with everybody in shock, to set up what has to be set up. We're going to need something new, something hungry, something that's not going to fuck around with paperwork and procedures and making sure the right asses get kissed. We put something together tonight, the three of us, guaranteed, we'll have the necessary Presidential and Congressional approvals, with the funding and mandate we need, within forty-eight hours. We wait another week or so, another month, and we'll be screwed. They'll reshuffle the deck chairs on the *Titanic*, that's what's going to be done, and we can't afford it.'

The other two men nodded. The CIA man knew that he should have felt pleased at their reaction, but he was still too damn tired, too damn wired. 'I'm thinking of setting up Tiger Teams. Know the phrase?'

'Sure,' the NSA man said. 'Specialty teams, brought in from the outside, to review and attack a problem and present a solution. Military to industry to almost everything else. Sure. Tiger Teams.'

The CIA man said, 'That's what we're going to do. Tiger Teams, recruited from our agencies, from outside, from colleges and media and think tanks and law enforcement. People who can think on their feet, poke and probe and not be satisfied with the ready answer. Tiger Teams for border control, bio-warfare, intelligence analysis, nuclear proliferation, everything and anything. We'll draw up a list, get something on paper and over to Sixteen Hundred by morning.'

'Think they'll be receptive?' asked the FBI man.

'The other night the President and his wife were asked to sleep on a pull-out couch in a White House bomb shelter. He'll be receptive. And both sides of the aisle in Congress, we can get them on board, too. The leaders in both parties, they were evacuated from the Capitol last week in helicopters and armored vehicles. That tends to focus one's mind.'

'What's the oversight going to be?' asked the NSA man.

'Not sure yet,' the CIA man admitted. 'But it'll be minimal. They'll have the mandate to get the job done. Performance will be what counts.'

The NSA man grimaced. 'I can see the Congressional hearings, decades down the road, where we'll be brought before the panel in wheelchairs, testifying on why the hell we set up a rogue intelligence group like this. Green light for almost everything, no oversight. A hell of a thing.'

'Sure is,' the CIA man said. 'And this is what we'll show them.'

From inside his suitcoat pocket, he pulled out a thin metal object, tossed it down on the conference-room table, where it clattered to a stop. The other two men looked on. He said, 'That's all it took. Some box cutters and knives, nineteen airline tickets, and nineteen assholes ready to kill themselves. That's all. And we lost several thousand people, four jet aircraft, the World Trade Center, part of the Pentagon, and billions of dollars in our economy. For any other asshole out there thinking to do us harm, that sounds like a hell of a bargain.'

The two other men stared at the box cutter, and then looked up at the CIA man. He said, 'And we'll tell those investigators, that's what we were up against. And why we had to do everything to make sure that the next nineteen guys from the Middle East who didn't like us or Barbie or Coca-Cola didn't come here carrying suitcase nukes.'

There was a pause. He said, 'You on board?'

The FBI man looked at the NSA man and said. 'Yeah.'

His companion nodded. 'Yeah. Let's get the fuckers.'

'Sure,' the CIA man said. 'But first, we've got work to do.'

CHAPTER TWO

In Lahore, Pakistan, the wind was blowing down from the Hindu Kush, bringing with it the smell of dust, cooking fires and burning coal. Nineteen-year-old Amil Zahrain paused in his quest for a moment, letting his left foot – the crippled one – rest some as it ached. He looked about the crowded sidewalks with wide brown eyes. This was the busiest place he had ever seen in his life, and he was quite scared, and quite lost.

A hand went into his thin cotton shirt, into the pocket his sister had secretly sewed for him, not more than a week ago. There, wrapped in paper, was his midday meal, a piece of flat bread, wrapping goat cheese and cabbage, and nestled next to his meal was a small fortune: one hundred Pakistani rupees, and an American twenty-dollar bill. And, between both of them, a thin piece of black plastic that was his weapon this day, to help kill the Jews and the infidels.

But he was lost!

Amil looked around the crowded streets again, looking vainly for a street sign or any other symbol that would help him reach his destination. He sighed, shifted his weight, winced again at the pain in his left foot. He had gotten up this morning before sunrise in his small village, about fifty kilometers to the east of Lahore. With other day workers there, he had scrambled aboard a wheezing bus that rode the bumpy Route A-2 that led into Lahore, and he had stood for most of the trip, taking in the kilometers after kilometers of crowded shacks and buildings that had been erected up against the old walls of the city. All along the way to the city, he had murmured to himself, repeating the holy prayers that he had memorized in the few short years he had spent in the local madrassa, asking for God's help and God's strength to do what had to be done.

The ride had been uneventful, except for one brief moment, along a place called Killorney Boulevard, when he had spotted a small fortress of a building, flying that hated red-white-blue flag, and he had stared at it with such contempt for a moment, until he'd remembered his instructions. Be quiet, do not bring notice to yourself, just do what you've been told to do.

God be praised.

But now, he was lost.

In Amil's hand was a dirty piece of lined schoolbook paper, with instructions and directions carefully written out in his scrawl that he was ashamed to show his sister, for her writing was much better than his. It was not fair, for his schooling had been the memorization and the glorification of the word of God, while their mother had insisted that his sister take part in some education and work program, administered by a women's council (as if such a thing could be believed!) that was getting money from some infidel bank from Europe. He had complained bitterly to his mother about the influence this was passing on to his younger sister, and she had snapped at him one night that with his empty head and God's words and a clubfoot, if he wished to do better, then by all means do better.

Amil looked up again and around, desperately seeking a sign. The instructions that had been dictated to him had been clear – he had been forced to read them back twice to the stranger who had first met him at the village mosque – and only then had he received the money.

The stranger – a tall Sudanese man – had said as they sat

on a stone bench near the center of the village, under a willow tree, 'I am looking for a pious young man, a man who wants to perform jihad. Are you that man, Amil?'

And he had replied, his hands trembling with excitement, yes, yes I am.

'You've wanted to perform jihad for some time now, haven't you.'

Yes, that I have, sir, he had said.

'You've wanted to take up weapons against God's enemies, to go to distant lands, but this has not occurred. Why?'

Amil had looked down at his feet in shame and sorrow, not able to answer.

The Sudanese had nodded. 'But your crippled foot . . . it has prevented you from traveling to Afghanistan or Yemen or Iraq, am I right? You cannot walk for long distances. So you have stayed here, in your home, with your mother and your sister. Instead of being a warrior for God.'

Amil had almost whispered, it is God's will. What else can I do?

The Sudanese had leaned in, his tobacco breath near Amil's ear, and said, 'There are other weapons to use against the Jews and the infidels, other ways to perform jihad without traveling too far or carrying a weapon. Are you interested?'

And Amil had said, his voice now strong, I am at your command.

The older man had smiled. 'You are at God's command, this is true. And this is what you shall do.'

And so Amil had learned and had written down the directions and the orders, and so it came to pass that he was now here, near where he had to go to do his jihad, to perform his holy struggle, and—

Lost!

The utter shame.

Two men made their way through the crowds and now eyed Amil, and he shivered. They wore uniforms of some sort, some type of policeman with large, fierce mustaches, and they carried long wooden staves in their weathered hands, and Amil started walking again, passing them, knowing instinctively that to stay in one place was to invite questions, and that was one thing that the Sudanese had taught him, over and over again, not to invite questions.

He walked up the street and thought for a moment, and then came back. Vendors and shopkeepers and buyers moved around in a chattering, bright flood, but he ignored the directions now for a moment, recalled what he was looking for, the bright sign the Sudanese said would be out there. The street sign was missing . . . how and where it went missing was not his worry. But the other sign that he sought . . . well, it must be someplace near. He could ask directions from one of the vendors, but no, with God's will and God's help, he would find it by himself.

And he did!

The sun had crawled higher up into the dusty yellow sky when in one of the narrow, unmarked side streets there had been the sign, in bright letters on a square piece of plastic. He looked down at the words laboriously written out in English on the paper, and matched them, letter for letter, with the overhead sign.

LAHORE NUMBER ONE INTERNET CAFE.

He murmured a prayer, thanks to be God, there is no God but Allah and Muhammad is his Prophet, and he went to the place.

*

The glass and metal door closed behind him, and Amil started shivering, both in fear and from the intense cold inside the place. He had never seen anything like it in his life. There were tables and booths and chairs, and while tea and coffee and pastries and other items were being consumed, at each table there were computers and computer screens, lined up, row after row. He took in the sight, jaw agape, at the men (and women!) sitting before the computers. A young man came over to him, frowning, wearing the foreign costume of a white shirt and necktie, and blue jeans, and said in a sharp voice, 'Yes?'

'I . . . I wish to rent a computer.'

The man sneered at him. 'You have the money?'

Amil fumbled in his robe, took out the American money, which he passed over to the man who grunted, held it up to the light, felt it with his fingers, and nodded, walking back to a counter. Amil followed and the man, with some papers and a small black object in his hand, said, 'All right, then, you can—'

Amil blushed with shame, remembered his instructions. 'I . . . must have a computer with a drive . . . a disk drive.'

The man shook his head. 'Very well. Come with me.'

Amil followed the man to one end of the place – a cafe, such an odd name – and he felt himself recoil as he saw two Western women – dressed like whores in T-shirts and shorts, their knapsacks resting against their booted feet – giggling and whispering to each other as they examined a shared computer screen.

They came to an empty booth in the corner, and Amil saw crumpled-up papers and napkins littering the floor and the table where the computer was, but the man made no attempt to clean it up. Amil sat down and the man presented a paper to him and said some long sentences that he had a hard time understanding, but even this had been part of his training. He just nodded and scrawled his signature at the bottom of the paper. The man took the paper away and put the small black object on top of the computer. It was a timer, with blood-red numerals, and it was set at 60, and as Amil watched it switched to 59.

The manager sneered again. 'Do you need any help, boy? If so, that will cost you more.'

Amil shook his head, now feeling anger at how the man was humiliating him. 'No, I do not need your help. I am quite able to do what must be done.'

The manager laughed. 'Maybe so, but it will be your fault if you do something wrong over the next hour. Not mine. The time is paid for. Not anything else.'

Amil watched as the man walked away, and when Amil felt like he was no longer being observed he went to work.

From his inside pocket again, Amil took out his directions, put the paper down next to the keyboard, smoothed it out. With fingers now seeming as thick as tree trunks, he started tapping at the keyboard, following the directions, feeling the twisted feeling in his guts ease away as the Sudanese's directions worked with no difficulty, as he set up the computer to do what had to be done. He remembered, during one of the sessions, asking the Sudanese why he was being sent to do what seemed to be a simple task, and the Sudanese had replied, 'Some of us are well known. We need to stay in the villages, in the forests, in the mountains. A young man such as yourself . . . with no history, no record, he can do much.'

And of course, that had made much sense.

There. It was time.

He took out the black rectangular piece of plastic, remembered what the Sudanese had called it. A disk. But weren't disks round? And this one was square! And was it true what the Sudanese had said, that so much information, so many words – and even pictures! – could be stored on such a thing?

He looked around the computer, found the slot that the disk went in, and inserted it. And as the Sudanese had predicted, there was a humming and a clicking noise, and when that noise ended, Amil continued, his fingers no longer seeming so thick and awkward.

On the screen something was now displayed and, reading with some difficulty, he saw that, again, the Sudanese was telling the truth. There were little cartoons on the screen, each with a number, from one to twenty, and the Sudanese had said that each little cartoon meant a photograph. And Amil had said, what kind of photographs? And the Sudanese had said, 'Of flowers. Trees. Mountains.'

Amil had been disappointed. Pictures? That was all he had to do? Send pictures to some other computer in some other part of the world?

And the Sudanese had laughed with delight. 'Not to worry, my son. You see, there is an infidel trick we have learned. Like a game or a puzzle. Even in a photo of a flower, an innocent-looking flower, there can be an important message hidden.'

In a picture? he had asked. How?

The Sudanese had shaken his head. 'Not for you to worry. It is enough that you know that these pictures are much more than pictures. They are messages to our brethren, important messages that must be sent.'

Now Amil went to work again, setting up e-mail messages, with an address that meant nothing to him – a string of numbers and letters – and he laboriously went through the instructions, somehow setting up a way where a message sent across the computer lines or wires or whatever they were would also carry the pictures that were represented by the little cartoons. The Sudanese had earlier led him through this process, over and over again, and it reminded him of the long days at the madrassa, sitting cross-legged on the floor, chanting the verses from the Koran. Amil was not sure of how the Prophet, God bless His Name, would think of these complicated machines, but Amil hoped that his work today would find favor.

There. One message sent out. One of twenty.

Nineteen more to go.

He flexed his fingers, surprised at how tired they seemed, for the work was not physical yet was hard enough. Strange how that would be.

Time for another message.

He went back to work.

And later Amil looked up at the timer. Eight minutes to go, and only three messages left. It had gone smoothly and there was plenty of time left to do the last messages, and as he bent over the keyboard – his fingers now quite stiff – he heard some raised voices and the opening of the door. He looked up at the cafe's entrance.

Two uniformed policemen were there.

He stopped, hands frozen over the keyboard.

And he could not believe it, but they were the two same policemen he had seen earlier, with the fierce mustaches and the wooden staves. He felt something gurgling at the back of his throat. Caught! But how? Did the policemen follow him here, did they know what he had been doing, how he had been contacted by the Sudanese?

And was his work here a failure? Before he could even finish it?

The policemen were now looking in his direction, talking to the cafe manager who was frowning. Amil tried to swallow, found his tongue was as dry as the dust outside his home. He forced himself to look away, to get back to what he was doing.

He looked up at the clock.

Just six minutes left.

Back to the keyboard, don't look up at the clock. Send out the e-mail message.

Two left.

The voices of the policemen seemed louder. They seemed to be walking towards him.

Time. Four minutes left.

God is great, he said over and over again to himself, God is great, God is great, God is great.

The policemen's voices were louder, there was no doubt.

They were coming closer to him.

Another e-mail successfully sent.

One left.

A glance up at the clock.

One minute.

His fingers typed out the e-mail address, and he cursed himself.

A mistake.

Erase and try again.

There. Complete.

Put the blinking little arrow over the send button and—

Click.

He looked up at the clock.

All four numerals read zero.

He looked up and saw the two policemen. Saw that they were standing only a meter or so away, and they were ignoring Amil.

Yes, they were ignoring Amil. They were talking and smiling to the two young blonde European women, the whores whose nipples were showing stiffly through their thin shirts. Hand shaking, Amil pushed the button on the side of the computer that released the disk, and he placed it back into his robe. He got up, swaying just a bit, for his legs seemed weak, and his clubfoot even more sore.

He limped his way past the policemen, smelling either their cologne or the scent of the European whores, and he went to the manager, who just nodded.

'I am done.'

The man shrugged. 'Is there anything else?'

'No,' Amil said.

'Then that's it.' And the man turned away, and for a moment Amil was tempted to grab the man's shoulder and wheel him around and speak to his face, saying, don't treat me like that, you scum. Don't you know what has just happened here, in your little place, a place that is obscene and should be burnt to the ground? A holy warrior came here, on jihad, and all you do is turn around and—

No, he thought. Remember what the wise Sudanese said. Do not bring attention to yourself. Leave as quickly as possible.

Which is what he did, and he gasped again, going out into the hot day, back to the noise and dust and people out in the street. Just a few more things to do, and then he would be done.

Amil walked along the crowded sidewalk until he found a grated opening at the side, for drainage, and he bent down as if to adjust a sandal, and he let the black plastic square fall into the stench-filled sewage. There. He stood up and kept walking, and as he walked he carefully tore up the piece of paper with his instructions until the little pieces were thick in his hand, and when he came to a series of trash bins, he scattered the pieces of paper amongst the piles of smelly trash, fat flies buzzing in and around.

Amil kept walking, his heart light, even his clubfoot not aching as much, and as he repeated, over and over again, Allah akbar – God is great – he remembered the last thing he had said to the Sudanese, two days ago, when he had asked if what he would do this day in that strange place, that Internet cafe, would make a difference, would strike a blow against the infidels.

And the Sudanese had squeezed his shoulders.

'Yes,' the Sudanese had said. 'You will have struck a mighty blow against the Jews and infidels in America.'

And will some die, he meekly asked, after this task is done?

'Many will die,' the Sudanese had said.

And, shyly, he had asked, sir, could you tell me how many? Hundreds? Thousands?

And Amil had thrilled to the answer of the Sudanese, who had grasped his young hand.

'Millions, my warrior,' he had said in a fierce voice. 'Millions.'

CHAPTER THREE

Just outside Greenbelt, Maryland, there are a series of office parks that stretch out like a series of glass and steel veins from the mighty concrete and asphalt arteries of I-95, traveling from Maine to Florida. One office park, called Lee Estates – for which the developer had received vicious criticism when the project was first constructed, from civil rights activists who were sure the place was honoring Confederate General Robert E. Lee – boasted a number of buildings, home to software developers, medical imaging companies, a temporary employment agency and, in one smaller building set off from the rest, an outfit called Callaghan Consulting. The building looked like a converted New England colonial-style home, complete with black shutters and narrow windows, and on this May morning Brian Doyle strode up to the quiet structure, yawning. It had been a late night the night before, and it looked like a long day was ahead, and he was not in a good mood. Thirty-five years old, a native of Queens, Brian was a detective first grade in the NYPD and still wondered how he had pissed God off so much that he had ended up here in Maryland.

A minute earlier he had parked his rental car in a parking lot set fifty yards away from the small building, and then made his way up a narrow sidewalk that led to the front entrance of Callaghan Consulting whose premises had been built underneath a number of tall oak trees. There were circular concrete planters around the perimeter of the house, and the sidewalk was flanked with odd-shaped recessed lighting with grillwork, and before entering the house one passed through an arch-shaped white trellis that boasted fake red

roses and vinery. An uneducated observer would think that
this small building had been set up by someone with an odd
and kitschy taste in architecture and landscaping.

An educated observer – like himself, Brian thought
grumpily – would know something else: the concrete
planters prevented a truck bomb from being driven
through the front entrance, the isolated parking lot prevented a car bomb from taking out the building, the way
the building had been built under trees, was to prevent
hijacked aircraft from getting a good read of the building's
location, and the sniffing devices hidden in the lighting
determined if visitors were bearing any explosives, and the
metal detectors in the trellis announced what those visitors might be carrying before they came through the front
door.

Which Brian now did, meeting the next line of defense, a
twenty-something woman named Stacy Luiz, who sat behind
a wide wooden desk set on thin legs. She gave him a big
smile as he came through the door and he smiled back. A
nice way to start one's day, even if it was on a Sunday morning.

'Good morning, detective,' she said. She wore a tiny
microphone headset that looked out of place in her thick
auburn hair, and held a small redialing device in her left
hand. She had on a yellow dress that showed a nice expanse
of cleavage, and because of the way her legs were placed
under the desktop the dress displayed a lot of leg as well.
There were no chairs or coffee tables stacked with *Time* and
Newsweek and *Adweek*, for Callaghan Consulting discour-
aged visitors, and Stacy – dressed as she was – was also part
of the discouragement process. The way she was positioned,
the way she was dressed, was to stop men – even dangerous

men, men who were on a mission – just for a precious second or two as they came through the door, and give her enough time to use her other hand, her carefully manicured right hand, which Brian knew right at this instant was wrapped around a Colt Model 1911 .45 semi-automatic pistol in a middle drawer of the desk.

Earlier on during his assignment with this oddball group, Brian had made clear his interest in seeing Stacy in a more relaxed, out-of-work setting, and she had eagerly taken him up on it, only insisting that she would pick the day and place. The day had been a Saturday, the place had been the indoor shooting range at the Berwyn Rod & Gun Club in nearby Bowie, and in the space of a half-hour she had out-shot him in every type of target and environment. That had been their first and last away-from-work encounter.

'Still carrying that nine-millimeter piece of junk?' Stacy called out as he walked past her desk to the short hallway behind her. Office doors lined each side of the hallway where some of the support staff worked.

'It's a lightweight piece of junk, compared with the cannon you're carrying,' Brian said, smiling back at her, seeing the carefully hidden consoles on the other side of the desk that gave immediate readouts from the explosives and metal detectors outside.

Stacy laughed. 'I know how to carry it, and how to use it, and that's all that counts.'

He yawned again. Up to the door at the end of the hall-way, a door that looked like wood, which it partially was: wood covering metal. At the lock near the doorknob, he punched in the number combination and let himself in. The door opened to reveal a small wood-paneled room housing an elevator with exactly one button. Brian got in, pressed the button, and felt that little surge in his stomach as the elevator went down into the Maryland soil.

The door slid open. Brian went out and through another door, along a short hallway, and into a small conference room. There were six chairs around the table, and three were already occupied. He nodded at the other people in the room and sat down, sprawling out his legs. One of the two remaining empty chairs awaited whatever guest might be attending this morning, and the other, at the head of the conference room table, was reserved for their team leader. Who was always late, and who had an office out at the other end of the underground complex, along with the other team members. Coffee and juice and pastries and doughnuts were set in the middle of the table. On the far wall was a thin plasma screen, displaying nothing save a pale blue light. Laptops were set up in front of the other three participants, and Brian didn't feel guilty that his own laptop was locked up safely in his own little cubicle.

At his left was Montgomery Zane, a black guy about his own age who was about the same height as Brian but who easily had fifteen pounds on him, all of it muscle around his neck and shoulders. He had on a dark blue polo shirt and grunted a greeting as Brian sat down, the good side of his face toward him. The other side – the left side – of Monty's face had ripples of burn-scar tissue running down to his thick neck. Brian sneaked a peek at Monty's laptop screen, saw that he was playing some sort of Tetris-like game, which immediately made him feel better about being laptop-less. At his right was Darren Coover, who was about ten years his junior and so slight and blond he looked like a stiff breeze would knock him over. Darren didn't even seem to notice as Brian sprawled out, and a quick glance at Darren's laptop screen showed streams of numbers and letters, nothing that seemed to make sense.

Across from Brian was Victor Palmer – or, as he preferred to be known, Doctor Palmer. Like Brian, he was on loan and was hating almost every minute of it. Brian quickly realized that he didn't like the look on the doc's face. Usually the doc had this air of superiority, like the rest of the group weren't fit to wipe his ass after he'd taken a dump, but not this morning. He was looking around the room and nervously licking his thin lips, eyes blinking behind his round, horn-rimmed glasses. That look made him seem scared, scared for the first time in a long time, and Brian said loudly, 'Anybody know when the princess is showing up?'

That brought a smile from Monty. But Darren continued to ignore everybody, while the good doctor still looked like he was trying to retain an enema in his bowels. Brian looked around at his fellow members of Federal Operations and Intelligence Liaison Team Seven, a/k/a Tiger Team Seven, and he remembered how it had all begun.

Months earlier there'd been a note on Brian's cluttered desk, at the First Precinct on Ericsson Place at the southern tip of Manhattan. 'See me soonest. L.'

L. Officially known as Lieutenant Lawrence Lancaster, known to everyone in the squad as Ellie but who was never called that to his face. Brian crumpled up the note, tossed it in a nearby wastebasket, and thought about going outside for a nice second cup of coffee. But he decided that wasn't going to solve anything. There. A detective joke – not going to solve anything – and he hadn't even tried. He looked at his cluttered desk, at the sparse collection of family photographs there, his ex-wife Marcy and their boy Thomas, and another one, showing a much younger Brian Doyle, a rookie in his fresh NYPD uniform, standing next to his dad Curt, wearing a NYPD sergeant's uniform, and a goddam proud look on his face. Across from his desk was another desk, just a shade cleaner, but empty. His partner, Jimmy Carr, coming in late from the dentist or something.

Brian got up from his desk, went over to the small office on the east side of the building. The lieutenant was sitting behind his own messy desk – Brian almost smiled at the memory of the biting memo that the Chief of Detectives had sent out last month, about how cluttered desks led to cluttered cases and court dismissals – and he rapped his hand on the side of the door.

'Looking for me?'

The lieutenant looked up, gazing at Brian over his half-rim glasses, which were kind of sissified for a squad lieutenant. But those nearly bloodless blue eyes behind the lenses never let anybody call the lieutenant sissy, even though his nickname was Ellie. He was squat, like a man whose intended weight and girth had been shoved into a frame built six inches too short. He waved a thick hand up at Brian and said, 'Yeah, Bri. Come in and close the door.'

Brian nodded, still hating the nickname Bri, wondering what in hell had gotten into the lieutenant that he needed an office visit. He sat down, noted the filing cabinets filling the office – at least those were neat, like they were part of the goddam wall system or something – and the lieutenant picked up a thin file folder, opened it up as he sat back. Brian kept quiet, kept his mouth shut. Better not to offer anything before knowing what the hell was going on.

The lieutenant was no longer looking at the file folder. He said, 'Last December.'

'Yes, sir?'

'There was a test we all took. Remember?'

'Vaguely.'

'It was an intelligence test, that's what most of us thought. Odd questions. Puzzles. Who's buried in Grant's tomb. Crap like that.'

Brian nodded. 'Yeah, I remember now.'

The lieutenant tossed the folder on his desk. 'Okay, Bri, we're now in confidential land, got it? Confidential such you don't tell your partner, you don't tell the ex, don't tell nobody. Understood?'

'Sure, boss,' Brian said, feeling better that the meeting wasn't for something he had screwed up on but was for something else.

'Okay. Deal is, we all thought the test was just another pysch-bureau bullshit project, but it wasn't. Maybe it was bullshit after all, but it wasn't ours. It's the Feds.'

'What do they want?' Brian asked.

'You.'

'Huh?'

The lieutenant grimaced. 'Don't like it at all, and you're gonna like it even less. The Feds are looking for people, on temporary duty. Six months, maybe a year, maybe longer. You'll be detached from the precinct, full pay and benefits and seniority accruing, plus you'll get a twenty percent pay bonus to make up for whatever OT you lose. Plus the usual travel and per diem goodies.'

'Lieutenant, I got cases to close, court appearances set for the next month, and—'

'It's all been taken care of.'

Brian heard his voice get heated. 'It has, has it? Excuse me, lieutenant, but what the fuck, okay? Don't I get a say in this? Don't I?'

The lieutenant seemed to choose his words. 'Apparently not. Because I've been raising a shit storm, too, losing a guy like you, but I've gotten the word, inscribed in granite letters ten feet tall from One Police Plaza, that it's a go. For some reason the Feds like the answers you gave on the test and what they saw in your personnel jacket. And don't take this the wrong way or the hard way, and you can be a royal Irish pain in the ass, Bri, but I'm gonna hate losing you.'

Brian clasped his hands together. 'Shit, boss, what the hell do they want me for, anyway?'

Lancaster opened up the thin folder, bent his head down and said, 'Something called Federal Operations and Intelligence Liaison. FOIL. Duties and responsibilities to be announced once you report in and sign a standard non-disclosure form, yadda yadda yadda.'

The lieutenant closed the folder. 'That's the official. Unofficial line, you want to hear it?'

'Christ, yes.'

'Unofficial, the Feds are cherrypicking people with different skills, putting them together in these teams. Thing is, Bri, you're going hunting.'

'Hunting? For who?'

The lieutenant made a gesture with his head, like he was pointing out something outside, and Brian looked out the window and knew what the lieutenant was pointing at. That near and terribly empty spot on the horizon, where the two buildings had once stood.

Brian said, 'Okay, I get it now. Shit.'

The lieutenant offered him a slight smile. 'Go and do

well, Bri. And maybe the Feds, looking at your record and all, decided that with your dad it makes sense that you—'

Brian interrupted, saying, 'So. When do I go? Next week? Next month?'

The lieutenant shook his head. 'Guess I wasn't clear, Bri. They want you now.'

'Now? Like what?'

His boss reached for a phone. 'Like now I'm calling a squad car, to get your ass to LaGuardia and to DC later this morning. *That* kind of now.'

And through the open door of the conference room, the princess came in, the leader of Tiger Team Seven, Adrianna Scott. Brian eyed her carefully as she came into the room. Unlike Stacy out in the front entrance, Adrianna didn't dress flashy, though there was something about the way she dressed and carried herself that Brian found interesting. Of course, if his ex-wife Marcy had been around, she'd laugh in that braying tone of hers (and why had he ever found that laugh attractive? He blamed Jameson's Irish Whiskey and Marcy's impressive chest) and say, sure, interesting. Another way of saying you're just a horny jerk, can't keep your eyes off the girls.

Adrianna looked tired, her long dark hair drawn back in a simple ponytail, with a tiny red ribbon. She had on a charcoal-gray skirt that reached mid-calf and a black pullover sweater. She carried her laptop under one arm and opened it up after she'd sat down. Brian looked around at the collection of characters, gathered here in this so-called undisclosed location, thinking of what weird shit had to have happened to have brought them all together. Himself, a New York City cop. Darren, the thin blond kid. Something to do with the

National Security Agency. The doc, from Atlanta and the Centers for Disease Control. Monty, an active-duty military officer – who for some reason kept his branch of service secret – with a quiet smile and the sharp confidence that if he had to, he could kill everybody in this room and leave while munching a doughnut, not even having broken out in a sweat. And the princess Herself, with brown eyes and mocha-colored skin, an officer with the Central Intelligence Agency.

She smiled and said, 'So sorry to have gotten you all here on a Sunday, but it could not be avoided.'

By now Darren and Monty had torn their gazes away from the computer screen, and Brian kept his hands folded on his stomach. On the far wall the plasma screen flickered into life as Adrianna started tapping away on her keyboard. Letters appeared, spelling out an Arab phrase.

Brian looked up and then glanced over at Adrianna, who – surprisingly enough – now had her elbows on the table and was slowly rubbing her temples with her long fingers. She said, 'The phrase shown here is the Arabic for May 29. That's a very special day for some fundamental Islamists, May 29. The day Istanbul – known back then as Constantinople – fell to the Muslim forces in 1453. A day celebrated in many parts of the Islamic world, a day in which the infidels suffered a defeat that shook the very foundations of the Christian rulers in Europe.'

Adrianna raised her head, no longer smiling. 'A special day, indeed. Its anniversary is coming up in less than four weeks, gentlemen.'

Brian felt something cold start to crawl its way through his stomach, like being on a stakeout and realizing that your radio batteries have drained away in silence, just as four or five assholes with guns are walking your way.

'And on that day, gentlemen, we are going to get hit.'

Monty spoke up, his voice lilting lightly with a Southern accent. 'Hit? Really?'

A sad nod.

'Hit, gentlemen – and hit hard.'

CHAPTER FOUR

On the island of Bali, in the tourist resort town of Kuta, twenty-year-old Ranon Degun stood before the blackened and twisted wreckage of the Sari nightclub in the light rain. Wilted and faded plastic flowers were scattered as offerings on the nearest pile of debris. Ranon kept his face impassive as he looked at what had once been a gathering place for foreigners, mostly Australians, loud and drunk Australians, swaggering through, acting like they were the rulers of this place. But some time ago holy warriors had attacked this nightclub, had killed more than two hundred infidels, and for that Ranon was pleased indeed.

But he kept his face still. Even now, it was still not seen as right in some quarters on this island to gloat over what had happened, even though a blow had been struck for righteousness. For ever since the bombing, the tourists had not returned in the numbers that Bali had become accustomed to. The Australians and the New Zealanders and the backpackers from Europe had stayed away from Bali, and those who lived from the tourists, including Ranon's own uncle and aunt, who had served as a houseboy and a chambermaid for one of the beach hotels had suffered. Seeing his aunt and uncle depart each day, clothed in some Western dress for the hotel, had caused resentment to burn inside him, as they scraped and bowed to the infidels. And he had mentioned that one night to his uncle, who had surprised him by standing up and striking him on the face. 'These "infidels" as you call them,' his uncle had cried out, 'these infidels pay good money, money that pays for your clothes and your food and this home. So shut up about the infidels, unless you wish to live someplace else.'

And living someplace else was not possible, for Ranon was a cripple, and he was dependent on the charity of his aunt and uncle. Years earlier, soldiers had camped near their village, soldiers fighting bandits in the hills, and he had snuck into their campsite one night, to watch, to observe, and, well, of course, to steal. Even though it humiliated him to think about it, he recalled stealing a slumbering soldier's belt, hoping that there was a wallet or something valuable hanging from it, and going home, the belt in his hands, a branch tugged at something hanging there, a small metal object that exploded in a flash and ruined his hands forever.

Ranon looked down at the pink stumps of his fingers that always made the young girls turn away, that made everything so hard to do, and the thought came to him that his own land of Bali was now a cripple, crippled by the foreigners. For Bali had long ago lost its own native way, of living off the land and the sea, and now she was nothing more than a whore for the foreigners, opening her legs for the chance of getting dollars or euros or yen.

Which was why the bombing had to happen. The infidels had to be expelled, from here and all other holy lands, and if sometimes people lost their jobs and innocents had to die, well, that was God's will. For had not God Himself said that there would be struggles and difficulties before going to Paradise?

Ranon wiped at his face with one hand, the other hand barely holding on to a small plastic bag with a firm object inside. The warm drizzle still fell from the gray skies, and in the wreckage of the nightclub there were those faded plastic flowers, left behind by relatives or friends, he imagined. He looked around, saw that nobody was gazing at his direction, and he placed his hand up to his face to hide the wide smile that he allowed himself. For here was a monument to what could happen when holy warriors did their work for God, and very soon, in a very simple way, he was sure that he would be allowed to join those holy ranks.

Ranon turned and started walking away, his feet splashing through the puddles.

Some blocks away, Ranon came to a store – really not much more than a shack tacked onto the end of a narrow alley – that sold wood carvings. A sullen-faced man in a soiled tank-top T-shirt sat inside, smoking a cigarette. Ranon went in, nodded in his direction, and said, 'I am here for a pickup.'

'Yes?'

'A pickup for a Mister Wilson. At the Amandari Hotel. If you please.'

The man stared at him through a cloud of cigarette smoke, reached underneath the counter and removed a small package fastened with string. Hands trembling, Ranon took the package from the man's hands and ignored the pitying look he gave Ranon's twisted finger stumps.

And Ranon remembered.

Weeks ago, at the small mosque that served his village,

just north of Ubud, a stranger had come to him. A tall
Sudanese who had called him by name, and led him away to
a cafe where they had shared small glasses of sweetened tea,
and where the Sudanese had peppered him with questions.
About his young life. His struggle with his crippled fingers.
His devotion to God. His thoughts for the future, even on an
island such as Bali, polluted with so much corruption and
with strange religions like Christianity or Hinduism. And
had Ranon ever made the hajj, to the holy place of Mecca?
And Ranon had said, no, he had not – though, of course,
like any good Muslim, he hoped to make the hajj before
he died. The Sudanese, his eyes bright with certainty and
strength, had said that, indeed, Mecca was a holy place,
and except during those times when he had been in the
Sudan and Afghanistan, he himself had made the hajj
many times.

Other questions had followed in the cool interior of the
cafe. The Sudanese had nodded at Ranon's answers, and had
said, 'Ranon, would you be willing to do a holy task for me,
a task that will strike fear in the infidels?'

And Ranon had hesitated, only for a moment, and the
Sudanese, smart and holy man that he was, had said, 'You are
reluctant.'

Ranon had nodded and had said, I am willing to do whatever you ask, but . . . would it take place here, in Bali?

The Sudanese had smiled. 'You are concerned, perhaps,
with the well-being of your family? Of your aunt and uncle?'

They are not very devout, Ranon had said, but they are
good-hearted people. What happened at the Sari had hurt
them terribly, and so many others. The tourists had left and
the jobs were lost, and the money dried up, and children
went hungry, and—

The Sudanese had interrupted him. 'But what about the Palestinian children, who are shot and bulldozed by the Zionists? And what of the Iraqi children, poisoned by the uranium-tipped weapons of the Americans and the British? And what of the Chechen children, burned in their homes by the thrice-damned Russians? The children here, they may go hungry and they may go thirsty, but at least they live.'

Ranon had been embarrassed. The righteous Sudanese had set him straight, had made him look at things more clearly. He had nodded and said, I will do whatever you require.

The Sudanese had smiled again, had gently tapped Ranon on his shoulder. 'Not to worry, my young warrior. What I will have you do, it will take place here, in Bali. But no one will die. No Hindu. No Christian. And especially no Muslim. No, the task I have for you, it will be simple, but in what it shall accomplish, it shall be deadly indeed.'

The Sudanese had looked around the cafe, seen that they were alone in this part of the building, and had leaned forward and spoken softly. 'It will be something so deadly that years from now, what happened at the whorehouse, the place where the men and the women danced together, that will be forgotten.'

The memory made Ranon shiver. He walked a while until he was sure that he wasn't being watched, or being followed, for the Sudanese had been quite specific in his directions. He sat on the wet concrete steps of a shuttered clothing store – whorish clothes for Europeans to display their bodies in on the sands of Bali – and clumsily unwrapped the package that he had received. The small plastic bag he had carried was now at his side. Unwrapping the rough paper revealed a carving of a kangaroo. A souvenir for some Australian. But what Australian would ever come here again after seeing what had happened to his or her countrymen? He put it aside and smoothed out the paper across his lap. There. A string of numbers and a collection of words.

His heart thumped harder as he looked at the simple scrawl. Something so simple, yet so simple a weapon would do so much harm.

The light rain had stopped. Ranon looked around him again, saw the empty taxicabs trundle by, the drivers looking bored and angry. He picked up the cheap plastic bag, took out the object. A bright green cellphone. He had bought it last week with one hundred Australian dollars that the Sudanese had given him. Again, the Sudanese had been specific on where to buy the phone, and how to buy it. Purchase it just before the store closes, so that the clerk is hurried and pays little attention to who you are or how you look. Pay with cash. Leave no record of who you are.

Which was what Ranon had done. Now he picked up the phone and switched it on, and then punched in the number scrawled on the packaging, being slow and careful, knowing how hard it was to do this with his injured hands. A man's voice answered.

'Yes?'

Ranon read off the first phrase. 'I am calling for our mother.'

The voice replied. 'Go on.'

'She is well.'

'Yes.'

'But her ankles still hurt her.'

'Yes.'

'She would like a visit from you soon.'

'Yes.'

'The south end of her roof is leaking.'

'Yes.'

'She sends her love, very much.'

'Yes.'

There. The last phrase. The Sudanese had been clear. Hang up immediately after the last phrase. Do not hesitate. Do not say anything more. But the man on the other end of the phone . . . who knew where he was. Perhaps he was in Bali. Perhaps he was in Hamburg or Paris. Perhaps even New York City itself! Ranon felt the shiver of excitement, sensing that this man was a part of something greater, a wonderful web of connections and phone messages and planners, all working towards jihad. This man . . . he could not just hang up.

'Sir?'

'Eh?'

'God is great.'

The man exhaled softly and said, 'Yes. He is.'

And there was a faint click as the man from far away, his comrade and friend, broke the connection. Ranon held the phone tightly in his hands, closed his eyes, thinking of what had just happened. Something easy, something simple, the Sudanese had said. And Ranon knew what he had just done. An important message had been transmitted, something important indeed, and when the news came out over the next days or weeks or months he would wave the newspaper at his aunt and uncle and proudly tell them of what he had done. For he had no doubt that something enormous was in the works, for that was what the Sudanese had said. What had happened at the nightclub would soon be forgotten. Let his aunt and uncle cry and worry about the infidels then.

Ranon got up and put the phone back in the bag, and

then he took the piece of paper. From another pocket he took out a small book of matches, and under the overhang from the shuttered store he lit the paper and watched it quickly burn down to ashes. Then he started walking away again until he came to a bridge arching over a narrow brown stream. Again, to make sure that no one was observing him, he stood on the bridge for a while, not moving even as a bus came by and sprayed him when the fat wheels went through a puddle. He heard laughter from inside the bus but didn't care. He was doing God's work, and when the bridge was empty, just for a moment, he turned the plastic bag upside down and let the cellphone tumble into the stream.

A pity, really, that such an expensive device had to be thrown away like that. But the Sudanese had been adamant. No trace, no evidence. Nothing.

Ranon looked down at his other hand. The silly wooden kangaroo had a carved smile on its face and seemed to be mocking him. He thought of tossing the carving into the stream, but no, that wouldn't destroy it. The wood would only float and it would still survive, perhaps, by washing up on a bank somewhere or on a sandbar.

Then he had a thought.

Ranon went back the way he'd come, enjoying the walk, heading back to where he had started, back to Haikon Street. And there the wreckage of the nightclub lay before him, unchanged. He looked at the faded flowers and even scraps of cloth – flags representing the infidel countries who had sent their crusaders here – and held the kangaroo in his hand. He leaned over and gently placed the carved kangaroo next to the red-white-blue flag of Australia, and just as he did that the morning sun broke through the clouds, warming his arms and his back.

A good sign.

A sign from God, no doubt.

And though he had been impassive on his earlier visit to the nightclub, Ranon had to let himself be free now. He couldn't help it. He started smiling and almost started laughing as he walked away from the place that had been a funeral pyre for so many unbelievers.

God was indeed great, he thought.

CHAPTER FIVE

In Maryland, Adrianna Scott took a breath to calm herself as she looked over the members of her team. She took a guess at what they were thinking. After Afghanistan and Iraq, there had been a feeling, no doubt a wrong feeling, but it was there, that the war on terrorism was being won. Not won in a flashy series of set-piece battles, like World War Two, but won in a steady series of bomb plots foiled, terrorist cells raided, and rogue bank accounts seized.

Now she had made it clear. Bad things were coming. The war was a hell of a long way from being over.

Adrianna looked over at the team again, nodded to her NSA man, and said, 'Darren?'

Darren's slightly bug eyes widened some more as he looked up from the screen. 'Yes?'

'Your report, please.'

Darren cleared his throat. 'Latest we have from our Level One intercepts show increased chatter from suspected cells in Pakistan, Bali, and Great Britain. All have referenced the upcoming May 29 date, and the fall of Constantinople. At first we thought that what we were seeing was idle chatter, talking up the past glories of Islam and the Caliphate, but it's clear that the talk is referring to the actual upcoming date.'

Monty spoke up. 'How do we know it's going to be big? Maybe it's just another spoof, something to scare us, get the threat color notched up another level, piss off the flying and traveling public.'

Darren said, 'There's a foundation to the increased chatter, a rhythm. After months of recording, you can determine pretty much the usual level of traffic. It's when you see a spike, especially within a certain range, that we feel we're onto something. Plus . . . there's a tone to the voices we're hearing. They're excited, they're thrilled that something's coming.'

Brian yawned and said, 'Could be bullshit that's coming, that's all.'

Darren was still looking in Adrianna's direction but his words were directed to his seatmate. 'And how's that, detective?'

Brian smiled now and said, 'Have to agree with my man Monty – maybe it is just a spoof, something to keep us all on edge. Their way of saying, "Hey, we're here, we're queer, get used to it." They want to pretend that they're still bad asses out there, ready to kill us all, get us all worked up.'

Adrianna nodded, keeping her gaze on Brian, and recalled the first time they had met.

The lobby of the Hilton hotel on Tysons Corner in McLean, Virginia. Adrianna Scott strode in and spotted Brian Doyle right away. He was sitting stiffly in a chair, watching everybody go past him without hardly moving his eyes. He was fit, with close-cropped black hair that was streaked with gray along the sides, and a clean-shaven face that looked hard indeed. She knew his age, knew his educational and professional background, knew of his recent divorce and monetary problems and what kind of car he drove and what his favorite drink was. But even with the NYPD-supplied photographs of him she noticed something right away that wasn't apparent from the briefing and the photos. Even sitting down he had this nervous, restless energy about him, like a herd animal out on the African savannah, tasked with protecting the group but desperately afraid of not doing the job well enough to save everyone.

He spotted her, stood up. She held out her hand and they shook briefly and then she sat down across from him, watching again how his eyes worked, knowing that he was using his own private male checklist to determine whether she was beddable material or not. She was surprised at how she wondered how she'd just rated.

Adrianna spoke first. 'Detective Doyle.'

'Miss Scott. Or should it be Mizz Scott?'

She laughed. 'Adrianna will be fine. How are you doing?'

Brian shrugged. 'All right, I guess. Still trying to figure out what the hell I'm doing here.'

'That should have been explained in your orientation.'

His hard eyes were still staring at her. 'The orientation was the usual crap of filling out forms, fifteen-minute coffee breaks in the morning and afternoon, and lots of Powerpoint presentations. How about you tell me, no bullshit, why the CIA wants a New York City detective to tag along.'

'It's not just the Central Intelligence Agency,' she said carefully. 'It's a number of—'

'Yeah, I know all that,' he said. 'Liaison teams, set up with representatives from Fed agencies, including the military and intelligence groups. Fine, that makes sense, as far as it goes. Still doesn't tell me why you've pulled me out of my precinct to spend time out here in the boonies.'

Adrianna folded her hands over a knee. 'It's simple, Brian. We need you.'

'Why?' he shot back.

She looked around at the lobby, knowing the type of people who were streaming in and out of here, day after day, setting up shop for the inevitable visits to departments and agencies sprawling out from DC, all within easy driving distance. Lobbyists. Software salesmen. Retired intelligence officers. All still filled with righteous indignation, even years later, for what had happened to their country on 9/11. All filled with a desire to wreak revenge. All filled with another desire, of course, to make some money while doing it.

And all doomed to failure.

Adrianna said, 'There are numerous reasons why we got hit on 9/11. I'm sure you can come up with a few yourself. But let me give you an important one, one that might have been overlooked.'

For the first time since she had met him, Brian smiled, just a bit. It was a nice sight. 'Go on. Sure you're not revealing any secrets?' he asked.

'You've already signed the necessary paperwork.'

'There might be eavesdroppers.'

'They can eavesdrop away. The real secrets can wait. Here's the deal, Brian. We got hit because we've lost our edge.'

'That's nothing new. Listen to those mad mullahs out there – all they preach about is the decadent West.'

Adrianna shook her head. 'No, I don't think you understand. I'm not talking about the West or our society losing our edge. I'm talking about my agency, other agencies. With very, very few exceptions, Brian, we've gotten fat, lazy, and complacent. Oh, we do a magnificent job intercepting and interpreting electronic intelligence, and our surveillance satellites do amazing things from orbit. There's no nation or organization on earth that can match our technical prowess in recording or intercepting electronic intelligence. But that's been our problem. Most everything's been done from here in the USA itself or in orbit. For example, let's say you're an intelligence officer, newly assigned to Langley. What kind of career path are you going to choose? One that puts you in a comfortable cubicle during the day and home by six p.m. every night with wifey and the kids, and Little League games and ballet recitals on the weekend? Or a career path that sends you to some Third World country with little electricity, no hot water, food that gives you the runs every other day, and unfriendly types who might walk up to you in a crowded marketplace and put a nine-millimeter round through the back of your head. What choice would you make?'

'I see your point,' Brian said. 'But I'm not one to choose living in a Third World hellhole, either. Just so you know.'

'And we don't intend to send you anywhere like that.' She leaned closer toward him, wondered briefly why she found that pleasant, and said, 'What we need from you are your skills, detective. Your street smarts, as they say. For the most part, our little group will be made up of people who are quite skilled in examining and interpreting intelligence, and presenting recommendations. What we're weak on are people with the smarts to ask the tough and embarrassing questions, not to put up with any bullshit, and to go with their hunches. Your service record is admirable, Brian.'

He looked uncomfortable with the praise. 'There are others who've done better. I've been lucky a couple of times.'

'Perhaps. But you have the combination we need. And luck is always a wonderful commodity. Which is why you're here.'

Brian stayed silent.

Adrianna said, 'And what happened to your father, well, we also thought that—'

She was surprised at his response. He said quickly, 'Please leave my father out of this, all right? This is my job, that's what it's going to be. It's not going to be personal. Understand?'

She nodded and he said, 'Thing I learned, right out of the Academy, you start to take things personally out on the street, your thinking gets fucked up, you don't see what's there, you make the wrong decisions. You're thinking with your heart or your balls, and not your head. And that'll get your ass in a sling, soon enough.'

Adrianna allowed herself a small smile. This tough guy was going to work out just fine. She said, 'Thanks for the anatomy lesson, Brian. Any other questions?'

'I'm sure I'll have a shitload, once we get going.'

'So. You're aboard?'

He nodded. 'Oh, yeah. Like I had a choice. But still . . .'

'Yes?'

Brian looked around again, like he was afraid that he was being listened to by the constant stream of guests and hotel workers walking through the lobby. 'It's just that I couldn't believe what I was hearing during those orientation sessions. About the level of authority you have. And the over-sight . . .'

Adrianna's hands were moistening up as she remembered the very first time her responsibilities had been outlined. Jesus Christ, she had said to herself, how can I possibly do this? How can I?

Because you have to, the answer had come back to her. There are no other options.

'We can talk about it in more detail later, Brian. When we're not in a hotel lobby. But what we'll be doing will be perfectly legitimate, perfectly legal. The proper findings have been reviewed and signed by the President and Congressional leaders from both parties. The oversight will be kept at a minimum. There's going to be a lot of trust put in us and our abilities, and with that trust comes responsibility. Responsibility to protect our people.'

Brian's look seemed to have hardened again. 'Especially when it comes to killing terrorists, suspected or otherwise, without benefit of arrest or trial?'

'We protect our people, Brian. Whatever it takes. Do you have a problem with that?'

There was a pause, and then he sat back in a comfortable chair in a comfortable hotel lobby in the most comfortable nation on earth.

'No,' he said. 'I don't have a problem with that.'

And with that, Adrianna kept her emotions in check. He was on board. He would do his job well. And that was the best news she'd had this day.

Adrianna observed the questioning look from Brian and knew he was doing his job, poking and prying, and she was glad that he was still performing well, months after his hiring. She turned to Victor and said, 'Doctor? If you please? The medical report from that gentleman in Vancouver.'

Victor coughed, wiped at his face, and started tapping on his laptop's keyboard. The plasma screen flickered into life and a man's face appeared, apparently a passport photo. He appeared young, with large brown eyes, thin face, long nose and scraggly beard.

'This is John Muhammad Akim. Originally from Brighton, in Great Britain. Twenty-four years old. Some records of juvenile crime when he was younger. Breaking and entering. Stolen cars. Entered Her Majesty's Prison at Maidstone more than two years ago. When he was there, converted to Islam. That's where he and his fellow pilgrims picked up their new middle names.'

Darren said, 'Unfortunately for all concerned, it looks like he didn't convert to the peace, love and understanding branch of Islam.'

If it had been an attempt at humor, the attempt failed. Nobody laughed.

'Late last year,' Victor continued, stammering a bit, 'he came to Montreal on a tourist visa. Was supposed to stay six months and depart. Never did. Dropped out of sight.'

Monty said, 'And Canadian immigration? Domestic intelligence? They just let him slip out?'

Adrianna said, 'He wasn't on any watch list. If anything, he was just a minor player. Oh, they did a day or two of surveillance on him in Montreal, just to say that they did something. But you know the pressures our northern neighbors are under. Can't afford to be seen offending anyone. Victor, go on.'

He coughed, punched a few more keys, and the passport photo was replaced by another. It depicted a slightly older, more fleshed-out John Muhammad Akim. The face was nearly chalk-white, and the man was lying on a slab of metal. A white sheet was pulled up to his neck, and near his throat a rubber-gloved hand was holding a slip of paper that showed Akim's name and a string of numbers.

Victor said, 'John Muhammad Akim. Now deceased. And at the Vancouver General Hospital in Vancouver, BC.'

Brian said, 'How did he get there?'

Now it was Darren's turn. 'We don't know. We have a theory, but we just don't know.'

'Well, shit,' Brian said, 'how about letting us in on the theory?'

Darren refused to rise to the bait, kept his voice calm and focused, and Adrianna was pleased to see that performance, as well. Despite everything out there, her team was still sharp, was still on the job, and would still do what was necessary. The NSA officer said, 'Traffic analysis showed a cell operating in Ontario for a number of months. Not much in the way of information. Just low-key chatter, but we were able to determine that one of the cell members had a distinctive Syrian accent. Then, for two weeks, silence. Nothing. Then the cell chatter started up again. In Vancouver, on the western side of Canada, and the same guy was talking, the one with the Syrian accent. During that two-week period Mister Akim was deposited at the Vancouver General Hospital. The theory is that the cell was traveling west when Mister Akim took ill.'

Brian said, 'Deposited? What does that mean?'

The doctor said, 'Exactly what he said, detective. Hospital records show that Akim was brought into the emergency room two weeks ago and dropped off by another man. No description or name of the other man, nothing on any local surveillance cameras. Nothing. It was like they picked this hospital on purpose, to be able to slide in and out without being recorded.'

Monty asked, 'And what was Mister Akim's problem?'

Victor returned to looking at his laptop screen. 'He was admitted with a high fever, shortness of breath. Usual and customary treatments were started, along with blood-culture testing and screening of his sputum and other bodily fluids. This testing was continuing right up to the point when Akim coded and died, not less than twelve hours after being admitted.'

Brian said, 'Damn it, stop dancing, will you?'

The doctor looked up. 'Excuse me? Dancing?'

'You know what I mean. Stop pretending like we're some hospital committee. Get to the point, doc. What killed this character?'

Victor looked in the team leader's direction. 'Adrianna?'

She took the ball, took the responsibility. 'Certainly. Brian, Akim died of acute respiratory failure, brought on by exposure to *bacillus anthracis*.'

'Bacillus what?'

Except for Brian, it seemed like the other members of the group, especially the good doctor, knew exactly what Adrianna was talking about.

She cleared her throat. 'Anthrax, Brian. Anthrax is what killed him. And that's what's going to hit us in less than a month'

CHAPTER SIX

The Brixton section of London is as far away from the London of Big Ben and Buckingham Palace as the tenement rows of Anacostia are from the Mall and the Washington Monument in the District of Columbia. Scarred occasionally by race riots and violent clashes between local gangs, it was also a place that Henry Muhammad Dolan proudly called home. In the cluttered basement of the flat he rented from the local council, he sat in front of a Dell computer, laboriously downloading files from an e-mail account, copying them to a diskette. He had no idea what he was copying or why he was copying; all he had been told was that it was important that it was done, and done quickly.

The basement was filled with cardboard boxes, unpacked from his family's last move, and some of the toys that he no longer allowed the children to play with, especially the Barbie dolls, which he has getting ready to toss out. His twin daughters had pleaded and wept and argued to have them back, but Henry had been stern: no such dolls would be allowed in his home.

He looked at the computer screen in satisfaction as he proceeded with his work, the light playing a bit of a trick on him so that he could make out his reflection in the screen. Before him was the ghostly image of a bearded man in his early thirties, a man with a shameful past and a very proud future. Only in his quiet brown eyes could he see the youth he once was, a drunken, ganja-using lout who had roamed the streets of Brixton at night, breaking into shops or parked trucks, stealing and drinking and whoring and drugging, showing no respect for himself, his family, or his neighbors.

A shameful past, for sure, but one that really didn't bring him to shame. That moment had come after his first arrest as an adult, when instead of going to the usual juvenile facility, he ended up at H.M. Prison at Maidstone, where—

Henry paused in his typing, swallowed hard. Even now,

it was difficult to recall what had happened there. Slight in build, he had still thought he knew how to handle himself, how to defend himself . . . but after just a few weeks he had been a broken boy (not a man – would a man have allowed that to happen?) who would cower in a corner, shivering, his asshole plugged with toilet paper to stop the bleeding.

Until . . . until deliverance came, in the form of a dark-skinned man, originally from the Sudan, who had offered him protection. His name was some indecipherable series of African syllables that Henry could not understand, so he called him Jack. At first he had turned Jack away, thinking that he was exchanging one tormentor for another, but no, the Sudanese had no interest in his body. Just his soul, and after one hairy tattooed thug had his testicles razored open in the shower Henry had been left alone. The Sudanese had begun teaching him, teaching him the prayers and history of the Prophet, and by the time he had been released from prison he had converted and changed his name – and, of course, his life.

He had owed the Sudanese everything, and in exchange for saving his life and his soul Jack had asked for only a few favors: for Henry to return to Brixton upon his release from prison, to begin a holy life, and, of course, to be available to perform a service or two. And Henry, still waking up at night shivering from the memories of his first few weeks in prison, had readily agreed to help.

The requests had always been minor. Gather up some of his new brethren from the local mosque and join a demonstration in front of the Israeli embassy. Help distribute copies of an Islamist newspaper in the district. And, once, report to two hard-faced men the names of those young men in the area, unbelievers, who were troublemakers. That particular task had worried him just a bit, especially when two of the troublemakers were found in trash cans, their arms broken. But a night of reflection and prayer, and memories of how the Sudanese had protected him in prison, had washed away any remnants of guilt.

Now this latest task was easier still. Set up an e-mail account with a particular password and address. Check the e-mail account three times a day for a specific message. And when that message arrived – as it had, just an hour ago – carefully copy the attached photo files to a diskette, and deliver the diskette to an officer at the local mosque.

Simple, quite simple, and Henry cared not for what was in the message, only that he was helping repay that terrible debt from his time in prison. He had met with Jack – out on his own now for over a year – at a local coffee shop where the talk had ranged loosely from their shared time in prison to gossip about neighbors attending the mosque to the current struggle. And at the mention of the struggle, the Sudanese had looked around himself for a moment, and then had leaned over to Henry.

'May I give you advice, brother – confidential advice?'

But of course, Henry had said.

'It must be kept completely confidential. I cannot impress on you how important this is.'

Henry had nodded in quiet excitement, thinking that he was being told something important, something no doubt to repay him for the small favors he had done over the years.

Yes, I understand the importance, Henry had said. You can always rely on me.

The Sudanese had smiled, his big teeth white and even. 'We have relied on you for many things, my brother. So listen, and listen well. It's true, is it not, that you have family in the United States?'

My wife does, Henry had said cautiously, not sure where the Sudanese was going with his questioning.

'We thought so.'

And Henry had thought that he did not recall ever, in prison, telling the Sudanese any details about his wife's family. The thought made him swallow hard. What was the Sudanese driving at?

Henry had told the Sudanese, Yes, my wife has a sister who lives in Detroit. Near Dearborn.

Jack nodded in understanding. 'Very good. So I tell you this, brother. Do not travel to the United States anytime in the next few months. Do you hear me?'

A little shiver of something had made its way to his chest at the words the Sudanese had said. Truly? he had asked.

'Truly.' The Sudanese had nodded emphatically. 'And that is all I will say about that.'

So that had been it. And now Henry was here, in the basement, fulfilling the latest request from the tall African. He remembered that chill, that—

Footsteps.

Coming down the stairs.

Working quickly, he worked a series of keys until the screen he had been working on was replaced with another. The sacred words of the Prophet.

He looked up. His wife Mariah was now there, plump and smiling hesitantly, black headscarf over her hair.

'Yes?' he asked.

'Sorry to disturb you, husband. It's just that . . . well, I have wonderful news.'

'You do?'

Her hands were clasping an envelope with American stamps on it. She said, 'It's from Azannah. Her husband's car dealership has had a wonderful spring. She wants to fly me and the girls to see her next month, and I—'

'No.'

Mariah stopped, looked at him, and lowered her voice. 'Henry, please, it's been so long since I've seen my sister and my nephews and—'

He shook his head. 'No. I will not allow it.'

'But Henry, it's—'

Another shake of his head. 'The discussion is finished. You and the girls are not to travel to the United States. Ever. Understood?'

Her face colored and she nodded. 'Understood.'

Mariah turned and went back up the stairs, her footsteps heavier this time, and Henry sighed as he resumed his work. No doubt there would be a week of cold meals and even colder words, but it had to be done. Others would have laughed off what Jack had told him, but not Henry. Not since that day in the prison shower when that tattooed tormentor of his had started bellowing like a bull, his hands clasped at his bleeding crotch. If Jack said something was going to happen, then Henry was going to believe it.

There. Finished. He shut down the computer and ejected the diskette, slipped it into a padded envelope. His work for now was done and he recalled that feeling he had experienced, that little shiver when Jack told him not to travel to the United States, that hated place, that cesspool of infidels . . .

The first time he noticed it, he had wondered: what was causing that shiver? And, of course, he had remembered that wonderful day, that September when he had watched with smiles and outright laughter those twin towers of Babylon burning and crumpling to the ground. The shiver was one of happiness, excitement, at seeing hammer blows struck against the unholy, and at the knowledge that somehow, with his work with Jack, he was helping to strike another hammer blow.

How wonderful.

Yet . . . Mariah's sister and family. Could there not be a way of warning them?

Henry stood up, thinking. A puzzle, a quandary, that he would have to think and pray over for the rest of the day.

CHAPTER SEVEN

Brian Doyle was now fully awake, the little fog of exhaustion that had clouded his thinking having been dispersed with that one shocking word: anthrax. He recalled the mailings, right after 9/11, and how it had seemed as though a reeling country was coming in for another blow, with newspeople taking Cipro and postal workers wearing rubber gloves and face masks. After a while, the panic had ebbed away – what the hell else could you do? – but now the boogeyman was back.

He said, 'Anthrax. All right. What else do you have?'

Adrianna said, 'Observe the screen, please.'

Brian turned, saw the flickering image of the dead Brit fade out, replaced by a burst of static. Then something snapped into focus, and the rest of the group turned as well, looking at the image. It was a moving image, with numbers and letters streaming across the bottom of the screen. An overhead shot, showing a city scene. Narrow streets, a hell of a lot of traffic, carts, vendors and shops. There was a flickering motion as the camera seemed to focus on one particular vehicle: a white four-door, maybe a Toyota, with rust stains along the roof. The vehicle was moving slowly through the crowded street.

Adrianna said, 'Aerial record, last month, from a Predator III drone.'

The doctor turned to Adrianna. 'I thought the Predator drones only went up two generations. Not three.'

She smiled thinly. 'Publicly, you're right.'

Monty asked, 'Where are we?'

'Western part of Damascus, Syria. Keep on watching, please.'

Brian watched the video, unease creeping around in his gut. He wasn't sure why but he remembered one of the last good times he had had with Marcy, before things had started crumbling between them. They had rented a cottage up in the Adirondacks, at some chilly lake whose name escaped him. Late one night, after a good meal and a bottle of wine, they had gone skinny-dipping in the cool waters of the lake, and in the moonless night they had made frantic love on the sands of their little beach. Marcy at first had been reluctant – 'Suppose someone sees us?' – but she had given in to his logical reply: 'Who the hell's gonna see us tonight?'

And the answer now, of course, would be that anybody and everybody with the right gear and the necessary curiosity could see you if they wanted to. And he remembered an event, during his first month, working for the team.

*

At first Brian had done the usual investigative grunt work, which had been fine, considering what they were paying him and how the burden of worrying about court appearances and getting one's story straight with whatever youngster assistant DA was assigned to your squad was no longer on his shoulders. The only thing was that he missed the reassurance of having backup. Back on the job, help was just a hurried radio call away: 10-13, officer needs assistance. But on this whacked assignment, he was on his own, which took a bit getting used to. He had flown alone out to Michigan, to interview some woman about her wayward nephew. The woman had emigrated from Yemen nearly twenty years earlier, and she had welcomed him into her living room with the quiet resignation of one who knew that her last name and ethnic background now meant that the giant searchlight of the government was glaring on her every move. Her house was sparsely furnished, with only one couch and two chairs and a tiny television set in the living room. She was worn and old, wearing a black dress and a headscarf. Brian felt like a fool, sitting in her room, asking a series of questions that he was sure had been tossed her way before, over and over again, from people as diverse as the INS and the Michigan State Police.

He went over the woman's childhood, her coming of age, her marriage to a man who had worked for the American embassy in Aden and who had managed to emigrate to the United States. Her two sons and daughter, all grown, all married and with lots of grandchildren. Her husband's unfortunate death five years ago. How difficult it was, making do in this community, even with a little money coming in every now and then from family mem-

bers. How humiliated she had been, the first time she had
received food from Meals on Wheels. So forth and so on,
and the only time the conversation got heated was when
she talked about her nephew – 'that accursed young man' –
and she had said, with emphasis by pointing a gnarled
finger at him, that she had not heard from the boy for years
and years.

Then, tears in her eyes, she had lowered her head and
apologized for raising her voice. 'You're just doing your job.
That's all. I understand.'

And as Brian made to leave, his interview over, she had
pointed proudly to a photo of a young man in an Army uniform, posed stiffly in front of an American flag.

'My son,' she had said. 'Halim. Serving as a translator in
Iraq. With the Third Infantry Division.'

So Brian had gone out to his car, thinking the trip had
been a bust – just low-level practice work for the team, he
guessed – and as he was about to start up his rental car and
head back to the budget motel that unfortunately was the
closest lodging to this neighborhood, he had stopped. Car
keys in hand.

Just stopped.

Something wasn't right.

He paused, listened to his gut tell him something was up.
It wasn't something that was taught in the Academy or even
in the few months on the street on the job. It was something
you picked up along the way, absorbing it until it became
part of who you were. And right now it was telling him that
something wasn't right.

Okay. Take a breath, take in the surroundings. A fairly
desolate area outside Detroit, tiny one-family homes, butted
up right against each other. Waist-high chain-link fences

separated each tiny lot from its neighbor. The poorer homes had no garages of any kind, those doing a little better had open carports, and the real up-and-comers had proper garages.

The woman's home just had a driveway. No garage.

Brian looked around some more. Most of the lots had the usual residential debris scattered around the small front yards: wagons, tricycles, bicycles, baseball bats and gloves, a skateboard or two, bright plastic toy furniture.

The woman's lawn was empty. Of course it was empty. She lived alone, it would only be strange, would only be out of the ordinary, if there were toys or kids' belongings on her front lawn, with the close-cropped grass and—

Grass.

Okay, then.

He checked out the other lawns. Most of them were just packed squares of dirt. Maybe two or three were struggling with crab grass, dandelions and brown grass, trying to make do in solid urban dirt.

But not this woman's lawn.

Her lawn was lush, green, well groomed and well maintained. There were ornamental plants placed along the foundation line of the small house. Brian recalled how painfully the woman had walked from the kitchen to the living room, limping heavily, saying she needed hip-replacement surgery and if God was kind her children would band together to help pay for it. He couldn't see her out in the yard, sowing fertilizer and weedkiller, or walking along the edge of the driveway, weed-whacker in her gnarled hands, trimming away.

Little money, he thought. Look at the rest of the house. The shingles curling up along the edge of the roof. The oil-stained and cracked driveway. The broken pane of glass in one of the small basement windows, plugged up with a piece of cardboard.

So how come she had a jewel of a lawn?

Brian shook his head, started up the car, and left.

He went one block, where he was sure that he would not be seen by the woman, parked the car, stepped out, and went back to work.

A couple of weeks passed. Brian had learned from the woman's neighbors about the landscaping company that came every other week to service her yard. Using his spanking brand-new Federal identification and credentials, he learned that a trust fund paid for the yard's maintenance. More digging showed that the financing for the trust fund came from an offshore account in the Cayman Islands. By then he had alerted Adrianna to what he had found, and he had briefed Darren, the young man from the NSA. And eventually, late one evening, he had been in the very same meeting room, watching the plasma screen, as Adrianna gently squeezed his shoulder and then played a few buttons on the keyboard of her laptop that was set up on the conference-room table.

'You did good, Brian,' she had said. 'That little ball of string you started unwinding has brought us to a very good place.'

'What was the deal?' he had asked.

'The woman grew up in a desert. All her life, all she ever wanted was a lush green yard, with grass and plants and shrubs, and the cool, moist feeling of a bit of paradise.'

'Near Detroit?'

'Paradise is where you can find it, and this particular patch of paradise was being fed, watered and groomed from afar by her favorite little nephew. We were able to trace that offshore account to another account in Khartoum, and then from there we just kept on tracing and tracing and tracing. Nicely done, Brian.'

'The hell you say.'

'Yes,' she said. 'The hell I say.' Adrianna glanced at a wristwatch, gold and shiny on her slight olive wrist. 'Take a look, then.'

Up on the plasma screen, an overhead shot from a Predator, showing flat desert. There was a plume of dust in the distance. The dust cloud grew larger, and the picture flickered some, as the Predator changed position. The dust cloud then revealed itself to be a dark blue Mercedes-Benz sedan, speeding along. Brian opened his mouth to say something when—

Flash of light. No sound from the screen but Brian could imagine what it must have been like. The flash of light merged into a black greasy cloud, and the Mercedes-Benz emerged through the cloud, rolling over and over and over. It came to a halt on its side, smoke and steam rising up and—

Men were there. Rising up from the desert floor, it looked like, where they had lain hidden in holes. Men in tan desert-camouflage gear with automatic weapons in their hands. They went to work, quickly enough, and five men were pulled from the wrecked car, stretched out on the desert floor, and then the helicopters came and the men were bundled in and—

Bodies. Taken from another helicopter. Brought over to the Mercedes-Benz. Awkwardly stuffed into the open doors of the sedan, and then the soldiers trotted back to their helicopters.

'Decoys?' Brian asked.

'Very good,' Adrianna said. 'Fedayeen who martyred themselves outside Kabul last year, by driving their pickup trucks into Bradley fighting vehicles. Score, Bradley fighting vehicle one, fedayeen pickup trucks nil. And we appreciated their martyrdom valor so much that we froze their bodies for later and decided to honor them by setting up a return engagement.'

The helicopters lifted off. Brian knew that he wouldn't have to wait long, and he didn't.

Another, larger flare of light. When the wind finally cleared away the smoke there was a crater in the desert floor, and scraps of blackened metal and what had once been bodies.

Adrianna reached over to her laptop, pressed a button. The plasma screen went blank.

'Yemen?' he asked.

'Doing well today, Brian. Yes, Yemen.'

'And when whatever Yemeni authorities get to the wreckage, all they're going to find are some scraps of metal and charred bits of flesh. They'll eventually figure out whose Mercedes-Benz that is, and they'll count up the body parts and make an educated guess as to what happened. They won't be in a position to do a DNA analysis of whatever's left.'

'Exactly.'

'And the evil nephew and his cohorts . . . their comrades will think that they're up in heaven, sipping strawberry smoothies and banging seventy-two virgins, when in fact they'll be in Gitmo, getting sweated out, offering up leads and other intelligence.'

Adrianna nodded. 'Exactly again, Brian.' She gave him a

large smile and Brian had felt good, having made that cool and composed woman smile. He suddenly decided that he needed to see her smile again.

Then he had a thought. 'The old woman. His aunt. Is she Gitmo-bound?'

Adrianna closed the laptop cover, shook her head. 'Why pick on an old Yemeni woman? No, we'll leave her be. But she will have to pay the price for her actions.'

'And what price is that?'

Adrianna looked at him, her gaze fixed and composed. 'Her lawn will probably die in the near future. You got a problem with that?'

'Not a bit,' he said.

'I thought you'd say that. Brian, welcome to the team.'

That comment nailed him, and he clenched his hands, just for a moment.

'A setup? A test?'

'No, no,' Adrianna said quickly. 'Not a setup. We just knew something wasn't right with that woman. Scores of interviewers had gone in and out of there without anything substantial. But you did, my friend. Went in there with your detective's eyes and detective's suspicions, and because of that five bad guys have been taken off the board. Permanently.'

Brian thought about that for a moment, and said, 'Okay. Not a setup. But a test.'

She shrugged. 'It could be said like that.'

'Any other tests out there for me?'

There, again, that damnable smile that seemed to light up something inside him.

'Brian, every day is a test. Every goddamn day.'

*

So now, on this testing day, the Predator was following the white Toyota with rust stains on its roof in Damascus traffic. Adrianna said, 'Darren?'

Darren said, 'A couple of months ago, somebody in Damascus made a mistake. One phone call. That's all it took.'

Monty laughed. 'Man, one phone call sure can fry your ass. What happened?'

'It was from a satellite phone that we've been monitoring in a neighborhood near Suq Hamadiya in Damascus. It was one of a parcel purchased by al-Qaeda members or supporters. The phone had not been used much, and when it was used the chatter was brief and low-key.'

Monty said, 'What's the mistake? Somebody use it to order some couscous?'

Darren managed a smile. 'Close. Somebody used it to call a local garage. Said he was tired of waiting for the transmission to be fixed. Wanted it fixed that afternoon or the mechanic's head would be on a pike, and his children would be forced to beg from the streets. So that was the break we got. Easy enough from there to find out who the car belonged to, and what it looked like. Put a tracking device in one of the tires. Easy enough again to put the car in the daily tasking orders for the Predators deployed in that area. And then . . . well, Adrianna?'

'Just watch,' she said. 'Just watch.'

Brian rubbed at his eyes, looked at the car, inching its way through traffic. Then it stopped at an intersection. A cop or traffic guy, standing on a little concrete island, tried his best to direct traffic, and it looked like he was being ignored. Then, strangely enough, vehicles in front of the Toyota moved, but it stayed still, just for a second. Then a hand appeared from the front passenger window, just for a moment, as it dropped something onto the sidewalk.

The car moved. Brian said, 'Can you freeze that, right there?'

Frozen. The car, the traffic, the frantic white-gloved hands of the traffic cop. Not moving.

Brian said, 'Play it back, slow.'

Like some comedy newsreel from the 1930s, the traffic moved backwards, and Brian stood up, leaned into the plasma screen, tried to see what was happening. Something flew up into the outstretched hand, and—

'Reverse it, right now.'

And the object was dropped.

Brian sat down. 'Okay. You can keep playing it.'

The tape ran for another thirty minutes, and twice more the white Toyota stopped at an intersection, and the passenger's hand reached out to drop something on the sidewalk. The bustling lines of people, pressed up against the walls of the buildings or the edge of the crumbling sidewalk, seemed to pay no mind for what was being dropped at their feet.

The plasma screen went blank. Brian turned and was surprised to see the team members looking at him, especially Adrianna. She said, 'There was something there you noticed, Brian.'

'Yeah.'

'What was it?'

He paused for a moment, wondered if he was being tested again. If so, what the hell. 'The guy in the passenger side of the Toyota. Looked like he was dropping something off.'

'What was it?'

He rubbed at his face, realized he had missed a spot on his

chin while hurriedly shaving that morning. 'If this was in the States, and if there was a radio car on its ass, lights flashing and siren sounding, then I'd guess it'd be a couple of drug perps. And that they'd be dropping off little baggies of whatever it is they were selling that day, to dump the evidence. But these clowns weren't being chased, near as I could tell.'

A pause. The group still looked at him. Made him still feel like he was trying to prove something to them, that even a non-Fed like himself could do the job, and he pressed on. 'Another thing, too. Perps in a situation like that, they're panicking. They're tossing out their merchandise, tossing it far, hoping that the cops on their ass won't find it. These guys weren't doing this. It was deliberate. It was—'

There. It came to him.

Brian looked over to Adrianna, now feeling slightly nauseous, wishing he hadn't had those two cups of coffee this Sunday morning on an empty stomach, and he said, 'They're deliberately dropping these plastic baggies. At intersections. Knowing that traffic and people walking will move over the baggies, rip open the plastic, distribute what's in there.'

Monty whispered, 'Holy shit.'

Victor said in a shaky voice, 'The perfect delivery system.'

Now everyone was looking at the doctor, whose face seemed even more pale. Victor went to his laptop and said, 'You get weaponized anthrax. You have a lot of weaponized anthrax. All right. What's the delivery system? The US Post Office? Good if you want to create panic like the fall of '01, not good if you're looking for mass casualties. Crop dusters over cities? Not good enough. Too much of a wide distribution, too much dispersal. A few people get sick and that's it. A bit of a panic but life goes on . . . Good Christ.'

Victor waited, and then bulled on, his voice coming quick

now, syllables rolling over each other, as he looked up at the blank plasma screen, as if recalling what had just been viewed up there. 'That's how you do it. You have a crew, ten, thirty, forty guys. Whatever number you need. You immunize them before they go in. They each get twenty or thirty baggies of anthrax. Respiratory kind. Anthrax spores weaponized so it's finely milled. Drive out to the middle of cities, Manhattan, Boston, LA, maybe three or four teams per city. Christ. Drop off the baggies at crowded intersections, during lunch. Baggies get broken, clouds of anthrax spores rise up, get spread around the streets. Infect scores – shit, no – hundreds, maybe even thousands. In a single day. The perfect delivery system. Time it right and you get respiratory-anthrax outbreaks in a dozen major cities, tens of thousands of causalities within a week. Maybe more. Holy fucking Christ.'

Now the silence was thick, still, just the hum of the laptops working merrily along. Brian had a sudden thought, the four of them clustered around this table, wheezing themselves to death, while the laptops merrily went on with their powered lives, outliving their owners by years.

Adrianna said, 'Monty?'

'Yeah,' he grunted. Brian thought the man looked ill.

'Seems to be a likely scenario, doesn't it? Question is, how can we defend against it?'

Monty looked at all of them and then shook his head.

'Bottom line, we can't.'

'Come on, there has to be something that we can do,' Brian said. 'I mean, look at it—'

Monty turned to him, glaring. 'Don't lecture me on my job, 'kay? Here's the deal, and you all know it, even if I have to spell it out for you. You heard what the good doctor said, what we're up against. Okay. Maybe ten, fifteen teams out there. Ready to hit us in less than a month. What do we do? Close down the borders? Do person-by-person, vehicle-by-vehicle searches for everything coming up through Mexico and down through Canada? Is that it? Clog up the airports? Or the seaports? And that's assuming these assholes aren't here already. Maybe they came here last year. Maybe they all got jobs at 7-Eleven and the local gas stations and they've blended in so well, they're acting like good citizens. What do you do then?'

Adrianna said quietly, 'At about four a.m. this morning, I left a department meeting of the Tiger Team director. There's a full-court press to pick up those Syrians, start interrogating them, start looking at what other intercepts and records might be out there. We even got the Canadians on board. One working theory is that the gentleman dumped at the Vancouver hospital was exposed to the respiratory anthrax before being fully immunized. But even if we do get some breaks, there's a good chance that we'll miss a number of these teams. It just stands to reason.'

Darren shook his head. 'Dark Winter.'

Brian said, 'Excuse me?'

'Dark Winter,' Darren said, and Brian noticed that Adrianna seemed to flinch. 'Terrorism scenario, run by the National Security Council, the summer of 2001. Before September eleventh.'

Brian said, 'Talk about timing.'

'Yeah, talk about it,' Darren said, now bent over his laptop, fingers moving rapidly along the keyboard. 'Scenario was held at Andrews Air Force Base in Virginia and was hosted by the John Hopkins Center for Civilian Biodefense Strategies. Reps from most federal agencies and three hospitals were in attendance. Former Senator Sam Nunn played the role of the president. Even had the governor of Oklahoma there. Scenario started with the usual Middle East bullshit. Rising tensions, threats here and there. And one fine day, smallpox outbreak in three areas: Oklahoma, Georgia and Pennsylvania. Started off small and then spread quickly. Didn't have enough vaccine for the population at large. There was conflict over who'd get the vaccine. People living near the outbreak areas, or National Guard and health-care workers? Casualties started to mount. Schools were closed and public gatherings were banned. Tens of thousands were infected within a month. Hospitals were overwhelmed. Shit.'

Brian's mouth was dry and he suddenly felt thirsty, but nothing before him was appealing. He had the feeling that if he drank another cup of coffee, water or orange juice, he'd puke up his guts under the conference-room table.

Darren stopped for a moment, as if not wanting to read any more from his laptop screen. Then he sighed and went on. 'The scenario got worse. Not enough smallpox vaccine could be produced in time. Canada and Mexico sealed their borders. So did some of the states. Governors declared martial law, the stock market collapsed, and there were food shortages in some of the larger cities. By the time the war game was completed, there were nearly a million deaths. A million.'

The silence returned, and it was like no one in the team could bear to look at each other's eyes. Brian rubbed at his face again and looked at Adrianna, who seemed to be thinking of something. A thought came to him and Brian said, 'There was another scenario, wasn't there?'

'What?' Adrianna asked.

'Another scenario. This one involved smallpox. I'm sure there was one involving a nationwide anthrax attack. What was it like? What are we facing?'

Now the mood in the room had changed, as Brian and the three others looked to Adrianna, as though waiting for her to confirm their worst fears. She coughed and said, 'Yes, Brian. You're right. There was an anthrax scenario held last winter. Similar to Dark Winter.'

She stopped. Monty said, 'Go on. Tell us more.'

Adrianna rubbed her hands together for a moment. 'Started off like Dark Winter. Simultaneous and multiple outbreaks of anthrax. Same challenges, same problems. Vaccine stock small, and what vaccine there was had to be administered in three doses over a period of a week. All the states' borders sealed, economic collapse . . .'

Another pause. It had to be said. Brian spoke up and said, 'Worse than the smallpox scenario, wasn't it?'

Adrianna pursed her lips. 'Much worse. Respiratory anthrax is a magnitude more contagious than smallpox. The scenario . . . it didn't end well.'

Victor said nothing, as if he knew what was ahead of them. Darren looked around, like a high school student suddenly thrust into a jury for a murder trial, deciding a man's fate. He said, 'How *did* it end, then?'

A slight shake of the head. 'Major cities depopulated. Refugees spreading out into the suburbs and countryside. Vigilantes setting up roadblocks. Casualties in the millions. Effective collapse of all governing authority, from national levels to state levels, including military. UN peacekeepers sent in to administer what was left alive and functioning. Other UN members setting up relief mandates, seizing oil, grain and other resources.'

Adrianna stopped for just a moment. 'Dark Winter was the name for the smallpox scenario, because it imagined that as dire as it would be to suffer a smallpox attack, there was room for eventual recovery, that the country and its government and its people could survive.'

She looked at each of them in turn. 'The anthrax scenario had no such assurance. Hence its name.'

The room was deathly quiet. 'It was called Final Winter,' she said.

CHAPTER EIGHT

Aliyah Fulenz was sixteen years old and knew that she was lovely and educated and lucky. Yet with all these good things, she still felt a terrible guilt over keeping a secret from her papa and mama, especially now, with another war being waged in the air above her home in Baghdad.

This was the second war she had lived through, but she'd been just a little girl during the first one. All she recalled from that war were the nights spent in the basement of their home, cuddled up with papa and mama, listening to the ghastly shriek of air-raid sirens and the far-off explosions from the enemy bombs and missiles. She had been too young to know who was fighting or why, and her most vivid memories were just the faces of papa and mama looking up with fear at the ceiling, like they were waiting for some warhead to burst through and kill them all. Even with the loud noises and the way her mama held her close and tight, she hadn't been that scared. It had been like an adventure, an adventure like that of some princess she had read about in her picture books, and if mama and papa were there, how scared could she be?

Plenty scared, she would learn later, plenty scared indeed.

Now she was sixteen, and a war had come back, and she was older and wiser and oh, so much lovelier, and the fear that came each night with the wail of the sirens and the thudding noises of the bombs was now outweighed by guilt, for she had never kept secrets from her papa and mama, and the secret she had now was one that she wasn't sure she could keep.

For Aliyah was in love.

His name was Hassan, and he was a nineteen-year-old militiaman who had volunteered as an air-raid warden for their neighborhood, and he was tall and dark and had brown eyes and a wide grin and a mustache that tickled her whenever he kissed her, for he had kissed her exactly twice, and she sometimes daydreamed, wondering what the third kiss would be like. And on this winter evening, mama had noticed her absent-mindedness, scolding her for not drying the supper dishes properly. Not complaining, like the good daughter she was, Aliyah had rewashed and redried each plate and fork and spoon, washing each item mechanically, trying to remember that firm touch of Hassan, the softness of his lips, and the way his sweetness stayed on her lips, minutes later after each kiss.

She closed the cabinet doors, went out to the main room of their house, where papa and mama were resting, sitting on a couch, the television on but the sound off. On the screen a man in a western suit was sitting behind a desk, reading what passed for news these days. She ached for a moment,

looking at her parents, knowing she was lucky indeed to
have such a man and a woman to raise her. Papa was a doctor
and worked in the Ministry of Health, in an office concerned
with pediatrics, and he would bring home piles of papers
and folders in an old, scuffed leather briefcase. Lately he had
been grumbling and examining these papers, late into the
night, trying to work with French and German pharmaceutical companies, trying to find some way of importing
medicines for the city's hospitals during the war.

Mama taught French at Baghdad University and had
promised Aliyah that this summer, once the war was finally
over, the two of them would fly to Paris and mama would be
her own personal tour guide to that magnificent and civilized
city. Paris! Aliyah had gotten books from her school library
that showed the monuments and museums and the Eiffel
Tower, and mama had laughed, gently brushing Aliyah's hair
one night, saying, 'Paris is a beautiful city, my daughter, but
remember this. Your own Baghdad was a center of culture
and civilization, for the entire known world, when Paris was
nothing more than mud and wattle huts, with peasants who
still prayed to the gods of thunder and lightning. Never
forget your heritage, Aliyha, never.'

Now she looked at them both, sitting there, her father
with the papers in his lap, mama knitting a pair of gloves for
her father, who suffered so much in the cold of winter. Mama
looked up at her. 'Are the dishes now done properly, Aliyah?'

'Yes, they are,' she said, her chest tightening with the
ache of what she was trying to do.

'Very good,' her mother said.

Aliyah remained standing. Her mother returned to her
knitting and looked up again. 'Yes, what is it?'

'I . . . I'm going for a walk. Is that all right?'

Her father looked up. 'Now? At dusk? It's not safe!'

'Only to the end of the block! Papa, I promise I will be careful!'

He shook his head. 'Suppose the bombing starts up? Eh? What then?'

'When the sirens sound, I will run right home.'

Her mother stopped her knitting. 'No, you will not run home. You will run to the shelter, that's where you will run.'

Father grumbled and said, 'I forbid it, wife. It's too dangerous to go out. Just one bomb, one missile . . .'

Mama smiled at Aliyah and reached up with a hand, gently rubbed father's bald spot. 'Not to worry. Our daughter needs to get some fresh air. That's all. And I know she will promise to run to the shelter and meet us there, if the sirens sound. Am I right?'

Aliyah nodded, though she hadn't liked the shelter that had opened up in their neighborhood. It was crowded and dark and children inside the shelter screamed and wept all night long, and she couldn't sleep. She had much preferred to take shelter here in her own home, in their basement, but her father had forbidden that, and for once her mother had let him have his way. He insisted that the new shelter was strong – 'built by the Finns and the Swedes, they know their engineering, and living next to the Russians for so long, they know how to build bomb shelters' – and that was where they had gone, night after night during the past week, when the shelter had been opened up to the neighboring residents.

'Yes, mama, you are right. When the sirens sound, I will run as quick as the wind, to the shelter. And I will find you there.'

Father grumbled some more and went back to his papers. Mama smiled sweetly up at her daughter and the ache of guilt returned, that she had not told them about Hassan. But perhaps she would tell them tomorrow. Yes, perhaps tomorrow. She came over and kissed papa on the head and mama on her cheek, and mama said, 'Wait, daughter, just for a moment.'

Mama's strong fingers went to Aliyah's neck, pulling at a thin chain that hung there. Mama smiled widely as she pulled the chain free and the crucifix was exposed. She tugged again and Aliyah lowered herself, allowing her mother to kiss the form of Jesus upon the cross.

'There. I feel better. God and His Son will protect you. Now. Go and have your fun, daughter. But if the sirens sound . . .'

'Yes, yes, I know,' Aliyah called out, racing to the door. 'I will run right to the shelter!'

Then papa said something else, which she did not hear, and to which she paid little attention.

There would always be another time.

Out on the streets, a scarf about her head, Aliyah walked quickly down the block, sniffing in distaste at the smell of burning garbage. Ever since the war had come to Baghdad, the trash services had faltered and failed, and electricity was spotty some days and nights. But she and her family were lucky, at least, that the water was still running. There was a rumor that a cousin of Himself lived just two blocks away, and that there would be no way that he would allow the water to be stopped.

She passed parked cars and there, up on the left and on the other side of the street, was a three-story apartment building with its windows blown out, the concrete scarred by shrapnel, the large extended family who had lived in there either dead or wounded. The newspapers had said that the place had been struck by an American bomb, by a terror pilot who only wanted to strike fear into the hearts of the Baghdad civilians, and Aliyah last week had asked papa if that was true, that it had been an American bomb. Papa had shaken his head and said, 'Daughter, you see how much artillery and missiles our brave forces fire up into the sky, do you not? Have you forgotten that old rhyme, what goes up, must come down?' And mama had shushed him and that had been that.

Aliyah reached into her blouse, touched the comforting pendant of Jesus on the cross. She and her family were Christians, and mama and papa were proud that here, in Baghdad, still the most civilized city in the Arab world, they were allowed to worship freely. Not like the barbarians in Egypt, who murdered their Coptic Christians, or the desert barbarians in Saudi Arabia, who allowed no other religion into their kingdom. 'We have many problems, Aliyah,' her father had once said, 'but being able to worship our own way is not one of them. Even Himself has a Christian as his foreign minister!'

Which was true, though it concerned Aliyah not one bit. Some foreign minister, to allow such a war to go on . . . but she kept such thoughts to herself. The only thought she had right now was to ensure that Hassan was going to be where he'd said he would be.

She approached the corner of the street, hesitated for a moment. She had told papa and mama that her walk would only take her to the end of the block. But it was such a cool, beautiful evening, and Hassan was only two more blocks away – what difference would it make? She hesitated again, thinking of papa and mama back home, and how easy it would be to turn around, walk back home, and stay in the living room with mama and papa, and perhaps mama would play some of her French music records, the women with such low and smooth voices, perhaps she should go back, back to where she belonged . . .

But the streets ahead beckoned to her. Hassan and his smile and his long fingers and his lips waited for her. Just a short stroll, that's all, she told herself. Just a short stroll.

Aliyah walked across the street, looked back, wondering if she could see her home, but all she could make out were the low buildings of the other homes and the jagged concrete of the destroyed apartment building.

The walk went fast, and up ahead there was a small pyramid of sandbags. Men in uniforms were standing around, talking and joking, automatic rifles slung across their young backs. Aliyah slowed her walk, not wanting to look too eager, but still, she was noticed. There was laughter from two of the men, who grabbed a taller man and thrust him forward. More laughter.

She stopped in front of him, smiling widely. Hassan nodded, smiling as well.

'Aliyah,' he said.

'Hassan.'

He said in a louder voice, probably for the benefit of his comrades: 'It's not safe to come out at night, you know that.'

'I know . . . but still, I had to go for a walk. It's so nice and cool.'

'So it is.'

The other young men – boys, really – laughed. Hassan looked at them, smiling, and he took her hand – how strong his own hand felt – and they walked away from the pile of sandbags. They sat on a bench and watched the traffic go by, listened to the sounds of the birds, even in this part of the city, and talked about school and soccer and other gossip and, here and there, just brief comments about the war. Aliyah felt such love for Hassan, sitting there next to her in his green uniform, his assault rifle held lightly across his lap, a young boy ready to protect her and her family from the invaders. She thought about how she would tell papa and mama about Hassan, maybe tomorrow, and a thought came to her, a thought so exciting that she could feel something racing through her: Paris. Mama had said earlier that if the war was over soon enough and the sanctions were lifted, there would be enough money that when they went to Paris, she could take a friend, and mama hadn't said whether the friend had to be a girl, and why not a boy like Hassan, from such a nice family and—

Hassan grabbed her hand, hard, as a siren began to wail.

Aliyah looked up, amazed at how dark the sky had gotten.

Oh, mama, papa, she thought, I am in so much trouble. She got up, ready to run back to their neighborhood, to the shelter, and Hassan said, 'Where do you think you're going?'

'To the shelter. With my parents.'

He held on to her arm as other sirens began to wail. 'No, it's too dangerous. You have to stay here.'

'Hassan, no, I—'

Hassan's voice changed from that of a smiling young man, flirting with a beautiful young girl, to that of an armed militiaman, charged with a duty. 'No! It's too far! You'll come here with us.'

He started dragging her away as his two companions joined him. They went through a narrow alleyway, past a squealing cat, and down one set of concrete steps, then another. The sirens seemed louder, and then there were two loud thuds as the evening's bombing began. A metal door was unlatched and lights were switched on. Another, longer flight of concrete steps led to a further metal door, which was open. Hassan led the way, followed by Aliyah and the two other men. Electric lights in the shelter flickered and glowed. There was a family there, father and mother and four children, bundled together, their eyes really wide, and Aliyah wondered if she had looked so scared and innocent during the last war.

She sat next to Hassan on a metal bench and said, 'My parents. They will be so cross with me, they told me to go to the shelter and—'

Hassan interrupted her, his voice so brave. 'Then I will take the blame. I will say that I was on patrol when the sirens sounded, that I brought you here to keep you safe. That is what I will do.'

Aliyah slipped her hand into Hassan's and squeezed it tight, thinking that yes, this would work so beautifully. She would present Hassan to mama and papa as a hero, a man who bravely took her in and comforted her. Surely mama and papa would see what a wonderful young man he was!

The lights flickered. More thudding. The children started whimpering.

Hassan raised his voice. 'It will be fine, just you wait and see. It will be fine. Our air defenses are the mightiest in the world. All will be fine.'

Aliyah squeezed his hand again. There was another thud in the distance, and the lights went out.

More whimpering from the children. It was so dark that she couldn't see anything, nothing at all.

But she could feel just fine, and in the darkness she felt

the tentative touch of Hassan's hand upon her face. She kissed his fingers and then his lips were upon her again, and in the darkness of the bomb shelter, despite the whimpering of the children and the thudding noises still coming in regular waves, she had never felt such pleasure, such joy, as Hassan kissed her, again and again, and then . . . his hand was upon her breast, gently squeezing, and her breathing quickened, as she felt a man's hand upon her for the very first time, my God, how pleasurable and how wickedly naughty, to be touched and kissed and loved in darkness and—

WHAM!

WHAM!

WHAM!

There was screaming, loud screaming, and Aliyah realized it was her. She closed her mouth, found that she was on the concrete floor of the bunker. The floor was . . . something was wrong. It was tilted. It was still dark and there was a flare of light, as the father in the corner lit a cigarette lighter. Hassan was standing over her, his face a mix of concern and fear, and she got up. 'I have to go, I have to go now!'

'It's not safe!'

'I don't care! I want my mama and papa, and I want them now!'

Aliyah staggered over to the door, tried to get it open. It seemed jammed. She pulled and pulled, and something wrenched free. The sirens were still screaming. She ran up the stairs, knowing that Hassan was following her, not caring.

Up and up she went, crying now, the sirens louder as she got closer to the surface. She broke free, out into the alley. Other sirens were sounding as well, ambulances and fire engines. She went out to the street, kept on running. The shelter. She would go to the shelter and find mama and papa and bury herself in their arms, and promise to be a good daughter, never again to leave their side, if only the sirens and shrieking would stop, if only it would be quiet and the war would stop and papa would work at saving sick children and mama would teach her French, and all would be safe and quiet and beautiful . . .

The shelter. Where was the shelter?

She ran up one block, and then took a left. More sirens from the distance, and then an ambulance shrieked by, and then another. She took another corner and—

Smoke. Chaos. Aliyah brought both fists up to her head and beat at her ears.

The shelter was across the street, but she could not get any closer. There were ambulances and fire trucks and masses of people, crowding in and around the structure. There was a barbed-wire fence around the concrete edifice, and people were tearing at it with their bare hands. A large plume of smoke was billowing from the rooftop, rising higher and higher into the night sky as if from a chimney venting the output of some horrible fire going on underneath the concrete and steel and—

A group of men emerged from the crowd, carrying a stretcher. They were chanting and screaming, and each held a fist up in the air as their other hand held the frame. An Iraqi flag was draped over the burnt body, barely concealing it. And another stretcher emerged, and another, and Aliyah was on the ground, prostrate, beating her forehead against the asphalt, praying to her savior, the Lord Jesus Christ, to save her and her mama and papa, and she stayed there all night long, as the hundreds of burnt bodies were dragged out of the destroyed shelter, her mama and papa among them, charred pieces of flesh and bone, and save for a distant aunt she was now all alone in the world, and when she finally stood up and saw the useless fire trucks still there in the morning, pouring water into the shelter, she was still sixteen, but she was no longer a young girl.

Hassan held no interest for her anymore nor did much of anything else. Not even her Lord Jesus Christ, who had permitted the Americans to come here and kill her family.

All that mattered now was revenge.

Revenge to make the Americans pay for what they had done to her and papa and mama.

And eventually that day, Aliyah returned home, and started to think and plan and work very, very hard.

CHAPTER NINE

In the conference room, Adrianna Scott could feel the greasy chill of despair come over her Tiger Team, but she would not allow it to get out of hand. She looked around the room and said, 'You know the weakness of scenarios. They assume the very best chances for our enemies, the very worst response by our agencies. But Final Winter was a war *game*. It was horrible. But it was just a game.'

The police detective said, 'A hell of a game, Adrianna. Jesus Christ, I thought weaponized anthrax was hard to produce, especially in quantity. Where the hell is this stuff coming from?'

Adrianna said, 'Darren?'

The NSA man said, 'Before the second Gulf War, the Secretary of State said that Iraq had produced hundreds of pounds of anthrax. Still hasn't been found yet. Not hard to figure out that the stuff was either sold or given away before the Third Infantry Division plowed into Baghdad.'

'Shit,' Brian said.

Adrianna said, 'Monty, there's no way to guarantee a one hundred percent success rate in sealing the borders or intercepting the teams. Correct?'

A morose nod of the head. 'You've got it.'

She turned to Victor, determined to keep things moving. In her experience since being chosen to head this Tiger Team, she knew that some teams collapsed in inter-service rivalry, bitter fights over who had said what in a year-old memo between the CIA and the NSA, and some teams were so cautious that nothing happened, except for strategy and long-range planning sessions. But her team and her people were quickly earning a reputation for coming up with solutions and making the solutions work, and that was a reputation she was determined to maintain.

'Victor, I'm afraid it's going to be up to you and your folks.'

Victor looked like a young rabbit, suddenly seeing a snake slither toward it. 'I don't see how.'

'The intelligence option and the military option are going to be of limited use,' she said, choosing her words carefully. 'That leaves the public-health option.'

'But I've told you already,' he protested. 'The typical vaccine regimen is three injections, spaced over a week. That and Cipro. I don't see what else we can do.'

There was a moment of silence, and then Monty spoke up. 'What do you mean, typical?'

'Just what I said. Typical.'

Now Adrianna saw the team members direct their gazes at Victor, who seemed to shrink some from the attention.

Darren said, 'All right, Victor. That's the typical approach. What's not typical?'

Victor looked at each of their faces, and when it came to Adrianna there was a pleading quality in his expression. 'Adrianna . . . it's highly experimental. It hasn't gone through the usual evaluation process and blind trials. The production line has been set up and there's been some progress, but it's at least—'

Brian said, 'What's usual about this, pal? Tell me that. C'mon, spill what you've got. What's going on down at the CDC?'

Victor looked down at his screen. 'All right. I'll brief you. But I'm not going to be held responsible for anything that—'

Adrianna tried to soothe him. 'No, you won't be held responsible, Victor. You know who holds the responsibility. So tell us what you've got.'

Victor still looked miserable. His fingers gingerly worked the keyboard of his laptop. He seemed to be struggling against something and Adrianna knew what it was: the desperate horror of screwing up, with the stakes so high.

Finally Victor said, 'It's been worked on since the first anthrax attacks, back in '01. Operational name is Clear Sky. Challenge was, just like now, goddamn it, how to maximize the immunization process for respiratory anthrax in the minimum amount of time. We had to get around the three-shot process. Wasn't working. How the hell can you get millions of Americans lined up and processed when it takes three injections to immunize them? The logistics were a nightmare. Even the one-shot process was a hell of a challenge, too. Then the working group for Clear Sky went at it from a different angle. Used a genetically modified version of the respiratory-anthrax virus. Modified it so that when an individual is exposed, he or she runs a slight fever, maybe a bit of nausea, but then they're immune. Immune up to five years.'

He looked up from his laptop. 'There you have it.'

'Have what?' Brian asked.

Monty said, 'Yeah. What the hell was the fuss all about?'

Victor had the expression of someone who couldn't believe the morons he was spending time with. 'Don't you see? It's a variety of the respiratory anthrax. You're not immunized through injection. You're immunized by breathing it in.'

Brian said, 'The hell you say.'

'The hell I do,' Victor said.

Adrianna said, 'Is there enough?'

'Enough what?'

'Enough vaccine to do the job.'

Victor shook his head. 'Maybe. I can find out later today. I know the production has been underway for some time, just in case we . . . well, just in case. But there's the biggest problem of all. Delivery. It's not like we can set up shower stations or breathing tubes on subways or train cars. Only possible delivery system would be airborne.'

Darren said, 'Hasn't it been looked at?'

'Sure,' Victor said. 'But the challenge of using an airborne vaccine is—'

Brian said, 'Oh, right. Like you said earlier. About wide dispersal. Crop dusters and such wouldn't work.'

Victor shook his head. 'That problem's been solved.'

Adrianna said, 'How?'

'Vladimir Zhukov.'

'Zhukov?' Monty asked. 'Who the hell is he?'

'*Was* he, we think,' Victor said. 'Nowadays, he's gone missing, after the break-up of the Soviet Union. Best report is that he got gunned down in Tashkent a couple of years ago for screwing some group out of money who thought they were getting smallpox viruses and ended up getting chickenpox instead. But during the bad old days of the USSR, he was head research scientist for the Kromksy Institute of Infectious Diseases, which was funded one hundred percent by the Red Army. Their own little biowarfare agency. They had the same challenge, too, of trying to weaponize respiratory anthrax because wind and air currents would cause such widespread dispersal that any attack would fail in the first few seconds. But Zhukov came up with a solution. Pretty goddamned elegant if you ask me. Way it works, it's like cluster bombs. You take—'

Monty said, 'Now you're into my playground, doc. I can do the explaining.'

'Go ahead.'

Adrianna watched the scarred face of her military man as he briefed them, not once looking at his laptop. She hated to admit playing favorites, but Monty was her favorite in her Tiger Team. Quiet, unassuming, smart and tough, with the look of a guy who could help deliver a baby in the morning, and in the afternoon break the neck of someone threatening the same newborn.

'Munitions,' Monty said. 'Always been the challenge of effectively delivering the most potent firepower with the most economic delivery system. You've got the problem of having enough munitions slung underneath fighter-bomber wings and in bomb bays to do the job, especially if you're flying over hundreds of miles of territory and your supply chain is thin. So here's the deal. You get one big bomb but it's really just a canister. That's all. Drop it over your target site. Maybe a staging area for infantry. Or an air base. Anything with nice, exposed targets. The canister is dropped, falls to a predetermined altitude, and pops open. Inside are hundreds of bomblets, packed away in little clusters that spread out. Each cluster about the size of a beer can. And when they get close enough, the little beer cans pop open and a lot of bad guys are having a bad day. One canister is dropped, but you're delivering munitions over a wide area. Lethal and effective as hell.'

Darren smiled. 'Sounds like you serve in the Air Force, Monty.'

Monty said, 'I'll never tell, and you know it.'

Brian was impatient. 'All right, you're saying that this Russian, he came up with a way of using cluster bombs to deliver the anthrax?'

Victor shook his head. 'Yes, but not in a mechanical sense. You see, Zhukov came up with an approach to cluster the anthrax spores using a membrane, about the thickness of a cell wall. And this membrane would last a number of seconds out in the open air before it decayed, releasing the anthrax spores. So you could have a release of respiratory anthrax from a rocket shell or a spraying device, and it would reach ground level before the spores were actually out in the open. Very elegant, very deadly. And what we did – well, the Clear Sky group, I mean – was to use Zhukov's approach to come up with a delivery system for the anthrax vaccine. Same method, using the membrane system. Initial tests looked promising. Anyone exposed to the vaccine would generally just need one exposure.'

'Good,' Adrianna said. 'We'll rely on you to—'

'But . . . but, Jesus, Adrianna!' Victor's voice raised a notch and she said, 'Yes?'

His face was mottled white, as though a surge of anger was now raging through him. 'You . . . I mean, all right, suppose we do have enough vaccine. That's a possibility. Considering who we are and the blank check we carry around in our back pockets all the time, we may be able to make it happen. But you haven't solved the delivery problem, not even close to it!'

'It's a problem, it'll be solved,' she said.

'Do you have any idea? Do you? My God, the last mass immunization we had in this country was the swine flu fiasco, back in 1976.'

Nobody said anything. Adrianna paused, hoped someone would pick up the ball, and thankfully, it was her New York detective.

'Going to need a history lesson there, pal. Most of us were pissing in our diapers back then. Go on.'

Victor wiped at his face with his right hand. 'In 1976 – February, I think – there was an outbreak of a respiratory illness at Fort Dix in New Jersey. An Army recruit died, and autopsy results showed he died from a variation of swine flu. That got a lot of people's attention. You see, a form of swine flu was believed to be the strain of influenza that broke out in 1918 and 1919. A lot of people died worldwide from that epidemic.'

Monty said, 'Define "a lot", doc.'

Victor's voice was now calmer, and icier. 'How does fifty to a hundred million people sound like?'

Brian said, 'Sick? You mean, fifty to a hundred million people sick?'

'Shit, no, not sick. *Dead*. Fifty to a hundred million people dead. Worldwide. In the space of a year.'

Adrianna's mouth seemed dry. So many dead . . . She said, 'Impossible. How could that many people have died without us knowing about it today? Something like that should be in all the history books.'

A sharp nod from Victor. 'Of course. But something else was crowding out the news about the pandemic. The end of the First World War. Tens of millions had died in the trenches and elsewhere. What was another ten or fifty or a hundred million? Which is why the CDC back in '76 freaked, thinking that the swine flu that killed this soldier was just the tip of the iceberg. Old reports I saw, the estimate was that if there was a swine flu outbreak that year, by the end of 1976 there could be a million deaths in the United States alone. A million. So there was a crash program, announced by President Ford, to immunize everybody in the United States against swine flu.'

Brian said, 'Sorry, doc, you're gonna have to continue the history lesson here. I don't remember this shit at all.'

'Can't see why you should – because it was a fiasco. It was supposed to be another Manhattan Project style of government management but those type of projects tend not to repeat themselves in terms of success, if you know what I mean. A global war against Nazis and Japanese militarists tends to focus one's mind and efforts. Not the threat of a possible flu epidemic. Anyway, pharmaceutical companies were pressed into service to develop the vaccine. One company spent all their time developing the wrong vaccine and had to start over. Insurance companies said they wouldn't pay out any claims against the pharmaceuticals. Congress had to step in to provide protection. The vaccine for children had to be administered in the two-dose system. Paperwork and administration was a nightmare. Then some elderly people started dying, the day they got the vaccine. And then it came out that people receiving the vaccine were at a greater risk of developing Guillain-Barré syndrome, a delightful and occasionally fatal form of paralysis. By the time it went down in flames, only a third of the population had been immunized, and the total cost reached almost a half-billion dollars. And there was no swine flu outbreak that year.'

'Christ on a crutch,' Monty said.

'And another thing,' Victor said, pressing on, 'they had nine months to do it, and they still didn't get it right. How in hell do you expect us to do the same thing in under a month?'

Adrianna was pleased at how calm her voice sounded, and felt a quick burst of pride – quickly suppressed– at how well she was doing. 'Victor, what other choice do we have? Wait for the outbreaks to start in Chicago or Atlanta or DC? It will be too late by then. You know it.'

'Another mass-immunization program . . . it can't work,' Victor said. 'You know it can't. Not in the space of time we have. Not to mention the media attention. Hell, the news medias' focus on the program back in '76 crippled it. Back when there were only three major networks, no news cable channels. Can you imagine what it would be like now, today? With the cable news channels? The twenty-four/seven coverage? The cameras outside the clinics? The interviews with people who have a bad reaction from the immunization? The chat rooms? The weblogs? It would be a disaster before it even—'

Monty interrupted, 'Not to mention that it would give the assholes with the anthrax an excuse to hit us now. Not wait until some special date on their fucked-up calendar. *Now*.'

Another pause in the conversations. It seemed like a moment had been reached, and Adrianna knew what it was. She had prepared for it, had practiced it, but still, it was hard, getting the words out.

'Then . . . then what we're talking about,' she began, 'is that perhaps the only option is to proceed with the immunization. But in private.'

There, she thought. It was out. From the looks on the faces of the other Tiger Team members, it was as though she had taken a baseball bat to the back of their heads. Darren, now looking even more pale, turned, stared at the other members, and said, 'What do you mean, private? You're talking nearly three hundred million people. How can something this huge be done in private?'

More voices, from Monty and Victor but not, she noted, from Brian. He seemed to be keeping his counsel, and Adrianna raised a hand and the voices quieted down for a moment. She said, 'Perhaps "private" wasn't the correct word. Secret, then. An immunization program in secret.'

Another blow to their heads. More silence. And now it was Brian's turn.

'You're looking at hefty prison sentences for all of us, if this goes through,' he said.

'Perhaps. And perhaps hefty prison sentences will be a worthwhile price to pay for saving millions of lives, for saving this country, for saving civilization.'

Victor said, 'Adrianna, we're facing terrible choices, we all know it, but hyperbole and exaggeration isn't going to help us—'

She let her voice rise. 'What hyperbole? What exaggeration? Come on, Victor. You know your history. You know what we're up against. Let's say we do nothing about immunization. Let's say that we depend on Monty and his bright young men and women to intercept the attack teams. I'm sure they'll be successful in most cases. But they're not perfect. Let's say a handful get through . . . what next? You're still looking at hundreds of thousands of deaths. Panic. Collapse of our economy. Perhaps even the end of us as a functioning superpower. What then? I'll tell you what then. Meetings are held in Tokyo and Moscow and Paris and Berlin and even in poor London, and decisions are made. Compromises. Appeasement. Surrender. From the politicians in those nations who don't want mass graves in football stadiums or wheatfields as a consequence of cooperating with us in our war on terror. And I know it's a fucking cliché and all that, but by then the terrorists win. And how long before sharia – Islamic law – is imposed in Paris, in Amsterdam, in some of the Asian countries? How long?'

Underneath the table, Adriana could feel her legs begin to tremble. 'You're correct, Victor. There are terrible choices ahead for us. Quite terrible. But there *are* choices, nonetheless. One choice is to do nothing, and hope that our border security and other forces intercept the attack teams. The other choice is not to wait on hope. It's to act, and I'm sorry, but that's the only choice I think is available.'

She was about to continue speaking when the lights flickered.

Flickered again.

And then there was a loud thump, coming from above.

And in a moment, Monty and Brian were standing up, their hands now gripping pistols.

The trembling in Adrianna's legs increased.

CHAPTER TEN

Hamad Suseel tried to ease the pain in his gut and the anxiety in his heart with the soothing thought that in a very few moments one of two wonderful things was about to occur. The first was that he was finally going to begin his jihad against the unbelievers, and if all went well he would be on his way home before the evening was out, thinking about the victory that he had achieved. And the second was that he was going to begin his jihad against the unbelievers, and if all *didn't* go well he would still enter Paradise and meet his mother and father and older brother, and feel joy at such a reunion.

He drove his rental car carefully into the lot of what was called an office park. There were buildings of stone and glass, plain cubes that showed no beauty, no design. Not even that mongrel in this mongrel country, Frank Lloyd Wright, would have enjoyed seeing these pieces of crap built on such rich land. As a younger man, Hamad had dreamed of being an engineer or an architect, learning to construct better homes than those concrete pieces of shit that the UN built for his family and others outside Jenin, but the education he dreamed about never happened, of course. His education involved the endless intifadah, stealing copper wire and other metals for money, throwing rocks and paving stones at Israeli armored cars and tanks, and going to bed hungry at night while his father dozed in the corner and spoke dreamily during the day of the family farm that had been lost, back in 1948.

There was an old black-and-white photo of the family farm, creased and faded, which was passed around family gatherings, like one of the relics the Christians loved to possess and collect, and Hamad never had any patience for this reminiscing. Remembering past glories was the sign of losers. Like the Greeks recalling their ancient knowledge and the Italians their ancient empire, many of his family members and others were content to sit still and moan about their misfortune at the hands of the Jews and the British and the Americans.

But not Hamad. And especially not after that night when an American-built helicopter – an Apache Longbow, built in Kentucky – had been aiming for some visiting Iranian mullah in a Mercedes, traveling down one of the narrow and dingy streets of his village, and the first missile had missed the speeding car and had gone instead into one of those concrete cubes put up by the UN, hiring out corrupt contractors who poured cheap concrete and not enough reinforcing bars, so that when the missile exploded the two stories pancaked into a heap of dust and debris, crushing the bodies of his mother and father and older brother.

No, not after that night. After that night, Hamad cared about one and one thing only: to do whatever was necessary so that in a very short time what was left of America would have *its* people dreaming about and remembering their past glories, their past achievements, before the righteous in the world had risen up and had ground them into dust.

There. An empty space. He parked his rental car, felt his hands shake for just a moment as he switched off the engine. Where to put the keys? In his pocket? Or leave them in the car? What made the best sense?

He looked at the keys, proud now that his hand was still, like the disciplined warrior he was. The keys went back into the ignition. He would leave the car unlocked. He stepped out into the cool morning air on this Christian Sabbath day and went into the rear of the car. He was wearing a light blue jumpsuit with the name Hank embroidered in red thread over the left breast, and over the right breast was a badge that said Colonial Flowers. He felt slightly disgusted at having to be dressed like a common trader. His intelligence, his dedication, his skills deserved better than this. But then he remembered how it had begun, back near Jenin, when the Sudanese had talked to him.

The Sudanese had been tall and very black, the blackest man that Hamad Suseel had ever seen. But he was a fellow believer and had come to spend some time in their village, speaking to the elders and the members of the brotherhood – the fighters, the holy warriors – and it was during these times when Hamad had sat alone in the corner, not saying a word, just watching. It had been a month since his family had been murdered by the Jews and the Americans, and never in his life had he been so cold. Even in the warmest nights he needed two or three blankets, for the coldness in his heart would cause him to shiver.

The Sudanese, with his piercing dark eyes, seemed to have noticed his quiet nature during the meetings, for on the third night he had spoken to him alone. The conversation had been quick and to the point.

'Al-es salaam,' the Sudanese had said.

'And the blessings of God be upon you,' Hamad had replied.

'I know what happened to your mother and father and brother. For that you have my sympathy.'

'You are too kind.'

The Sudanese had cocked his head for a moment. 'I am told

that during the month since the attacks, you have not fought back. Why is that? Are you waiting for the right moment?'

Hamad clenched his fists, standing in the dark alley that stank of garbage and the open sewer. Why, he had thought, why had it come to us that cities in other countries – and on their flickering television, they all knew what other cities looked like, even if they could not actually smell them – never had this kind of stink, this kind of filth, this kind of grinding day-to-day oppression from invaders with clean uniforms and good meals and warm homes to go to at night?

'No,' he had said. 'I am waiting for the right target.'

The Sudanese had nodded at that. 'Go on, my friend. I would like to know what you mean by a "right target".'

Then it came out, in a torrent.

'What use is this kind of fighting?' Hamad had said. 'Our brave boys and girls wear martyrdom belts, they go into pizza shops and buses and playgrounds and kill themselves and other boys and girls, and sometimes old men and old women too. Oh, such glory, such honor, such bravery! For generations their actions will be celebrated in song and verse, like those of the blessed Saladin!' he added in a mocking tone. And he wondered if he had spoken too harshly, but the Sudanese seemed to appreciate what he had said.

'Yes, yes,' the black man had said. 'I agree.'

Hamad had then said, 'The bombs, the shootings, the rock-throwing – what does it accomplish? It makes us bitter. It makes us beggars to the world, asking for scraps of money and support, for bags of rice and beans from the UN, for occasional kind words from the French and the Russians and the Americans. And for what? The Jews have gotten stronger, we have gotten weaker, and when we are not ignored, we are laughed at. Laughed at!'

The Sudanese had said, 'And? What is to be done, then?'

Hamad had said, 'What is to be done is to strike hard, and to strike hard at the heart. That is what must be done. To wait patiently, to plan, to think ahead . . . and that is what I have been doing these past days, as I continue to mourn my mother and father and brother. I am planning to kill some big shot, some important American. They come here, every now and then. All puffed up and proud. The head of the CIA. The Secretary of State. The Secretary of Defense. Somehow . . . somehow, I will find out when such a man or woman is coming here, and then I will kill them. By a bomb in the street. Or from the air. Or from a bomb around my own waist. Whatever it takes. And no doubt I will die in the process, but justice will be done.'

The Sudanese had suddenly shaken his hand. Hamad had felt queasy for a moment at having the man's dark skin touch his own, and the Sudanese had said, 'We will speak later.'

And speak later they did. In the early morning hours the next day, as the Sudanese was preparing to leave, he had said, 'There is need for a thoughtful man such as yourself, Hamad. Will you come with me, to fight your war? And not here, but in America?'

'Of course,' Hamad had said and had left at once, not even bothering to pack anything. For the Sudanese said everything would be taken care of, and the Sudanese, Hamad quickly learned, always told the truth.

Hamad opened the rear door of the rental car, took out the long cardboard box with the red and white ribbons. Again, he felt like a fool, but the moment was a fleeting one. He was no fool. He was a warrior.

He walked the distance to the squat glass and metal building, pasting on a phony smile that all Westerners loved to see on dark-skinned men who came to their country. He took his time going up the walkway, the box in his hands. He supposed it should have felt heavy and awkward in his grip but it was as though he was carrying a bag of rose petals, it was so light.

Up ahead was the arched trellis, and Hamad recalled what was there. He'd been told by the someone who had sent him e-mail messages once he got to the United States who had also told him what was beyond the trellis and the glass doors. He took a breath, and just as he reached the trellis—

He broke into a run. The cardboard box falling open in his hands, the bandoleer with the Russian-made RGN-86 fragmentation grenades coming out and over his shoulder, in his grip the folded-up and cut-down Chinese-made SKS-12, a cheap piece of shit that wasn't good at long distance, but distance wasn't his concern, what mattered was close-in firing, and in seconds he was through the doors. There, just as predicted, a large-titted whore sat behind the desk and before she could even react he fired three times into her chest, making her fall back with a squeal and a spray of blood and tissue on the wall behind her.

Discipline, Hamad thought, discipline. There were videos out there of brave fellow warriors, standing and holding their rifles like they were fire hoses, proudly spewing dozens of rounds at a target. Oh, how mighty they looked – and how stupid! For it took whole seconds to empty a clip, and for a disciplined force facing you – like the British SAS or American SEALs or the Israeli Shin Bet – all it would take would be one or two well-placed shots in response to send you to Paradise. Which was why he had only fired three times. There was neither time nor ammunition to waste.

A quick check to make sure that the whore was dead – she certainly was – and Hamad started towards the hallway behind the desk. There were office doors on either side, both of them unlocked – such bad security! – and he opened each one and tossed into each small office a hand grenade. Women and men were there, at their desks, looking up at him with surprise, with fear, with concern, but none of them reached for a weapon, none of them did a damn thing. He felt this sudden rush of exultation, knowing that the Sudanese had been right, it had been right to fight them in their home, for here, they were not brave, they were like children, and like children in his village they died where they stood or sat.

After tossing in the hand grenades, he slammed the doors shut, ducked down and placed his hands against his ears and opened his mouth as the explosions ripped through each office. Perfect, it was going perfectly. He got up and kicked open each door again, and this time he let the fire discipline slip just a bit as he hosed down each room, but making sure that his shots were well aimed at the slumped bodies sprawled on the floor, over the desks, and against the walls.

There. Done on this floor. Hamad popped out the spent magazine and punched in a fresh one, worked the action, got to the entrance of the elevator, and slid open the keypad. The number sequence from the e-mail message that he had memorized over and over again came into his mind and he punched in the numbers. Waited. Managed to hear the whine of the elevator coming up to this level. Stepped back and held the Chinese assault rifle up to his shoulder. The doors popped open and his finger was tight on the trigger.

Empty.

The elevator car was empty.

Praise God.

Hamad stepped into the elevator, pressing the button for the lower level so hard that he hurt his thumb. Moved to one side. The elevator went down and the anxiety and pain in his gut were now gone. Gone, gone, gone. This was what it must have been like to be under arms with Saladin, defeating the Crusaders outside Jerusalem, watching their banners with their Christian symbols tumble to the dust. To be at the outskirts of Constantinople, moving in through the walls, seeing the Christians cover their faces in fear. To be in the cockpit of that American Airlines aircraft, flying towards Babylon, seeing the tower of Babel, the hated one, grow and grow in one's view.

The sweet feeling of the Holy Warrior.

The elevator came to a halt. The door slid open.

He went forward, to continue the fight.

Brian Doyle looked over at Monty, surprised at how quickly the man had gotten his weapon out, not even knowing that the military guy carried. Damn, he was good.

Monty said, 'Elevator?'

'Only place in and out,' Brian said. 'Adrianna, get to the farthest office. Mine, I guess. Lock and barricade the door, start working the phones.'

'Brian, I—'

'Lady, shut the fuck up and move. We don't have time to talk.'

Monty said, 'We've wasted enough time already. C'mon!'

They went out of the conference room. Darren at least was moving right, he shut and locked the conference-room door behind them. He and Monty raced down the hallway. Brian's weapon felt heavy in his hands. He looked around, thought about dragging some furniture out for cover, but there was the sound of the elevator motor working as the elevator car came down. Monty was kneeling down, flat against the far wall, his own pistol held out in a two-handed grip.

Brian instantly knew what Monty was doing. Holding the weapon out, flattening himself, narrowing his silhouette for whatever offensive fire might be coming from the elevator car. Brian imitated the serviceman's stance. He held his own pistol out, wished for a hand-held radio right at this moment – wouldn't it be fucking excellent to call in a 10-13 and get some serious backup here? Like the muscle boys from Emergency Services. That would be—

Monty said, 'Care for some advice?'

'Would love some advice.'

'That door opens up, we see anybody we don't recognize, anybody not showing proper ID, anybody threatening in any way, we blow their asses into next Tuesday. Got it?'

'Yeah, got it.'

'Another thing. If Stacy's there, if she's being held as a human shield, if she's being held hostage—'

'No time for that. It begins and ends right here.'

'Yeah.'

It seemed like the elevator motor was louder. Brian thought of something and said, 'Monty?'

'Yeah?'

'How come you won't tell anybody what branch of the service you're in?'

'No time for that, pal.'

The elevator doors slid open.

*

Hamad stepped out, SKS-12 ready. He thought he saw movement. He wasn't sure. He moved forward and—

Brian felt his finger squeeze the trigger as he noticed the barrel of a weapon sticking out through the open elevator door and—

Hamad came forward, seeing nothing, moving and—
    A blow to the head.
    And it was done.

Brian caught his breath. Coming out of the elevator, a 9mm Uzi in her manicured hands and a protective vest over her lovely torso, was Stacy Ruiz. She was alone. Brian and Monty stood up and she said in a measured, even voice: 'We're in lockdown for a while.'

'What's up?' Monty said.

Stacy kept her voice even, though Brian sensed there was trembling going on somewhere back there. 'Just got word. Tiger Team Four got hit, outside of Hartford.'

'How bad?' Brian asked.

'Bad enough. We're at Threat Condition Delta for a while. We've shut down the upstairs.'

Monty nodded, put his weapon away. 'The noise we heard down here – shutters?'

Stacy slung the Uzi over her left shoulder. 'Yeah. Doors locked automatically, the metal shutters slid down over the ground-floor windows. And I switched us over to auxiliary power, just in case. You probably saw a power flicker down here. We're now on recycled air. Pretty much nothing can get in here and hurt us except for a suitcase nuke, and I don't think one will be wasted on us at the moment.'

Brian said, 'Good move,' as he returned his own 9mm to his shoulder holster.

Stacy's eyes flashed at him. 'Just doing my job, that's all.'

Monty said, 'Thank the Christ somebody is. Come on, let's spread the news.'

They went back to the conference room door, still locked, and their pounding and shouts didn't produce any response. Monty said, 'Guys back there are too good. Phone?'

'Inside the elevator,' Stacy said.

Back to the elevator and Monty handed the phone over to Brian, pulling the receiver free from a receptacle under the panel. 'Hope you can remember your own extension.'

'I believe I can.'

He dialed the four digits and it was picked up after the first ring. 'Scott.'

'Adrianna, it's all right. Stacy's with us. We're in lock-down. Threat Condition Delta.'

He could hear her breathing on the other line. 'Brian?'

'Yes?'

'If you're under any duress, please say the phrase "not a chance". If everything's all right, please say the phrase "you bet your life".'

He said, 'You bet your life, and your fucking ass, that we're fine. Okay?'

Adrianna hung up. Monty looked on. 'That's the second time you've dropped an f-bomb on the princess this morning. She's a sensitive lady. I don't think she's gonna like it.'

'Yeah, well, what's she going to do? Send me back to New York? I'd love to go to New York City right now, honest to Christ I would.'

There came the sound of the conference room door being unlocked and opening up, and Brian shook his head as he led

Monty and Stacy into the room. Only one of the two doors was open, and Victor was there, hands shaking, aiming a fire extinguisher at the three of them. Frozen carbon dioxide cloud versus automatic weapons. A hell of a last stand, if it had to be done. Then they all sat around the conference room table, Stacy now looking embarrassed, holding the Uzi in both her manicured hands, and Brian noted that after she put the weapon's safety on she slid it under the table.

But she kept the vest on, which Brian found distracting. He'd rather looked forward to the view of her cleavage, he thought as the afternoon dragged on and the phone rang a few times and they received word that nine of their colleagues had been killed up in Connecticut. None wounded. There were six survivors from the lower level of the building.

Adrianna looked around at them and said, 'We're done for the day. We'll take the Final Winter matter up again, tomorrow morning, seven a.m. Please be prompt.'

As he stood up, Brian was surprised that Adrianna hadn't looked right at him with that comment about being here on time. Then he was surprised again when she came up to him and said, 'Brian, do you have plans for dinner?'

'Not a one.'

'Good. Please join me at my place, will you?'

Brian thought back to how the day had started, with the news of the upcoming anthrax attacks. Then he pondered on the thought that they would have to come up with a plan to immunize hundreds of millions of people without their knowledge and consent and tried to absorb the implications of the news that a terrorist attack had knocked off some of their comrades.

And now there was a dinner offer from the princess.

'Sure,' he said. 'That'd be fine.'

All in all, Brian thought, walking with Adrianna to the elevator, it had been one hell of a day.

CHAPTER ELEVEN

Adrianna Scott lived a fifteen-minute drive from the office park, in a collection of townhouse condos that called themselves Fox Hollow Estates. Brian followed her Toyota Celica with his own rented Lexus – why the hell not, if you're working on the road, why not rent something fancy? – and he took a space next to hers. Within a minute or so they were in her home, a narrow two-story building that was the end unit of a row of dwellings.

Adrianna turned on the lights in the kitchen as they went in. She said, 'I get to pay extra each month for the privilege of living on an end unit, and most days I think it's worth it. Means there's at least three walls that don't bring in sound from the neighbors. Hold on, will you? I want to go upstairs and change. I'll be right back down. Grab something from the fridge, if you'd like. Oh. And one house rule, if you don't mind.'

'I've been here sixty seconds, and already you're tossing rules at me?'

She ran a hand through her hair, the gesture making her look tired. 'No shop talk, not for a while. About today or about what happened up in Hartford. We'll have plenty of time to talk about it later.'

'Usually I hate rules, but that's a good one.'

Adrianna went upstairs to the left and Brian went to the kitchen, which was off to the right. The kitchen was small but tidy. Even the cookbooks seemed to be sorted by size. He went to the refrigerator, opened it up. Saw a collection of Heinekens on the bottom shelf, picked up one of the green bottles and popped it open. He debated whether to pour it in a glass or not and decided what the hell. He took a sip from the ice-cold bottle as he wandered through the rest of the condo. The floor was polished hardwood and next to the kitchen was a small dining area – round wooden table with four wooden chairs. Beyond the eating area was a living room – couch and two chairs, television set on a dark wooden stand, and a set of bookshelves.

He went up, examined the books. Medieval art history, it looked like. And the history of Rome as well. Some reference books. And a Second World War history book: *The Army That Never Was*. He picked it up, gave it a quick glance, saw what it was about. The story of General George Patton and how he was assigned during the build-up to the Normandy invasion in 1944 to be in charge of a mythical army group that the Germans thought was going to invade France. He remembered seeing something about that in the George C. Scott movie. He put the book back on the shelf.

Near the bookshelves was a fireplace, closed off. On the mantelpiece were two old brass candlesticks, flanking a photograph in a thick frame. Brian went forward, examined the photo. A much younger Adrianna Scott, standing behind an older woman who was sitting in a formal chair. Both women were wearing black velvet-like dresses trimmed with lots of white and red ribbons. Adrianna's hands were on the shoulders of the older woman. He took another sip of beer.

'My aunt,' Adrianna announced, coming into the living room. Gone were the charcoal-gray skirt and black pullover, replaced by dark blue sweat pants and a white sweat shirt that said NAVY in big blue letters. The ponytail was gone as well. Now her hair hung loose, and she suddenly looked smaller and younger.

'Nice photo,' Brian said.

'Thanks,' she said, reaching up to gently stroke the frame. 'It was taken right after I graduated from high school in Cincinnati. Auntie Elyse raised me after my parents died in a car accident. She was the only real family I had, and I splurged some money to have this photo taken. Auntie Elyse said no, I shouldn't spend the money, but I did. And I'm glad I did . . . she passed away soon after the photo was taken.'

'Sorry to hear that,' he said. 'Sorry, too, about your parents.'

'Oh, it's all right,' she said. 'I lost mom and dad when I was five years old. Don't have many memories of your parents when you're five years old. And I was fortunate – well, if that can be said – I'm fortunate that I got to stay with Auntie Elyse. I couldn't live in our old house – and she was a good mom to me, as good as a woman could be, taking care of her niece.'

Adrianna turned to him, still looking small and young. 'Now it's just me.'

Brian didn't know what to say. She shrugged and said, 'And I know it's been a while, too, but I'm sorry about your dad.'

The beer bottle felt slippery in his hand. 'Thanks. And thousands of other people lost loved ones that day, too. I'm no different.'

Adrianna said, 'All right. We drifted into shop talk and that was my fault. I'll get dinner going, if you promise to take off that jacket and try to relax.'

Brian raised the Heineken bottle to her in a toast. 'That's a deal.'

The coat did come off, and Brian debated for a moment about taking off the shoulder holster. What the hell, it was dinner – the holster and the pistol came off and he put the rig on one of the living-room chairs, draping his coat over it. He then joined Adrianna in the kitchen. She worked well and efficiently, defrosting and then heating up some alfredo sauce, quickly stir-frying some chunks of chicken and pieces of vegetables, boiling some pasta, and within a half-hour they were seated at the round table, eating the fettuccine dish and drinking glasses of a Californian pinot noir. A few minutes after he started eating, Brian said, 'You're not very talented, you know.'

'Excuse me?' Adrianna said, fork held in mid-air.

'You heard me. You're not very talented as a chef.'

'I'm not?'

He was enjoying the expression on her face but decided to take a bit of mercy on her. 'No, you're *extremely* talented. This is the best meal I've had in a long while.'

'Thanks,' she said. 'I think.'

'No, I'm not being a jerk,' he said. 'I save that for other times. After a while, Adrianna, Red Lobster or Chili's or any other variation of a chain restaurant gets to be boring. This is a treat.'

Now Adrianna smiled. 'Okay, thanks. This time, for real. No thinking.'

'Very good.'

They ate for a while longer and she said, 'Ask you a personal question?'

'Go right ahead.'

'Why did you become a cop?'

Brian smiled at her. 'What makes you think I had a choice?'

'Hmm?'

'Sorry. Old and no longer so funny joke. You see, being a cop was the family business. Dad was a cop, granddad was a cop, both uncles and a number of cousins were cops. There you go. I got out of high school, worked a couple of jobs here and there, and took the test. There was no real thinking about it. I just did it. That's all.'

'Uh-huh.'

He took another bite, chewed and swallowed. 'All right. That was my boring story. Now it's your turn. How did you end up being an officer with the CIA?'

'Very good,' Adrianna said, rewarding him with another smile.

'How's that?'

'Most people call us agents. We're not agents. We're officers.'

'Yep. And I'm not most people, as you've noticed. So. On with your story, boss.'

She shrugged. 'Not much to it. Went to college after high school – Northwestern. Majored in medieval history. Got good grades but towards the end of my four years came to that chilling conclusion: what use was a medieval-history major? Only thing ahead of me was grad school, and I was getting tired of the school routine. Then the student newspaper ran an advertisement, saying the CIA was recruiting college grads, and I went in for an interview, did an okay job, and got a follow-up phone call a couple of months later. That's it.'

He shook his head. 'No, that's not it.'

'What?'

'Good try, boss, but that's not it. There's a hell of a jump from being a medieval-history major to entering the CIA. It's not like dumping all that book learning about the Middle Ages to become a lawyer or an accountant. That's not it. So. What was it?'

She toyed with a piece of pasta with her fork, looking down at her plate, and then she looked up. 'Nicely done, detective. Nicely done. You still looking for an answer?'

'That's what I do. Ask questions and look for answers. Go on.'

Adrianna carefully put the fork down, like it was a move she had practiced by herself. She dabbed at her lips with a napkin and said, 'Remember what it was like in the early '90s?'

'Sure. I was there.'

'Uh-huh. The collapse of the Soviet Union, China coming around to a market economy, peace even breaking out in Central America and parts of the Middle East. It was the "end of history" – remember that? Everyone was going to play nice and everyone was going to adopt the Western ideals of democracy and freedom. Yeah. Right. That's when I looked at my history and remembered the last time this old globe had a solitary hyperpower, around the time of Christ.'

'The Romans.'

'No gold star for that answer, detective, because it was an easy one. So there I was, looking at my beautiful country, and I got scared. I had a sense that history *hadn't* gone away, was still out there, ready to bite our ass. That while we were obsessing over who controlled Congress, who got a blow job in the Oval Office, and how many stock options certain dot-commers were getting, serious men with serious grievances were getting ready to do us harm. That was when I decided to respond to that CIA advertisement, and I've never regretted it, not once.'

'And when was this?'

'A few years before 9/11.'

'And what were you doing then?'

'Classified.'

That made Brian smile. 'Please, boss . . .'

Adrianna laughed. 'Truth be told? Your basic research analyst. That's all. Then after 9/11 . . . lots of things changed at Langley. Stuff that still isn't known publicly.'

'Like to share?'

A small shrug. 'You know what's the biggest problem the CIA faces?'

'A good dental plan?'

Again, he was pleased to see her smile. 'Actually, we have an excellent dental plan. No, the problem with the CIA is that there's a huge gap between the management and the officers, whether those in the field, in embassies or in Langley. Whatever work the officers did . . . we called it the silo effect. Information from different departments and groups would go up to supervisors, without cross-checking, without cross-referencing. Like grain silos on a Kansas plain, reaching up, inaccessible to each other. And that was within the CIA. Within the so-called intelligence community – more like a dysfunctional family than a community, if you ask me – it was even worse, with silos marked NSA, CIA, FBI, National Reconnaissance Office, so forth and so on, reaching up. Before 9/11, I was tasked to an inter-agency group that recommended breaking barriers, designing small, mobile intelligence teams that would have maximum authority and minimal oversight. When our report was done, it was filed and forgotten, and I went back to analyzing crude-oil output in Kazakhstan. Then the planes hit, my name and others were pulled from that group, and there we are. Hopefully, problem solved.'

Brian eyed Adrianna curiously as she talked, sensing something was going on behind those quiet brown eyes. This was the longest he had ever spoken to her, face to face, and he was surprised at how much he was enjoying it. He said, 'Seems like lots of problems yet to be solved.'

'Yeah, ain't that the truth.'

They ate in silence for a while, and he helped her bring the plates and silverware and glassware into the kitchen when they were done. The crockery was rinsed and placed in the dishwasher, and from outside he heard the yelps and squeals of children playing. Through the large living-room window he could see three or four boys and girls on a grassy lawn, playing with large plastic balls and bats. Adrianna stood beside him and folded her arms, watching with him. Something felt out of place inside Brian as he thought about his son Thomas. Growing up without having his boy near him, not being able to teach him those one hundred and one important things – how to play basketball, how to rollerblade, how to correctly hate the Red Sox – sometimes made him clench his fists in anger at the oddest moments. Like right now. He shouldn't be in Maryland with this attractive and odd woman. He shouldn't be working with the Feds. He should be home where he belonged, working out the difficulties of his new relationship with Marcy and seeing Thomas as much as possible.

Adrianna said, 'You know how many places there are in the world where this can't happen? Where children can't go outside and play without fear of being shot or bombed or stolen? Plenty of places. Plenty.'

She motioned to the lights coming on in the surrounding condo units. 'There are people out there who have put their trust in us, Brian. Who trust us to protect them and their children. Trust us so that they can wash up their dinner dishes and send their children out to play without worrying that they will be kidnapped, or blown to pieces by a suicide bomber, or die choking to death from something invisible dropped upon them from the sky.'

Brian said, 'I guess the time for shoptalk has arrived.'

'It has.'

'All right.'

Adrianna turned to him and he was conscious of how close she was, the light fragrance of whatever scent she had on (so unlike Marcy, who would sometimes drench herself with some flowery concoction after spending time and money with an aromatherapist), and just how delicate her eyes looked. She said, 'I'm going to need your help tomorrow, Brian.'

'In what way?'

'Come,' she said, 'let's sit on the couch, where we can talk comfortably.'

Brian sat down on the couch while Adrianna went to the kitchen and returned with two tiny glasses that each seemed to hold a thimble-sized amount of sherry. He wasn't particularly fond of sherry, but he decided that being polite wasn't going to kill him. He sipped a bit at the sweet liquid and said, 'Once we thrash out the Final Winter scenario and the immunization options, what are you looking for?'

'I'm looking for you to speak up for the only immunization option that can work. That's what.'

He shook his head. 'Don't like the idea of secretly immunizing a couple of hundred million people. Too drastic, too overwhelming.'

She seemed to sink down into the couch cushions. 'I agree.'

That surprised him. 'You do?'

'Of course.' Adrianna put her glass down on the empty and clean coffee table and put both of her hands behind her head. 'It could turn into an utter fiasco that would make that swine flu screw-up look like the greatest public health project of the last century. There's no doubt that some people out there will react poorly to the vaccine. We will end up putting some people in the hospital, will no doubt kill some very old and very young people, as well as some who are already very ill. News of what we've done could send all of us to jail for life, if it gets out. It would bring the Tiger Teams out into the open and destroy the progress we've been making in protecting those kids out there and their families. And, of course, the damn vaccine might not work.'

'Good points,' Brian said.

'Yes,' she said, dropping her hands to her legs. 'Yes, all good points, and I keep on looking at it and looking at it and . . . damn it, Brian, what else *is* there? What else can be done?'

Brian tried to think of what to say. Different things went through his mind as he heard the squeals of the children out there, safely at play. What to do? Remembered his Academy training, the times when his shooting skills were challenged by pop-up targets that either posed a threat or didn't. Shoot or not? Live or die? Don't just stand there, the instructor had said. Do something!

'I don't know what else can be done, Adrianna. I really don't. I only know that the option that's out there, if it's the only one, sucks.'

She nodded. 'Sucks wind.'

'And what do you want me to do tomorrow?'

Adrianna rubbed at her eyes and said, 'Monty will be in support of the immunization. Victor and Darren will be arguing against. But I guess that you'll be supporting it. Even if you don't like it.'

'Why?'

'Because of who you are, Brian. A cop. A cop who's been out on the streets, knows the depths of evil that some people can sink to, and knows how to cut through the bullshit and be realistic. For Victor, his universe begins and ends in a laboratory. For Darren, it begins and ends on a computer screen. Intellectually, they know what we're up against. But you, Monty and myself, we know the evil that men can do. Up front and personal.'

'You know about evil, eh? And where did you come across that knowledge?'

And by God, for the briefest moment Brian felt as if he had burrowed through her defenses and seen the real Adrianna, for her expression flickered like a picture coming into snap focus and then broke up, back into something indistinct. And when she'd been in focus, her expression had been bleak and had suddenly reminded him of a case from a couple of years ago. An old woman, a survivor of the Holocaust, in her apartment, sitting in a stiff wooden chair, looking down at her husband – another Holocaust survivor – who lay on the floor, dead. Knifed in the heart by a sixteen-year-old boy who could barely spell his own name and who had been trying to rob the apartment. The look on the old woman's face . . . as if God, having tortured her years earlier, had saved up one more awful torment for the end of her life.

'I'm sorry,' Adrianna said, her voice now snappish. 'That's classified, Brian.'

'Oh. All right, then. Look, why don't—'

'Hold on,' she said, a hand scrambling around the couch cushions. 'It's the top of the hour. I want to catch the news.'

Her hand emerged with a television remote, which she pointed at the television screen. It popped into life and she selected a cable news channel. The young male anchor looked somber and at his side on the screen was a graphic, showing a map of Connecticut with a rifle superimposed over it.

'. . . We go to Bloomfield, a community north of Hartford, Connecticut, where a workplace shooting has left nine dead earlier today.'

The anchor tossed the link to a young blonde female reporter who was standing in front of a length of yellow police tape, microphone in her delicate hand. 'State and local police are investigating a workplace shooting here at Tompkins Consulting, a business firm specializing in software in Bloomfield, Connecticut. While no police official will speak on camera, it is believed that a disgruntled former employee – not yet identified – entered the workplace and began shooting. Eight employees were killed before the shooter turned his weapon on himself and committed suicide.'

'Kimberly, do police have a motive yet on what caused this former worker to return to kill these people?'

'No, they don't, and—'

Adrianna clicked off the television. Brian shook his head. 'Some cover story, Adrianna.'

'Has to be done.'

'How the fuck did it happen?'

'Intelligence leak, someplace. How else? You can bet the lights will be burning late tonight in Langley and other places, trying to find out how those clowns learned about this.'

Brian said, 'Too fancy.'

'Excuse me?'

'Intelligence leak. Sounds very hush-hush, very *fancy*. Like somebody in the pay of al-Qaeda or whoever, giving out information for money or because they're being blackmailed. Somebody high up. Hell, they'll probably find out it was something as simple as somebody getting drunk or getting laid and letting out the story of who actually worked at the site of Tompkins Consulting. Adrianna, look, people talk, people gossip. Information loves to travel, loves to find a welcoming place. All it took was a piece of information finding its way to a cell here in the United States, and there you go. Nothing fancy. Just rather fucking direct.'

Adrianna smiled. 'See? That makes a lot of sense. In fact, I'll pass your suggestion along, at our daily conference call. Told you I liked your cop mind. Suspicious, cuts through the chatter . . . a true asset, Brian. A true asset.'

Something about that made Brian laugh and when he saw her expression he said, 'Just for a second, I thought you said something about my ass. A true ass.'

She laughed in return and said, 'Oh, you have quite a nice ass, Brian.'

That got his attention. 'Really? You think I have a nice ass?'

Adrianna seemed to blush – if that was possible. A hand rose up to her lips and she said, 'I'm sorry. That's the sherry talking. Or the wine. Or both.' She got up from the couch and Brian followed, sensing again that whatever he had learned about her these past months had only revealed the faintest background glimmer of what made her tick.

And damn it, that flip comment, about his butt . . . why had it made him grin like a teenager, happy that the It Girl in high school had noticed him in the hallway between class? Before he knew it, his coat, gun and shoulder holster were in his hands as Adrianna gently shepherded him to the front door.

At the open door Brian turned to say something and she was there. His free arm went out and around her slim waist, and he pulled her close. He kissed her and she responded, folding her body into his, pressing her pert breasts against his chest. He felt the eagerness in her open mouth and smooth tongue. The embrace went on for long seconds until she pulled away and kissed him firmly on the lips. He returned the favor.

Adrianna smiled. 'Later, Brian.'

'How much later, boss?'

'When we get Final Winter under control . . . it's going to be a good time to take a long break from running a Tiger Team. I . . . it's a lot of pressure, my dear friend. A lot of pressure. And right now, engaging in a somewhat improper relationship with a subordinate—'

'One of my favorite positions is being subordinate,' he responded, liking what the phrase did to her expression.

'Maybe so, detective, but now's not the time.'

Brian was still holding her and she stood still, seeming to enjoy his touch. Then her tone grew somber and she said, 'Bloomfield.'

'Yeah.'

'I knew two of the Tiger Team members up there. Man and woman.'

'There are survivors – that's what the news said.'

She shook her head. 'No, I got the call earlier today. They're both dead.'

'I'm sorry.'

Tears came to Adrianna's eyes and she said, 'I am, too. But that doesn't mean we stop.' She took a deep breath. 'September eleventh. I was in my cubicle when the word came down about the attacks on the World Trade Center and the Pentagon. We got the order to evacuate, because Langley's a goddamn easy target to find. So we did. Later on, we found out about something else that had happened that day. It seems the director wanted the entire building evacuated, everybody out, and the head of the Counterterrorism Center at Langley said no, we needed to keep some of his people working up on the sixth floor, at the Global Response Center. And the director said, they're at risk. They could die if the building was attacked. And the CTC head said, well, then they're just going to have to die. Just like that, in the space of that conversation, the entire culture of the CIA changed. Just like that.'

Another kiss on the lips, and Brian knew that was not a 'wanna spend the night?' kiss but a 'come on, get your ass out of my house' kiss. Adrianna said, 'That's where we're at, Brian. The war isn't over there, it's right here. In Bloomfield, or in the airstream over our cities. And this is a war we have to win. Have to.'

He reached up, touched her cheek. 'Okay. You got me, boss.'

'Good.' Another smile.

And as Brian turned to go out into the evening, he said,

'Oh. One other thing. You also have me for tomorrow, to support you. Got it?'

'Seven a.m., Brian. Seven a.m.'

Adrianna Scott folded her arms and from her kitchen window watched Brian Doyle make the short walk to his parked car. He did have a nice ass, she thought, smiling. Then another thought came to her, about what had just happened this evening, and she was surprised at the spike of guilt that shot through her. She'd thought that guilt was something she had under control, over the years of experience and training, but there it was. Guilt at having lied to poor Brian Doyle, her own personal New York cop.

She hoped that when the time came he would forgive her.

Brian Doyle got into his car, tossed the shoulder holster, gun and coat next to him, and backed out from the parking space. He looked up at the lit windows of Adrianna's place, and thought about the day just gone and what had happened up in Bloomfield. He guessed he should have offered to spend the night – on the couch, of course – pistol within easy reach, because he had a thought of another nameless holy warrior breaking into her home tonight, to do her harm.

But hell, she was CIA. Trained in counterterrorism and God knew what else. She could take care of herself.

Still . . . there was a feeling, and as Brian headed back to his own place he knew what that feeling was. Guilt. At having lied to Adrianna tonight and on many other occasions. Brian had lied before on the job, often and with great gusto, but this particular spate of lying . . . it stuck in his craw.

He hoped that when the time came she would forgive him.

CHAPTER TWELVE

It was now seven p.m. on Monday. Tiger Team Seven – a/k/a Foreign Operations and Intelligence Liaison Team Seven – had been meeting for twelve hours, and now, finally, it was done. The arguing had gone on, back and forth, back and forth, throughout the long day, and at one point Adrianna had had tears in her eyes, and so had Darren, her NSA guy. Voices had been raised, hands had been slammed down on the conference-room table, and now Adrianna had called a halt. It had gone on too long. Her mouth tasted like it was filled with fuzz, her legs had been quivering off and on all day, and now she held her knees firmly together.

It was time.

She said, 'My friends . . . we've talked and debated our response to Final Winter for the whole day. This evening, at midnight, I need to make a recommendation to the Tiger Team director. I need to tell him what the group feels, what our response to Final Winter is going to be. So the question before the house is: What is your reply to this question? Do we or do we not recommend that our response to Final Winter should involve the covert immunization program? Monty?'

His dark brown eyes looked at her, unblinking. 'Yes. Without a doubt. I don't see how else we can do it.'

She nodded, switched her focus to her cop. 'Brian?'

'Yes.'

'Nothing else to add?' she asked.

'Enough talk. You're just going to have to sell it to the Director later on. That's when the talking will resume.'

'True. Darren?'

The tears were back in the eyes of her NSA representative. 'I . . . God help us, yes. We can't allow the population to be exposed to what's being planned. Not doing anything is worse than what we've outlined.'

The shaking in Adrianna's legs resumed, no matter how hard she pressed them together. 'Victor?'

His face was pale and sweaty, and it looked like his horn-rimmed glasses were about to slide down his nose. He played with a few keys on his laptop and said, 'Before I answer, I just want to reaffirm one thing. All right? Just one more thing.'

'Victor . . .'

'It will only take a second, Adrianna. Please. Can't you give me one more goddamn second?'

'Say your piece, doc,' Monty said. Adrianna kept quiet. The doctor said, 'The very first field trials on the airborne vaccine show that in one one-hundredth of one percent of cases there will be an acute reaction. And in the majority of those cases the reaction will lead to respiratory seizure and death, especially among the elderly, the very young, and those with deficient immune systems, like AIDS patients or cancer patients undergoing treatment.'

No one said anything. The doctor looked around and said, 'People, I just want to make sure that you understand. The most optimistic scenarios say, if this is approved and proceeds, that we might be able to expose about one hundred million people to the airborne vaccine. And based on what we know from the field trials, within a month or so of this happening there will probably be ten thousand dead. Do you understand that? Do any of you fucking understand that? We in this little room and those few people who oversee us, we're about to condemn ten thousand Americans to death over the next several weeks. And why? Because we're scared. That's why.'

The silence was heavy, oppressive, as though some inert gas had slipped into the room and rendered speech impossible. Monty cleared his throat and said, 'Doc, we know the numbers. You threw them at us this morning, right when they started. Ten thousand dead . . . a hell of a number, doc, a hell of a fucking number. And I'm gonna have nightmares sleeping tonight, trying to get my mind around that number. But I'm thinking about another number. I'm thinking, even if we get every attack team out there that's coming in except for one – if just one slips through, in the space of a few weeks from now we'll have a hundred thousand dead. Or two hundred thousand dead. And that's only if we're very, very lucky. And then we'll have to live with the fact that we could have saved most of those people, if we had acted instead of sitting on our hands. And if we're not that lucky, if two or three teams make it into Manhattan and Chicago and Los Angeles, then you're talking a million casualties. A million casualties and a collapsed economy and UN peacekeepers in the streets and—'

Victor raised his voice. 'You don't have to tell me that! I know that already!'

Monty shrugged. 'You were repeating yourself earlier. I was just repaying the favor. C'mon, doc, shit or get off the pot. Adrianna needs your answer.'

Victor took his glasses off, rubbed at his eyes. 'I just want all of you to know the cost. That's all. The cost. Because when we go to trial – and we will, one of these days, someday down the road – I want my conscience to be clear. I'll want to know that I told everyone the cost.'

Brian said, 'Yeah, we'll remember that doc. And I'll be

happy that we're sitting in a functioning court room in a functioning country to go to trial. Like Monty said, you've got to—'

'Yes,' Victor said.

Victory, Adrianna thought, sweet and total victory. 'I'm sorry, Victor, could you repeat that?'

'Yes,' the doctor said. 'Yes, and God help us all.'

'Yes,' Darren said. 'God help us all.'

With the decision having been reached a sense of energy and purpose came over the group as if, having put the decision behind them, they could now move on. Adrianna felt the mood change but wasn't fooled by it: these few people in here would be haunted for the rest of their lives for what they were about to do.

She picked up a pen, went to a legal pad. 'Victor? To reaffirm what you said this morning, we'll have enough vaccine by month's end?'

'Just barely,' he said, his voice sullen. 'We're looking at immunizing the top five or six population centers, ten if we're lucky – which means a lot of rural areas will be on their own. But the war-gaming all shows the attack teams striking at city centers. No other place makes sense. The rural areas will have to muddle through.'

The doctor moved from his chair, reached under the table and pulled out a shiny metal case. He undid the clasps and opened it up, revealing black foam inside. Nestled inside the foam was a metal cylinder about the size of a small fire extinguisher, colored dark green, with yellow letters and numbers on it. 'Here's a mock-up of one of the dispersal units. Each one like this can administer about one hundred fifty thousand vaccine units . . .'

Monty whistled and Darren said, 'The fuck you say.'

'Nope, that's right. One hundred fifty thousand vaccine units. Now. Here's the challenge, and I'm sure this is going to be the second question you're asked tonight, Adrianna, by the coordinator. The first question being, of course, are you out of your ever-loving mind?'

She nodded, knowing what Victor was saying. 'Absolutely. The second question will be, how do we administer the vaccine by a covert method. Victor, haven't your folks come up with any delivery options?'

The doctor passed the cylinder to his right, to Darren, who examined it before passing it on to Brian. His hands now free, Victor said, 'Yeah. Initially, the vaccine was going to be kept in ready reserve, at CDC and infectious-disease centers across the country. Way it was figured, if there was an anthrax attack on a city the first response would be to quarantine and treat those exposed with Cipro. Secondary response, outside of the quarantined area, would be to set up the airborne dispersal area. Like major parks, boulevards, sports centers. Anyplace where you could get a concentration of the population so you could immunize them quickly and in large numbers. Oh, there wouldn't be much in terms of efficiency – some of the vaccine would end up drifting away – but to do it quickly, with large numbers, that's how the preliminary plans came to be developed.'

Now Victor looked directly at Adrianna. 'But now . . . well, we're in a whole different universe. First, doing it covertly, and second, doing it over a large number of cities. Any suggestions?'

Wait, Adrianna thought, just wait. Monty came to her rescue. 'Airborne dispersal, of course. Helicopters? Crop-dusters?'

Brian spoke up. 'Not possible. Don't you think it'd be all over the news, crop-dusters and helicopters arriving at the same time over the ten largest population centers? And how do you keep it secret, an operation like that? Not going to happen.'

'Military, then,' Darren offered. 'Best way of doing this, keep it all in-house.'

Monty shook his head. 'Maybe you could do it for a couple of cities, but not for ten. Most military craft don't fly in and out of civilian airports, or transit civilian airspace. Same problem with news coverage. If you start having military aircraft suddenly appear over civilian airspace, then the questions will start.'

Victor seemed to want to say something, but kept his mouth shut. His hands on the tabletop in front of him seemed to be trembling. Adrianna said, 'Those canisters, Victor. How can they be installed on aircraft? What kind of support mechanism would you need? Would a pilot have to activate the canister?'

'No, you wouldn't need a pilot,' Victor said sullenly. 'You could have it set up automatically, as simple as possible. You'd have a dispersal-control mechanism hooked up to the canister. Place the canister in a secure location. Set a radio altimeter switch in the canister so that when the aircraft carrying it rises up to three thousand feet the radio altimeter arms the canister. When the aircraft goes below three thousand feet, the canister begins dispersing the vaccine because of the change in altitude registered by the radio altimeter. In fact – shit, you know, that might work. That just might work.'

Adrianna kept quiet. It was important that the entire group take part in the process, have a stake in whatever outcome was chosen. Darren said, 'Well, tell us, doc. What would work?'

'What do all these population centers have in common? Airports. That's what they have in common. Aircraft coming into airports all the time. Not a problem. Nothing unusual. Nothing to attract attention. If you time it just right . . .'

'Shit,' Monty said. 'It could be done in just one night, right?'

Brian said, 'Who are you going to get to do it? American Airlines? United? You think they'd take part in something as crazy as this? Not going to happen. Not in a million years.'

'Then perhaps somebody else, another outfit,' Adrianna said, the shaking of her legs continuing. 'Not a passenger airline, but an airline that—'

Darren spoke up, and Adrianna had to prevent herself from shouting in glee at his suggestion.

'The General,' he said. 'We get the General to do it, that's how.'

The expressions on everyone's faces changed. Nobody needed an explanation of what Darren had just said. Former Air Force General Alexander Bocks, nearly ten years ago, had used his experience as a cargo-shipping officer in the Air Force to create one of the most successful airfreight airlines in the world, AirBox. His black-and-yellow Air Boxes could be seen on most streets in major cities in the United States and Canada, and the men and women delivering the packages coming out of the Air Boxes wore uniforms that were clear knock-offs of Air Force apparel. He was also a firm supporter of the current administration and of the latest installment in the round-the-clock struggle that characterized the new war on terror.

Darren spoke up again. 'Adrianna, this is more in your department's line but it's always been rumored, at least in my agency, that General Bocks has always been . . . well, co-operative when your agency or others have needed transportation assistance. True?'

Adrianna tried to keep her voice calm and level. Finally, at long last, success . . .

'Yes,' she said. 'General Bocks has been very cooperative in the past in helping us move assets from parts of the world where traditional air service is under constant surveillance. Air cargo doesn't get the kind of scrutiny that the typical airlines receive.'

Brian said with a smile that made her shiver for a moment, 'Care to say what you mean by assets?'

She smiled right back at him. 'Packages containing sensitive equipment. And, on a few occasions, packages that contained sensitive *people*.'

Monty said, 'Can it be done? Adrianna, do you think you can do it?'

She looked at each and every one of them and said, 'Yes, I do. I really do.' She took a breath. 'Victor, I'm going to need a timetable of when the canisters will be available to be shipped, and where they can be picked up. Darren, I need the latest information you have on the traffic analysis and intercepts of the anthrax attack teams. Monty, come up with a briefing on border security and the hunt for the Syrians, and what recommendations I need to bring to our border people. Brian, give me a recommendation of how we can bring in local law enforcement to look for the attack teams without word getting out.'

Adrianna yawned suddenly, which caused the men to laugh – a good sound. She looked at her watch and said, 'I'll need this information by eleven p.m. At midnight I'll be making a presentation to the Director. And tomorrow . . . Tuesday, right? Right. Tuesday, I want this place empty. You're all going to take the day off, all of you – and that includes me as well – because we need to come back to work rested and refreshed. It's going to be one long fucking haul to do this right.'

Adrianna stood up, her legs no longer shaking, her stance firm and strong, and she said, 'Thank you. Thank you all for your work. You can't even begin to understand how much this means to me.'

And then she turned aside to hide the expression on her face.

CHAPTER THIRTEEN

The meeting of the Tiger Team leaders took place in the basement of an obscure building on the outskirts of Andrews Air Force Base in Maryland. The conference room's main table was long and the mood was somber as Adrianna took her seat and looked up at the Director sitting at the other end, overseeing the twelve Tiger Team leaders, all of whom sat still and quiet, their laptops open in front of them. He had once been a Deputy Director of her own agency – a former colonel in the US Army Special Forces – promoted after a tour of duty in Afghanistan in that bitter fall of 2001. Outside Kandahar he had lost most of his left leg to a Soviet-era land mine, and had been tapped to head the Tiger Teams after his recovery. It was midnight and coffee, tea, doughnuts and juice drinks had been placed on a table in the corner of the room, but nobody was eating, nobody was drinking. It seemed to Adrianna that the mood in the room tonight just didn't go with people munching goodies.

The Tiger Team leader sitting closest to the Director was an older woman from the National Reconnaissance Office, whose name Adrianna had already forgotten and whose hands were quivering as she presented her report. She had been stationed at the facility in Connecticut, and was the senior surviving officer from yesterday's assault. Though her hands shook as she went through her report, her voice was clear and to the point. The terrorist had gained entrance by moving quicker than anyone had anticipated. The female security officer on the ground floor had apparently just returned from a bathroom break when the terrorist entered. The personnel on the ground floor also did not respond in time to the assault, though the alarm system should have been activated. Due to a security breach that was still being investigated, the terrorist had had the proper keypad author-ization to use the elevator to descend to the lower level, where he had been shot by one of the personnel on that floor who had responded to the alarm activation.

Adrianna joined in the discussion with the other Tiger Team members, being careful not to probe too deeply or too forcefully. She knew that she was going to be in for a rough time of it later, and wanted to save her energy and her voice for then. The other Tiger Team leaders persistently and quietly interrogated the National Reconnaissance Office woman, and when the questions finally dribbled away she gave a quick glance of thankfulness to the Director that her ordeal in the conference room had ended.

The Director said, 'Jonathan . . .'

A heavyset man with a thick, black beard streaked with gray spoke up from the other end of the table. 'Sir?'

'I want your team to take the lead investigating the intelligence failure that led to the Connecticut facility being breached, and summarize the lessons to be learned. Within twenty-four hours, I want a directive to all Tiger Teams with your recommendations for increasing security without decreasing operational effectiveness. Understood?'

'Perfectly, sir.'

'Good. I also want an interim report within a week on the shooter: who he was, and how in hell he knew where to go and how to get there. I know you won't have all those answers, but I'll want some of them.'

'You'll get it, sir.'

The Director turned his attention to the woman at his side and said, 'One more question, Leslie, if I may.'

'Certainly, sir,' the NRO woman said.

The Director said, 'Who killed the intruder?'

'Simon Hannity. On loan from the Marine Corps.'

The Director nodded. 'Why?'

The NRO woman looked confused, but Adrianna had an idea where this was going.

'Sir?' the NRO woman asked, her voice no longer so confident.

It seemed like the Director was trying to keep his temper in check as he spoke clearly and slowly. 'Why was the intruder shot and killed? Why wasn't he captured? Or wounded?'

She said, 'Simon felt that it was the only option available to him. And . . .'

'And what?'

Her voice quivered. 'Simon had been talking to one of the personnel on the ground floor. He had heard the grenade blasts, the shots, the screams. He . . . wanted that man dead.'

'Don't we all?' the Director said. Then he leaned forward: 'But only after we capture the fucker and wring him dry and find out everything we can about him. Do you get that?'

The NRO woman nodded. The Director said, 'I want this Simon character released from service, and sent back to the Marine Corps with our thanks. By tomorrow. All right?'

The NRO woman nodded again. Adrianna felt sorry for her. It was the only thing the poor woman could do.

But her feelings of sympathy quickly evaporated as the Director narrowed his gaze, focused on her and said, 'Adrianna? You're up.'

Adrianna activated a program from her laptop as she stood up. 'Thank you, sir.'

When Adrianna first started, she was so tired that she fumbled some of the words and, once, a PowerPoint slide was triggered too early. But as she continued talking she found that she gathered strength and confidence, and she laid out her presentation for Final Winter. She talked about the intelligence findings, the interpretation of these findings, and the recommendations from the other members of her team. She would pause occasionally to see if anyone was interested in asking any questions, but the only response she got from the Director was, 'Go on, please.'

So she did, right up to the very end. She stood still, her legs not quivering at all, a tiny victory but one she was pleased to have.

The Director said, 'Anybody have any questions?'

Silence.

'I have a couple, though,' he said.

'Certainly, sir.'

'General Bocks. Do you think you'll have any problem bringing him on board?'

'No, sir, I don't,' Adrianna said. 'I know of his past participation in Agency missions. I'm sure he can be convinced to take part in this one.'

'And you're calling it Final Winter?'

'Yes, sir.'

A slight smile. 'Seems fairly ominous.'

'The whole matter is ominous, sir.'

The Director scratched at his chin, looked up at the nearest plasma screen. 'And you'll be ready to deploy in just under a month?'

'That's correct, sir.'

Another scratch of the chin. 'And I want to be sure that this is understood, because if word gets out over what's being attempted, there'll be merry hell to pay . . . you understand that, right?'

Adrianna nodded. 'That was the focus of many, many hours of discussion, sir.'

'I'm sure.'

She waited, the trembling still not there. Would it end now? Would it?

'But there's one more question I have, Adrianna, before you'll get my approval.'

She couldn't speak. She just waited.

'This . . . bacterial agent that you're proposing to disperse from these aircraft: it's completely safe, am I right?'

Adrianna took a breath. 'Absolutely, sir. It's been field-tested in many other areas, over the years, by private medical personnel and biowarfare defense units of our military. As I mentioned in the briefing, it's a variant of the *b. sofia* bacterium, completely benign to human ingestion. But it perfectly mimics the possible dispersion of an airborne anthrax attack. With the ground sensing stations that are already in place in these target cities, we can detect the bacterium once it's been dispersed and be able to design computer models that will enable us to better prepare for when we're attacked with real anthrax. It's a large-scale research exercise, sir, one that has the potential to give us very valuable defense information in a short span of time.'

The Director looked right at her, like he was trying to psych her out or something, and she stared right back at him. Bring it on, she thought, bring it on. I've got everything in place. Everything.

He said, 'When are you planning to see General Bocks?'

'Two days, maybe three.'

He said, 'Good. You look tired. Take tomorrow off. And Final Winter . . . Adrianna, it's approved.'

She could barely speak. 'Thank you, sir. Thank you.'

Adrianna sat down, her legs quivering now like she had just run a marathon, and the screaming inside her mind started, victory, victory, holy victory. She was startled when a man at her right – Gideon, a Tiger Team leader stationed in Los Angeles – leaned over and said, 'That was something funny you said just then, Adrianna.'

'What was that?' she replied, barely focusing on what he was saying.

'The Director asked about an anthrax attack, and you said, "when we're attacked". You're that certain – that it's going to be when, not if?'

Adrianna turned and gave Gideon her best smile. 'Absolutely. It's going to be when. Not if.'

CHAPTER FOURTEEN

Several hours after the meeting of the Tiger Team leaders, the members of Tiger Team Seven followed their own leader's instructions and took the day off. Each one of the members did something that day that partially revealed who they were and where they came from, though each would seriously challenge anyone who tried to analyze their activities. It was just a day off, a jewel to be cherished, that was all, and trying to read anything into it was so much bullshit.

Which was true for all the Tiger Team members, save one.

In the small garage in Monty Zane's rental home outside Greenbelt – he had never owned property in his entire life, though that was going to change once he became a civilian – Monty lovingly polished the bright red gas tank of his Harley Davidson Road King motorcycle. Every piece of chrome and exposed metalwork was bright and reflective, and even the fat tires of his hog had been polished with Armor All. He wiped his fingers on the rag and stepped back, admiring the look of the beast, bad-ass and powerful, all that energy just tied up and bundled in that lovely Twin Cam 88 engine of pure Pennsylvania energy.

The door of the house opened and Charlene stepped out, frowning, her blonde hair freshly washed, just barely touching her shoulders, a towel wrapped around her lovely midriff. 'Are you going to ride that damn thing or just drool over it?'

Monty laughed, wiped his hands again. 'You know, babe,

sometimes drooling comes from riding things . . . as you know.'

Charlene smiled and then stuck out her tongue at him. 'You should be so lucky – which you will be, if you get your muscular ass back here before two o'clock, 'fore the kids get home. Deal?'

'Deal, love.'

'Good,' she said, walking back into the kitchen, flipping up the towel to show off her shapely butt. 'Now have a good ride and don't get killed.'

Monty kept on smiling as he toggled the garage door opener. When the way was clear he straddled the bike and switched on the ignition, gave the start-up lever a good pop. The Harley roared into life with a satisfying *thump-burble-burble* and in a few seconds he was down the driveway and out on the road. He checked his Timex. A good four hours of quality driving time ahead of him, no highways, no urban centers, just get out into those blue country lanes that still crisscrossed this marvelous land of his, and he remembered those sweet last words of Charlene. Don't get killed. Maybe a joke but there was a bit of seriousness back there, remembering what happened to him back on September 10th, that awful year. Monty liked keeping secrets from the civilians he worked for – made his image that much meaner and more mysterious – and he knew that everybody gossiped about the burn marks on his face. There were questions about where he had gotten burned – Yemen, Iraq, Afghanistan – and everyone assumed that he had been torched in the line of duty, on some heroic mission, and they all assumed wrong. He had been burned on his day off, and in Mary-goddamn-land, when some kid with a week-old driver's license had blown through a stop sign and punched through the side of another car in front of Monty. He had dumped the cycle, sliding into the car just as the gasoline cooked off and toasted part of his face. And the day and weeks after, when the hammer came down in Afghanistan, he had been stuck in a burn unit, cursing his luck, as his comrades went out and did a job that they had trained their entire lives for.

Not a heroic story at all, damn it.

The motorcycle now seemed like an extension of him as he drove east, not caring what particular road he took or where he was going. The trip was the destination, that was all, just the feeling of the wind in his face, the scent of things growing, the sights of the farmland out there, still being tilled, year after year.

Monty grinned, thinking of what it must have been like out here a couple of centuries ago. Some of those farm buildings had been out there then, fresh new, home to farmers and grazers, and Monty had no doubt that some of his ancestors had been out there as well, working for the Man, dying and living and praying out there in bondage, and here he was, a descendant of theirs, not only prospering in this country but actually sworn to defend it, and man, that was a good feeling.

He kept on riding.

All right, there was another feeling, the one that gave him a quiet warm glow every time, especially when he was around Charlene, the former Miss Charlene Taylor, second runner-up five years ago in the Miss Virginia USA beauty pageant. For when Monty had started dating that fine specimen of Southern womanhood he had been curious about her past and had done a little checking.

He leaned into a corner, felt the way the tires just gripped that pavement, like the firm touch of a masseuse, never letting go.

Okay, a *lot* of checking. Monty had always been interested in genealogy and had done a lot of work here and there, trying to trace his family back, which was easy enough until you got into the latter part of the nineteenth century. Then the records became spotty at best – and for good reason, of course, because the black men and women of the South back then had been like survivors in some post-nuclear-war landscape, wandering around shellshocked, trying to scratch out an existence in what was left of the Southern economy, fighting off hunger and cold and the nightriders and the Klan. Keeping good records for a safe and prosperous future would sure as hell have been low on their 'to do' list.

Leaned into another corner, really picking up speed, thinking for a moment what might happen if that damn vaccination program didn't work. What kind of life would it be for his children? Growing up a dead country, scrambling around in the looted and empty cities, hearing tales of what it had been like to be the world's only superpower, being here and now, starving, wondering what it must have been like to live when you didn't go to bed hungry at night, every night . . .

Well, fuck that shit. It wasn't going to happen to *his* children.

Then Monty laughed. He knew that he shouldn't have. But his kids – Grace and Marilyn – wouldn't Charlene's ancestors have dropped dead from horror at the sight of those light-brown children? For during his genealogy work on his own side of the family, he had done some investigation into her side and had found out that one of her great-great-great-grandfathers had been a prominent slaveholder and a colonel in the Army of Northern Virginia. Monty had always gotten a big-ass kick out of how that proper Southern colonel would have probably shot himself in the head at the knowledge that one of his descendants would be marrying the descendant of a piece of his property.

And as he rode, the laughter kept coming back, as it always did, loud enough to be heard over the roar of the Harley.

Victor Palmer walked into the store, almost sighing with pleasure as the smell of old paper and ink came to him. The store was in an otherwise unimpressive strip mall outside Greenbelt, with a Pizza Hut franchise, a Jiffy Lube franchise, a bunch of other franchises and this little store, called Pulp Planet. Sometimes when Victor came here he thought the only thing Americans were good for were setting up franchises so that a strip mall in Maine looked exactly like one in California.

He stood on the scuffed-up linoleum, looked around at the open bins set up against the walls. He walked slowly to the nearest bin, just savoring the anticipation of what lay before him. Rows and rows of old magazines in plastic sleeves were stacked in rows and he let his fingers brush over the plastic, looking at the brightly colored and lurid covers of the pulp magazines from the 1930s and 1940s and 1950s. Ah, he thought, that had been the time, back fifty and sixty years ago, when there'd been dozens of pulp-fiction magazines published each month, from westerns to men's adventure to mystery to science fiction and fantasy. The colors were garish, the stories were often poorly written and the advertisements for becoming a 'he-man' or getting rid of blackheads were always hilarious. But there was an energy and spirit to the pulps that had always appealed to him, especially during the grueling days of med school and residency. For he enjoyed losing himself in the spirit of the pulps, written during the Depression and the Second World War and the opening decades of the Cold War when the stories had suggested that, no matter how grim the news, anything was possible. Anything.

Victor rummaged carefully through the magazines, looking for his particular favorite, *Doc Savage*, a pulp character that lived from 1933 to 1949. Doc was the subject of more than a hundred serialized novels, involving adventures all around the Earth, fighting crime, fighting evil, working to make the world a better place. A brilliant physician with the crime-fighting abilities of Sherlock Holmes, Doc kept his offices in the Empire State Building and had a Fortress of Solitude in the Arctic. Ridiculous stuff, Victor knew, but he loved these tales of black-and-white morality, about evil men with death rays and secret poison clouds, not with hijacked airliners and weaponized anthrax.

Victor weaved a bit on his tired feet, looking through the *Doc Savage* magazines, and he remembered one particularly fantastic aspect of Doc's world: the man believed in the ultimate goodness of humanity and thought that it was diseased minds that created criminals. Doc had a secret medical facility in upstate New York where criminals he had captured were operated upon, to correct the imbalance in their minds and thereby allow them to become useful, productive and law-abiding citizens.

Poor Doc. Victor went to another bin of magazines. Doc never realized – as Victor had, during his first residency at an ER in an inner-city hospital in Atlanta – that some men (and a few women, to be honest) liked hurting people, liked killing people, liked being evil, and there was no miracle operation in existence that could change that. He remembered a bull session with Monty Zane late one night, when Monty had said, 'You know, when it's all said and done, the best way to protect this nation is to locate a certain number of men out there who hate us, and dispatch them with a nine-millimeter round to the forehead. Problem is, of course, knowing who they are and where they are.'

How true. Victor rubbed his fingers across the clear plastic, remembered the joy in reading these pulps in those few hours available to him, early on in his medical career. He wished for the simplicity of that time, wished he had never heard of the CDC or weaponized anthrax or any other damnable thing. At the moment he thought it would have been a fine thing to enter the Public Health Service and end up as a small town MD in rural Arkansas or something, married to some local gal who'd worship him because of his education, and where he could haunt the used-magazine and book dealers on the Internet.

What a life that would have been, instead of the nightmare he was in now. A nightmare that was going to get worse, for Victor had no doubt that details of the Final Winter immunization program would most certainly become public, if not this year then next.

And he had already planned that as part of a plea agreement for quickly cooperating with the government, he'd be sent to a minimum-security facility, and be able to bring his collection of pulps with him.

It would only be fair.

Darren Coover sat in a comfortable easy chair in his apartment, the Bose Wave radio in the room set to a local classical station, as he worked on a *New York Times* crossword puzzle from 1950 while his laptop hummed away at his elbow on a portable desk. He looked over at the laptop, saw that the program he was running was doing its business, quietly surfing sex sites on the Internet – with an emphasis on busty women – and went back to his puzzle. He had long ago lost interest in doing contemporary crossword puzzles – he usually finished the Sunday *New York Times* one in under an hour – but he did love the challenge of solving posers and he found that doing old puzzles was a hell of a nice challenge.

For one thing, there was a whole universe of cultural phrases and words that were a half-century old that one had to ruminate over before completing a fifty-year-old puzzle, which was a delight. Darren subscribed to a special service that recovered old puzzles from the *New York Times* microfilm records and mailed them out to subscribers around the world. It was one thing to solve a puzzle involving a play on words; it was something else when you had to remember the name of a Broadway star from the late 1940s.

Remembering. Darren looked up at the laptop, merrily moving along the program that he had sent into its innards. The line from his Dell laptop was linked with a cable modem, and he spent a few moments just imagining the intricacy of sending those packets of information back and forth, back and forth, along the cable line. One cable here out to a utility pole to a switching station to . . . another memory, this time of a lecture being given back at the NSA campus – known as Crypto City – when a lecturer from MIT came in and stood in a secure conference room, yapping about something. Darren had sat at the rear, idly listening to the guy drone on, when the man had said something interesting. The lecturer asked, 'How many computer networks are out there in the world today?' There had been a low murmur and Darren knew it was a trick question, and he had kept his mouth shut until the lecturer had triumphantly said, 'One. There is just one computer network in the world.' Everything else was just a subset of this huge network. There had been a low titter of laughter, and the lecturer had just let it slide right over his pointy head.

Because the right answer wasn't one. Darren wasn't sure what the right answer was, exactly, but he knew that the numeral one wasn't it. For there was another network out there, one that belonged to the NSA. It was called HARD-WIRE, and it was a network with a 526-bit encryption technology, based on a new quantum mechanics computing system that existed only in Crypto City. HARDWIRE allowed NSA operatives – like himself – to chat with one another.

He looked down at the crossword puzzle, thinking yet again how the current puzzles were no longer much of a challenge. Ah, a challenge – now, getting a handle on Final Winter and what Adrianna had set in motion, that was one hell of a test, and he knew that he should have been satisfied with what was on his plate. But there was something there that he wanted to dig around, something that just didn't quite make sense. If he dumped that porn program he was running and logged into HARDWIRE – which could take a while: the verification and password protection system made entering the White House look like buying a day pass at Disneyworld – he could chat with some of his co-workers and see what sniffings they had on Final Winter. Not that he didn't trust what was going on with his Tiger Team. No, sir, not at all. It was just that – well, he liked things to work out right, to make sense. And right now something wasn't quite making sense. He wasn't sure what it was. There was just a tingling back there in his mind that bothered him.

Darren glanced up at the impressively built women flashing in and out of existence on his computer screen. Some women – every one of them, in fact – that he saw flash by were merely representatives of binary numerals, like 1001011101001110100011100111, and the merest adjustment to that number stream, say, changing the second zero to a one, could make the photo out of focus. Or blur it completely. One switch of a digit could turn something originally designed to arouse men into a frustrating blend of colors and static.

He looked away from the screen. The unfilled puzzle was still in his lap. He remembered his boss's orders. Take the day off. We need you fresh.

True enough.

Darren picked up his pen and went to work. Now. Who in hell had been the female lead in the Broadway premiere of *South Pacific*?

Brian Doyle spent part of his day off heading out to a small park near Greenbelt that looked like it hadn't been maintained since it had originally been slapped together. The park memorialized some cavalry unit from Maryland that had fought for the Union during the Civil War and save for a few benches and a statue of a man on a horse there wasn't much to the place. Late-night drinking and sex bouts by local high-school students were probably the main recreational activities. Brian pulled into the gravel parking lot, noting with satisfaction that the place seemed empty. Good. That suited him well.

He got out of the Lexus, went to the rear door and took

out a heavy black box with a handle in the center. He walked past the statue, down to a grassy field that overlooked a stream. The grass was ankle high but that didn't bother him. It seemed to be a good day. He put the box down on the grass, looked around. No picnickers, no witnesses. Brian remembered how, some years ago, in a similar park, the body of the White House counsel had been found, an apparent suicide. Now *that* had been a time, and an eight-year vacation from reality. All that spilled ink and recorded news tape about a pudgy intern and a lecherous president, leading to an impeachment and an incredible waste of media energy and resources.

So. Nobody had asked his opinion about it. All he knew was that Adrianna was correct. While most folk were focused on the trivial, serious men with serious grievances were preparing to do the American people harm. And were continuing their preparations.

Brian kneeled down in the grass, undid two brass snaplocks and opened up the cover of the box. There, nestled inside and folded, was a set of Highland bagpipes. He took the ungainly tangle of pipes out and stood up. The ebony finish of the tubes was shiny in the sunlight, and he tossed the three drones over his left shoulder, placed the mouthpiece between his lips, and began inflating the bag. As the bag came to life, he recalled the brief and unsatisfactory conversation he'd had with his son Thomas that morning. He had asked questions about school, about Thomas's friends, about his pitching status on his school baseball team, and most of the answers he received had been the same grunts or 'Yeps'. About the only time Thomas had been anything like himself was when he'd asked the last question he always asked: 'Dad, when are you coming home?'

Good question. A *damn* good question, one that Marcy always asked in that acid tone that shot right through him. 'What kind of father are you, spending so much time on the road?' she would always say. 'What in hell are you doing to your son?'

Brian closed his eyes, felt the leather bag inflate under his left arm. He fingered the chanter with both hands, squeezed the bag, heard the drones – one bass, two tenor – explode with that steady tone, and a second later the chanter squealed into life. He dipped his left knee, slid right into 'The Heights of Vittoria', a good tune celebrating a British battle in Italy during the Second World War. From 'The Heights of Vittoria' he went into 'The 42nd Black Watch Regiment Crossing the Rhine' and then to something more cheerful, 'Highland Laddie'. The tone and depth of the music cut right through him. He played for a while, letting the music relax him, playing the tunes he loved, which most certainly did not include what he thought were the two most overplayed bagpipe tunes of all time, 'Amazing Grace' and 'Scotland the Brave'. Brian had taken up the bagpipes, just like Dad, after joining the force, and he had become a member of the NYPD's bagpipe band, playing at functions throughout the city, from ribbon cuttings to parades to funerals . . .

God, especially funerals. As he went into a slow march – 'Skye Boat Song' – Brian remembered that dreary fall in 2001, playing at funeral after funeral all over the city. Save for one, that of his father, and he never quite forgave himself for one thing: the tears. He had shed plenty of tears for his fallen brothers in the police department, as well as for the firefighters, EMTs and Port Authority cops. But for one funeral he had remained stone-faced and silent – for his own father's.

And what kind of son was he, that he would not cry at his father's funeral?

Brian opened his eyes, played another march, 'Johnny Cope, Are Ye Walkin' Yet?' and tapped his left foot in time with the music, thinking about the pipes themselves, how he hadn't wanted to pick them up, but now he was enjoying both the music and the history. The history, of course, was of war, for the Highland pipes were known for inspiring Scottish fighters and frightening their foes. Killers in kilts, the Scots soldiers were called, and Brian wondered briefly if the pipes had been played by the British troops a couple of years back when they took Basra from Saddam's forces.

There. He sensed something, spun around.

A man was standing there with a woman and two children. Holding on to their mother's hands. Boy and girl. All were dressed for a day off, maybe a drive in the country, a picnic in a deserted park. The man seemed apologetic.

'Sorry to disturb you, but . . . well, we were enjoying your playing.'

Brian smiled. 'Thanks.'

'And I was wondering . . . would you mind playing something for my kids?'

'Sure. What would it be?'

The guy grinned. 'My favorite. "Amazing Grace".'

Ugh, Brian thought. He was going to say something short and sharp – like 'I've never heard of it' – and then he looked at the eager and expectant faces of the man's children. Thought about Final Winter. Thought about these kids, coughing and wheezing, being brought to an overwhelmed emergency room by their terrified parents. Or maybe even worse . . . this boy and girl, alive and well, but trying to wake up mommy and daddy in their bed, mommy and daddy who had been so sick and now seemed to be sleeping, but they had been sleeping so long and their skin was so cold . . .

Brian rubbed at his dry lips. 'Sure. "Amazing Grace". Coming right up.'

And he played for the man and his wife and his children, all still alive on this glorious spring day in the United States.

Adrianna Scott looked at herself in the mirror, didn't like what she saw, and didn't particularly care. Her face was made up more than she was used to, really highlighting her eyes and her lips. Her aunt would say that she looked whorish and, for once, Auntie would have been right. Adrianna stepped back, looked at the crop-top white tank top that she was wearing, with no bra underneath. Her nipples were showing through fine and clear, and her brown tummy was nice and flat. She supposed that maybe she should have had her navel pierced – some guys seemed to get off on that – but that was too drastic, and besides, her time was short. She spun around, examined the tight white slacks she had on. Underneath she was wearing a tiny bright pink thong and the colored fabric could be seen clearly through the white of her slacks. Perfect. Hot and slutty. Just like she wanted.

She walked out into her apartment, saw up on the mantel the photograph of her and Auntie that Brian Doyle had been admiring the other night. That had been close. She touched the thick frame and then went to the closet, put on a knee-length light green coat, and left the house, carrying her heavy purse in one hand. She got into her car, backed out of her lot, and went to the new Summergate Mall, about a twenty-minute drive from her condo. She checked the time when she got to the mall and drove into the underground garage. Time for once was on her side, and she left the car and strode quickly into the mall, looking like any one of the hundreds of women packed in there tonight.

A good night, a good night for shopping. But Adrianna didn't plan to buy a damn thing.

Instead, she relied on her training from her early CIA days at Camp Perry – also known as The Farm – where basic tradecraft was taught, everything from using mail drops to shaking a tail, which helped her feel completely confident, an hour later, as she drove away from the underground parking garage in a stolen Chrysler minivan, that she wasn't being followed at all.

Adrianna allowed herself to feel a quiet tingle of excitement. Her day off was proceeding just as planned.

CHAPTER FIFTEEN

Adrianna Scott drove west for almost an hour, going over the state line into Virginia. As each mile slid on by a little voice insistently whispered at her, saying that she really didn't have to go out here tonight, that it was too disgusting and too dangerous, picking up strange men like that. She let the little voice drone on. Sure, it would be easy to turn around and drive back – hell, she might be able to get the minivan back to the mall parking garage before it was even missed – and go home and just have a glass of wine and try to unwind.

But the little voice, while it could be heard, was certainly going to be ignored. The next few weeks were going to be hell indeed, and Adrianna needed this break tonight, needed it bad, and there was nothing that was going to stop her. Her mouth was dry and her tummy was fluttering with excitement, and she wondered if this was what gambling addicts or drug addicts or Internet sex addicts felt like, just before scoring whatever it was that they needed to soothe their frayed nerves and jumpy imaginations.

Maybe so.

But tonight would be the last one. Honest.

Sure, the voice said, just like the one in New Jersey, three months ago. That was supposed to be the last one, right?

Right.

Now Adrianna was off the highway, navigating narrow state roads, heading to her target. She had scoped it out weeks before, and was confident that it would suit her needs. There. Up ahead. There were neon lights there, red, white and blue, marking a local VFW hall. It was a two-story wooden building, white, with darkened windows. Pickup trucks and other vehicles were parked in the gravel lot. She drove into the lot, found a place to park the minivan so that it wouldn't be spotted from the street, and stepped out into the cool dusk. She shivered. She knew what she had to do. There was no turning back.

Adrianna walked up to the entrance, teetering a bit on the black high heels she was wearing, carrying her heavy purse in one hand.

Inside the place was dark and smoky, a jukebox in one corner playing a country and western tune. The bar was a square structure in the center, surrounded by tables and chairs, and off to one side was a polished wooden dance floor. The place was about half filled, more men than women, and Adrianna sat down in the corner at an empty table. There was a candle in the center of her table, unlit. She looked around, took in the atmosphere of the place. There were framed items on the wall, old Second World War recruiting posters and photographs of tanks, aircraft and ships. There were flags and banners as well, along with the usual bumper stickers plastered along the side of the bar:

9/11: Never Forgive, Never Forget.

United We Stand.

These Colors Don't Run.

Adrianna had to hide a smirk. Imperialism through bumper stickers.

A waitress, a sagging middle-aged woman, came over, wearing jeans and an old gray sweat shirt. Over the sound of the twanging guitars, Adrianna ordered a Budweiser – and then, slipping the waitress a folded-over ten-dollar bill, she ordered something else.

The waitress stood up, her expression shocked. 'Tell me again what you want?'

Adrianna repeated her order. The waitress looked at the folded bill in her hand and said, 'Well, I suppose Henry would fit the bill. He's single, not bad-looking, but I tell you . . . he's not the sharpest knife in the drawer, if you know what I mean.'

Adrianna sipped from her beer. 'I know exactly what you mean.'

The waitress left and Adrianna sipped the cold brew again, wishing she had ordered something different. But in this place, she reckoned, she'd be lucky if imported beer meant a Coors from Colorado. It was warm sitting there, her long coat over the few clothes she was wearing underneath, but she left it on. She was making an impression, no doubt about it, but she didn't want to cause such a big stir that a lot of people would remember her later.

There.

A man was coming over, a glass of beer in one hand, a pool stick in the other. She judged him to be in his late forties, close-trimmed beard – which was fortunate, since she liked men with beards, Brian Doyle notwithstanding – and had on khaki slacks and a red flannel shirt. There was a bit of a beer belly developing but, thankfully, there wasn't a heavy gut. The man grinned and she was relieved again to see that he seemed to have good teeth. This night was turning out to be fortunate indeed.

'The name's Henry Spooner,' he said. 'Are you really looking for me?'

She looked up at him coyly. 'My name is Adrianna, and yes, I really was looking for you. Or somebody like you.'

'How's that?'

'Please,' she said, motioning to a chair, 'do sit down.' And of course, as she motioned to the chair, she let the coat slip open so that the white tank top was revealed in all its braless glory, and Henry definitely caught a good glimpse as he sat down. His grin was wider and he said, 'Karen told me that there was a pretty girl sitting here by herself, looking to meet a single man. A vet who'd served in the Gulf. Was she right?'

'Yes, she was,' Adrianna said, gently running a finger around the tip of the beer bottle. 'But you served in the first Gulf War, am I right? Back in 1991?'

He nodded. 'That's a big affirm, lady. Gulf War One, which would have been the last Gulf War, if Daddy Bush had had any balls.'

'And what did you do when you were there?'

A satisfied smile. 'Gunner on an M-1A Abrams Tank, First Army Division, Big Red One.'

Adrianna made a point of licking her full lips. 'Really? That sounds so fascinating . . . and dangerous.'

A manly shrug. 'We did what we had to do, that's all.'

'Did you . . . did you kill many Iraqis?'

Another manly shrug. 'Some. It was real easy for us, in the M-1A. Called it a turkey shoot. Our thermal imaging could spot a T-72 out there, hundreds of meters before they knew we were even coming after them . . . sometimes you'd get a T-72 popped and we'd have crispy critters out there, smokin' . . .'

She reached out and gently touched his left wrist. 'Thank you . . . thank you for your service.'

His smile was still there but she sensed he was suspicious and she was right – thank you, Camp Perry training – and he said, 'So. Why are you asking me all these questions? Something wrong?'

Adrianna shook her head. 'Not at all. You see . . . my uncle, he was in the Army as well. Served in the Gulf. He was a driver on one of those armored vehicles – the ones that carry troops – what're they called?'

'Bradley Fighting Vehicles.'

'Yes, yes, that's the one,' she said, sitting up straighter, making sure that her chest was nice and prominent. 'He served there as well, and was seriously hurt.'

'Oh. Sorry to hear that.'

Sure, Adrianna thought, sorry that I'm not flashing you my naked boobs, that's what you're sorry about. Aloud she said, 'Oh, he survived. Somehow an anti-tank round hit his vehicle, damaged it severely. He was trapped inside and would have died, except another soldier, from another unit, pulled him out and saved him. My uncle never knew his name.'

Henry said, 'Well, sorry to disappoint you, miss, but that wasn't me. Never did see anything like that, though it sure did happen in other sectors over there.'

Adrianna touched his wrist again. 'I'm sorry, you don't understand. You see, my uncle died last year, and he was upset that he had this debt, this obligation, that had never been paid off. That somewhere out there was an Army trooper who had saved his life, and he'd never got a chance to thank him personally. And before he died, so he could get some peace, I told him that I'd go out and find this man, and I would thank him. I travel a lot on business, and I knew I would have an opportunity to find him, whoever he was.'

Henry said, 'Oh. Okay, I get it.'

Another touch of her hand upon him. 'But . . . you see, it's nearly impossible for me to do this. I've checked the official records of the incident, and there's no record of this soldier's name. So I'm doing the next best thing. When I travel, I go to the local VFW or American Legion Hall, and try to thank all the veterans from the first Gulf War that I can. I figure that this way, I just might thank the right soldier, without even knowing it.'

Henry seemed confused, which was fine, especially since the waitress had warned her that he wasn't particularly bright, which would serve her purpose so well. He took a swallow from his beer glass and said, 'But there's one other thing I don't understand.'

'Yes?'

'Karen, the waitress . . . she said that the girl sitting here wanted to meet a Gulf veteran, but that he had to be single and kinda good-looking. What's that about?'

Adrianna picked up her beer bottle, gently suckled the top as she took a swallow, and then reached out for the last time and caressed the man's wrist, making sure he got a good look at her tight slacks, in addition to the white tank top, her nips so hard now that they almost hurt.

She lowered her voice. 'Maybe I want to say thank you in another way. Interested?'

Henry's eyes lit up, like little horny diodes back there had just clicked on. 'God, yes.'

She leaned forward, close enough so that her hair tickled his face. 'Good. I have a room at a motel, a couple of miles away. Let's get out of here.'

'You got it, babe.'

The motel was called the Longstreet Arms, and Adrianna had earlier rented an end unit there. She was on Henry the moment the door closed. She dropped her coat on the floor and her purse as well, and the man grabbed her by the shoulders and pulled her close. His beard scratched her face and she kissed him, kissed him hard, and his mouth was open and slobbering and she started bumping and grinding against a thigh, and that got him going, too. His hands grabbed her ass and she forced herself to giggle as she dropped to her knees, started unzipping his jeans.

'Jesus,' he said. 'Jesus, you are one hot babe . . . God!'

Sure she was, Adrianna thought, deftly pulling his hardening member free from his soiled white underwear – ugh. She was hotter than any other small-town babe he had gotten in the past few years, she thought, he'd have been lucky to get some chain-smoking overweight hausfrau with bad teeth and tattoos from high school sloppily inked on her shoulder blades. Adrianna forced herself not to grimace, not to give in to the gag reflex as she took him into her mouth.

Henry shuddered and leaned back against the door, his hands now in her hair. She continued the repulsive act for a few moments before pulling away and looking up at him, smiling. 'Time to get comfortable, don't you think?'

He was grinning, breathing hard, eyes glassy. 'Oh, shit, yes, babe. You got it.'

Adrianna stood up, took him by the hand, led him over to the bed. The room had light green wall-to-wall carpeting, a TV on a stand, and a bathroom that looked like it got cleaned regularly, every spring and fall. Henry worked fast to undress himself, and she helped him along. She didn't protest when he pulled down her tight white slacks and pulled her tank top over her head. Now that her breasts were exposed, he growled and grabbed them. She couldn't help herself when she winced as he worked on her nipples. She gently took a hold of his hands and said, 'Don't worry, hon, they'll be there later. Lay back, now, why don't you?'

He fell back on the bed and she straddled him, grinding her butt on his erection. His hands went back up to her breasts and then she leaned down to kiss him and whispered in his ear, 'Want to try something kinky?'

'Shit, yes,' he said, grinning. 'Would love to.'

'Then close your eyes.'

Henry did as he was told, and Adrianna clambered off the bed, thinking joyfully, there he goes, just like the other ones, thinking with the wrong head. She went down to her purse, snapped it open, took out the two metal instruments, and within a very few seconds she had handcuffed his hands to the headboard of the bed.

'Hey!' he protested. 'What the fuck do you think you're doing?'

She was amused to see how small the other head was, now that it was shrinking away. She straddled him again, kissed him on the lips, and said, 'Shhhh, dear one, everything will be explained shortly. Just keep quiet.'

'The hell I will!' he yelled, yanking at his cuffed wrists, the metal restraints rattling against the headboard. 'You get me out of here, you crazy bitch, I'm not into *this* kind of kinky stuff, this goddamn bondage, not at all, and if you don't let me out of here right now, I'll—'

As he was raving, Adrianna went back to the floor, retrieved her purse, and came back up onto the bed to straddle him. She opened her purse and took out a Black Attack folding knife, which she snapped open. She poked the very point of the blade into his chin, right through his beard. A bead of blood suddenly appeared in the whiskers. Henry froze, his eyes wide with shock and fear, his arms now trembling.

'Got your attention?'

No reply. She gently moved the point of the blade again, and Henry moaned.

'Got your attention?' She asked again.

'Yes,' Henry said, his voice thin. 'Yes, you do.'

'Good.'

Adrianna took a deep breath, felt the shuddering shame of thrill and excitement flow through her like a heavy slug of maple syrup, just sliding down one's throat. She leaned over him and said, 'I want to know more, Henry. Tell me more about your war in Iraq, back in '91. Do tell me more.'

'Wh-why?'

'Hmm, a good question,' she said. 'Hold on. Don't move, and maybe I won't hurt you.'

Back to the floor and to her purse, from which she took out a thin leather wallet. She returned to her handcuffed man on the bed – noticing right away the stench now rising up from him, wondering how automatic that was, the body reacting to being put in unavoidable danger – and straddled him again. She was conscious that she was naked, save for the pink-thong panties, but she didn't really care.

Adrianna held up the leather wallet, flipped it open. 'See the photo? Not a bad likeness, is it?'

'Noo . . . nooo, it's not.'

'See what it says?'

'It says . . . Adrianna Scott – and, Jesus Christ, you're a fucking CIA agent! What the hell *is* this?'

The knife point went back to his chin. He winced and she said coldly, 'For someone who can walk and breathe at the same time you're pretty stupid, Henry. We're not CIA *agents*. We're CIA *officers*. Got it?'

He moaned again. 'Please . . . what the fuck do you want? Huh? What the fuck do you *want*?'

Adrianna leaned into him again. 'I want you to tell me a story. A story about killing Iraqis. Tell me a story. That's all. Is that so hard?'

Henry closed his eyes. Another bead of blood appeared in the bristles of his beard. His chest moved rapidly, up and down, underneath her splayed legs. He said, 'A story . . . that's all? A story?'

'Sure,' she said. 'And to be fair, I'll tell you a story in return, all right?'

Eyes clenched shut, Henry said, 'Our tank was called Killer Kobra. Part of K Company. All tanks had names beginning with the letter of their company. We . . . we . . . set off at 0300 hours, H-Day, the day we made our swing out east, heading up into Iraq. The classic left-hand hook. It was flat, rocky land. Great terrain for tanks. Lots of room to maneuver . . . we'll probably never have an advantage like that, ever again. We were about twenty klicks north of the border, when we had our first contact . . . three Soviet-era BMPs, personnel carriers—'

Another jab of the knife. 'I know what BMPs are, you fool. Go on.'

'Then . . . then we saw a T-72, coming up over a sand dune. The poor son of a bitch probably didn't even know we were there . . . Bruce, our tank commander, called for a Sabot round . . . I pulled it up, chambered it . . . boom! . . . god-damn thing, we could see the turret spin up . . . those T-72s were goddamned deathtraps, they were . . . we motored up and a few minutes later, we slowed down as we went past it . . . no reason 'cept none of us had ever seen anything like that, in a real war . . .'

Adrianna said, 'What did it look like?'

Henry's eyes flashed defiance. 'What the hell do you think? The tank was still burning when we got there . . . and there were a couple of crispy critters, hanging over the side – didn't even fucking look like humans . . . but you know what? They were the enemy – that's what – we had to do what we had to do . . . so . . . anything else?'

She shook her head, feeling her breathing quicken. 'No . . . no, I don't think so, Henry. I think it's my turn, I do . . .'

She shifted her weight, felt sweat trickle down her naked back. 'Before I start, I need to ask you a question. Have you ever heard of Amiriyah?'

'Amir what?'

'Amiriyah. It was a bomb shelter for civilians, in a nice neighborhood in western Baghdad. You never heard of it?'

A shake of the head, a clatter of the handcuffs.

Adrianna took the knife, gently moved it across Henry's right cheek. 'I don't doubt it. Why bother? It was just an unfortunate part of the first Gulf War. Everybody remembers Kuwait and the Highway of Death and Stormin' Norman Schwarzkopf and the yellow ribbons and the victory parades after the war. Right? Pretty parades in pretty towns, flags and cheering. I bet you went to a parade like that, Henry, right? A nice parade, nothing like those poor Iraqi boys got when their war was over. Most of the Iraqis killed were just poor ignorant farmboys, many with their first pairs of shoes, and they ended up burned or blown to pieces or turned into dust by you and your weapons.'

Her breathing was really quick now, and she went on, the words tumbling past each other.

'But let's get back to Amiriyah, shall we? It was a bomb shelter that was used by hundreds of civilians every night, when the air-raid sirens howled in the air. Ever hear an air-raid siren, Henry? It makes a wailing noise that cuts right through you, turns your guts into water, as you wait for the bombs or missiles to strike. But the civilians who got into Amiriyah, they thought they were safe. It was a bomb shelter. Everyone knew the Americans had smart weapons. Everyone knew they would be safe if they got inside Amiriyah.'

Adrianna had to stop, her breathing was so hard. To her own ears, her voice was changing, the way the syllables were coming out, it was all different. She said, 'But the Americans weren't as smart as we thought they were, and they weren't as smart as they thought they were. For early on the morning of February 13, 1991, the shelter was bombed by the Americans. More than three hundred civilians – mostly women and children – were incinerated. Instantly. Including my papa and mama. Do you understand? My mama and papa, two of the sweetest, kindest and most intelligent people in the world, struck dead by your bombs.'

Henry's mouth was moving, like he was trying to say something, and she grabbed the identification wallet she had shown him earlier and flung it across the room, spitting out the words. 'My name is not Adrianna Scott. It is Aliyah Fulenz. I am an Iraqi Christian woman, and I am here to seek justice.'

'But . . . but . . . the CIA . . . how in God's name did they . . . I don't believe you . . .'

She felt herself smile. 'For even as a young girl, I was quite smart, Henry. After my parents were murdered by you, I came to the United States. I lived with an aunt, and soon after I came here I started with my work. My story. My setting up of false identification papers was so easy, even at a young age. And the CIA? Once they started going through my background, they went as far as my high school years. Which was typically American, save that I was an orphan child, adopted by an elderly aunt, who had passed away. So there was no one left alive to contradict my story. No one. No one at all. It was so easy . . .'

Adrianna brought the knife up to Henry's chin again. 'So that was my story. And here's another one.' She pushed the knife in again while Henry groaned. 'I have schemed and worked and planned and now find myself, with God's help, I have no doubt, in a position of power. Of authority. Of trust and responsibility. And the people who have put their trust in me, they have no idea, not even a concept of what I am about to rain down upon them. For you see, in a few weeks' time, aircraft will be flying out at night, to all places in the

United States. Secreted aboard them will be canisters. Those installing the canisters will believe that they contain something benign. But they won't. They will be carrying weaponized anthrax, Henry, weaponized anthrax that will be spread across your largest cities. And panicked people, already infected, will stream out into the countryside.'

Henry was whimpering as she twisted the knife against him. 'Everyone you know and love and cherish will be dead in less than two months, Henry, including your bastard whore empire that runs across the world like some elephant run amok, crushing everything in its path. Do you hear me, Henry?'

'Please . . . please, no, don't tell me any more . . . why are you telling me this . . .?'

Another twist of the knife, another moan. 'Because I'm human, Henry. I couldn't have gone all these years without telling someone, so every now and then, when the pressure becomes too much, when I feel I'm losing my focus, my anger, I seek one of you out. One who has killed my countrymen, who helped kill my parents, and then I unburden myself . . . and I feel so much better when I'm finished.'

Henry was crying now. 'Please . . . please don't tell me any more . . . please don't say anything more about you or anthrax or anything else . . .'

'Why, Henry?'

Snot was oozing out of his nose. 'Because . . . because I'm afraid you're going to kill me, that's why . . .'

She nodded.

'Henry, you're absolutely right.'

And with that, Aliyah Fulenz took her knife and slit the man's throat.

PART TWO

CHAPTER SIXTEEN

Ten miles out of Memphis International Airport, Carrie Floyd stretched her fingers for a moment, above the control yoke of the AirBox McDonnell Douglas MD-11 that she and her co-pilot, Sean Callaghan, were piloting in the last few minutes of AirBox Flight Twelve, San Jose to Memphis. She was thirty-five years old and a veteran of the US Navy, and while she loved flying for AirBox – truth be told, she was lucky to be flying for any commercial outfit with the current airline industry slump – she hated the hours. AirBox was one of the handful of companies that guaranteed overnight delivery in the continental United States, which meant a hell of a lot of flight crews and package handlers worked vampire hours. Not fun for a single mom, and she thought briefly about seven-year-old Susan, down there dreaming, safe and snug in her own home and bed.

'AirBox Twelve, switch to the tower now on one one nine point seven,' came the quick, professional male voice of Memphis Approach Control through her earphones.

'Roger, AirBox Twelve, switching,' Sean said, toggling the radio-microphone switch on the control yoke.

Before them were the bright lights of Memphis, home to a hell of a lot of history and to Graceland – which Carrie had yet to visit, and doubted she ever would – and the international airport. Stuck in Tennessee but home to lots of cargo carriers like FedEx and Airborne and AirBox, and the number one airport in the world for moving packages. A hell of a thing. She focused on her flying, let her co-pilot handle the communications.

'Memphis Tower, AirBox Twelve, checking in on the visual to three six right,' Sean said, noting the number of the runway ahead of them, 36R.

'AirBox Twelve, cleared to land, three six right, winds at five zero four zero.'

Sean replied crisply, 'Roger, AirBox Twelve, cleared to land, three six right.'

In front of Carrie now were the lights of the airport, and the white marker lights that outlined all nine thousand feet of their runway. Compared with what she'd had to deal with during her Navy career, flying S-3 Vikings off and on aircraft carriers, the airport runway looked huge, as big as the county. There was plenty of room to land, and with light winds and a clear night it should be routine. Now, try landing on a couple of acres of steel, rolling and heaving and pitching, with no room for error, no room for anything going wrong – though, of course, things *do* go wrong and maybe that was the real reason she was shuttling packages at midnight across CONUS and not ferrying passengers to London during the daylight and working for a real airline—

Her co-pilot said, 'Five hundred feet, on airspeed, and sinking seven hundred feet per minute. Looks good, Carrie.'

She blinked her eyes. Damn woolgathering.

'Yep.'

One last scan of the instruments: everything looked good, airspeed at 135 knots on glide slope, flaps down, wheels down and locked, the yoke in her hands trembling just a bit as she imagined she could feel the entire vibration of the cargo jet, letting her know through the sense of touch and her other senses what was going on. And what was going on was a nice, normal landing, and . . .

Here we go, she thought.

The last few seconds, it seemed like the runway surface was on a giant elevator, rising right up, fast and fast and fast, and—

Slight bang.

Main gear down and . . .

Nose gear down.

Sean next to her, calling out the decreasing airspeed as she reversed the engines: 'One hundred knots, eighty knots,' and Carrie applied the brakes, and 'Sixty knots.'

Good. Now they were at taxiing speed, no longer an aircraft, just a big old bus on the ground, and in her earphones Memphis Tower said, 'AirBox Twelve, switch to ground control, point nine, on Yankee one.'

'Memphis, ground,' Carrie said, toggling the radio switch on the yoke. 'AirBox Twelve is clear on Yankee one.'

A different voice now: 'AirBox Twelve, proceed to ramp AB12.'

'Roger.'

Now the jet felt heavy and slow, like an overweight Greyhound bus, waddling its way into the Port Authority terminal. With gravity now in control and working its magic touch, Carrie felt like she was driving a luxury car whose power steering had just cut off.

She made the left turn, headed to the processing terminals up ahead. She switched on the number two radio on the center console, allowing her now to talk to the AirBox dispatcher.

'AirBox center, this is AirBox twelve,' she called out.

'Evenin', Twelve,' came the soft twang of the dispatcher working tonight. Hank something-or-other.

'Where do you want us tonight?'

'Ramp four,' came the reply.

'Ramp four it is, thank you kindly,' she said.

A chuckle. 'Not a problem, Splash.'

Her hands tightened on the nose-wheel-steering tiller bar. She could sense Sean stiffen up in his seat, decided not to say anything about that crack. Okay. Carrie turned and said, 'Got that? Ramp four.'

Sean had the post-flight checklist already in hand. 'Ramp four, boss. And we're five minutes ahead of schedule. The General will love that. Get a jump on getting all those letters and packages on their merry way.'

'It's what we do, Sean. It's what we do.'

Now that they were nearing the ramp, fatigue started setting in, especially around Carrie's shoulders and hips. With only one other crew member, there wasn't much down time flying from San Jose to Memphis, and with most of the cabin space back there taken up with cargo there also wasn't much room to walk around. There were rumors that General Bocks was considering expanding his reach to the Pacific Rim countries, which made perfect business sense, but Carrie knew that something would have to change before she'd be up to make that kind of grueling flight.

There. Halted and everything else was on auto, and in a matter of minutes she and Sean had de-planed, carrying their heavy kit bags full of manuals and charts. Both were now wearing the uniform caps of AirBox. Sean didn't seem to mind the uniform – he had flown C-141 Starlifters for the Air Force and was still in the Reserves – but it was too Air Force for Carrie's taste. She preferred the old Navy flight suit, which reminded her of something . . .

They walked to the entranceway leading to the inside of the

AirBox terminal system. Around them workers in AirBox jumpsuits were hustling to unload their flight, and Carrie spared a glance back to where the scissors-cargo unloaders were sidling up the fuselage. With the way they worked, the damn plane would be empty in less than twenty minutes. A hell of a system. Still had to give the General credit, though the damn penny-pinching during the last quarter had been a royal pain in the ass. Everything from reduced fuel burn and landing reserves to the per diem being cut back – there were struggles going on out there, and she hoped the General would win this one without too much of a fight. She really needed to fly, and with her record she really needed the job.

Then she spotted another man out there in the unloading crew, with a jumpsuit that looked cleaned and ironed. This guy wasn't manhandling pallets of freight off the MD-11. He was standing there, holding something in his hand, wearing a set of earphones that connected to the wandlike piece of equipment in his grasp. Every now and then he went over to one of the passing pallets. The other crew members ignored him.

Sean saw where she was looking and said, 'Homeland Security on the job again.'

'Yeah, but it still gives me the creeps.'

'What's the matter? Afraid we slipped a suitcase nuke into Memphis, on its way to Manhattan?'

'Nothing to joke about,' Carrie said, and she walked across the tarmac, her co-pilot at her side. She knew she had been snippy but she was tired and she was in no mood for jokes about terrorism.

As they climbed up the stairs to the main floor of the freight terminal, she said, 'Sean, see you in a bit.' Sean looked over, a bit surprised.

'What's up?'

'Got to see a man about something.'

'Where?'

'Dispatch.'

He frowned. 'Be careful.'

Carrie smiled at him. 'There are old pilots, there are bold pilots, but there are no old, bold pilots, and I'm not feeling too bold. Just a tad cranky. But I'll be careful.'

'Thanks,' he said, and added: 'I like flying with you, Carrie. Don't screw anything up.'

'I won't.'

Sean went on, while Carrie kept walking down the hallway, noticing with her mom's eyes how untidy parts of the building were beginning to look. Despite the cheery commercials on television and the media's continuing love affair with the General and his somewhat unorthodox way of doing business, AirBox was barely hanging on. And when you're hanging on from a cliff by your fingernails, worrying whether your hair was combed was way the hell down on your list of concerns.

Down the hallway, up two flights of stairs, and she was outside the dispatch center. There was a row of light orange plastic chairs – and why in hell did these chairs always have to be light orange? Why not blue? Or yellow? – and she took one, placing her kit bag down by her feet. In front of her was a door marked *Dispatch* with a keypad by the doorknob, and she waited. She should have been checking out with Sean. She should have been getting ready to get home and spend some time with Susan before her daughter went off to school. She should have been doing something else instead of sitting here, but instead she waited.

Carrie hoped that she wouldn't have to wait long.

And what the hell, her hopes came true.

The door clicked open and two people came out, a heavyset woman and a tall, thin guy with a stringy mustache. Hank, the soft-spoken dispatcher. He must have just cracked a joke because the woman was laughing as they stepped through the door, which snapped shut behind them. Either they didn't see Carrie or didn't care. Just another pilot. Down the hallway they went, to the restrooms, and as the guy went into the one marked *Gentlemen* Carrie stood up and went down the hallway, carrying her kit bag.

She caught Hank as he stood in front of the sink, a comb in his hand. She noted the look of shock on his face as she came through the door. Then he gave her a brief glance of recognition, and started out with a little joke. 'Hey, Carrie, didn't you notice the sign outside, the one that—'

Not a word from her side. She stepped up and swung her black leather case at the back of his legs, hitting him hard, and followed that up with a kick to the ankles. Hank yelped and fell down in a tangle and then she was on him, her knees slamming down on his chest, her hand now on his throat.

'Hey, hey, hey!' he called out. 'What the hell do you think—'

Carrie grasped his thin throat and squeezed, making him squawk.

'You shut the fuck up and listen,' she said, leaning down to him. 'Shut the fuck up. Got it?'

A muffled squawk, his eyes wide.

'Good,' she said. 'Listen and listen well, pal. You call me Splash one more time, either over the air, in private, or in your home while you're whacking off in the bathroom, then

I'm gonna come back and tear your balls off and feed 'em to the catfish. You got it?'

Yet another squawk that she figured was an affirmative signal, and she relaxed her grip, got up. Her legs were shaking. She hoped he didn't notice.

Hank sat up, face mottled red, his hand to his throat. 'You . . . you crazy bitch! I'll have you fired! Today!'

Carrie bent down again and he tried to scramble away, like a crab with broken legs, and she was sure that she surprised him when she kissed his forehead. 'Sure, Hank. You do that. You tell everyone how a girl beat you up in the boys' bathroom. Just like high school, right? You go on and do that, and just remember what I said. No more Splash. Ever.'

Carrie picked up her bag and walked out, and within two minutes had joined Sean in the checkout process. He kept silent as they signed and processed forms, and then he said, 'You okay?'

'Never been better.'

'Sure?'

'Positive.'

He didn't seem to believe her. 'Okay,' he said. 'Give you a ride home?'

'Absolutely.'

The ride home took about twenty minutes, ten of which were spent nodding in sleep against the passenger's-side door of Sean's Ford Explorer. He kept the music low and his mouth shut, a perfect co-pilot. At the northern end of Memphis's sprawl, where there were pleasant neighborhoods with one- and two-family duplexes, Sean stopped to let Carrie out as the sun was coming up.

He looked over to her and then leaned over and gave her

a kiss. She kissed him back and said, 'Knock it off. You know the rules about fraternization.'

'Screw the rules.'

'Another kiss and you'll be wanting to screw something else. Later, co-pilot man.'

'Tomorrow?'

She smiled. 'Call me and we'll work something out.'

'I want to raise Topic A again, you know.'

'Raise it and we'll talk. Honest.'

Another kiss. 'All right, then'

She got out and Sean drove off. It looked to be a beautiful day. She let herself in the side door and let her bag drop in the kitchen. Dishes piled in the sink, and she felt a flash of anger. Work all night and come home to dirty dishes and . . .

Carrie was tired, but she also tried to remember what it had been like when she was nineteen. Somewhere in this duplex two young girls were still slumbering. Her seven-year-old daughter Susan and her cousin Marilyn. Poor Marilyn. The young girl was struggling to make it through her sophomore year at the University of Memphis, and Carrie recalled her own times, joining the Navy ROTC to get a degree in history – like that was going to do anything for her – and then, after graduating from ROTC, finding out that she actually thrived in the Navy. Hard to believe but there it was. One of her heroes when she was younger had been Sally Ride, the first American woman in space, and through her aviation training at Pensacola that had been one thought at the back of her mind: that she would someday take Sally Ride's place up there in the cosmos. Maybe the first woman on the moon. That would have been something.

Carrie went out of the kitchen and into the small living

room, and then to the bathroom. Washed her hands and then her face. Looked at the tired eyes, the short blonde hair. Hat hair again, and she recalled the really vicious helmet hair she'd get out on deployment, flying her S-3 Viking jet, off and on the USS *Enterprise* . . .

And there you go. From Smash to Splash.

For 'Smash' had been her call sign, indicating who she was in the pantheon of aircraft carrier pilots. The real gods of this particular pantheon were the fighter jocks – and just a few jockettes – who wrestled F-14 Tomcats up into the air and down onto the deck with vim, vigor, and a few touches of arrogance. She hadn't quite made it to F-14s but had done all right with the S-3 Viking. That little jewel of a four-seater had originally been designed for ASW work – anti-submarine warfare – for if there was one thing that the admirals overseeing carrier task forces were terrified of, it was some sub sneaking its way into the defensive cordon around an aircraft carrier and sinking the damn thing. But with the Cold War over and what was left of the USSR submarine force rusting and sinking at the dockside, the Viking went through a few changes to make it a new aircraft. There was the airborne-surveillance Viking and the cargo Viking and the airborne-refueling Viking, and one humid night, in the Sea of Japan, Smash was doing a routine landing after a routine mission – topping off a number of F-14s – when that evening's landing quickly became everything but routine, as she slammed the aircraft down and powered up the throttle, as the tailhook snagged one of the arresting wires, and there was a movement to her right, as her co-pilot, one Tom McGrew, jerked against his shoulder harness.

And with the sound and the lights and the force and everything else, there was a thump and trouble, my God, the trouble in River City for – as Carrie later found out – that damn tailhook had snapped clean off so instead of coming to a nice and abrupt halt, the Viking bolted on the deck and started tilting off the port side, and slamming the throttles to full power didn't do a damn thing, as the Viking slewed off and both her gloved hands reached down and she tugged the lower ejection handles, and maybe she yelled, 'Eject, eject, eject' and maybe she didn't – depended on what day the remembering was going on – and she and her co-pilot, Lieutenant Tom McGrew of Seattle, Washington, blew out of the doomed aircraft. Carrie had been plucked out of the water, legs and arms bruised, coughing up sea water, to find out that her multimillion dollar aircraft was now several thousand feet below them in the water, and that her co-pilot had actually drifted under the damn bow of the *Enterprise*, steaming ahead, where he was either drowned, crushed, or shredded into pieces by one of the four twirling propellers.

Well.

There were investigations and a hearing and eventually Carrie was returned to flight status, but her little steps up on the way to the top of the female flying pyramid were faltering. She would shake and tremble during each landing. More and more times, she would miss the very last arresting wire and would have to bolt from the carrier deck and come around for another approach. Soon enough, she was under the spotlight as a possible candidate for grounding and while this was going on her well-earned and hard-earned call sign had mutated, thanks to the rough humor of carrier pilots, from the proud 'Smash' to the shameful 'Splash'. A pilot who couldn't make it, a pilot who didn't have what it took to take a hit and keep on flying. A pilot – God forgive them for using such a cliché – who didn't have what that writer had called the Right Stuff. Though she was never grounded, her flying reputation was permanently blackened.

Soon afterwards, Carrie left the Navy. And trying to get a regular airline job, flying passengers . . . well, the airline industry was still grinding along in its recession – isolated from the rest of the goddamn US economy, it seemed – but she was finally able to get a job for the General, flying for AirBox, for the General had a soft spot for all ex-military pilots, male or female, perfect records or not. She was lucky, she knew, even though she never flew into any exotic locales, and she grew intimately aware of which motels were safe enough around some of the places she flew into – AirBox pilots never could afford to stay at a regular chain motel – and the hours sucked. Especially around Christmas, where a young girl always wanted to know why mommy couldn't attend those special parties or recitals . . .

Carrie walked to the rear of the house, down a narrow hallway. Past the first door, and through that door she could hear the snoring of her cousin Marilyn and the soft droning of a television set. Marilyn had this awful habit of falling asleep while leaving the television on all night, and since it didn't keep Susan awake Carrie put up with the waste of having the damn thing suck electricity all night.

Now to the second door. She opened it gently and then stepped in, taking a breath, enjoying the scent of her little girl and her little-girl things. There. A little routine she did, whenever coming back from a flight, was to step into this little cocoon, this little-girl universe, and just let the stress and tension ease on right out of her. She walked to the bed where Susan slept, and knelt down, barely seeing her light blonde hair spread over the pillow. The bedroom was neat and orderly, nothing like her own room down the hallway, and nothing like how Carrie had treated her own things when she'd been a child. That little piece of Susan's genetic makeup must have come from her father, one Robert Francis O'Connor, another pilot from UPS and with whom she had had a brief and satisfactory affair six years ago, an affair that had produced some wonderful pleasures, some good times, a quick and harsh break-up, and this little bundle of joy beside her.

Carrie took another breath of the room, leaned over and kissed the top of her girl's head. In this little room, at least, Carrie was known as mom or mommy, but never, ever, was she called Splash.

In the darkness and quiet of his kitchen, Randy Tuthill sat at the kitchen table, his first mug of coffee before him, just resting. It was just after five a.m. and already he was dreading the day ahead. From the light over the stove the kitchen was barely illuminated but he could still make out the bay window overlooking the small yard – installed several years ago, after more years of gentle nagging from his wife Sarah – and the nearby refrigerator. Its white enamel was almost entirely obscured by recipes, doctor's appointment cards, and photos of their two sons – Eric and Tom, both serving in the Air Force – and their grandchildren.

Randy picked up the mug, took a sip, put the mug back down. Looked down at the table. The mug was bright yellow and black, advertising AirBox, his home for the past fifteen years. He stared at his hands . . . huge and scarred and heavily callused from years of moving machinery and tools and parts in and out of aircraft. First in the Air Force, traveling across the world to bases like Incirilik in Turkey and King

Khalid in Saudi Arabia, Anderson in Guam and Utapoa in Thailand, hot and cold places, rain and wind and snow, making sure those big damn gray birds flew and flew well. A twenty-year man, he would've been content to pull the plug and fish and chase his wife around the house for the rest of his life, but a retiring general had caught his attention, a retiring general who said he was going to set up an airfreight company and needed a good wrench-turner to set up the very first mechanic bays in a rented hangar in Memphis . . .

Another sip of coffee. Many years ago, many ups and downs ago, many union contracts negotiated and debated and settled. And now . . . well, not so good.

Randy looked down at his hands again. Funny how when he was younger, that was the thing that bothered him the most. Whether or not he would ever find a woman who wouldn't be put off by these rough fingers and palms. And then Sarah had come along . . . Sarah who had worked as a civilian clerk-typist at Nellis in Nevada, and after their courtship and eventual engagement he finally had asked her that important question: hadn't these rough hands been a liability of his, something she would have to overlook, in the years to come?

Sweet girl! She had kissed the top of his head – at a time when there had been a lot of hair up there – and said, 'Dear heart, I've been with a number of boys, boys with soft hands and soft skin and soft minds and bodies to go with them. When I'm with you, either at work or at play in the bedroom, I like the feel of your hands on me. It lets me know I'm with a real one, a real man, one who's not soft.'

And as if on cue, there was a murmur of noise and Sarah came into the kitchen, yawning. 'Up early again.'

'You know my habits.' True enough, for at any point in

time, when it was possible, Randy liked to get up before anyone else. His own private little oasis of time. Sip his coffee and plan the day and just let those thoughts come right up to the surface . . .

Sarah ambled over to the coffee pot, poured herself just a tiny bit. Being polite, she called it, since she didn't like coffee that much, and he smiled at her as she came over to the table. Twenty-five years of marriage and two boys later, she had added on a number of pounds and a few laugh lines, but he still felt like he had come out on top. She had on a thin robe and a knee-length nightgown that had a nice expanse of cleavage, and even at this early hour her short brown hair didn't look mussed at all. Most of his own hair was gone, his love handles and gut were a daily embarrassment, but she still would smile and say he was the sexiest man alive, and during some brief moments he sometimes fooled himself into believing her.

'What's going on in that mind of yours?' she asked as she sat down.

There was a snappy response back there, like 'seeing you topless', but Randy knew her moods and tone of voice, and said, 'Teeth.'

'Teeth?'

'Yeah, teeth. Like dental plan.'

'Oh,' Sarah said, raising the mug. 'Dental plan. The contract talks.'

'Yeah,' he said, shifting his legs under the table. 'The damn contract talks.'

She eyed him as only a wife married to a lead machinist and union local president could, and he said, 'The talks have been dragging on for months. We're without a contract right now. We've made progress on a bunch of items . . . but it's

the damn dental plan. We pay a twenty-buck-a-month premium, with eighty percent coverage. The General wants to
double the premium, reduce the coverage to seventy percent. And he won't budge.'

'And you won't either, will you?'

That familiar flash of anger sparked through Randy.
'We've had years and years of concessions, givebacks and
cutbacks. This is where we're gonna make our stand, Sarah.
I know it sounds petty and crappy and all that, but we've got
to draw the line sometime. And this is where it's gonna
happen, and if they don't budge, then by this time tomorrow
the talks will be off. Shit.'

He took a swallow from his coffee and Sarah rubbed her
hand across his right forearm. She said quietly, 'Times sure
have changed.'

'Shit, yes, they sure have,' Randy said. 'Time was, contract
negotiations like this would take up an afternoon. Me and a
couple of guys and the General and his accountant, we'd
have a catfish barbecue, drink a few beers, and by the time it
got to cigars and cognac we had a contract. Shit. Didn't
even have to sign any paper that night. Just a handshake,
that's all. Worry about the details later, and you know what?
Didn't have to worry about the details. The General's word
and handshake were his bond.'

'Still are, aren't they?'

He shook his head. 'Back when we flew from Memphis to
Seattle, Memphis to LA, and Memphis to JFK. Back when
the aircraft we used were one step away from being sent to a
boneyard in Arizona. Back when payroll was sometimes met
when the General maxed out his credit cards. That's when
his word was bond. Now . . . Christ, the goddamn number
crunchers and pencil pushers are in charge. The General's

forgotten what made him rich, what made the company work. It wasn't the pencil pushers. It was us.'

Sarah stroked his arm again. 'So what happens next?'

Another shrug. 'The talks will break down. Today or tomorrow.'

Sarah said, 'And what then? Take a break? Begin again?'

Randy looked down at the coffee cup, with its bright and cheery logo for a company that he had helped found, all those years ago, and whose success had been due in part to some very long working hours, some very hard dedication, and even a little blood, here and there, spilled onto aircraft tools and hangar floors.

'No,' he said, his voice just a tad shaky. 'No. The talks won't begin again. And we won't take a break.'

Sarah was one bright woman, and he was sure that she already knew the next answer. But she pressed on, like she needed to hear those words.

'Then . . . what will happen?'

'Strike,' he said. 'We'll go on strike. And AirBox will be grounded.'

Sarah brought her coffee mug up to her face, stopped, and then lowered it to the kitchen table. 'I read the newspapers, Randy. That might drive AirBox out of business.'

'Then that's what's gonna happen. AirBox will go out of business.'

Sarah shook her head. 'Over teeth.'

'Yeah,' Randy said, looking out the bay window, to the brightening sky in the east. 'It's all about teeth.'

In his sixth-floor office Brigadier General Alexander Bocks, US Air Force (retired) sat behind his desk, looking across its clean and shiny expanse at the man he had depended on these past six months, and a man he admired for his intelligence, tenacity and imagination. And, also, a man he had come to despise.

Frank Woolsey, his chief financial officer, crossed his legs and said, 'Alex, you know and I know there's no way around it.'

He looked at the lean man who – even at this early hour – looked like he had been well-dressed and groomed since two a.m. Outside there was the faint gray of an approaching dawn, and Bocks heard the low-pitched hum of his airfreight empire out there, bringing in and sending out packages, flying hither and yon across the United States. Right now, as his CFO sat before him, this whole empire was being held up by fraying black threads, ready to part and toss everything down to disaster.

Bocks said, 'I know you're making sense. I just hate hearing it again.'

Frank looked down at a yellow legal pad and said, 'The numbers are what they are. To keep AirBox flying and working, you're gonna need to expand. And if you're planning to expand into the Pacific, you're gonna need investors. And you're gonna need investors who have confidence in what you're presenting, what you're planning, and how you're gonna deal with your mechanics' union.'

Bocks eyed his sharp-eyed and smooth-shaven CFO, knowing that the bright little bastard had been passing one test after another. Bocks knew his strengths, knew his weaknesses, and one particular strength was that he knew he got his best ideas and best output early in the morning, while everybody else dozed or worked-out or grazed through their morning breakfast. He had thought Frank here would have balked at getting his gym-buffed body out so early, to break bread with the company president and CEO, but the sharp little guy had done it without complaint.

'"You"?' Bocks asked. 'What do you mean, "you"?'

'Excuse me?' Frank was questioning but he wasn't rattled. It was like he had the supreme self-confidence of either knowing the answer to the question instantly, or knowing that he had the answer's source.

'What you were saying, back there,' Bocks said, leaning slightly back in his chair. 'You kept on saying "you". What you're planning, what you're going to need. There was no "we" spoken, Frank. Don't you think you're part of the team?'

'Of course I am.'

'Not saying "we" doesn't give me a good feeling.'

A brief pause, and Bocks knew what the man was thinking. Frank was the outsider, the one member of the AirBox hierarchy who had never served in the military, had never belonged to a group that looked out for each other, who were part of something bigger. Bocks hadn't wanted to hire Frank in the first place, but the financial crisis he and the other airfreight carriers were still facing – thank you very much, al-Qaeda, you fuckers – meant that something drastic had to be done. Like hiring a sharp outsider and number cruncher who could come up with the tough recommendations.

Still didn't mean he had to like it.

Frank said, 'Nothing implied there, Alex. Just the way the words came out.'

'Yeah,' Bocks said, leaning forward now in the chair. He rubbed at his chin and said, 'What's the latest on the labor committee?'

'The contract negotiations are probably going to collapse today. Over the dental-plan issue.'

'And our fallback?'

Frank's gaze was steady. 'Once the union goes on strike, we give them one last chance. Then we bring in the contract force.'

'Scabs, then.'

Frank said, 'Scabs that are going to save this company. Scabs that will ensure that you still have a job, the AirBox drivers and package handlers still have a job, and the pilots and the ground crews. Sometimes sacrifices have to be made, Alex. Surely you know that, because of your history.'

Bocks felt his hands clench into fists. He took a breath. 'Frank, in the time I've known you, I've come to admire your skill, your fortitude and clear-thinking.'

A slight nod of appreciation, it seemed.

Bocks said, 'But if you ever again try to bring in my military experience of life-and-death decisions to try to score a point about some budgetary problem, then I'm going to punch out your fucking lights, and then fire you. And no doubt you'll come back at me with a civil complaint of assault and a lawsuit for improper dismissal, and I will gladly mortgage my home here and my vacation place up in Maine to settle it. Just for the satisfaction of punching you out and firing your ass. Have I made myself clear?'

'Quite,' Frank said.

'Good. Now get the hell out of my office.'

And when Frank left, Bocks slowly swiveled his chair, to look out at the aircraft arriving that were part of his empire, an empire that was slowly crumbling away.

Damn this day, he thought. Damn these times we live in.

CHAPTER SEVENTEEN

Adrianna Scott emerged from her third shower in as many hours, carefully wiping down her body with the towel, checking underneath her fingernails and examining her body carefully to make sure that there was not a shred or piece of anything on her – tissue, blood spatter, even dandruff – that had once belonged to the late Henry Spooner, whose flaccid body was no doubt still cooling down at the motel about twenty miles away.

Even though the bathroom was warm, she shivered as she wiped her body down again. It was always like this, always – and how many times, this was the ninth, right? – she felt depressed and blue and angry and everything else, like it would be for a drunk the morning after an all-night bender after successfully navigating years of sobriety through AA.

She took a brush, started working it through her hair. Number nine. Another shiver. She knew what it was, why it happened. Easy enough. She had been in this country for years and years, holding herself in tight, living a lie day after day, always wondering if today, this day, the CIA's Office of Security would come into her office and take her away to a safe house somewhere out in Maryland, to be injected full of babble juice and squeezed dry of what she had been planning all these years.

All these years. From the very start, when Adrianna knew she was going to get revenge against her parents' murderers, she knew that it would be something big, something spectacular, something lethal. And she knew that the only way to do that was to get into the power centers of this mongrel country and to take that one chance to do something spectacular, something that would make them pay for what they had done to her and to her family . . .

It had been hard, long, bitter work. And keeping everything closed up led to sleepless nights, shaky days, and a feeling that somehow, somewhere, she had to let off steam, make her feel sharp again, and to resurrect those old feelings of rage.

An accident, the very first time. Adrianna had been working for the CIA for two years, and the burden of carrying the secret had seemed almost too much to bear. She had been lonely, too, and had occasionally dated the sharp and muscular young men who worked for a number of agencies and administrations that sprouted immediately outside that enormous ring of power known as DC. Yet in dating those men – who'd always been track stars or football stars or baseball stars at college – she had often remembered those innocent but loving touches from her first boy, poor young Hassan, probably dead now, after all these years, no doubt wondering to the end what had happened to his special girl.

Ah, yes. His special girl. And her first special man. Craig Poulton. Some sort of liaison to Congress with the Department of the Army. First date, back in his apartment, he showed off his war souvenirs, for he had served in the first Gulf War, and proudly displayed a framed Iraqi flag, tattered and stained with blood, that he had retrieved from the Highway of Death after the ceasefire. When he had turned to put the framed flag back up on his apartment's wall, Adrianna had picked up an unopened bottle of wine and had smashed it against the back of his skull.

Again and again.

And had finished him off with a knife.

The very first one. Never caught. And after the shock had

worn off that first night, when she hadn't been questioned, hadn't even been considered a suspect in Craig's murder, Adrianna had felt a thrill that she had killed, had killed the enemy in his own home, and never had she felt better.

That had lasted for many months, before the tension returned, the sleepless nights, the jittery days. Then she realized what she had to do. To keep that edge up, that hate, that anger that allowed her to pass through this American culture day and night with a smile and bright eyes, meant that occasionally she had to strike back.

Just like tonight. Against that lumpy Henry Spooner.

She sighed with satisfaction. The last one, no doubt, until . . .

Until Final Winter.

That brought forth a smile.

She looked in the mirror again, just before leaving the bathroom. Adrianna Scott was not looking back at her.

It was Aliyah Fulenz.

And she knew it was going to be a good day.

Brian Doyle waited impatiently outside the man's office, sitting there, reading the day's *Washington Post*. His left foot jittered a bit while he waited. The wait-and-see tremor, his old partner called it. Whether on surveillance at some bodega in Queens, or waiting in an ER while one of his precinct buddies was being worked over, or waiting outside some office like this one, the old wait-and-see tremor would start.

Especially when waiting outside an office. Brian had no good memories of waiting outside any such place while on the Job, especially when it involved something with Internal Affairs, a/k/a the Rat Squad, and this time it was worse.

Instead of being interrogated by some flunky from the Rat Squad, this time Brian *was* the Rat Squad, and he hated it, hated every second of it.

The door opened. A tall man with broad shoulders that indicated lots of weights being tossed around in a gym somewhere leaned out.

'Detective?'

He stood up. 'Sir.'

'I'm ready to see you now.'

Brian walked into the office, heard the muted roar of jets taking off and landing from the base outside, Andrews Air Force Base, and he idly wondered where the hell Air Force One was being kept when he sat down across from the Director, the man in charge of Foreign Operations and Intelligence Liaison, the so-called Tiger Teams. The Director, a former Army Special Forces colonel, was limping as he went around his desk and sat down with a muffled grunt.

The Director said, 'You did a good job on the Darren Coover investigation.'

'Thanks.'

The Director seemed to eye him in a peculiar way. 'Your tone of voice suggests otherwise.'

'It does, does it? If you don't like my tone of voice, then release me from my Tiger Team. I wouldn't mind going back home.'

The Director smiled. If the gesture was meant to cheer him up, Brian thought, then it didn't work. 'We all have places we don't want to be, detective, but there are places where we belong. For now, you work and you belong with us. And again, you did good work on Darren Coover.'

The Director opened up a file folder and Brian said, 'So. What happens to Darren?'

The older man shrugged. 'He enjoys viewing pornography of large-breasted women on the Internet. So what? Any other place, especially in the private sector, such interests can get you fired. We're at war. And in wartime, when you have someone talented working for you – like Darren – I don't give a shit if he enjoys looking at some knockers.'

'Some war,' Brian said.

'Only one we've got,' the Director said. 'And don't sell yourself short. You're playing an important role.'

'Some role,' Brian said, rising to the conversation. 'You know what I am? I'm a fucking rat, true and simple. I work with these people and do missions with them, travel with them and eat with them, and you're asking me to betray them, one right after another.'

The Director said, 'Catholic, are you?'

'What does that have to do with anything?'

'Too young to have gone to the Latin Mass?'

'Yeah,' Brian said. 'And I haven't been to Mass in a hell of a long while. Look, sir, what I'm saying is—'

The Director interrupted with a sentence of Latin words. Brian stopped, and said, 'All right. Say that again, will you?'

'I said, "Quis custodiet ipsos custodes?" A Latin phrase from the first century. It loosely translates as, "Who will guard the guardians?" Or, "Who will watch the watchers?" Different phrases, same meaning.'

The Director spread an arm out, as to emphasize a point, and said, 'Since 9/11, we've been working in the shadows. The Tiger Teams – thank God – haven't received any news-media attention at all. If any of our work ever does get out to the public, it's always attributed to intelligence agencies. That's it. The title and concept of the Tiger Team hasn't been revealed. Which has allowed us to do tremendous work, here and abroad, in disrupting terrorist cells, disrupting terrorist planning, and even helping some regimes see the error of their ways. We have been given great power to protect this country.'

The Director leaned forward slightly over the desk. 'But with that great power comes great responsibility. A little secret for you. Just after 9/11, after the shock and terror, there was an opening, and some took advantage of that opening. We knew there was only a slim opportunity to set something up that would protect us and kill our enemies. Not merely reshuffling office cubicles in some government agency, or setting up a color-coded alert system. Speaking of which . . . what color are we at today?'

Brian shifted uncomfortably in his seat. 'Don't know. Orange, I guess.'

The Director smirked. 'Here you are, a valued member of Tiger Team Seven, and even you don't know our alert level from the Department of Homeland Security. So there you go. And as I was saying . . . with this power comes great responsibility. We have minimal oversight, but what oversight there is has to be tough. Which is where you and a number of other Tiger Team members come in. In addition to your regular duties, you check out your comrades. You see what they do. You take a fresh look into their background. Nine-hundred ninety-nine times out of a thousand, there's nothing there. And what is there is something minor. Like looking at porn while on company time. Big deal. But we can always say later, when the Congressional investigations start – and, my friend, they will start, that you can believe, it's the nature of the beast – that we had oversight in place. That's your job. To guard the guardians.'

'The job sucks.'

The Director said nothing for a moment. Then his voice changed, became softer, more reflective. He said, 'Two months after 9/11, I was in Afghanistan. I was a liaison to an anti-Taliban group that was operating near Kandahar. We were moving at night and some of the mujahedin had stopped a Toyota pickup truck, running without lights along this long dirt road. Took the men out of the truck. There were four of them. They weren't from Afghanistan. They were Saudis – volunteers who had come there to fight for the Taliban. To the Afghans there, they were outsiders. Interlopers. Arabs. So you know what happened to them?'

'Something not nice, I'd imagine.'

The Director said, 'Here, let me help you with your imagination. Besides myself, there were two other Americans there. And a few dozen mujahedin. And those mujahedin took the four Arabs away and took turns buggering them, and when they were done their throats were slit. Our allies had raped and murdered these men, and left their bodies in the Toyota truck as a warning to other outsiders about what happened to those who were captured by Afghans. And our Afghans were happy and were singing, and there we were, representatives of twenty-first-century America, witnessing a war crime, and we didn't do a damn thing. That, detective, is what sucks. Sorry you don't like your job. Get over it.'

The Director opened up a desk drawer, pulled out a folder which he tossed in Brian's direction.

'Your next assignment,' he said. 'As soon as possible.'

Brian picked up the folder, opened it up. Adrianna Scott's photograph looked up at him. He looked to the Director and said, 'Adrianna? Are you sure?'

'Nobody is immune from oversight. Not even myself, not even her.'

Brian said, 'It's going to be busy this month, with . . . well, you know. Final Winter and all.'

The Director nodded. 'I'm sure you'll find the time. If you'll excuse me, detective, I need to get ready for my next meeting. And by the way, the Homeland Security threat level today is yellow. Not orange.'

Brian was dismissed. So what? He got up and left without a word, the bad feeling leaving an even worse taste in his mouth. The Rat Squad membership was to continue. How joyful. Out in the hallway he looked at the folder and thought, Adrianna. My apologies already. What a fucking job.

And as he was walking down the hallway, something odd came to him, what the Director had said back there. Or hadn't said back there.

About Final Winter.

With Final Winter breathing down everyone's neck, you'd think that the Director would have given him a pass about looking into Adrianna's background.

Yeah. You would think that.

But the Director had almost brushed aside Final Winter. Like it wasn't as important as finding out whether or not Adrianna Scott had really, truly lettered in soccer when she was in high school or some damn thing.

Odd.

And before Brian could think about that anymore, his pager started vibrating at his side.

Darren Coover woke up, groggy and tired, mouth sore, body sore, whole damn body aching. Last night had been a wild one, he had just felt the need to let loose, so it meant a night of clubbing and drinking and . . . well, a few minutes of fumbled passion in the back seat of a Toyota 4Runner, like he was a college kid or some damn thing.

He just stayed quiet in bed, let his eyes rest, let the seasick feeling in his gut ease. He probably shouldn't have gone out last night, but with Final Winter and the thought of what was out there pressing against him . . . he'd just needed it. That was all. The next few weeks were going to be hell and he needed all his energies and focus to pay attention to that. Nothing else.

Darren opened his eyes, looked up to the white plaster ceiling. He rolled over, checked the clock. Damn. He was late. He reached over to the phone, knocked over a pill bottle, picked up the phone and dialed.

It was going to be one hell of a day, and he could hardly wait to see this man's face when he was done.

Montgomery Zane yawned as he left the bathroom after a nice long shower, rubbing his head and back with a soft white bath towel. Charlene was sitting before her vanity unit, running a brush through her hair, and he bent over and kissed the back of her neck. She had on a bathrobe and he enjoyed the view of her freckled cleavage as he brought his head up.

Charlene noticed the gaze and gently thumped him with her elbow. 'Get your eyes where they belong and get dressed. You're gonna be late for work.'

Monty smiled and tossed the towel back towards the bathroom. 'Babe, you're the best excuse for being late there ever was.'

'Hah. Hush and get going now.'

He started dressing and thought about the day ahead, and about how much he had enjoyed that long motorcycle run,

out into the countryside. Probably the last piece of relax-
ation he was going to have for a long, long time, and he felt
queasy for a moment, remembering what he had thought
about, out there in the deserted countryside.

A deserted country. For years and years to come.

He quickly finished dressing and went back to Charlene.
He rubbed her shoulders, kissed the top of her head, did
some quick calculations and said, 'Four weeks from now.
What's going on with you and the kids?'

She lowered the hairbrush. 'Four weeks? Hell, hon, trying
to figure out what's going on four *days* from now is a hell of
a stretch. Why four weeks?'

Monty tried to keep the tone light. 'Thought you and the
kids might go on a trip. Visit my aunt in Georgia, at Miller's
Crossing. That's all.'

He noticed her hand tightening around the handle of the
hairbrush. 'Aunt Clara? Honey, God bless your aunt and all,
but she lives in a town with one street light and four stop
signs, and . . .'

Monty kept quiet. Charlene was a very bright woman.

'Georgia,' she breathed. 'There's a reason, isn't there?'

Not worth trying to fool a military wife. 'Yes.'

'Good enough reason?'

Final Winter. Suppose that damn vaccination program
didn't work? And suppose the children got sick from whatever stuff was going to be sprayed from overhead? Then those
obscure men in rental cars would start driving around his
country, dropping off plastic baggies of death in his cities,
and . . . Jesus.

'The very best,' he said.

Tears came to her eyes. 'Can you tell me anything else?'

'No. And you can't ask any more questions, Charlene.'

Her hand went from her hairbrush up to his hand on her shoulder. A gentle squeeze.

'Yes, my love,' she said through the tears. 'I think a visit to your aunt will be a wonderful idea. Can you come, too?'

A pause.

'No. No, I can't.'

Charlene squeezed Monty's hand tighter as her tears continued to flow.

Victor Palmer was in the kitchen of his small apartment, about a half-hour drive from his Tiger Team's offices. He had just finished breakfast and unread copies of the day's *Washington Post* and *Baltimore Sun* were on the kitchen counter in front of him. Next to the newspapers was a cellphone, a bulky object that most kids would have sneered at for being large and ungainly and without a camera included in the handset.

Ah, but if those benighted children only knew the things this cellphone could do, the way its classified technology allowed one to make an encrypted and untraceable phone call with the greatest of ease.

He picked up the phone, looked at the keypad, and then started scrolling through the directory until he reached a number beginning with a 404 area code. He keyed the dial pad and brought the phone up to his ear.

It rang twice. On the third ring, a woman's voice answered: 'CDC, operator four, may I help you?'

He gave her a four-number extension. Waited.

'You have reached the Alpha Directory,' an automated voice said. 'Please enter the subsequent extension.'

Take a breath. Could drop the phone here, leave. The call unfulfilled. Miss the late-afternoon meeting with the rest of the Tiger Team. Head north. Maybe Canada. Nice simple village. Probably could survive Final Winter or anything else. Nice Canada. Quiet country. Nobody lining up to fly airliners into the CN Tower in Toronto or the Parliament building in Ottawa or to drive suicide trucks into embassy buildings. In this bloody new century, there was something to be said about living in a country that didn't attract so much hate.

The voice returned. 'You have reached the Alpha Directory. Please enter the subsequent extension.'

He sighed. Slowly keyed in the six numbers. Waited again.

There was a low-pitched tone, followed by a series of high-pitched ones. The encryption device in his government-issued cellphone, synchronizing with the encryption device at the other end. Hey, how you doin'? One phone to another. Boy, wouldn't Doc Savage be impressed with that. And maybe this phone's being answered in Atlanta at the Centers for Disease Control, but maybe not. Doubtful such delicate work as this anthrax vaccine went on in Atlanta, though everything obviously went through the central phone station and—

A man's voice. Definitely not automated.

'Harrison.'

Victor cleared his throat. 'This is Doctor Palmer calling. I need a status report on the packages you're developing.'

'Hold on.'

Victor waited. Looked around the rented apartment, the rented kitchen, the rented kitchen table. Rented by some-one whose soul was being rented. How goddamn appropriate. He closed his eyes. Hoping that Harrison would say it wouldn't work. Hoping Harrison would say that the whole Final Winter scheme had been overruled. Hoping Harrison was struck dead by a coronary before coming back with—

Harrison returned to the phone. 'Slightly ahead of schedule. The canisters will be in place at the Upper Mississippi Delta Storage Facility in two weeks.'

'Two weeks,' Victor said. 'Got it.'

'Good.' Then a pause, as if the prim-and-proper government man just had to know. 'Ask you a question?'

'Sure.'

'Is . . . is this really going to happen?'

'Looks that way.'

'God help us all.'

Victor said, 'Think God's a bit busy nowadays.'

And then he hung up.

In the Pacific Ocean near Vancouver Island it was barely daylight as the ferry plowed its way through the cold waters, heading through a fog bank. The visitor stood at the bow, bundled up, hands in his pockets, seeing nothing but the tendrils of gray swirling around him. The wide bow of the ferry rode up and down in the waves, and the visitor kept his balance on the trembling deck.

A movement at his elbow. The young man called Imad Hakim stood there next to him, shivering, wearing a long wool coat and gloves, a hat and scarf wrapped around the top of his head. Imad held a cup of tea in his gloved hands, the steam rising up past his dark face.

Imad muttered something and the visitor said, 'What did you say?'

'I said, I cannot believe how cold it can get in this cursed land, that's what,' Imad said. 'I spent six years here, growing up with my mother's brother, and still I can't get used to the cold. I feel like my balls have turned to ice.'

He stood there, proud that he could stand next to this barbarian who kept his head uncovered. The man said: 'Cold? This is nothing. I will tell you what cold is, my friend. Cold is when you step outside and you spit into the snow, and you hear a crackle as your spittle freezes before it hits the ground. Cold is when you can shatter metal with a sharp blow of a hammer. Cold is when the slightest bit of exposed skin turns deathly white from frostbite, in a matter of moments. That is cold. This . . . this is nothing.'

'Bah,' Imad said. 'You stay out here if you like. I'm going back inside to try and get warm. If that is possible.'

'Very well. Go back, then, and dream of camels. If that is what you dream of.'

Imad spat on the metal deck and went towards the lit windows of the main cabins of the ferry. The other man stayed behind, hands in his pockets, feeling the cold breeze around his ears and hair, wondering and thinking. Just how far he had traveled in these years, to finally have the opportunity to come here and do what he had trained to do, years ago, when he had been a proud member of the greatest empire the world had ever known.

Recently he had been living in some Third World shithole country, advising the Health Ministry – and, Mother of God, the laboratories they had there were nothing more than children's chemistry sets, set up proudly in rooms that had no consistent heat or air-conditioning or pure water – when the first messages had arrived. At first he had thought that it had been an elaborate trap: some enemies of his out there – no matter the news of reconciliation and understanding – still had long memories and even longer-lasting hatreds.

But the messages had intrigued him. He had answered the first one, waited. And his Caymans bank account had seen a dramatic increase within a week. Then he answered another one, replying to a highly technical question that established the bona fides of whoever was on the other end of the line. And with that answer, another bump in the bank account. One test after another, to see if the message sender had actually been for real, including one particularly deadly request on his part, just to see how serious the message sender was.

Sure. That had been something. In the Health Ministry was an even more corrupt-than-usual doctor, who had been distilling cancer medications supplied by the United Nations and selling them on the black market. The adviser's own wife, years ago, had died of cervical cancer, and the sheer greed and evilness of this particular doctor had galled him. So he had requested of his message giver his own test of that person's abilities. Remove the doctor from the scene.

And it had happened, just a week later. A car bomb.

A few more messages, here and there, and here he was now, on the deck of a ferry, heading towards his enemy of so many years, now face to face, with a childish Arab at his side to help him along.

He coughed, shifted his weight from one leg to another. Strained his eyes, looking out at the fog.

There. Coming clear. One light, then another, and then an entire constellation, appearing now ahead of the ferry, and, as if on cue, the ferry horn sounded. His chest tightened with glee and pleasure. The enemy he had sworn years ago to smite was finally in front of him.

'Hello, America,' the man called Vladimir Zhukov, once of the Kromksy Institute of Infectious Diseases, murmured, as the lights of Washington State finally appeared through the fog off to the starboard side of the craft. 'So nice to finally be here.'

CHAPTER EIGHTEEN

At home again, Adrianna Scott took one more shower – for luck, she whispered to herself, as she scrubbed her body clean one more time – and with a towel about her hair and a bathrobe about her body, she went over to the mantelpiece where the photo of herself and her aunt was placed. Even knowing that she was home alone, she looked around to make sure no one was watching. She took the photo down and deftly undid the snaps at the rear, holding the cardboard placement against the frame with her fingers. Now she could stick a fingernail behind the loose cardboard and drag something out.

The something, of course, being another photo. Of a very young Aliyah Fulenz and her mama and papa, seated on a couch in some photo studio for a formal portrait. Mother and daughter were wearing identical dresses, some white and black lace piece of magic that mama had gotten from Paris, and father was in his Ba'ath Party uniform, standing firm and proud behind the two of them, his protective hands on their shoulders. Father hadn't been much of a party member – to go anywhere in that society, you had to belong to that gangster organization – and the tales he told could have—

Enough, she thought. Quite enough. No time for reminiscing. She gently kissed the faces of her dead parents, replaced the photo in the frame, and put the frame back up on the mantelpiece. Another touch to the glass and wood, and then she went down to the basement of her condo unit. The floor of the basement was concrete and it was cool and slightly damp. In one corner was a workbench, unused since she had moved in – the previous owner had had a wood-working hobby, making toys for underprivileged children, how sweet – and most of the rest of the basement was taken up by old moving boxes and bits of furniture that she had never had the energy to sell or donate to Goodwill.

Adrianna padded across the concrete floor in her bare feet, wincing at the cold. She went around to the other side, behind the stairs. There was a wardrobe bureau standing there, heavy and immovable. She reached behind the wardrobe, flipped a switch. Inside the wardrobe, hidden casters at the bottom were suddenly released. Well-oiled and balanced, the casters allowed her to move the wardrobe easily to one side of the cellar.

Now revealed beneath the stairway was a small door with a combination lock. Flipping through the combination with ease, she unlocked the door and ducked down, entering the small space underneath the stairway. A light came on and she closed the door. Then she relaxed, sitting down on a small office chair. Before her was a horizontal wooden plank, serving as a desk, and on the plank was a laptop computer. She switched it on, waited for it to power on and boot up. She looked around the small space, which had a network of cables running across the wooden walls and the concrete floor and the ceiling which was also the bottom of the steps. She had spent months putting the wiring in place, working quietly and taking her time, making her own bubble.

Ah, yes, the bubble. An open secret for many members of the media and readers of obscure books about foreign policy: whenever American diplomats went overseas and were not staying at their own embassy, they would use a bubble – sometimes the size of a small tent – to discuss matters they wanted to be kept secret, knowing that if they were within the bubble, they were impervious to any forms of electronic surveillance. Bubbles were kept close to the chest and weren't something one could pick up at the local Radio Shack, but someone smart and dedicated (like moi, Adrianna thought) could make one at home.

Which was what she had done. Which meant no electromagnetic radiation at all could leave this small space under her cellar stairs. Not a bit. And with sensing devices available to certain intelligence agencies that could record the minuscule signals created whenever a laptop keyboard was used, that meant a lot.

She moved the laptop closer. It was in a black case and had no identifying insignia at all: no Apple or Sony or Dell or IBM. Zilch, because this particular laptop had been made within the CIA's own Technical Services Division, and she had stolen it nearly four years ago. Pretty simple: it had been left in someone's car in plain sight in one of the satellite parking lots at Langley, and Adrianna knew that particular lot's surveillance camera gear was out for maintenance that month. So, with the skills learned at Camp Perry, she had entered the car and stolen the laptop. Later she learned that the analyst who had allowed the laptop to be stolen had been fired.

Oh well. Collateral damage.

But it meant that she had one of the most powerful and secure laptops in the world for her exclusive use, and my, had she put her own little laptop through its paces these past years, even managing to upgrade it here and there by doing some deft access work to one of the CIA's mainframe systems.

There. The screen snapped into focus. She typed in the password that allowed her entry and got to work. So many files, so many records, so many dead ends over the years . . .

Yet look at what she had accomplished, all she had done, from the safety and security of this surveillance-proof cubbyhole in her condo unit. Something that would make a wonderful book or movie, if the world would allow such a thing when she was done.

There. A file opened up and she stared at the list of names there. She rubbed her chin, shivered some in the cool cellar air.

Amil Zahrain of Pakistan.

Ranon Degun of Bali.

Henry Muhammad Dolan of Great Britain.

Three men from around the world, three men who had similar things in common: living on the edge, crippled in some way, and all infused with an undying hatred of America and all it represented. Easy enough to locate them – being a Tiger Team leader meant so many case files and intelligence briefings were open for your perusal – and it was also easy enough to figure out what to do with them once you had their locations and their backgrounds in your eager little hands. For one of the perks of being a Tiger Team leader was being able to see what kind of message traffic was flowing among the various terrorist cells out there, and to see what the messages were saying.

And once you knew what kind of codes were being used, and once you knew the way the codes were passed from one cell to another, from one cell member to another, it was also quite easy to plant fake messages. Fake messages that increased the 'chatter'. Fake messages that made the cell members think that they were part of some grand, glorious plan.

And fake messages that let her own people think that an anthrax attack was imminent.

She had to smile at that. There was no attack. There were no cells. Nothing. It was all made up, made up by one Iraqi Christian woman, working from her cellar.

Such a life! Such a country!

A wonderful joke, of course, and what made the joke even more wonderful was that there *was* going to be an anthrax attack upon this country, in just a few weeks ... but it wouldn't be coming from the ground, from plastic baggies, from Arab men in automobiles.

It would be coming from the air, and it would be coming from her.

Brian Doyle stepped outside the building at Andrews Air Force Base, cellphone in his hand, returning the page he had just received. A familiar voice answered and Brian said, 'Darren? What's up?'

A slight cough coming from the receiver. 'Sorry. Rough night. Look, Brian, I've got to see you, right away.'

Brian looked at his watch. Less than two hours to go before their next meeting, and he still had to review Adrianna's file, and he owed a phone call to his son, the boy's Little League season was about to start ...

'Is it important?'

'Yes.'

A jet roared overhead, and then another. Brian looked

up, saw two F-16s crawl their way up into the sky. Any other place, any other time, they would be two Air Force fighter jets, up for a routine patrol, but these weren't routine times. Brian knew that the two Falcons were going up as part of the CAP – Combat Air Patrol – over the Washington DC area. News accounts rarely reported on their presence, sometimes noting they were dispatched whenever there was an uptick in the Homeland Security threat level. But Brian knew differently. The CAP was always up, and had always been up there since a certain September 11.

'Come on, Darren,' he said. 'Can't it wait until our meeting?'

'No.'

'Why?'

'Because it's personal, that's why.'

Brian said, 'Look, Darren, I need to know—'

'Brian, how do you think the other Tiger Team members will react when they realize you're a snitch, reporting on us to the Tiger Team Director? Think they'll be happy? Do you?'

Brian lowered the cellphone for a moment, shook his head. Shit. Caught. He brought the cellphone back up and said, 'All right. I'll see you. When?'

'Soon as you can get here.'

'And where the hell is here?'

'My apartment, silly,' Darren said. 'And don't say you don't know where I live. I already know that you know that, Brian, with a lot of other stuff as well. See you soon.'

And then the call was cut off.

Damn it. Brian shoved the cellphone back in his coat pocket, started walking to his car, as another brace of F-16s went up into the clear and dangerous sky.

*

Montgomery Zane went into the garage, just as Charlene followed him out. Her face was puffy and she had been crying, though she tried to hide it. She said, 'No more questions, hon, except this one. Are you gonna be safe?'

He grinned at her, gave her a big hug. 'As safe as I can be, babe. As safe as I can be. Now. You just worry about gettin' the kids ready and your bags packed over the next couple of weeks. You go on to my aunt's place and don't worry a bit.'

'The hell I won't,' she said. 'The hell I won't.'

He went to his Jeep Cherokee, black duffel bag in hand, and Charlene, arms crossed, said to him, 'How long do we stay there for?'

'Until I send for you.'

'A day? A week? A month?'

Monty shook his head. 'Less than a week. That's all I can say. You just keep on packin', girl, all right?'

And she nodded and he knew he should go over and give her a big hug. But he was late already, and these days he couldn't afford to lose any more time.

Monty backed out of the open garage, waved to his wife, who waved back, trying to look cheerful, trying very hard to look happy, and failing miserably on both counts.

Darren Coover opened the door to his apartment, noted right away the severely pissed-off expression on the face of Brian Doyle. The face in question was reddened and his lips were pursed, and Darren knew he had just a few seconds before the detective started blowing up in his face. Darren had always found himself liking the scrappy New York guy, nothing like the actors on *NYPD Blue* or any of the other detective shows on television. Brian was the real deal.

Through the clean kitchen he took him, to the small

living room, where one of his laptops was running on a coffee table, next to copies of the *Washington Post* and *Washington Times*. Darren sat on a couch and Brian sat down across from him on a chair as Darren said, 'Okay, I used harsh language there a while ago. I apologize, Brian.'

Brian nodded, and Darren said, 'No offense was meant. Seriously. My goal was to get you over here to talk.'

Now the anger in Brian's face was replaced by puzzlement. Darren liked what he saw. Brian said, 'Mind telling me what the hell that's supposed to mean?'

He smiled at the cop and said, 'I've always enjoyed having you on our Tiger Team, Brian. Just so you know. There are some – and I'm sure you know who they are – who think having a detective working with us is somehow beneath them and their abilities. So be it.'

Brian said, 'Tell me something I didn't know. Go on.'

Despite himself, Darren enjoyed this feeling, enjoyed being in charge, knowing secrets that either the person sitting across from him was supposedly holding or had no idea existed. It made up for his lousy childhood, the way he had kept to himself through high school and college, always knowing he was the smart one, the bright one, but also that he was the different one.

Darren said, 'I'm used to giving out information in briefings, so please bear with me, all right? Trust me. It'll be worth your time.'

'Go ahead.'

Darren smiled. He was enjoying this. Most briefings there was always somebody senior in rank or somewhat senior in smarts, putting on bored airs, but this guy seemed to want to know what was going on. He wasn't going to disappoint him.

'Information is what we play with, day in and day out,'

Darren began, sitting back on the couch. 'Sometimes that information is dramatic, like an Order of Battle for the Medina Armored Corps of Iraq, back when they had an armored division to play with. And sometimes that information isn't so dramatic, like that misused and popular phrase, chatter. The trick is to identify the sources of your information, and to make a best guesstimate of what it means now, and what it might mean in the future.'

Brian said, 'I've heard about a dozen different versions of that little speech since I came aboard, Darren. Thought you weren't going to waste my time.'

A nod. 'All right. I'll get specific, then. Since you came aboard, I've known from the start that one of your roles was to play . . . Rat Squad, I guess is the correct term . . . for the Tiger Team Director. The Colonel. Your job was to follow the directives of Adrianna and work for the team, but your other job was to look into the backgrounds of your fellow Tiger Team members. Correct?'

Brian's face was colored red again. 'How did you know?'

'My dear boy, before I was detached to Tiger Team Seven, I worked for the National Security Agency. The biggest and baddest information-collection agency in the world. Finding out what you were doing was quite simple. The matter of finding one memo sent through the ether that should have been encrypted. There you go.'

'And you're telling me this . . . why? A threat? Blackmail?'

Darren tried to put a shocked expression in his voice. 'Not at all. My goal is to make sure you do your job better.'

Now the confusion was back on Brian's face. Oh, this was so much fun. Darren said, 'Surprised, aren't you?'

'Yeah.'

'Then here's another surprise. I bet I know what was said

in your report. That Darren Coover is a valued member of the team, has problematic social skills, and has one flaw. And here's that one flaw. He enjoys viewing on-line pornography of women with large breasts. Am I correct?'

Brian said, 'I shouldn't be saying so, but yeah, you're correct. That's what the report said.'

Darren grinned, got up from the couch, went to the coffee table and spun the laptop around. Brian looked at the upright screen and then raised his head. 'Why are you showing me this? A big titty page. So what?'

'Ah, but watch. Tell me what's going on.'

Brian returned his gaze. 'The pages – they're moving on their own. They're bringing up photos and . . . videos. Quicktime videos. That's what I'm seeing.'

Darren turned the laptop around again, and returned to the couch. 'Delightful program that I found on the net, and which I tweaked on my own time. It's an avatar program. Do you know what an avatar is, Brian?'

'Enlighten me, why don't you.'

'Very well. An avatar is a construct, an artificial person. If you go on-line and play a computer game against somebody else, you might want to call yourself Brian the Magnificent, Slayer of Dragons and Savior of Maidens. That would be your avatar.'

Darren pointed to his laptop. 'That's my avatar, Brian. For somebody monitoring my computer usage – like you did, no doubt with the assistance of my agency's Technical Security Department – would quickly determine that I was a heterosexual male with an unhealthy fascination with large mammary glands. Correct?'

Brian nodded slowly. 'Correct.'

He reached into his pants pocket, pulled out a black and

gold matchbook, which he tossed over. Brian caught it and Darren said, 'What's it say?'

'It says The Wilde One. What's that?'

'It's a private club outside of Baltimore. A members-only club. The membership requirement is quite simple. One has to be a male homosexual. Guess you and the agency didn't spend any time performing a surveillance on me, tailing me to see where I went and what I did.'

Brian's response was better than Darren had anticipated. He just nodded again and tossed the matchbook back, and Darren was pleased that he was able to catch it. Having always been bad at student athletics, it was a very small but fun victory.

'Okay. So you're gay. I don't care and probably most of the team doesn't care either. What's the deal with the surfing of the titty sites?'

'To prove a point.'

'Point being . . .?'

'Information. What you can trust and what you can't trust. Brian, you probably had a checklist of items to review for me. Am I correct? Schooling, contacts with friends and neighbors, bank accounts, credit-card debt, and everything else. Lot of work for one guy to perform, especially with a deadline handcuffed to you. So you did what you could. You looked again at old interviews. Maybe made a few phone calls. And relied on others who went before you to really look at my background. I was able to spoof the investigators quite easily. You see, they tend to look for secrets, for embarrassing little background items. A perfect person doesn't exist. So if you give them something to write about – like a preference for women with huge breasts – they're satisfied. They have found the flaw that they've been looking for, and they go on to other assignments. Especially during these troubled times, when so many people are being investigated, from Cabinet secretaries to Saudi students to FBI job applicants. The investigators were able to check off their little boxes. But their jobs weren't done. Not by a long shot.'

Brian now seemed amused. 'You want I should go back and rewrite my report? Say that you're gay?'

Darren shrugged. 'In these alleged enlightened times, it doesn't make much of a difference anymore. Back during the Cold War, there was the fear of having homosexuals in sensitive areas because their background meant that they could be blackmailed by the KGB or others. But nowadays . . . hell, there's nothing there to blackmail about. But I do enjoy keeping the secret. It keeps me on my toes, and it tells me how we're managing information.'

Brian said, 'Secret's safe with me, and thanks for the lesson.'

'You're quite welcome.' Darren was enjoying this moment with the detective and didn't want it to end. He folded his arms and said, 'We all need to do a better job about the information we receive. Yet we don't.'

'I don't get what you're saying.'

Darren paused, and then said, 'Oh, what the hell. You've got the proper clearance, or you wouldn't be part of the team. It's just that . . . well, you know what the big advantage is of having the Tiger Teams in place?'

'Unless it's going to screw with my pension, tell me.'

Darren unfolded his arms, leaned forward a bit on the couch. 'It's broken down the barriers. Information was kept in the different agencies, like big old vertical office buildings, everybody guarding their little turfs, their little pools of information. Very little in terms of cooperation and information-sharing. But the Tiger Teams broke that all apart. It's like these huge office buildings suddenly had sky-walks installed between the different floors, letting information flow side to side, besides bottom to top, like it used to. Which means a lot of shared information. But a lot of shared questions, too.'

'Like what?'

Darren said, 'Just my paranoid nature, I guess. It's just that . . . well, I've been poking around into other agencies. Like Homeland Security. FBI. Border Patrol. You would think that with Final Winter barreling down on us within a few weeks, that they would be on heightened alert, would call back their people, cancel all vacations and overseas trips. But if it's happening, I'm not seeing it. And there's another thing.'

'Which is?'

'The chatter,' Darren said.

Brian shook his head. 'I swear to God, I'm sick and tired of hearing the word. Chatter, chatter, chatter. Makes me think of those old dime-store chattering teeth you wound up and put on your kitchen table. Chatter.'

'I'm sick of it too, Brian, but I've been reviewing the chatter. And you know what?'

'What?'

'It's exactly the amount and level of chatter one would anticipate if a major attack like Final Winter was being undertaken. A lot of code phrases and sentences, being sent to and fro among a number of terrorist and support cells. And coming from different parts of the world. Pakistan. Great Britain. Bali. Among others. And then there's the Predator surveillance of that car doing a test run in Damascus. Not to mention our dead Syrian friend in a

Canadian hospital. It's all pointing to that one thing: Final Winter, and coming soon to a metropolis near you.'

'And what's the problem?' Brian asked.

Darren rubbed at his chin. 'The problem is what I just said. Don't you see?'

Brian, sharp operator that he was, picked right up on it. 'I get it now. The amount and level of chatter you're seeing is exactly what you'd expect. Nothing less, nothing more. It's like . . . it's like somebody is trying to warn us beforehand. Nothing dramatic. Quiet. So he or she isn't putting themselves at risk for giving away secrets. Like somebody within the cells wants us to know what's going to happen. A sympathetic ally, buried deep within the organization? Someone who secretly enjoys Britney Spears or X-rated video or racks of beer?'

'Perhaps. I mean, that's a simplistic answer to a complex problem, but as one of our late lamented presidents said, sometimes simple answers are just the hard ones. I just don't know. I'm just one analyst, Brian. I know that there are better and more experienced analysts out there who are probably looking at the same problem, right now.'

'So if you had the power, what would you do?'

'I'd recommend that the people who are performing this chatter, that some of them get picked up and squeezed. In fact, I'm surprised that it hasn't happened yet. And I may do just that at our meeting this afternoon. Ask Adrianna to have some of these characters picked up.'

Brian said, 'Typical response from those who make the rules. If I knew about some low-level street dealers setting up shop in my precinct, sometimes we'd string them along. See where they went and who they saw. Makes sense.'

'Sure, but if the intelligence is correct, a major terrorist attack is set to take place within a month. I'd think you'd want those people in your control, debriefing them, before that date arrived.'

'Well, that's for the higher-ups to decide, I guess. All I know is that I've got lots of work to do and precious little time to do it.'

Darren said, 'Adrianna's the next one on your investigation list, am I right?'

Brian said, 'Christ, is there anything you don't know?'

'Sure. Lots. What are you going to do?'

'I don't know, smart one, you tell me. What should I do?'

Darren thought for a moment and shrugged. 'Hell, I'd wait until after this Final Winter thing is completed before digging into the Princess's background. What's the point?'

Brian seemed to agree. 'My thoughts, too.'

Adrianna noted the time from a little clock icon up on the corner of her screen. Time to get out of this little hole and get dressed, but not before one more task was done. She toggled open a familiar file and looked again at the names.

Amil Zahrain of Pakistan.

Ranon Degun of Bali.

Henry Muhammad Dolan of Great Britain.

They had performed their roles, and had performed them well. They had taken messages and rebroadcast them, and had added to the din of the chatter out there. They were good soldiers.

Just like poor Hamad Suseel of Palestine. Brought over to the United States for one purpose, to raid the offices of Tiger Team Five. Things had been too quiet the past several months. She needed something to shake up the increasing complacency, to make the higher-ups and her own Tiger

Team members fearful of the hard-core men out there who wanted to kill for the sake of their God.

Of course she felt bad about the deaths in Connecticut. Two of the Tiger Team members she had counted as friends.

But it had had to be done.

Just like now, with what was going to happen to the men from Bali, Britain and Pakistan.

Adrianna wrote up a file protocol, with information and JPEG photos of the three, plus their home addresses and habits. All placed into a file which was compressed and encoded.

There. Done.

She disconnected the laptop's power cord, picked the machine up, and left the cubbyhole underneath the stairs. Walking back out to the cellar, she left the door open and walked upstairs, carrying the laptop, her bathrobe still fastened around her waist.

Now she was in the small dining room where she had dined the other night with Brian, that good-looking, interesting young man from—

Cut it out, she thought harshly. No time for that.

She placed the laptop on the table, moved the screen around so she could look at it properly.

Took a breath.

Pressed a key.

A quick dialogue box appeared.

FILE TRANSFER COMPLETED.

There. It was now in somebody else's capable hands. Just a second or two earlier, a compressed chunk of data had been uplinked from her CIA laptop to a satellite 23,000 miles overhead in geosynchronous orbit. The transmission had lasted less than a second, if that. Any type of surveillance being conducted at her home – quite unlikely – would have registered, if the watchers were very, very lucky, a tiny burst of static. That would've been all. But the data package squirted up to the CIA satellite had been received and the information was being extracted and expanded, and with the proper code phrases and authorizations the data now stored in the memory banks of the overhead satellite would be rebroadcast to certain individuals back on the ground.

And the satellite's own data-processing software would indicate only that it had received a burst of data from a certain point in Maryland, where dozens and dozens of offices that could have been the source of the information were located.

Quite simple, quite delicate – and quite deadly.

Especially for those three men.

Adrianna powered down the laptop and then looked outside. It was a sunny afternoon and there were children at play on the lawn outside her window. About half a dozen children, maybe six or seven years of age, playing with a couple of large rubber balls. They were laughing and yelling and bouncing into each other, and she smiled at their energy and youth. How wonderful. How purely joyful, to see them at play, and she looked at them . . .

And thought of something else.

Adrianna thought of these children, their parents. How much love their parents had for them. How much work their parents did to feed and clothe them and keep them safe. How they had chosen this comfortable suburban condo complex as their own little shelter, to keep their loved ones – My God, with such hope, dreams and love invested in those tiny little bodies – safe from the ravages of the outside world.

Safe. So safe.

And she thought of what it would be like, in just a few weeks, when the illness came, for she had no doubt this place would be one of the blighted ones.

At first it would start like any other respiratory illness. Fever, chills. Then labored breathing. Frantic phone calls to the doctor's office. The doctor's office crowded. The ER overwhelmed. Patients lining up outside for treatment. Television and radio reports, breathless and shrieking in their reporting of what was going on in New York and DC and Los Angeles and elsewhere . . .

These poor children out there. Would they die in their perfect little bedrooms, choking to death, with their parents watching them? Or would they wander through their pretty condo units, wondering why mommy and daddy weren't waking up, and why wouldn't somebody feed them or take care of them . . .

What would happen to them?

She knew what would happen. She knew because she was going to do it.

Adrianna looked again at the laughing children.

Odd, when you got right down to it, it was easy to plot and plan for years and years to take your revenge. But when she looked right at those pretty faces, the faces of the children who would play on the sidewalk outside, or ring the doorbell at Halloween, she had to ask herself, could she do it? Could she kill them, just like that?

Adrianna snapped the laptop cover shut.

Of course she could.

In a war, there was always collateral damage.

Just like mama and papa.

CHAPTER NINETEEN

Vladimir Zhukov stood in the motel parking lot outside Bellingham, Washington State, sipping a cup of coffee, hating the taste but knowing he needed the caffeine to stay awake. He would have preferred to have a cup of tea, ah, now that would have been something. A nice freshly brewed pot of tea in a samovar, pulling the little toggle, letting it settle in a china cup. Drink it in the old way, a cube of sugar tucked inside your cheek, my God, how many cups of tea he had swallowed over the years, back at the Institute, back when . . .

He sipped at the coffee. Back when things made sense. Back when things worked. Back when he was privileged, was someone, was part of the elite, the *nomenklatura*, the ones who would work very, very hard to protect their Fatherland and their Party. Which was what he did, all those long years of studying, everything from molecular cell structure to Marxist theory, climbing up that long, rugged path to be someone, to be respected, to devise weapons to protect everything he held dear . . .

And to be betrayed. By Gorbachev and the rest of the lackeys who had rolled over on their backs and spread their legs, like whores or whipped dogs, begging for mercy, begging for hard currency credits from the West so they could buy Sony or Chrysler or any other damn thing. And he . . . he had left, had peddled his wares to various shit-holes around the world, knowing in those dark places in his soul at two a.m. that he was a veteran, like one of those Japanese bastards hanging out in an island jungle decades later, never knowing the war was over.

Well, that was the truth. The war might have been over for everyone else, but not for him, not for Vladimir Zhukov, he who had the same last name as the famed Marshal of the Soviet Union, Giorgiy Konstantinovich Zhukov, who had led millions of Red Army soldiers to crush Hitler and destroy the fascists . . . and whose own people, decades later, would allow the Germans to reunite and become one again. And who would later toss in their lot with the capitalists, with the West, with those who would have crushed them if the spirit had moved them.

He looked around at the buildings, the roadways, at all the hustle and bustle of what appeared as progress. Some progress.

Vladimir finished the coffee, tossed the cup to the ground. One more piece of garbage to join the others. And speaking of garbage, here he came, his comrade, his partner, who was to help him in this very last battle. A Freightliner tractor-trailer truck, bright red, with no trailer behind it, roared its way into the parking lot, Imad sitting proudly behind the wheel, smiling like a trained chimp from the famed Moscow State Circus, showing off his talents. Imad parked the truck and switched off its engine. Vladimir went over to join him. Imad opened the cab door, leapt out, still grinning.

'See? I told you I could drive this. Not a problem, no problem at all.'

'So you can,' Vladimir said, looking over the truck, seeing that the tires appeared to be in good shape, the bodywork was clean and recently washed. 'And you rented this for the agreed amount of time?'

'I did,' Imad said proudly. 'One full month. They were eager to rent it. There were many more in the lot, but I chose the best one.'

Vladimir got on his knees, examined the truck's underside. Nothing blatantly out of place, but he was not a mechanic, nor was he a diesel-truck driver. Which was why he was burdened with this child to accompany him. A gift from his mysterious benefactor. He got up, brushed gravel and dirt from his knees. A cold wind was blowing, smelling of salt and exhaust.

'And the paperwork? You used the proper credit card, the proper identification?'

Imad's smile faltered. 'Of course I did. Do you think I am a fool?'

'I don't know,' Vladimir shot back. 'You tell me. The first time your friends tried to take down the World Trade Center, one fool went back to the rental agency, to get back his deposit for the truck that carried the bomb. That led to his arrest and the arrest of many others, and it's only because the Americans wanted to arrest you instead of kill you that you fools succeeded the second time around. Will you do that here, Imad?'

'No,' Imad said, his face darkening. 'No, I will not. And remember this, my friend: despite whatever that "fool" did, we *did* come back. We came back and we did it right. So don't forget that. No one else has.'

Vladimir shook his head. 'No, it has not been forgotten.'

Imad grabbed his upper arm. 'And do not forget this. My own cousin . . . my own cousin, I did what had to be done. I did what I was ordered to do. The poor boy . . . all he wanted to do was to come to Canada and marry a Canadian girl and someday own a small restaurant. And I infected him with that awful anthrax and dumped him off at a hospital like a bag of shit, so that whatever must be done is happening. So don't doubt me.'

Vladimir shrugged off the boy's touch. 'I don't doubt it. Just do your job.'

'And you do yours, Russki. You do yours.'

'I shall,' Vladimir said, walking back to the motel room. 'And get your belongings ready. I want to be over the border by nightfall.'

Imad kept up with him, now smiling, like a man who would cheerfully feed you a sumptuous meal and then strangle you later that night. Imad said, 'Very well. Over the border at nightfall, all to defeat the enemy.'

'Yes,' Vladimir said, finding himself finally agreeing with the child. 'To defeat the enemy.'

Montgomery Zane was driving to his Tiger Team office when his pager started vibrating at his side. He grabbed the pager, toggled it, and then read the text message. He shook his head. A hell of a fucking time for a trip. He looked ahead, found a place to turn around, and did just that.

No Tiger Team visit today.

Brian Doyle looked out the window of the Delta airliner, saw the city of Memphis and the Mississippi river unfold beneath him. Elsewhere in the cabin was the Princess, Adrianna Doyle, looking very quiet and unflappable over there by the other aisle, and behind her sat a very unhappy and apparently nervous Dr Vincent Palmer. Although they traveled on the same flight, there were rules against sitting together, probably to prevent some idle chitchat that could be overheard by either a *New York Times* reporter or a terrorist cell leader, both of whom were hated to different extents within the Tiger Team management.

Below Brian the view of Memphis seemed to tilt up and

down as the aircraft descended. He hated flying. Not that he was some Luddite who thought that transportation progress had ended with the arrival of the steam locomotive; no, he just hated being strapped into a thin aluminum tube and having his life completely in the hands of a pilot he had never met, a mechanic whose work he didn't know, or an aircraft assembler who might or might not have had a bad day when putting together an intricate piece of machinery.

So there you go. He much preferred to have his life in his own hands, thank you very much, and being in control of the situation. Being 30,000 feet above the earth in the hands of somebody else didn't strike him as being in control.

The descent continued, the ground getting closer and closer, and Brian couldn't help himself, he closed his eyes for a moment as the wheels hit the runway. In control. The past several months, being at the beck and call of Adrianna and her bosses, that sure didn't meet the definition of being in control, now, did it?

After long minutes of wading through the people exiting the aircraft, each juggling a piece of carry-on luggage, and passing the poor flight crew with their robotic ''Bye now' – and did they do that because some marketing whiz a thousand miles away thought such greetings would mean a point five percent increase in return flyers? – he joined Adrianna and the not-so-good doctor outside the jetway. Adrianna nodded to him and Vincent just looked miserable. He was holding a silver metal case in one hand. Brian went up to him, grasped the doctor's left wrist for a moment, and said, 'The joys of technology, doc, am I right?'

Victor looked surprised. 'What? What do you mean?'

Hand still on the doctor's wrist, Brian tugged at a thin steel cable running from the handle of the case to a handcuff hidden under the shirt sleeve. Brian said, 'Back in the bad old days, there was a thick chain running to the case. Now it's just a thin steel cable. Harder to spot. But still, it's easy enough to get the case off your wrist.'

'How's that?'

Brian couldn't help himself. 'Just use an axe. That's all.'

Adrianna said, 'Brian . . .'

Vincent said, 'But I was told the cable was resistant to all cutting devices.'

Brian grinned. 'Who said anything about cutting the cable? All it'd take to get the case away is to cut off your hand.'

Adrianna came around, grabbed his upper arm. 'Come along. No time for games, Brian.'

Despite it all, he enjoyed her touch. 'You got it, Adrianna. No time for games.'

They exited the terminal, got into a cab, and the cabbie snorted when he heard the address from Adrianna. 'Man, what a waste of time . . .'

Brian was sitting in the front, letting Adrianna try to cheer up the doctor. 'Don't worry, pal. We'll give you a big tip, just the same.'

'You will?'

'Sure,' Brian said. 'Unlimited expense account. For anything and everything we want. Even if it's for a cab drive a couple hundred yards away.'

The cabbie got them out into the steady flow of airport traffic. 'Must be nice, throwing money around like that. You guys must have one hell of a job.'

Brian said, 'Pal, you have no idea.'

*

Alexander Bocks stood alone in his office, looking out the window at the collection of hangars and outbuildings that belonged to him at the Memphis International Airport. Oh, lawyers and bankers and accountants would put up a hell of an argument, saying that these structures did not belong to him, they belonged to AirBox and a bunch of subsidiaries and stockholders and this and that, and Bocks would nod at all the right places and then say, fuck you, they're mine. They weren't there before I started, and they are there now, and they belong to me.

He raised a hand, touched the window, felt the vibrations that came from the jet engines and ground equipment and luggage handlers. He pressed his hand tighter against the glass, as if trying to remember well what the sensation was like, what it was like to stand here and feel that thrumming sensation against your skin, that sensation that meant decades' worth of work and dreams were finally being fulfilled, that he had something he could call his own, something that in a very few hours would—

The door opened. Bocks dropped his hand as if he was a twelve-year-old boy caught in a bathroom by his mom, a copy of her *Cosmo* magazine in his hands. He turned and Elizabeth stood there, Elizabeth Bouchard, a retired warrant officer from the Air Force, who had taken early retirement to come join him at this crazy venture, to go after the big boys at UPS and FedEx, and who was now a very wealthy woman, stock options and all, but still preferred to come to work every day for the general.

He said, 'I really wanted some quiet time, Liz.'

'I know, sir, but you have a visitor.'

Bocks went over to his desk, to the clear piece of square Lucite that stood up six inches and which held his day's schedule, like the menu of some restaurant or something. He glanced down, then looked up and said, 'First appointment isn't for an hour. Who is it?'

'An Adrianna Scott. With two associates.'

'Tell her to go away.'

Liz came forward, her fiftyish body still looking uncomfortable in civilian clothes, like she should be wearing BDUs instead of a ridiculous pants suit from Talbots, and she passed over a business card. He looked down, saw the woman's name and the very familiar emblem and main phone number of the Central Intelligence Agency.

Bocks handed the card back to her. 'Sorry, I don't go all weak in the knees anymore when unannounced visitors from Langley turn up. Tell her to make an appointment. Preferably for next week.'

Liz held the card and said, 'She asked me to say something to you.'

'And what's that?'

'Sky Fall, sir,' she said. 'She told me to say "Sky Fall".'

Now there's irony for you, Bocks thought, for when Liz said those two words something indeed made his knees quiver for a moment. Good goddamn. Well, another day shot. And the possibility was now there for a whole host of nasty days ahead.

'All right,' he said. 'Show her and her associates in. And be prepared to cancel everything else for today.'

'Today?' Liz replied. 'Are you sure? I mean, it looks like—'

'Yes,' Bocks said, heading back to his desk. 'Everything. And no phone calls, Liz. And give me a minute before you show them in.'

'Very good, sir,' she said, walking out. Bocks sat down in his chair and then let his head rest in his hands, started rubbing at the temples, and closed his eyes real tight. In this position, he thought that the vibrations had returned, but no, it was probably just an illusion, make-believe – which he desperately hoped was what this entire day would become.

Adrianna Scott walked into the general's office, Victor and Brian right behind her. There was the quick exchange of handshakes, and she said, 'General, allow me to introduce my two associates. Doctor Victor Palmer, of the Centers for Disease Control, and Detective First Class Brian Doyle, of the New York Police Department.'

The general looked fit and trim, like most military men she had ever known, and as she expected the mention of Brian's rank brought a quick smile to his face. 'NYPD? What are you doing here? Going to come after me for some unpaid parking tickets in the Big Apple?'

Brian smiled back at him. 'It can be arranged. If you'd like.'

'What's that? Arranged to be arrested, or arranged to be let loose?'

'Whichever makes sense,' Brian said. The general laughed and they sat down and Adrianna was so glad she had worn the longest skirt she owned, for her legs were really trembling with the tension of being this far along. Before leaving on the trip she had taken a dose of acrimophin, a beta blocker that was supposed to ease her racing heart, but she guessed that she should have taken another dose, for her heart rate was roaring right along.

She took a quick glance around the office, saw something that surprised her, and the general picked up on it, right away. 'Something wrong, Miss Scott?'

Good for you, Adrianna thought. Don't underestimate this one, don't even come close to having him think you're bullshitting him, because it could collapse and end right now, with her on a flight to Guantánamo Bay in Cuba and all those years of dreaming and working would be gone in an instant.

'Forgive me,' she said, 'it's just that I find your office . . . well, different.'

The general eased back a bit in his leather chair. 'Different how?'

She nodded in the direction of the solitary framed photo, up on the wall. There were bookcases full of books and what looked to be a tiny bar in the other corner, but just the one photo, of a young man with big ears in an Air Force enlisted man's uniform, looking very young and very serious. Over the many years the chemicals in the photo had faded out, giving the man's skin a greenish-yellowish tinge, but she could still recognize a young Alexander Bocks.

Adrianna said, 'Where's everything else?'

'What do you mean?'

'The plaques, the photos, the—

'—framed photos, framed certificates, all that framed crap,' Bocks said back to her. 'Yeah. The ego wall. Look at me shaking hands with the President. Look at me with the Pope. Look at me, getting pinned when I became a general. The hell with that.'

Bocks swiveled in his chair and said, 'See that? That's a skinny kid with big ears who grew up in a small town called Arapahoe, Nebraska, and who knew he didn't want to farm like his father and grandfather. So he joined the Air Force and worked hard and the Air Force found a place for him, educated him, sent him around the world a few times and made a man out of him. That's the only thing that's on my wall. To remind me where I came from, to remind me what I had to do to get here.'

Adrianna stayed silent as Bocks moved his chair back. His gaze was now focused right on her. 'All right. You didn't travel here unannounced to admire my empty walls. You need something. You used a coded phrase, telling me who you are and establishing your bona fides. You've got my attention, miss. Use it well.'

She nodded. This was where it was going to pay off, for she had been practicing this presentation for months – years, even! – and being so close, she wasn't going to fail. She said, 'General, we need your help.'

'How?'

'We're going to be attacked in just under three weeks, simultaneously and across the country. Major metropolitan areas. Our best guess is that the twenty largest population centers have been targeted.'

'Nukes?'

'Anthrax.'

'Delivery system?'

Adrianna said, 'Teams of four or five operatives in each city. Each has a vehicle, a rental car or truck. They have weaponized airborne anthrax virus in baggies. Delivery system is absurdly simple. Drive into each major city and drop Baggies off at intersections, where foot and vehicle traffic will spread the spores.'

Bocks's gaze never wavered. 'Casualties?'

'Horrific. Tens of millions of deaths within weeks. Total collapse of economy and government. We—'

He held up his hand. 'Don't need to go into any details. And you need my assistance? How? Transport of medical supplies? Evacuation? What the hell can I do that the government can't?'

Adrianna said, 'Doctor Palmer will explain, sir, if you permit.'

'Go ahead.'

Now it was Victor's turn, and Adrianna was even more nervous. During the past few days, Victor – never a calm one to begin with – had become more erratic. He did his job just fine, but there'd been a day or two when she'd noted a patch of stubble on his face where he had missed shaving. And food stains on his shirtsleeves. And a frayed necktie. Telltale indications of stress that had never been there before.

But he rose to the occasion as he opened up the silver case, removed a dark green canister with the yellow stenciled markings, and started talking. Though Victor's voice was a monotone, Bocks paid rapt attention to details of the experimental vaccine, the spraying mechanism, and the radio-altimeter switch that both armed and triggered the canister's operation. Victor's briefing went on for eleven minutes exactly, and when he was done and had replaced the mock-up canister in the metal case the only thing audible was the sound of the aircraft, out in Memphis, taking off and landing.

Bocks shook his head. 'A hell of a thing. And where exactly does this canister go?'

Adrianna said, 'Your air fleet consists mainly of McDonnell Douglas MD-11 jets, retrofitted from passenger use to cargo use. In each aircraft, in the aft portion of the fuselage, there is a port and starboard exhaust system for the on-board air-conditioning system. Our aircraft analysts believe that the vaccine canisters can be installed as an add-on to the exhaust system. The pilots would have no control over the distribution. The radio-altimeter switches would take care of that. It would be automatic.'

'So you want to use my aircraft to secretly immunize millions of Americans against anthrax,' Bocks said, his voice rising some. 'Is that it?'

'Yes.'

Bocks paused, then said, 'And that's all you're going to say?'

Adrianna felt the trembling increase again. 'I'm sorry, sir, I was answering your question. That's why we're here, that's why I used the "Sky Fall" protocol. We would not have come here if there was any other option. To immunize publicly would tip off the attackers that we knew they were coming, and would allow them to advance their schedule. To start a public immunization program would result in chaos, confusion and panic. The only alternative – and not a good one, but at least better than doing nothing – is a secret immunization program. We're calling it "Final Winter". And using government or military resources would simply not work. We need to use aircraft that are seen publicly every day. Aircraft that travel to every major metropolitan center in the United States. Aircraft owned by one man who has shown his commitment and dedication to this country. General, you're our only option.'

Bocks glared at each of them. 'Again, a hell of a thing. You realize the kind of liability I'm being exposed to, just by sitting here and listening to you? I could go to jail for conspiracy, for one thing. Not to mention that if I do go along I'll be partially responsible for a number of deaths and injuries. Am I right? You've war-planned this out, haven't you? How many deaths will occur if I lend you my airfleet one night for your secret immunization? Don't bullshit me.'

'No bullshit, sir,' Adrianna said. 'Doctor Palmer and others have gone through the numbers. Best-guess scenario is an additional ten thousand deaths over a period of a month. Infants, the elderly, those with weakened immune systems. Cancer patients, transplant patients, AIDs patients.'

Bocks stared right at her again, and she wondered what it must have been like to be in the Air Force and to have this man in command over you. 'Just so we're clear on this, then, you're asking me to take intimate part in a venture that will result in the death of ten thousand Americans. Just so we're clear. Ten thousand people killed. By me and you and your nice doctor with his green canister.'

'True, sir,' Adrianna said, keeping her voice level even as his rose. 'Ten thousand will die. Which is truly unfortunate, and the thoughts about those deaths have given me many a sleepless night. But what keeps me going, what has brought me here, is that we will also *save* tens of millions of Americans. Ten thousand will die to save scores of millions. An awful equation, but one we must face. We cannot see any other way.'

A pause, and Adrianna waited expectantly, knowing that whatever counter-argument or point the general would raise she was ready, ready for anything. She had an answer for anything that Bocks would bring up, and she waited.

And in two seconds, she was proven wrong.

The general's voice softened. 'Miss Scott, you've made the start of a compelling argument, but I'm afraid I can't help you.'

'Why?'

Bocks looked at his watch. 'Because in ninety minutes, my machinists' union will be going on strike, and my air-fleet will be grounded. That's why.'

Adrianna couldn't help herself. She closed her eyes, just for a moment.

Oh mama, she thought. Oh papa. How I've failed you.

CHAPTER TWENTY

In the small village of Goresh, about fifty miles away from Lahore, Pakistan, nineteen-year-old Amil Zahrain leafed through a copy of the Karachi *Daily Jang*, the country's largest newspaper, feeling that little knot of anger and depression grow inside of his chest. Since his meeting with the Sudanese weeks ago and his visit to the Internet cafe in Lahore – which still gave him the shakes sometimes at night, thinking how close it had seemed, when the two policemen had entered the place – he had scanned the newspapers and had listened to the BBC and watched al-Jazeera at his uncle's store and . . .

Nothing!

Nothing at all!

The Sudanese had promised him that something would happen, something dramatic, something that he, Amil, would have helped along through his dangerous journey to Lahore. He couldn't sleep at night that first week, knowing the news would come out, like that glorious day when New York and the Pentagon were attacked, and that he could take praise from his family for having taken part in such greatness.

But the papers had been silent. Al-Jazeera had said nothing. All had been quiet, save for the usual gunplay and atrocities in Palestine and Jordan and Iraq and other places.

And there had been no death in America. Nothing.

Had the Sudanese been lying?

Amil crushed the newspaper in his hands, stood up from the stone bench where he had first met the Sudanese all those months ago, the Sudanese who had promised him everything: fame, pride, and at last, a sense of belonging, of being part of a jihad, of something that would make his clubfoot irrelevant. He walked awkwardly out of the village center, past the stores and booths and stone buildings with the loud radios playing immoral music, knowing that nothing really awaited him when he got home, save for his mother and his sister, and they would argue with him and demand that he find work, even with a clubfoot, he should do something for the family, and even though he was the sole male he knew he deserved better, and—

A man's whisper caught his ear, coming from a narrow alleyway. He turned.

The whisper was louder. 'Amil?'

'Yes,' he said. 'Who wants me?'

'Come here, my friend. You'll know me when you see me.'

He turned, saw a man standing there in the shadows, barely lit by the gas lamps from the dirt street he had been walking on. The voice did seem familiar . . . he walked into the shadows and then the man stepped forward, and Amil's heart started thumping. It was the Sudanese!

'Amil,' the man said, smiling. 'You do remember me, don't you?'

'Yes, yes, of course I do . . . tell me, what has happened? Why are you here? What news?'

The Sudanese smiled. 'So many questions from such a brave young warrior. I do have so much to tell you, but we need to go to a place that is private, out of sight. There are Jews and Americans out here, even in a place like this, who seek to halt what work we have done.'

Amil nodded in excitement. 'Yes, yes, I know of a place. Follow me. It's not far.'

They exited the alleyway. Amil had spoken the truth, but he wished that he hadn't, for the place was indeed nearby, but he would have rather walked a distance with the Sudanese, with hopes that he could meet friends or cousins or aunts or uncles, and say to them later, that black man, the Sudanese, he is truly a holy warrior, and he has asked for my help.

A short distance away – Amil walked as fast as possible with his poor foot – there was a home that was being built. The home had a view of the Hindu Kush and it was said that the rich man who was building it for one of his wives had run out of money, so the place was only half-built. A wire fence surrounded the property but Amil and others knew how to get in, and long ago the place had been stripped of its wiring, windows and piping. There was a gap near an old pine tree and though it was dark there was light enough from the other buildings to light their way. Amil led and the Sudanese followed until they were on the property, near a half-built brick wall.

Amil turned to his friend. 'Sir – please tell me what is going on.'

The Sudanese clasped Amil's shoulder. 'Yes, all is going to plan.'

'But . . . nothing has happened! You promised that I would strike a mighty blow against the Jews and infidels, but I've not seen a thing!'

'All in God's time, my mighty warrior,' the Sudanese said. 'All in God's time.'

Amil was confused but happy. 'I understand now ... I think I do ... but tell me, sir, why have you come back? Is there more to be done?'

The Sudanese said, 'There is always more to be done. But I need to know something. Your work that day, going to the Internet place in Lahore. Did you tell anybody what you did there?'

'No.'

'Did you see anybody in Lahore who would recognize you?'

'No.'

'And you have kept your secret well, all these weeks?'

Amil nodded eagerly. 'Yes, yes, I have.'

The Sudanese slapped him gently on the back. 'You have done so well, my friend. You truly have. Here, I must show you something.'

Amil watched as the Sudanese reached into his robes and pulled out a small pistol. It was a dark and ugly thing, and there was something odd attached to the end of the stubby barrel, like a short length of pipe wider than the barrel itself. Amil eyed the pistol as the Sudanese raised it.

'Is ... is that for me?'

'In a way, yes.'

'But I have no experience in using such a thing!'

The Sudanese shook his head. 'No experience is necessary. But I have one more thing to tell you, Amil.'

'Yes, what is that?'

The Sudanese's easy smile disappeared in an instant. 'Greetings from the people of the United States of America.'

And the end of the pipe-length was pressed against Amil's forehead, and all was darkness.

On the island of Bali, Ranon Degun looked out through a window of his aunt and uncle's home, watching the rains fall. The exhilaration and joy he had experienced at making that cellphone call and feeling that he had been doing something great and exciting had dribbled away, like ice melting in a glass. What worth had it been? What great thing had he accomplished? There was so much to do and he thought he had done his part . . . and silence. Nothing. He looked back into his uncle and aunt's home, saw the disarray of dishes in the kitchen, laundry to be folded, floor to be swept – women's work, not work for a man, yet his uncle had demanded that the home be cleaned before he and his wife came home later that night. 'You must do something here to support yourself,' his uncle had shouted, 'for we cannot feed you for free! You understand? We are not your slaves, to feed you and clothe you at your demands!'

So there it was. Women's work. When just a while ago he had been a proud jihadist, taking the first step to fight against the enemy, to free his beautiful island from the filthy—

A man was coming down the pathway, a tall man, a black man—

The Sudanese!

Ranon ran out of the small house, went down the stone path, the sodden leaves on the tree branches slapping him in the face and on the shoulders, and the Sudanese gave him a wide grin as he met up with him. He grasped the black man's hands with his and said, 'How wonderful! How wonderful! Do you have any news?'

The Sudanese smiled back at him. 'Yes, wonderful news . . . but only if we can speak quietly. Can we do that?'

Ranon released the man's hands, quickly nodded. 'Yes, yes, right here. I know the place. Come along!'

He walked quickly, not minding the downpour, as the Sudanese kept pace with him, following behind him, as he peppered the older man with questions. Did his phone call really make a difference? How goes the jihad? Why was there no news of a major strike against America? Was the day coming soon? Could he, Ranon, join the Sudanese and leave Bali to do God's work?

They came into a small clearing. Almost out of breath, Ranon said, 'This is my secret hiding place. It's where I come to pray and think when my uncle and aunt . . . when they yell at me too much. This is where I come to be alone.'

The Sudanese nodded, and Ranon noted something odd, as if the man was troubled by what he said. But the Sudanese simply said, 'And of my visit. And what you did. Was anyone told?'

Ranon shook his head. 'No one. I swear.'

'Very good.'

The Sudanese slid a large hand into his clothing, took out a pistol. Ranon was fascinated with the black shape. The Sudanese said, 'Ranon, do you know how to use one of these?'

'No, I do not.'

The Sudanese shrugged. 'It does not matter. I do, and that is all that is important.'

And while Ranon was trying to figure out what the man meant, he felt the touch of the cold metal upon his forehead and flinched. Something inside him froze when the last words he heard were, 'Greetings from the people of the United States of America.'

Henry Muhammad Dolan yawned as he exited the Tube station, carrying a plastic bag of groceries. It was a five-block walk home and his feet hurt with every step. He didn't like picking up groceries – women's work, of course – but since his wife was ill he had no other choice. He walked slowly, burdened not only by the weight of the bag in his hand but by other things as well. His wife had nagged him in that gentle way which wasn't nagging, asking why she and their daughters could not go to Detroit to visit her sister. He had forbidden it, over and over again, but still she had come back to it, like a cat circling a meal, going around and around, until late one night he had lost his temper and said, '*Because*, woman! There will be something bad happening in America, and soon, and I do not want you or the girls to be there when it happens!'

Oh, curse it, for what had happened then was the probing and nagging and questioning. While Henry had said very little, he had said something about his meeting with the Sudanese and the work he had done and the warnings he had received and . . .

He stopped at an intersection. And another thing. The Sudanese should have come back. Should have told him more. Should have—

And, God's beard, like something out of a fairy tale, the Sudanese was there, standing next to him!

The Sudanese smiled. 'You look surprised, my brother. Hide your shock well. I do not want to draw attention to either of us. Continue your walk.'

'I . . . I was just thinking of you, and what you asked me to do . . . tell me, can you tell me when—'

'Hush, now,' the Sudanese said. 'I cannot tell you a thing. Not yet, at least. But I need to talk to you in private. Do you have the time?'

'Of course!'

They walked among the crowds, the lines of people flowing about him, and Henry Muhammad Dolan was proud that the Sudanese had returned, for it meant something of importance was going to happen. Of that he had no doubt. None whatsoever. Like the vision he had once, that the black flag of Islam would one day fly over Whitehall, there was not a doubt. It was to be a reality, and sooner than anyone would think—

At a small hostel, the Sudanese went through a side door, up a narrow set of stairs. Henry followed. A television was playing loud and there was music and cooking smells, but it all meant nothing to him. All that mattered was the tall Sudanese dressed in a shabby dark brown suit, walking ahead of him. The Sudanese took out a key, opened another door. He walked ahead of Henry, put his own grocery bags on the floor. The room was simple, with a small bed, a table with a television on it, and a washbasin in a corner. The window shade was drawn, and on the floor was the oddest thing: a square of green plastic, two or three meters to a side.

The Sudanese said to Henry, 'Before we begin, I must ask you something.'

'Go right ahead.'

'The task I assigned you – did you tell anyone of what you did?'

Henry felt his face grow warm and was wondering what to say when the Sudanese looked at him sharply and said, 'You will speak the truth to me. Did you tell anyone?'

Henry looked down at the floor. 'My wife. I told her a little. About you.'

'And what else?'

'Only that she was forbidden to travel to the United States next month. To visit her sister. I told her something bad was going to happen to America. That she had to stay home.'

The Sudanese seemed upset at something, but not at what Henry had just said. It was like some inner struggle was taking place. Then the Sudanese closed his eyes for a moment and said, 'Very well. What is done is done. But no harm will come to your wife and children. None.'

'Very good,' Henry said, confused. 'But what does all of this mean?'

The Sudanese reached underneath his coat, pulled out a pistol of some sort, and Henry knew what was about to happen, could not believe it. He started to say a prayer and the shock of what the Sudanese said next – 'Greetings from the people of the United States' – caused him to halt in mid-sentence, just before a split-second flash of light preceded a final darkness.

The man known as the Sudanese was now in a men's room, staring at a mirror. He had the room to himself. He looked at the dark face and brown, impassive eyes. Water was running in the sink, and before him was an open container about the size of a yogurt carton. He took a washcloth, dipped it in water, and then dipped it again in the container, and started rubbing at his face. Rub, rub, rub, and the dark color started to wash away, revealing a lighter skin, brown but not as black as before. More rubbing and something else began to emerge, a pattern, a display of scar tissue, of facial skin that had been badly burned, years ago. More rub, rub, rub, and when he was done there was no longer a Sudanese looking back at him from the bathroom mirror.

Instead, it was Montgomery Zane, of Tiger Team Seven.

'Welcome back to the world,' he whispered to the mirror.

Outside the restroom, Monty walked into a wide, open room with a low ceiling. There was country and western music being played somewhere, and in the middle of the room were a number of tables and chairs. Men were there, eating and drinking and smoking, and some were playing cards. Men were also two-deep at the bar, on the other side of which was a grill, open 24/7, where someone could order anything from frog's legs to bacon and eggs to a milkshake to Maine lobster to caviar. Anything and everything. The men's voices were loud and boisterous, though some of the men were quiet, sitting by themselves, reading or sleeping or listening to music through headphones or watching a movie on a hand-held DVD.

Monty felt his body relax, for that was the purpose of this room. It was in a nondescript building stuck in the corner of a training facility at Hurlburt Air Force Base in western Florida – home of Air Force Special Operations – but there were about a dozen other facilities like it scattered around the world. Its purpose was simple: it was an oasis, a recharging place, a room to re-enter The World after doing the dirty work of the United States. For each and every man in this room was a member of an elite, either Special Forces or Delta Force or Navy SEAL or Air Force Special Ops or any other black-budget group, who in fact were known as the 'point of the spear', and here they relaxed for a while, after killing the enemies of the United States.

At the bar Monty leafed through a thick menu, ordered a plate of barbecued ribs. After getting a Sam Adams, he went back to a table and sat down. There was a day-old *USA Today* newspaper there and he started looking through it. He yawned. Man, going through so many time zones in just a few days fucked up his inner clock so bad the poor thing probably didn't even know what year it was anymore. The beer was cold and good and as he sat there, feet stuck out, he thought about the past couple of days. Some strange shit, though he was no newcomer to strange shit. His job was to be the hammer. Somebody's else's job was to be the architect, the designer.

Another swallow of the beer. But what kind of design lay behind his latest run? He had spent a fair amount of time over the past few years playing around with these contacts and others, passing along spoof information, knowing that it was for a good cause. The spoof information could cause enemy higher-ups to react, to make plans, to be caught on the radar of all the God-loving forces involved in this war on terror. So that had been the job, and he had done good with it, playing the devout Sudanese, paying attention to terrorist-wannabes.

So why were they whacked? What possible threat could they have posed?

Somebody kicked at his feet. He looked up, and smiled in recognition. 'Yo, Bravo Tom, have a seat.'

'Don't mind if I do,' said the other man, a bulky redhead whose hair was cropped short and whose muscular shoulders looked like they were about to burst through his black T-shirt. Bravo Tom was a second-generation Croatian, whose father had taken him to the United States when the Yugoslav civil war began in earnest. He

had a twelve-syllable first name that began with the letter
'B' and, thankfully, his middle name was Thomas. His last
name was also a jumble of consonants and one vowel, and
everywhere he was deployed he was just called Bravo Tom.
Monty had met the man in a SEAL refresher course a few
years back, and had run into him, off and on, all across the
great globe.

'Buy you a beer?' Monty asked, and Bravo Tom laughed
back at him. Everything was free, and buying a beer just
meant walking up to the bar and retrieving same. Bravo Tom
said, 'Nope, I'm good for now. How you been?'

'Good. And you?'

'Just fine,' Bravo Tom said. 'Good to see your ugly mug.
How's business? Still with the Tiger Teams?'

Monty smiled at the easy give and take. This was one
part of the military that civilians never quite understood.
You made a friend, a good friend, and despite deployments
hither and yon you could run into that friend in the most
Godforsaken places and they'd show you the ropes and help
you fit in and watch your Six. It was a big organization, the
military, but it was like one big-ass family if you looked at it
right.

'Busy, quite busy, but it's all right. Tiger Team is treating
me okay. And you? Still with the Hymen Squad?'

Bravo Tom seemed to blush at that. Monty knew that his
friend had been stationed with a secretive group that was
tasked to provide quiet and clandestine support to the US
Border Patrol and Customs. There were very strict rules
against the use of military resources in domestic law-
enforcement affairs – rooted in the old concept of the
posse comitatus – but since a certain day in September 2001,
rules were pretty much what whoever made them – and who

could get a Federal judge, usually in secret, to sign off on them – wanted to make them. Officially, Bravo Tom's group was known as the Border Support Task Force and, using Kiowa helicopters and cut-down armored Humvees, they worked both the Canadian and Mexican borders to interdict smugglers of drugs and smugglers of people. But since their job was, as some wise-asses had noted, to protect the purity and sanctity of the nation, their unofficial name was the Hymen Squad.

So far their work had gone well. They'd intercepted nearly a dozen teams trying to infiltrate, said teams either being killed in vicious firefights never reported in the news media or captured and sent to the tender clutches of the rapidly growing prison system in Guantánamo Bay.

Bravo Tom shrugged at the question and said, 'Hymen Squad's doing all right, I guess. I'm going on a thirty-day leave this weekend and, let me tell you, I am counting down the hours.'

Monty lowered his beer bottle to the table. 'Leave? You're going on leave?'

'Sure. Why not?'

Monty looked at his friend to see if he was joking but there was no humor there. He said, 'You're going on leave. For thirty days. Tell me, you guys spun up about anything coming down in the next couple of weeks?'

Bravo Tom shrugged. 'Nope. Everything's about as normal as it can be, Monty. Some training down in Lower Baja, and some work going up north with the Aussie Special Forces, out in Montana, but that's it.'

'Regular schedule? Regular ops?'

'Yeah. Hey, no offense, mind telling me what the fuck is going on?'

Monty toyed with the edge of the Sam Adams label. His fingers felt cold, his feet felt cold, the whole damn room felt cold. 'Bravo Tom, you ever hear of something called Final Winter?'

His friend thought about that for a moment and said, 'Nope.'

'You sure?'

'Damn sure I'm sure. Look, pal, I know who you are. Your name is Monty Zane. You sure as hell weren't named for a street, but you should have been, 'cause the traffic's all been one-way. And if you don't start yapping, I'm moving to a friendlier table.'

Monty was stuck but he knew that fair was fair. At this level of classification, Bravo Tom didn't have a 'need to know', but Monty sure as hell needed to know what was going on with his buddy's unit. If that meant horse-trading with information, so be it.

Still toying with the beer label, he said, 'My Tiger Team has been riled by something coming up in a couple of weeks. Something known as Final Winter. Major attack on a number of cities. Those doing the attack are supposed to be Syrians, infiltrating through the borders. I did some background work, passed my recommendation up the usual and customary chain of command. Thought for sure you guys would be heading up any response. I can't fucking believe you're not at high-level alert.'

Bravo Tom said, 'Sorry, pal, we're not And if we were, I'd know about it.'

'Shit,' Monty said.

Bravo Tom said, 'Looks like somebody in your group has some explaining to do.'

Monty nodded, saw that his plate of ribs was coming over,

carried by a male airman wearing BDUs. 'You better fucking believe it,' he said.

CHAPTER TWENTY-ONE

Vladimir Zhukov sat next to the Arab boy as he drove the tractor-trailer truck through the confusing maze of roadways and parking areas of the Port of Vancouver. There were three terminal areas that handled container cargo – Deltaport, Centerm and their destination, Vanterm – and Vladimir was pleased enough to let Imad do the driving and dealing. The place was filled with parking areas, service stations, railway yards, and long lines of belching tractor-trailer trucks, coming out with their containers firmly fastened at the rear.

Imad was singing some high-pitched tune that grated on Vladimir's ears, but he let the boy go on. Even though Imad probably weighed no more than sixty or seventy kilograms and looked like such a child behind the wheel of the Freightliner he handled the massive truck with ease. Between them was a metal clipboard with a sheaf of papers and documents, and Vladimir smiled at the memory of crossing the US Customs station not more than an hour ago. The Americans didn't care who was leaving their benighted nation, and Canada was only too eager to allow tradesmen and businessmen and truckers through. Their papers had gotten a perfunctory glance and then they'd been on their way, passing from US Route 5 to Canadian Route 99. Imad commented immediately on the rougher roadway.

Vladimir said, 'The joy of a socialist economy. They would rather spend money on making immigrants feel good than on good roadways.'

Imad grunted. 'This is one hell of a bad road.'

'So it is. I will tell you a story. After the end of the Great Patriotic War, the—'

'The what?'

Vladimir folded his arms. 'What others call the Second World War. We call it the Great Patriotic War. As you call the Six Days' War between Israel and the Arabs the Great Betrayal. At the end of the Second World War, Canada had the third-largest navy in the world, after the United States and Great Britain. They were a world power, and they pissed it away, like a drunk peasant getting a fortune and spending it on vodka. Now they have an Air Force that relies on American castoffs, a Navy that depends on leased ships, and an Army that cannot even fill a football stadium. Pathetic.'

Imad had laughed. 'Like a nuclear-armed empire that sees half its land given away, its mighty submarine force rusting at the dockside, and an Army that is still getting its ass kicked in Chechnya.'

Vladimir felt his fists clench. 'We've lost our way. We will be back.'

Imad laughed again. 'Surely you will, Russki. You keep on believing that.'

Now they were in the middle of the Vanterm container terminal, having followed a map provided by a security guard. Imad had opened the window and the smell was of diesel fuel and chemicals and salt air and exhaust. Imad sang another little ditty as he drove, irritating Vladimir with its stupidity, but the Russian let the boy do his job. Other vehicles traveled on the access roads as well, mostly tractor-trailer trucks like themselves, hauling away containers that just a number of hours ago had been transiting the Pacific Ocean. He found that the palms of his hands were moist. He wiped his hands on his pant legs. Everything would be fine.

They came to another gate. Imad passed the paperwork over, chatted to the terminal worker. The man was Chinese. Lots of workers here were Chinese, and Vladimir hated the sight. The damn Chinese were pressing against his homeland, buying up land and mineral rights and pulp mills in the eastern part of his Russia, and the damn people were here as well, taking over the western part of Canada. Were the Canadians so blind that they fretted and complained about the behemoth to their south – who usually ignored them, except when it came to UN votes – and overlooked the true behemoth to the west, who was going to overtake their pretty little country by buying and breeding, two things at which the Chinese excelled?

The truck barked into motion again. As they went down a narrow roadway, flanked on each side by overhead cranes, more containers that marked the oceanwide business here – P&O, Freightline, Haatz-Merlin and Stagway – Vladimir said, 'Are we there yet? Are we?'

'Just another minute,' Imad said. 'Aaahh . . . here we go.'

There. Vladimir could feel his pulse racing at the sight of the bright yellow Comex container and trailer, sitting by itself off to the left. Imad honked the air horn in celebration as he slowed down and passed the trailer. Working the gears and looking in the side view mirrors, he backed up the tractor-trailer and Vladimir winced at the sudden jolt as the truck seemed to hit something.

'Damn fool, what did you do?'

Imad's head was turned but his voice was sharp enough. 'I am young but I'm no fool, you pampered doctor. Haven't you ever ridden in a truck before? We've just hooked up the trailer. Nothing unusual. Damn fool yourself.'

Imad opened the driver's door, leapt out. Vladimir followed him and dropped down to the cracked pavement, enjoying stretching his legs. He looked around at the mess of containers and cranes. He felt a flash of anger that such a place existed here, in a joke of a country. Canada! Something like this should be in Vladivostok, an ocean away, feeding his home country, helping it to grow strong again. Not in this Western fairyland of a place . . . He walked to the rear, saw Imad at work, connecting cables and hoses from the Freightliner to the trailer.

'How much longer?'

'Just a few more minutes, that's all. What's the rush?'

Vladimir rubbed his cold hands, looked to the south and the horizon and the haze that marked the homeland of his enemy.

'You're right, no rush,' he said. 'I've waited decades. I can wait just a bit longer.'

Imad laughed. 'We've waited more than five centuries. We too can wait a bit longer.'

In Memphis, Alexander Bocks spent just a few seconds looking over at his three visitors, gauging their reaction to the news he had just given them. The doctor looked like he was relieved, as though something bad he had signed up for was not now going to happen. The detective just looked uncomfortable, like he knew he didn't belong here but should be back home in Manhattan, investigating an assault at a bodega or something. And the CIA woman . . . when he had told her that AirBox was going to be grounded in less than two hours, something more than disbelief or anger had flashed across that pretty face. It had been as if something she had cherished and hoped for had been snatched away at the very last moment.

Adrianna Scott said, 'Less than ninety minutes? Are . . . are you sure?'

'Sure I'm sure,' Bocks shot back. 'What the hell kind of question is that?'

Yep, the CIA woman was rattled. He wondered how in hell she had gotten to the position she was in. She seemed to pull herself together and said, 'Yes, you're right. Of course. The question I should have asked is, why? Why are your mechanics going on strike?'

Bocks managed a small smile. 'Over teeth.'

'Teeth?' the detective asked. 'What's the matter, they don't like their dental plan?'

The general turned to look at Doyle. 'Sure they do. That's the problem. They love their dental plan, but they don't want to pay more than their fair share. In order to be more competitive, we've got to cut costs even more. Neither side is going to budge, so by the time you nice folks get back to your hotel rooms the strike will be on.'

'But don't you have contingency plans?'

Plans, Bocks thought, sure, plans thought up by my slug CFO. Aloud he said, 'Sure we do. We have mechanics lined up. Scabs, the poor bastards. But the FAA isn't going to allow us to shut out our old mechanics and bring in a new crew without certifications and training being checked. So we'll be down. A week, maybe two. Maybe even three.'

'Over teeth,' the CIA woman said, a tinge of wonder in her voice.

'No, not just teeth. It's more than that. It's a struggle, like other companies struggle. How to make it to the future. How to survive. Hell, how to thrive so you have jobs, and stockholders have dividends, and nice little people get their nice little packages on time.'

Adrianna said, 'That's very nice, general, but unless we do what we have to do there isn't going to be a future, most of your stockholders will be dead, and those nice little people won't be looking for nice little packages. They're going to be looking at digging graves in their front lawn to bury their children, and they're going to worry about getting food this winter. That's the reality. And teeth isn't going to cut it.'

Bocks was going to say something but the woman plowed right over him. 'By my side is Doctor Victor Palmer. One of the best and smartest physicians working at the Centers for Disease Control. He could quit this afternoon and by tomorrow have his own hospital wing in New York or Los Angeles or Phoenix, to do whatever kind of research he wants. But he gets paid shit by the government and puts in tremendous hours, and suffers for it, all to protect his countrymen. And for what? Knowing he might fail, that millions might die, and that even if he succeeds people alive this instant will be dead by this time next month because of what he's devised.'

Adrianna shifted in her seat, her voice sharper. 'Then you have Detective Doyle. He'd rather be home in New York, rather be involved in his son's Little League team and schoolwork, and put bad people behind bars, than be working for us. He's sacrificed time with his son, he's sacrificed his career with the New York Police Department, and for what? For being involved in something that could see him disgraced, see him sent off to jail. A New York detective whose own father was killed on September eleventh.'

Bocks looked at the detective. 'That true?'

Doyle looked irritated. 'Yeah.'

'Tell me about it.'

He shrugged. 'Thousands of people lost family or friends that day. My story's no different.'

Bocks said, 'Maybe so, but still I want to hear it.'

Doyle cleared his throat, shot a glance at the woman seated next to him – Bocks wondered what kind of dynamic was at work there – and said, 'The story is simple. My dad's name was Sean Doyle. Spent nearly thirty years on the Job. Raised me and a brother and a sister. Retired as a sergeant, decided he was going to be a handyman and single-handedly renovate the family home on Ridgeway. But the poor guy didn't know one end of a hammer from the other and thought heat magically came out of the basement by itself. And my mom – well, she was used to having him out of the house during the day, and truth be told, he was used to being out too. So he got a job as a security officer, for a finance firm in Tower Two. He and nearly everybody else in that firm was killed that day.'

'Did anybody see him that last day?'

'An admin aide – Jackie somebody – she thought she saw him go into the offices, to try to get the people out of there, just as the smoke got real thick . . . that's about it.'

Bocks looked at the quiet detective, tried to imagine what it must have been like to lose one's father like that. In his years in the Air Force, Bocks had lost many friends and acquaintances, and tragic as their deaths were they made sense, in a grim sort of way. Aircraft crashes in bad weather or enemy fire or mechanical problems . . . in the back of your mind, what you expected could happen to you or somebody you knew. But to die in one of the world's tallest buildings, from a terrorist attack, when you had retired safely after years on the street? Not only did it not make sense, it was obscene.

Bocks looked at the detective and said, 'Your dad was a hero. You should be proud.'

'No, he was just doing his job. That's all. And nothing else.'

'I respectfully disagree, detective. He was a hero.'

The detective didn't say anything else. Bocks shifted to the CIA woman again, and said, 'You've told me about the good doctor and the good detective. But nothing about yourself.'

'There's nothing to say,' she said.

'Of course there is, and I want to hear it,' Bocks said.

Adrianna Scott looked at the sharp face of the general, knowing what she'd like to say. She'd like to say:

Arrogant man, it was men like you, men from your Air Force, who killed my family that February morning. Arrogant and powerful men, thousands of miles away, choosing which targets in my blessed city should be destroyed. Men in comfortable offices eating fine meals at the end of the day, choosing the targets here and there, deciding who would live and who would die. And then other arrogant men, in their high-powered machines, flying high above the ground, high above a place where the people would have fought you hand-to-hand if possible, but, the cowards in their machines came far above my land . . . and in a matter of seconds incinerated my family and hundreds of others.

Now you sit here, she thought, one more arrogant man among others, showing no regret, no remorse, no apology for what you and so many others did to my country, and to other poor countries, from Vietnam to Bosnia to Somalia and so many others, blundering around with your sledgehammer weapons, speaking of piety and democracy and human rights, and slaughtering all those who get in your way.

This is what I would say, arrogant man, that the time has come for this Iraqi woman to use your machines, your arrogance, your power against you, and in a matter of weeks the world will not be able to sleep at night for the crying and rending of the robes and the gnashing of the teeth from those cold and huddled and scared survivors in what was once known as the United States of America.

That was what she wanted to say.

Instead, Adrianna said, 'The story is nothing exceptional. Nothing like those of the good doctor here and the detective. My parents died at a young age. I lived in a poor neighborhood in Cincinnati. Raised by an aunt who passed away while I was in college. Decided then in college that my country – my homeland – was in danger. No matter what the talk shows or newspapers or opinion polls said, I just knew my country was in danger. I entered the CIA and worked well and quietly until September eleventh.'

She kept her steady gaze on the general, who was looking right back at her with a direct expression. She said, 'Now we're approaching an imminent threat that will make September eleventh and everything that followed it look like a schoolboy brawl. Something that will destroy what Lincoln called the world's "last, best, hope". And I cannot believe that you, General Bocks, will allow this nation to face something like this without your help, your aid, over the matter of a union and a dental plan. I cannot believe that a man as powerful and as dedicated as you will allow that to happen. Am I right?'

The air seemed heavy. She knew that Victor and Brian, flanking her, were no doubt looking at her but she kept her stare fixed on the general. She wondered what machinations, what thoughts, were going on behind those eyes. The general stared and stared and then he smiled, and she caught herself. No, she thought, not yet. Too soon, too soon.

'Very well put, Miss Scott,' he said, shifting in his chair. 'Very well put. Yes, you're right. I'm not going to let a simple matter of a dental plan derail what you've asked of me. That's not going to happen.'

Brian said, 'If you've got a strike going down in less than two hours, how in hell are you going to stop it?'

Bocks said, 'By going back to the past. By going to my roots. By seeing someone who I once thought of as a good friend, and bringing a six-pack of beer and some ribs. And we'll work it out.'

Adrianna forced herself to breathe slowly, not to let any excitement show. 'So . . . so we can count on you and your carrier company?'

A hammer blow, right to the gut. 'No,' Bocks said. 'Not yet. I require something else.'

She could not speak. Only nod.

Bocks said, 'No offense to you and your companions here, Miss Scott, but I need to verify your bona fides. All right? Every other op I've ever done for the CIA and anybody else in DC, I've checked and rechecked what's been requested of me. Everything from sensitive packages to sensitive people, I've risked equipment and aircrews for my nation. But this one . . . this one dwarfs everything, miss, and I'm not going to proceed until I'm comfortable. So. Who do you have?'

'Hold on, general,' Adrianna said, and he wasn't sure, but the woman seemed more pale than when she came in. What was going on there? he thought. The pressures? The responsibility? The burden of having to come to this office and plead a case that could end with all of them going to prison?

She went to her leather bag, took out a notepad, scribbled something and passed it over. Bocks glanced at the name and number, nodded. 'I recognize the name. That's a big point in your favor. We ran some items into Bagram couple of years back on his say-so. How's his leg?'

'He never talks about it.'

'Figures.'

He put the slip of paper down, picked up the phone, dialed the number. It rang just once and a female voice answered the phone by repeating the last four digits of the number.

'Four-one-twelve,' she said.

'This is General Alexander Bocks, of AirBox air freight,' he said. 'I need to speak to your Director. The Colonel.'

'Hold on, sir,' came the voice.

Dead silence.

Bocks looked over again at the trio sitting across from his desk. 'I'm on hold,' he said. 'At least there's no elevator music.'

No reply, nothing, just the somber looks on their faces. He had no envy for what they did and what they lived with, day after day. Running a multimillion-dollar business was tough, but the spreadsheets he worked with didn't have collateral damage of tens of thousands of civilians.

A click. 'General Bocks?' came a male voice.

'That it is, colonel, that it is.' He switched the receiver to his other hand. 'I have before me three people who say they work for you. An Adrianna Scott. Doctor Victor Palmer. Detective Brian Doyle. True so far?'

'You've got it.'

'I've just been briefed by Adrianna Scott of an operation called Final Winter. You're familiar with it?'

'Yeah, quite familiar. And I'll remind you, general, we're not on a secure line.'

'Understood. Question I have for you, has Final Winter been vetted?'

'Yes.'

'You're comfortable with what's been presented, its outcomes and variables?'

A sigh. 'Never comfortable with something like this, but as best as I can say, yeah, we're comfortable.'

Bocks kept his eye on Adrianna. She looked like she had been carved out of marble. 'I'm concerned about the liability on my part.'

'There's protocols that have been signed with you and your company and the Justice Department, am I correct?'

'Yes, five or six years ago. When I first started . . . doing favors.'

The colonel laughed. 'Now that's a word. Favors. Yeah. General, the liability is covered. Don't worry about it. The question I have is that Adrianna probably mentioned a tight deadline. Can you do it?'

Bocks took a breath, looked at the solemn faces of the people sitting across from him. 'I don't think I have a choice, now, do I.'

'I don't have to tell you the debt we'll owe you if you're able to provide this assistance, general.'

'No, no, you don't.'

Another pause. Bocks said, 'All right, then, you've answered my questions. Thank you.'

'No, sir, thank you . . .'

Bocks hung up the phone, looked at his visitors.

Adrianna had one thought, and one thought only:

Don't throw up. Don't throw up. Don't throw up.

Somehow she knew the general would have to do something to verify what she was proposing, but she hadn't thought that he might go right to the colonel heading the Tiger Teams. The briefing she had given the Director a few days ago had so far worked well; all that anyone knew in the Tiger Team oversight was that Final Winter was merely a harmless bacterial test to determine air patterns and detection methods over various American cities. My God, if Bocks had said one word about anthrax, one word about deaths being caused and lives being saved . . .

Could she have gotten out of the building in time?

Don't throw up. Don't throw up. Don't throw up.

Bocks shook his head. 'All right, I'll take care of my machinists. In the meantime . . . Miss Scott, it looks like you've got me and my aircraft.'

'Thank you, sir,' Adrianna said, disgusted at how weak her voice sounded, exhilarated at what she had just pulled off.

My word, wouldn't papa have been proud.

CHAPTER TWENTY-TWO

Now there was a line of traffic forming up before them, as Vladimir Zhukov and Imad drove south to the American border. They had left the Port of Vancouver with their cargo, and while Imad wanted to chat about what mighty blows the two of them were preparing against the infidel oppressor – blah, blah, blah – Vladimir was more concerned about what was ahead of them. Back again on Canadian Route 99, Vladimir was under no illusions of what they were about to face, for the Americans were finally beginning to tighten up their long border with their dull Canadian neighbors, years after that glorious Tuesday morning in September.

At his side was the long leather wallet that held his identification, Imad's identification, the papers from the Port of Vancouver, and the bills of lading for what they were supposedly carrying back there in the shipping container. According to all the paperwork – which had originated from Shanghai, China – there was nothing back in the trailer but a collection of children's toys, from dolls to footballs. Which was true, for about the first six feet's worth of packaging. Once you got past those brightly colored boxes, other items began to appear, specially constructed canisters of metal and plastic, packed in foam and securely fastened, for not one of the canisters could have been put in place with a risk of breakage or rupture, since an accident like that would have quickly killed everyone on the container ship, and the crew of any curious vessel coming by to see why things were amiss on a ship manned by corpses.

Vladimir folded his arms. So far it had gone well. From that shit-hole of a tribal state that dared to call itself a nation, to a number of other hotels and hostels and way stations on the route across Asia and Siberia, his hidden contact out there had pried, prompted, promised, and, of course, had paid him. He had no idea if his contact was a man, a woman, a committee, part of some group or some nation. All he knew was that the contact knew a lot about him, and knew just how to interest him enough to get him to do what he was doing.

It had worked out fine, so far, and Vladimir's Cayman Islands account had grown fat indeed. But late at night, in the quiet stillness when he opened his eyes and stared out into the darkness, he liked to think that of course it was more than just the money, more than grabbing his chunk of the capitalist system that was strangling the globe. He saw it as a perfect revenge, a perfect dish served so very cold. A time that—

Imad said, 'We're getting close.'

'I see,' he said.

Up ahead there was an exit for COMMERCIAL TRAFFIC, which he and Imad and this truck certainly were.

Imad looked over at him, licked his lips. Vladimir smiled. 'Nervous, boy?'

'Don't call me boy!'

'Very well – nervous, child?'

Imad's face was tense, his lips trembling, as he downshifted the big truck, easing into the Customs lane. Ahead were a number of other tractor-trailer and container trucks, pulling over for inspection, and Imad said, 'Watch your fucking mouth, Russian. I don't take that from anyone.'

Vladimir said, 'Watch your own fucking mouth, Arab, because we want these Customs people to see two ordinary truckers, entering their ordinary country, not knowing that we're going to slaughter millions of their ordinary people in just a few days. Understand, child?'

Imad said nothing, braking the truck, the air brakes sounding like the howls of some Siberian creature out there on the taiga. Vladimir smiled, couldn't help himself. It was fun, needling the little shit. Needed to be put in his place. But he had to watch it, he knew: there were many more kilometers left ahead of them.

In Memphis, they were in Overton Park, about five miles away from her home, and Carrie Floyd watched as her daughter Susan flew a kite, her chubby legs pistoning back and forth as she giggled while the little piece of plastic fabric and string struggled to get up into the sky. Next to Carrie was a light blue blanket, the remains of a picnic lunch and one satiated and somewhat groggy Sean Callaghan, her co-pilot and companion. He was dozing, his head in her lap, and she almost had a fit of giggles at what to call him. She was really too old to be calling him a boyfriend, and 'companion' was a term that belonged to those members of the gay community – not that there was anything wrong with that, of course (which almost caused her to burst into laughter again), and 'significant other' seemed too cold and sterile. Sean was many things, but cold was not one of them, and she was sure – though she had no evidence – that sterility wasn't an issue either.

This time, the giggles burst through, and Sean opened his eyes, smiled up at her. 'Did I say something funny in my sleep?'

Carrie touched his forehead, smoothed aside some of his hair. 'No, you didn't.'

'Didn't burp or pass gas?'

'Nope.'

The smile grew wider. 'Then I must be as damn near perfect a man as you'll ever see.'

That caused a laugh and he laughed with her and said, 'Marry me, then.'

'Oh, Sean.'

Carrie looked up and saw Susan now dancing with glee as the kite held steady in the breeze. Some great genes the kid had, for even at this young age she was getting the hang of aerodynamics and lift and wind pressures and—

'I'm serious,' Sean said.

She leaned down, kissed his nose. 'I know you are. But you know the rules.'

'Yes, I know, and I've been thinking about that.'

'Oh? Care to share?'

'That's what I'm doing, love. Sharing. I know the rules. We get married, one of us has to leave. And you have seniority. Got that. But I've got a line on a good flying job, out west.'

'How far west?'

'Anchorage.'

'Alaska!?'

The cocky grin that endeared him to her, looking up with confidence. 'Sure as hell don't mean Anchorage, Arizona.'

'Uh-huh,' she said. 'Didn't know Alaska Air is hiring.'

'They're not. It's a corporate deal. Some CEO nut, moved his corporation headquarters up to Anchorage so he could be close to the best huntin' and fishin' in the world. Air Force Reserve buddy of mine, O'Toole, he's decided to re-up and get activated, so the CEO's pilot job is opening up. Great salary, good bennies, best thing is that you don't do much flying at all. Just some bush stuff and occasional trips to

Seattle or Portland. You've got to be on call 24/7, but O'Toole said you can go for weeks without getting paged, and still pull a salary.'

'Sounds good. For you.'

Sean grabbed her hand. 'No. For *us*. It'd be a stretch but we could do it, the three of us, without you having to hold down a full-time gig. And you could spend some quality time with Susan. Isn't that all I've heard about, these past months: seeing your girl growing up without being there for her? Just seeing her on the occasional weekends, early mornings and late nights? You'd be off the cargo-air treadmill, Carrie. You'd get a life back. And we'd have a life together. All of us. Besides, who in hell knows if the General can keep AirBox afloat?'

Something started aching inside Carrie as she watched Susan running back and forth, knowing how she would cherish this sight. How damn attractive, she thought. Not to juggle schedules, doctor's appointments, school appointments, school plays and presentations. Just retro out and be Donna Reed, staying at home, doing something else for a change, instead of the cargo treadmill. How attractive . . .

Yet . . . never to fly again? Never to be the boss of your air machine, ever? Be a hausfrau in Anchorage and swap cookie recipes with the neighbors? And Alaska! Sure, a pretty state but she was used to the Memphis weather and—

'You're thinking too hard,' Sean said.

'No, I'm thinking quite straight,' she said.

'All right, then think about this,' he said. 'Alaska will be good not only for us, but for your daughter.'

'Susan? Why's that?'

Sean shifted his head in her lap, looked over at her daughter and her kite, and the tone of his voice changed,

changed so much that it quickly terrified Carrie. 'Last time I had reserve duty, I was ferrying an intelligence unit over to Hurlburt for a briefing. Stayed the weekend, went out drinking, met up with them. We had a nice chat. Nothing classified, you understand. Just general bullshit. Guy was telling me about our glorious war on terror. You want to know how long they estimate it's gonna last? Do you?'

She shook her head. 'I don't know. Six, seven years, maybe.'

'Uh-huh,' he said. 'Try sixty or seventy years. Or a hundred. Understand that? The past few years, we've been in the opening shots of the next Hundred Years' War. That's what we're facing.'

Carrie felt chilled and said, 'I've never heard of that. A hundred years . . . that's crazy!'

'Of course it is, and of course it's been kept quiet. Do you think Joe American, do you think he and his family and friends, do you think they have the stones to put up with a fight that's going to involve their children and grandchildren? Do you? No offense to Joe American, they pay the taxes that paid our salaries when we were on active duty, but he puts up with higher taxes, two-hour security lines at airports, and a lessening number of countries each year that welcome American tourists because he believes this war is worth winning, and that we'll win it, one of these days.'

Sean moved his head again. 'But how much stamina do you think he'll have, knowing that this war is going to last another century? He'd say to hell with it, and the hell with the world, and he'll listen to those politicians and pundits who think Fortress America can keep all the bad guys away.'

'Maybe it can,' Carrie said.

'Hah,' Sean said. 'How secure are our borders, Carrie? Tell

me that. All it takes is one guy slipping across, carrying a suit-case nuke designed for the KGB back in the 1970s and bought on the black market, and overnight we lose DC or a good chunk of Manhattan or LA. And that's why the war is going to last for decades. Every other previous war, including the first Hundred Years' War, was a war between states. You could con-quer that state by killing its armed forces and holding the ground. But that's not the war we're fighting. We're fighting an idea, a radical version of a religious belief, and the only way to win that war is to change societies, change people's minds. And that's going to take decades. We'll fight them by killing terrorist cells and overthrowing nations that support them, but the only victory will be when young men growing up in Karachi or Riyadh or Jakarta or even in the slums of London and Marseilles, when those young men decide they want to live and have families and have good jobs, when all of that is more attractive than strapping on suicide belts and going on jihad. It's not going to happen in our lifetimes, Carrie. It might happen in Susan's, if we're very lucky.'

Carrie felt cold, though it was a beautiful day and a warm breeze was caressing her skin. 'Why Alaska?'

Sean said, 'Because except for the pipeline and a military base or two, it's safe. There're no real target areas up there. Terrorists like big targets, like big shopping malls, big office buildings, big cities. We could find a place up there and raise a family, and be much safer than living here, in the lower forty-eight.'

'Sounds like running away.'

'No, we've done our duty, you and me, in the Air Force and Navy. We've given our time and talents to the military, put our lives on the line, eaten bad food and slept in strange places, and now it's time for us to look out for each other.

You know I'm making sense, Carrie. You know I am. So marry me and let's get our lives in order.'

'North to Alaska?' she asked, smiling.

'More like northwest to Alaska,' he said.

Carrie bent down, kissed Sean's lips, kissed him again. 'I'm not saying yes, but I'm not saying no, Sean. Give me some time to think. All right?'

Sean said, 'Sure. But you know I'm right.'

'No, I just know you have good taste,' she said.

'How's that?'

Another kiss. 'Because you spend time with me, that's why.'

At the US Customs checkpoint at the Route 99 crossing in Washington State, Tanya Mead of the Customs Service walked up to the Freightliner that was hauling a bright yellow Seamarsk container. She carried a clipboard in her hand, and she eyed the truck as she approached it. The license plate was clean, not having been flagged on any of the search-&-seize lists, and the neutron-emission detectors buried along the decorative shrubbery flanking the off ramp to the commercial vehicle crossing area hadn't flickered as the truck went by. There was a driver and a passenger, both looking down at her as she approached.

She went up to the driver's side, looked up at the open window. Young guy, dark skin, Mediterranean type. Greek, maybe, or Turkish. Who knew?

'Good morning,' she called up to him. 'What's your destination?'

'Julius Distribution, Port Bellingham,' he said. His voice had a trace of an accent. Sounded Middle Eastern but please, let's not get into racial profiling, all right?

'Cargo?'

'Toys. Bats, balls, dolls.'

'Your paperwork, please.'

'Sure,' he said. He ducked in, leaned back out, handed the papers down to her, and then – son of a bitch – he let them go, obviously on purpose. The papers fell to the ground and as Tanya bent down to pick them up she was sure she heard the driver say two words, the first being 'dumb' and the second being the n-word, that nasty n-word that she wasn't going to allow any male fucking driver to use in her presence, and she stood up, glaring at him. Tanya Mead had been with the US Customs service for three years and she loved her job and took it seriously, and the fuck she was going to let anybody push her around.

She smiled sweetly up at the driver. 'All right, pal. You and your friend get out of the truck. Hope you don't have dinner plans tonight, 'cause for the next few hours your ass and his ass and this fucking truck and all its cargo belong to me.'

Also in Memphis, Randy Tuthill was in his small backyard, his head buzzing a bit from the beer and the strange and wonderful thing that had just occurred. A while ago he'd been at the union hall, going through the hundred thousand or so details that had to be taken care of just before a job action, when his wife had called. 'You need to come home, right now,' Sarah had said.

'Why?'

'Don't ask why, just do it,' she had said.

'Are you okay? Is it about the boys?' And his heart had almost seized at the thought of something happening to Tom and Eric, their young bodies burnt or shattered or blown up or—

'The boys are fine. I'm fine. Come home now.'

'Look, babe, I've got so many—'

'Randy Buell Tuthill, you've known and trusted me for years, so trust me on this,' she had said. 'You need to get home. Now.'

Sarah had hung up the phone, Randy had sworn and hung up his own phone, and he had left, and less than a half-hour later he was home, smelling the barbecue out back, Sarah meeting him with a cold Coors, and then shoving him out the back door.

And there, standing in Randy's backyard like nothing had happened, nothing had changed, was the General himself, with a barbecue apron wrapped around his torso and a set of tongs in his hand, and he had said, 'Hungry?'

'Damn straight.'

'Feel like eating and straightening everything out?'

Oh my, a long pause there. Randy thought of the guys and girls back at the union hall, depending on him and the contract-negotiation committee and the strike committee and the relief committee, and Randy knew what was proper and what he should do, and what he should do was politely excuse himself and say, shit no, General, we've gone too far. We've got to do it by the book.

So he had looked at the General and had said, 'Pass over those tongs, General, 'fore you burn up my backyard. And then, yeah, we'll eat and straighten everything out.'

Which is what they had done. It hadn't taken that long and both he and the General had to make some phone calls to head off certain things, but it had taken place. There wasn't going to be any strike.

Now, the barbecue eaten and the beers drunk, and Sarah having shuffled them off to the flagstone patio, Randy sat next to the General, cigars and cognacs in their hands – just like the old days! – and listened to the hum of the night insects out there in the brush.

Randy said, 'Okay, I'm sure I can get this deal through. Question is, how about you?'

'What do you mean?'

Randy laughed. 'Word out on the hangar floors is that shiny new CFO of yours has your balls and checkbook in his back pocket. You think he's gonna let this deal go through?'

'It's my company,' Bocks said.

Randy sipped from the cognac, taken out only on very special occasions. He would have preferred another beer but cognac was what they had drunk during previous successful contract negotiations, and he wasn't going to spook the tradition. 'Beggin' the General's pardon, but it isn't just your company. It belongs to stockholders and mutual funds and your board of directors, and I'm wondering what they're going to say when they see what kind of deal we reached. They might even force you out in a month or two.'

'A month or two?'

'Shit, yes,' Randy said. What the General said next chilled him right to the core.

'A month or two . . . that's plenty of time. After a month or two, they can do what they fucking want.'

Randy whipped his head around to look at his boss. 'You feeling okay, General?'

'Feeling fine. Why you ask?'

'Christ, what you said right there, makes it sound like you don't expect to be around in a month or two. Like you got cancer or something. You *sure* you're okay?'

'Had a company physical last month. I'm all right, Randy. Just like you. And how're those boys of yours?'

'Both fine,' Randy said. 'Eric is assigned to a maintenance wing out at Lakenheath. Tom . . . well, he's a disappointment. Not following in dad's footsteps.'

The General chuckled. 'Randy, you old fool, the boy's flying a KC-135. He's doing fine.'

'Shit, yes, but a pilot? Only thing a pilot is good for is taking a perfectly maintained aircraft and screwing it up somehow.'

They both laughed at that. The cognac and beer and full barbecue were settling in, and Randy looked at the tiki torches flickering in the yard that Sarah loved, and thought about what had happened, how everything had just come together, right at the last minute, and Christ, it had looked like a strike was going on, something must have happened, something must have—

Oh.

Shit, yes.

That's what.

Damn.

'General?'

'Yeah, Randy?'

Randy's fingers were tingling some, holding the cigar and the cognac glass. 'This settlement – what happened?'

'Happened? Decided to settle it, that's all.'

Randy let that comment sit in the air for a moment, and said, 'Sir, no offense, but that's a load of shit. You came here and we have a settlement and for that I'm damn proud for what I did for my union, but you got practically shit from this agreement.'

'You complaining?'

'I'm observing, sir. That's what I'm doing. And what I'm observing is that we were about an hour away from a job action and something got under your ass to make you move. Something that made you come to my house and get something settled out real quick.'

'I just didn't want a strike, Randy.'

'Yeah, but that could have been settled last week or last month. General, seems to me that you got a hell of an incentive to keep AirBox flying. An incentive coming from DC or Langley.'

'Don't know what you're talking about.'

'Sure you do. Look, most of AirBox is ex-military. We know the score. We know how to do our jobs and keep our mouths shut, and we know that sometimes favors get done. Small favors, big favors. And the fact this strike's not gonna happen – some big favor is coming due, right? A favor that needs AirBox up and running. Am I right?'

The General took a leisurely puff from his cigar, looked up at the darkening sky, and said, 'Randy?'

'Sir?'

'Next couple of weeks . . . I'm going to need your crews working their best. Oh, I know they always work hard, but this is going to be an important time. I'm going to need a hundred and ten percent effort. Our airfleet . . . there's going to be some unanticipated but very important installation work that's going to be scheduled over the next fourteen days. About thirty aircraft are going to be retrofitted, and don't ask me why, or what for. I'm just going to need to have it done. No arguments, no discussions, minimal paperwork. It just has to be done, Randy. Got it? It just has to be done.'

It was a tone and manner of voice that Randy had heard from the General only once before, when they were both active-duty and the General had been a major, overseeing a maintenance unit on Qatar, just before the first Gulf War had kicked off, when men and women were going to fly into harm's way with the equipment that Randy and his crews were servicing. Randy swallowed. Some heavy shit was going down, no doubt about it.

'General,' he said. 'We won't let you down.'

The General said, 'I knew you'd say that, Randy. And I can't tell you how pleased I am.'

Vladimir looked over at Imad, stunned at what the stupid boy had just done. What had gone through that simpleton's mind to cause him to insult the American Customs officer like that? The Arab had a silly, triumphant grin on his face, like he had machine-gunned a school bus filled with Jewish children or some such, and Vladimir hissed, 'What the fuck are you doing, idiot?'

Imad said, 'I don't bow to any woman, especially not to a nigger woman like that.'

'You fool, you're going to—'

Imad said sharply, 'I acted like a man! Like you should!'

A woman's voice, from outside. 'Come along, fellas. I want to see what's in that truck, and now.'

Vladimir's head and hands felt thick as he let himself out of the truck, descending to the asphalt. It was noisy, with the other tractor-trailer trucks rumbling by, heading for the open highway, only meters away. But because of this . . . creature, this mis-spawned creature from that hellhole of a region that produced only oil and fanatics, all his years of dreaming and planning and all his hopes of revenge were about to come tumbling down.

Imad joined him at the rear of the truck, by the locked rear doors of the shipping container. A small black box with a thin cable secured the rear lock. Vladimir looked at the

Customs officer striding over to them, a fierce look on her face, and he bowed and said, 'My apologies, officer. My young driver has been on the road for a very long time. He didn't mean what he said.'

The woman was having none of it. 'Don't care if he gets down on his knees and kisses my ass. He did what he did and now I'm gonna do what I'm gonna do. The rear of the trailer is getting opened, and after I get the drug-detecting dogs over here to look at every single package in there, you'll be on your way. Probably by tomorrow.'

Imad stood there, smirking, and Vladimir knew now there was more going on than the boy's attitude towards women. The boy was challenging him, was trying to see how Vladimir could pull this off, how he would do anything to prostrate and humiliate himself before this black woman so that they could get into the country.

Vladimir took a breath. 'Again, madam, our apologies. We are behind schedule. Please. This time. Could you let us proceed? If we are late, we do not get paid. We could lose our business. Please, madam.'

The Customs officer shook her head. 'Not going to happen, pal. Open it up.'

Vladimir's legs refused to move. He could not believe this was happening. The trips across the dusty plains of Asia, following diesel buses belching thick clouds of soot, working and wheedling and bribing, all his years of schoolwork and study and lab work and Party membership and kissing the right asses of the right overseers – that it should all come to this? So that the great-great-granddaughter of some slave or tribe member from the Dark Continent would thwart his plans? It could not happen!

The woman was now in his face, her eyes flashing. 'Get a

move on, pal. Unless you and your buddy want a full body-cavity search as well. Is that what you're gunning for?'

'But . . . the lock, it's a lock secured by—'

'Mister, shut the fuck up and open the door. Now.'

The keys. The keys were in Vladimir's coat pocket. How long could he stall her? How long?

Imad was looking over, still grinning.

Vladimir's hand went into his coat. Felt the hard metal of the keys.

'Move,' the woman said.

The keys were now out of his pocket and in his hand. He moved up to the door.

Imad had disappeared. Where had the little shit gone?

Vladimir's throat was dry. This could not be happening, could not be happening. He looked over to the woman again, to see if he could once more appeal to her. But there was no possibility of appeal there, not with that anger.

He went up to the lock, the key in his hand, and—

'Tanya!'

Vladimir turned, as did the woman. An older Customs officer stood there, clipboard under his arm.

The woman's tone changed instantly. 'Sir?'

'What's the problem?'

'No problem, sir,' she said. 'Just pulling this one out for a random check.'

The older man came over, looked at Vladimir, the truck, and then eyed the square black box under the lock. From his own coat pocket, the older Customs officer pulled out a scanning device, ran it over the black box, and said to Tanya, 'Cut them loose.'

Her mouth was agape. 'Sir?'

'You heard me, cut them loose.'

Vladimir could hardly believe what he was hearing. The older Customs officer said, 'You haven't kept up with your circulars, Tanya. Recognize the box?'

'Sir, I know it's a SmartSeal, it's just that—'

'Right, a SmartSeal. Which means one of your brother or sister officers overseas, either in Tokyo or Singapore or Shanghai, cleared and verified what's in the container. The scan I just did shows that nothing's been disturbed since it was loaded last month. So Customs has already taken a look inside. Don't waste your time or my time . Let 'em go.'

'Sir, I just wanted to do a random——'

The older man said, 'You've already surpassed your quota today for randoms, Tanya. Now let's get a move on, before the fucking Chamber of Commerce people start howling again at how we're strangling international trade, all right? So they go south and you get back to work.'

The male Customs officer walked away and the younger, female Customs officer stared at him with such contempt and hate. Vladimir knew that he should feel triumphant, but all he felt was cowed. This had been, as the Duke of Wellington had said about Waterloo, a close-run thing.

And where in hell was Imad? He walked over to the driver's side, saw Imad standing there, grinning, arms crossed, the door to the cab still open.

'Come along,' Imad said. 'Didn't you hear the man? We're free to go.'

Vladimir shook his head, still not believing what had happened.

Tanya Mead stood there silently, still furious at what happened, as the truck containing the young boy and the man with the Eastern European accent drove away. The young snot looked triumphant, the older guy looked like the two of them had just gotten away with murder.

Sure, she had gone over quota, but so what? Something was still hinky about those two and she hadn't liked their attitude, even before the little dark-skinned one had called her a nigger. And then there was her supervisor, Herbert Comer, known to everyone – except himself, of course – as Captain Commerce. He was a regional office hack who had been demoted and sent down because of some indiscretion – the latest rumor had him surfing for Internet porn during his lunch hour – and his single goal was to keep the wait times down, the searches to the minimum, and the business concerns in Washington State and elsewhere happy.

Some damn attitude, Tanya thought.

She also thought about her heroine, Diana Dean, a Customs officer on duty years ago, back on December 14, 1999. Dean had stopped a guy coming in on the Vancouver ferry, to Port Angeles. Something about the guy had made her look twice at him and his car, and when Dean went to talk to the character – later found to be a member of al-Qaeda – the little fuck had fled, before being tackled to the ground. And in his rental car? In the trunk, they found 130 pounds of plastic explosives, two 22-ounce plastic bottles full of nitro-glycol, and a map of LAX, Los Angeles International Airport. That had been going to be al-Qaeda's contribution to the millennium festivities on December 31 – blowing up the airport at Los Angeles. And that plot had been stopped dead in its tracks. Not because of the FBI or CIA or NSA. Not because of some whizbang satellite in orbit, snooping on cellphone conversations and e-mail messages. And not because of some multibillion-dollar agency.

No, the airport had been saved from destruction and people who would've been killed had lived because some sharp Customs officer had been doing her job.

Just like me, Tanya thought. Just like me.

Except for goddamn Captain Commerce.

She watched as the suspect truck made its way to the clear area, on its way into the United States. She took out a small memo pad and wrote down a description of the truck, its two occupants, and the British Columbia license plate number.

Tanya Mead had an idea that she would hear about this truck again.

As the truck crossed into the United States, photo equipment hidden in light poles, highway signs and ornamental planters at this station and so many other border crossings continued their quiet work, documenting every male and female who passed through into a frightened and increasingly paranoid nation.

Imad laughed as they made their way onto the American Interstate 5, heading south. Vladimir felt his hands shake, his arms quiver. How in the name of God had they made it through . . .?

His voice was low and even. 'What were you doing back there?'

Imad laughed again, pounding the steering wheel with his fist. 'I was putting that bitch in her place. Did you see it? I put that bitch right in her place. And her boss came over and backed me up. Oh, the joy, it was so funny!'

Vladimir said, 'You realize what you did back there? You almost compromised everything. Everything! And all for your stupid boy ego!'

Imad shifted gears as the truck grumbled its way south. He said, 'You're overreacting.'

'Overreacting! That Customs officer was only moments away from having me open that door. And what do you think would have happened after that? Hmm? After she went through the toys and the dolls and the soccer balls, and found the compartment with those canisters. What then?'

Imad turned, grinning. 'It wasn't going to happen. You had that SmartSeal there, just like the older man said. The container had already been checked overseas. Right?'

'That's not the point.'

'Ah, but it *is* a point, my friend. You see, I never knew about the SmartSeal. You never told me. Care to tell me now?'

Vladimir looked around him as he entered America for the second time in less than a week. He said, 'Part of the arrangement to ease Customs bottlenecks after 9/11. The United States set up overseas Customs offices. They would inspect containers at the point of origin. Seal the doors with an electronic lock and tracing device. Container coming into the United States didn't have to be reinspected. I had this container inspected a month ago.'

'Some inspection. How did this happen, without your mystery canisters being discovered?'

'A hefty bribe to a Customs officer suffering through an opium addiction will work wonders.'

'But suppose he changed his mind afterwards? Decided to confess all?'

Vladimir said, 'A boating accident took care of that.'

'And you didn't tell me this earlier? About the SmartSeal and the bribed Customs officer? Why?'

'Because . . . because I didn't think you needed to know, that's why. You just needed to drive. That's all. Which doesn't excuse a thing. You could have still jeopardized everything. Suppose that woman's boss had not come over right then. What would you have done?'

'Taken care of everything, that's what.'

'And how would you have performed this miracle?'

Imad was still smirking as they made their way south. He reached under the seat, pulled out a leather case, tossed it on the seat between them. Vladimir picked up the case, unzippered it, and looked inside. A semi-automatic pistol was in there. Holy shit.

He zippered the bag shut and threw it across the cab, where it bounced off the windshield.

'Hey!' Imad protested. 'What the fuck is your problem?'

'The problem is that you smuggled a pistol into Canada and then resmuggled it into the United States, you stupid shit – *that's* what the problem is.'

'Didn't get caught, did I?'

Vladimir felt his breathing quicken. 'Stupid fool. Worthless pile of shit.'

Imad said, 'Well, I had a plan, which is more than you had. Shoot that black woman between the eyes and then roll across into the highway. Who could have stopped us?'

Vladimir knew that he could no longer have a reasonable conversation with the boy. He folded his arms, looked out at the Washington landscape. A kilometer or two passed.

'Well?' Imad demanded. 'Why don't you answer me?'

Vladimir took a breath. 'Imad, why didn't you tell me about that? About having a pistol with you?'

Another bout of laughter from the boy. 'Maybe it's because I didn't think you needed to know. Hah. How does *that* sound?'

No reply. The truck and its cargo continued to speed its way into America.

Twenty miles east of the US Customs crossing station, Dan Umber sat in front of his computer terminal, trying to stifle a yawn as he came close to the end of his shift. He worked for the Department of Homeland Security, and his office was in the basement of an anonymous glass and steel cube that had sprouted up around Redmond after Bill Gates started making some serious change.

All around him in the dimly lit room were waist-high cubicle walls and terminals, just like the one he was sitting in front of. In front of him on the large plasma screen was a collection of faces – brown, white, yellow, red and every color in between, and male and female and a whole bunch of 'I'm-not-really-sure'.

Another yawn. The photos were coming in at a rapid pace from the Customs station just up the coast. Must be having a busy day there, for Dan was already over quota, and it might mean a chunk of overtime, if it played right. Which was not a problem, because he had his eye on a new WaveRider, and the extra cash would be just fine.

Face, face, face. Dan's job was to set them in some sort of order, following a template of ethnic appearance and background – hello, racial profiling – and then feed it along another chain of command until the photos, using the latest facial-matching software, were compared with the CIA, FBI and everybody else's watch-list of terrorists. Or, as some memos primly put it, 'persons of interest'.

Another sip of coffee. Most of the photos were straight-on head shots, but sometimes you had to deal with other types as well. Like those two. He clicked on the mouse, froze the program. Two guys standing outside, arguing, it looked like, with a female Customs officer. The head shots weren't so bad, but he had seen better. One guy was white, the other dark-skinned. Maybe Mediterranean. Hell, maybe Caribbean. Who knew?

Dan clicked the mouse one more time, as the program went on its merry way. He finished off the coffee. Just another day, he thought, in the front line against terrorism.

CHAPTER TWENTY-THREE

Brian Doyle sat in his room at a Sheraton Hotel in Memphis, staring at the phone. Another in a series of lousy phone calls with the growing young boy who was his son, and who still couldn't understand why dad couldn't do a better job of being around. Good question, boy, and time to get somebody to answer it for you.

He got up and left the room. It was late at night: he didn't know the particular hour and he didn't particularly care. The hotel was nice, with an outdoor cafe covered with canvas awnings and an outdoor pool, but he didn't give a shit about that stuff right now. He strolled down the hallway until he found the door he was looking for, and he gave it a good pounding.

No answer.

He resumed the hammering on the door.

Down the hallway, a young guy poked his head out from an open door.

'Hey, will you shut the fuck up down there?' he called out.

Brian turned and glared at the guy. The guy rubbed at his face, muttered something, and went back into his room. Brian raised his hand again and then the door opened. Adrianna was there, yawning, wearing a white terrycloth robe.

'Brian . . . what is—'

He pushed by her and went into her room. 'We've got to talk now, princess, and I mean now.'

He turned to her, just as she closed the door. She tightened the robe around her neck. There were a couple of lights on in the room but the television wasn't on. He guessed that he had woken her up. He didn't care.

'All right, then,' she said. 'What's up?'

Brian said, 'Lots of things. Let's start with the first. Why am I here?'

'You know why.'

'No, I don't. Explain.'

Adrianna said, 'I needed some security assurance, with what Victor was carrying. It was essential that Victor and his package arrived at General Bocks's office without any difficulty.'

'Bullshit.'

Her expression didn't change. 'That's not bullshit.'

'Sure it is,' he said. 'Except for our regular meetings, most of us are out in the field, working on our own little assignments, whatever they are. When was the last time I was assigned security for anything? Short answer: never. So. Why am I here?'

Adrianna was silent. Brian stepped up to her, feeling the blood and the anger race through him. 'You know why I'm here. I'm the super-patriot sock puppet, brought out to help close the deal. The good general was waffling there yesterday and then you went into this God-bless-America routine that mentioned my dad died in the World Trade Center. That's why you brought me along. Nothing more than that. When it came to crunch time, you trotted out the story of the bereaved New York cop and his dead hero dad. Don't tell me anything else, Adrianna. Don't insult my fucking intelligence.'

She pushed at her hair with a free hand. 'I won't insult your intelligence, Brian. Security was one aspect of why you are here. And I confess the truth. Your personal history is another reason you are here. For that, I make no apologies.'

'Well, goodie for you. I'm getting the hell out of here, and the hell back to my job.'

Brian started to brush past Adrianna and she held on to his upper arm. 'Please. Just for a moment. May I say something?'

When Brian was in a pissy mood like right now, and especially when he was on duty, having someone grab his arm usually meant a quick slap and takedown or something equally violent. All right, but not now.

'Okay. Say whatever the fuck you want. But I'm still leaving here and paying whatever I have to pay to fly out of Memphis tonight and get back to New York and my boy and my job. And I don't care if the big nasty Feds cause me to lose a grade on my job or even bust me back to patrolman. So you say your piece.'

Her hand was still on his arm. 'I used you. For that, I apologize for hurting your feelings, but I do not apologize for using you. Brian, this war has been on for a few years and it is going to continue for a very long time. And if I use what I can to shorten this war, to protect my country, I will do what it takes. If it takes long hours and using trickery and bribes to achieve our objectives, so be it. And if it means causing the untimely deaths of ten thousand of my fellow citizens to save millions, then, I will do it. And if it means using a trusted colleague's heartbreaking story to help sway a man who can help save millions of Americans, then I will do it. With no more apologies than what I have given you.'

'All right,' Brian said, when she was done. 'Fair enough. Now it's my turn to say something.'

'Of course.'

He took a breath, felt the hot hammering in his chest. 'You talk about my heartbreaking story. You want to hear my real heartbreaking story, princess? Do you?'

Adrianna nodded, her touch still light on his arm. He said, 'All right, then. Here's a story for you. A story about a dad who got never higher than a sergeant in the department because he loved the bottle as much as he loved the job. And his family . . . who in hell knew what he loved there. He beat me and he beat my brother and he beat my sister. My sister is living somewhere in California, don't ask me where, because when she moved out she never told anybody where she was going. Only California. My brother is a psychologist on Long Island, no doubt because he wanted to learn more about what my dad was like and what made him tick. My father came home mean most every night, and you know what, sure, he died on September eleventh. But he was no fucking hero.'

The breathing was quicker now, and he was stunned that his cheeks were moist, which meant he had to be crying. But why in God's name would he be crying? 'And the day he died, like all those others, the story about him going back to look for people was just that. A story. He was in a men's room, probably sleeping off what had happened to him the night before, and when the plane hit his tower he got up and stumbled out. Knowing drunk old dad, he took a wrong turn and never made it out. That's the story of my dad, the hero, the story that you wave around like a pair of black lace panties, trying to get your way.'

'Brian, I—'

'And one more thing. At my dad's funeral, I couldn't cry a single fucking tear, and neither did my brother. But my mother did, she cried these big long bouts of tears, and in the funeral-home car, heading back after my dad was buried, she sat between us, her fists clenched, and she whispered something, something I think she let slip out, because she never repeated it, not once. But you know what she whispered?'

'No, Brian, I don't know what she whispered.'

'"Finally, he's gone,"' Brian said. 'That's what my mother said, after burying a man she'd spent nearly forty years with. "Finally, he's gone." And this is going to sound like the worst blasphemy, but she's been a happier woman ever since September eleventh, ever since that old drunk never came home. That's the story.'

Now Adrianna's hand went away from his arm, up to his shoulder, up to his cheek, to gently touch the tears, and he took a deep breath and lowered his head and kissed her and kissed her and kissed her, and she moved towards him, and he stepped back, and together they fell back onto her bed.

They drove east, along the long stretch of Interstate 90 that was flanked by forests and rocks and desert and scrub grass, and up ahead the silent and sharp peaks of the Rockies rose. It was night and the grumbling of the diesel engine made Vladimir sleepy. Up ahead, just a few more kilometers, was their destination, a small town in Idaho called Pinehurst. Imad was driving well, he had to give the little shit that, but the boy's smell and his incessant singing irritated him no end. There was a radio in the truck but the country and western twang-twang shit that they all played out here was enough to make him prefer Imad's singing.

Imad yawned and said, 'Such a big country.'

'Not as big as ours.'

Imad laughed. 'Still pissed at losing the Cold War, eh?'

'We didn't lose the Cold War. We were betrayed.'

'Bah. Same outcome, that's all. Your country humbled and prostrate. America astride the world. And here we go, fighting for what is right.'

'What is right . . . what do you think is right?'

'Me? What is right? I'll tell you this. What is the meaning of Islam, eh?'

'I don't know.'

'Islam means submission, submission to God and his holy word, through the Koran. Submission. The world will be at peace only when all submit to God's will, when all are believers. Islam. When the black flag of Islam flies over the White House and the baseball fields and football fields and schools here and elsewhere, then there will be peace. And I am fighting to secure this peace. This is what is right.'

After leaving the highway, they passed a street sign: WELCOME TO KIRKLAND: POP. 1661.

'We are almost there,' Vladimir said.

'And you? What do you fight for?'

'Later,' he said. 'Later. Find the address. Here.'

From his leather folder, Vladimir pulled out the directions for their destination. Imad eyed them and soon buildings appeared, one- and two-story buildings – how depressing to be out here in the middle of this desolate area. How to survive? How to live? And how did these odd people in this even odder country get the energy and the drive to accomplish everything they had done?

'Slow it down,' Vladimir said. 'I don't want some constable or deputy sheriff pulling you over for speeding.'

Imad muttered something. Vladimir knew it was an obscenity and didn't care. Imad took a left and they headed out from the center of town to a small shopping plaza. It was late and the stores were closed, but there was one place, well lit. The Space Station. Shoshone County's Finest Self-Storage Area.

'There,' Vladimir said. 'Pull over.'

The truck grumbled to a halt and he opened the door, stepped down, wincing as a cramp shot through his left leg. They were at a chain-link fence and a central gate, secured by a keypad. Vladimir punched in a series of numbers and there was an audible click. The gate automatically creaked open, its electric motor whining. When the gate was fully open, Imad shifted the Freightliner and the truck drove into the large parking area. Ahead of them were four low-slung buildings made of concrete blocks with slanted metal roofs, and with rolled-down doors that were secured by locks. Imad drove over to the furthest building on the left and Vladimir followed. Imad pulled ahead until the rear of the trailer was adjacent to one of the locked doors.

Vladimir walked up to the door, took the combination lock in his hands. The metal was cold. He waited for a moment before working the tumbler. For the past several months, his unseen handlers out there – he doubted it was a single man, for who could have done this all by himself? – had enticed him from his self-imposed exile in Central Asia, across Asia to Shanghai and elsewhere, paying him and pleading with him, and easing his way out here. From money transfers to package deliveries in out-of-the-way post offices, he had secured his fake identification, the travel papers, even the trucking documents that had gotten him and Imad through Canada.

At first he had thought the whole thing was an elaborate trap, to pull him out of his exile and to place him in a position where the American Special Forces could seize him and what he'd made . . . but that no longer made sense. They could have gotten him and Imad days ago – hell, weeks ago! If he had been left unmolested by the desire of some intelligence agency out there to find fellow travelers or co-conspirators, then by now the intelligence agency must know that they didn't exist. There was just him and Imad, the driver, and when this was through he had plans for Imad.

So.

Vladimir jiggled the lock in his hand. To carry on, or to walk way? There was enough money in his Cayman Islands account for him to live comfortably for the next decade or so, but he wanted more. And the 'more' he wanted wasn't just money.

Imad stuck his head out of the passenger's side window. 'What are you doing?' he called down. 'Have you forgotten the combination?'

Vladimir didn't bother to reply. He started turning the tumbler. There was a chance that it would all end here, that when the lock was unsnapped – like now – and the lock was pulled away – like now – and when he rolled up the metal door, black-suited American military men would tumble out, seizing him and Imad and beating them to the ground, and—

The door rattled up. From the outside illumination he could make out a light panel. He flipped on the switch.

Save for three black plastic cases, about a meter long and a half-meter wide, the storage compartment was empty.

So we go on, Vladimir thought. We go on.

Late at night in Maryland, Darren Coover sat in his easy chair in his condo unit, his NSA-issued laptop on his lap, the encrypted-data line working just fine, and everything was just fine, save for the throbbing headache he had at the base of his skull.

He was ego surfing, something most people did by keying in their names to Google and other search engines, to see what was out there on them. Big deal. He was ego surfing in a whole 'nother realm, trying to find out just how much weight his Tiger Team was carrying under the Final Winter scenario. He did that by searching through the various classified message boards out there to see what references there were for either Final Winter or Tiger Team Seven. Little-known fact after the cluster-fuck known as 9/11 was the extent that information sharing was going on among the various intelligence agencies and groups out there. Oh, the heads of the intelligence agencies would troop up to Capitol Hill every several months to get grilled by the senators and congress-critters on why intelligence sharing wasn't proceeding, how come agencies weren't talking to each other, haven't we learned anything since September 11 – and the whole damn thing was a fake and a fraud.

Truth was, communications had improved, communication was taking place, but why in hell would you want to publicize it? So it wasn't publicized, even as it grew. Poor intelligence-agency heads. Darren was certain that in their classified job descriptions there must be a sub-section or paragraph that stated, 'When required, the Director of Central Intelligence (or fill in the blank here of whatever agency you would like) will proceed to Capitol Hill, to experience filibustering and questioning from a group of people with the collective inquisitive intelligence of a tree sloth, and during that time the Director will express shock and dismay and will promise to do better concerning the state of his intelligence agency.'

Blah. Hope they got tidy bonuses for putting up with that shit.

So. Here he was, this late night, going into secure chat areas and message boards, trying to see what was there in preparation for Final Winter. And what he saw there terrified him.

There was nothing.

Nada. Zilch. Nothing.

Key in Final Winter and there were old reports about the anthrax-attack scenarios that Adrianna had previously outlined, and really old reports about Japanese attempts to bomb the Western (US) mainland with bubonic-plague-infested fleas during the Second World War by using huge helium balloons, but now ... Anything about Final Winter and what was coming down the pike shortly, which had caused him and his Tiger Team such heartache and grief?

Nothing. Except a cryptic comment in a minutes report for a Tiger Team meeting held last week at Andrews Air Force Base, where it was stated that A. Scott had briefed the Director about Final Winter, and that authorization had been granted to proceed.

Authorization? All right, then, but where in hell was everybody else? The security hunts for the Syrian teams supposedly moving in the States, with their rental cars and plastic baggies of anthrax spores? Where were the public-health and CDC teams? Hell, where were the classified call-ups of certain National Guard and Reserve units?

Nothing.

It was like Final Winter didn't exist.

Darren paused, chewed on a thumbnail.

But if it didn't exist, what in hell were they doing? What was going on?

Puzzles and questions. As a proud member of the NSA, he hated them both.

Adrianna Scott rested her head on Brian's shoulder, her heart still pounding, still reeling a bit from what had just happened. It shouldn't have happened, couldn't have happened, it threw a lot of things in the air, it put a lot of things in jeopardy. Just a few minutes ago, when their breathing had eased and things had calmed down, the two of them had had The Talk about how this was a mistake and it shouldn't have happened, enjoyable as it had been, and things were too hectic and Final Winter took precedence over everything, and after The Talk she knew everything should have been fine. But it wasn't.

Adrianna could not help herself, but something about this New York City cop was calling to her, was making her giddy like a schoolgirl, a feeling she had not experienced for many, many years, all the way back to that sweet young boy in Baghdad and—

'Hey – you okay?' Brian asked her, in the darkness of the room.

'Yes, yes, just fine,' she said.

'Okay,' he said, squeezing her shoulders with his strong arms, kissing the top of her head – ah, how sweet the touch – and he said, 'You shook there for a moment. A tremble. Like you were falling asleep and suddenly had a bad dream.'

A bad dream, yes, a dream about Baghdad . . . and she pushed that thought away.

'Yes, I was falling asleep, but no bad dream,' she murmured. 'I was just thinking . . .'

'About what?'

Adrianna rubbed her face against Brian's hairy chest. She liked hairy chests. She said, 'Work, what else? I think the team should come out to Memphis. Stay close to here and oversee the project at AirBox. Perhaps we should take rooms in the hotel.'

She sensed his smile in the darkness. 'Perhaps. And perhaps we will share room keys?'

Adrianna raised her head and kissed Brian on the lips. 'Perhaps. We will talk about it later . . . right now, no . . .'

'Okay,' he said, pulling her down again with his strong arms. Adrianna felt safe and secure – and puzzled at how this man was affecting her. He said, 'What do we do now?'

She snuggled into his arms again, feeling content and sleepy, and smiling at the thought that this was the first man she had slept with in a very long time that she had not killed. It was an odd and glorious feeling.

'Nothing,' she said. 'We do nothing.'

In Idaho, the switch took just a few minutes, the time it took to empty out some of the Chinese-made toys from the trailer and fill up the empty space with the heavy black containers that had been in the storage facility. Vladimir and

Imad then put some of the toys back into the truck. There. Still looked nice and peaceful. Imad leaped up, grabbed the leather strap at the rear of the trailer and pulled down the sliding door. The rattling noise was loud in the empty lot. Vladimir went back to the storage trailer, closed the door, locked it. There were probably ten or twelve cases of toys in there.

Imad joined him. 'So what happens to those toys now?'

Vladimir said, 'They will stay here forever, I suppose.'

Imad said, 'A pity. I know some children from poor families in Vancouver. They would enjoy them. Forever, you say?'

Vladimir looked around at the empty parking area, the lights from the sleeping town. This is what it will be like, he thought, in so many places across this country. The streets will be empty and there will be no traffic and, so long as the power generators keep working, the lights will come on at night, all the while the bodies in the bedrooms and living rooms and hospital rooms will decay and dry out and rot . . .

He said, 'I suppose the owner of the facility could open it, but what for? In a matter of weeks, there will be much more important things to concern themselves about than toys in a storage area. No, they will be here forever, until archeologists from Russia or China or Brazil come here to explore the dead cities and dig up the bones.'

Imad rubbed at his hands. 'I'm cold. Let's get out of here.'

'That sounds fine.'

In a few minutes they were back on the highway, heading east, and Vladimir felt more awake. Being outside in the Idaho air had woken him up, and seeing another checkpoint's assignment successfully carried out cheered him. Just a few more things to do before they reached their destination – and before he reached his destiny.

Imad shifted the truck into a higher gear and said, 'I asked you earlier, before we got to that town. What do you fight for?'

'Excuse me?'

'What do you fight for, Vladimir? Do you fight to see the red banner rise again? To see the Soviet Union come back upon the world stage and take its leading role? Do you want to have Russians take over this land? What do you want?'

Vladimir looked out at the painted lines flashing before them as they rolled along the highway. He said, 'Nothing as complicated as that. I just want to smash. And kill. That's all. There are times for politics and discussion and great thoughts, and there are times to be barbarians. I want to be a barbarian. I want to smash and kill.'

Imad laughed at that. He kept a merry smile on his face as they continued their drive, and the sun rose on their faces.

In a chair that had been occupied a day earlier by Dan Umber, Blythe Coonrod worked the evening shift in a part of the government archipelago in the United States that was the Department of Homeland Security. It had been a quiet evening, just going over the previous shift's downloads, making sure the in-house servers were chugging along merrily. But as she sipped her first cup of tea of the evening and thought about heading out of the room for a comfort break, it looked like the screen on the monitor had frozen.

Everything on the screen had turned black.

'Christ,' Blythe whispered as she leaned forward – her ID badge, hanging from a thin chain around her neck, clinked against her keyboard – and then she dropped the cup of tea when a bright red icon with a flashing light appeared.

A real-time hit. Be damned.

She moved the cursor, double-clicked on the icon.

WATCH LIST MATCH.

ENGAGE YOUR PROTOCOLS.

WATCH LIST MATCH.

ENGAGE YOUR PROTOCOLS.

'Holy shit.' Blythe couldn't remember the last time – if ever! – her shift had experienced a real-time hit on the watch list. She made another move with the mouse. Waited. Somewhere deep in the pedabytes of information that the numerous American intelligence agencies stored were thousands of photographs of men and women of interest who were on the watch list. The system she was working matched those photos with all the people coming into the United States at any recognizable crossing – JFK airport, LAX, San Diego, little burgs in Maine or Vermont, for example – and it looked like she had just received a live one.

There.

Photos came up . . . and . . .

'Fuck,' Blythe whispered.

Both shots taken yesterday at the Customs crossing in Washington State. The original photos were displayed, showing two men talking to a Customs officer. And there, the photos in the intelligence database, showing what had been triggered. She didn't know all the particulars, but she did know that the facial-recognition software looked at key points on a person's face, everything from the size of the nose to the distance between the eyes to hair length and color.

First up, Yemeni national called Imad Yussef Hakim, age twenty-three, connected to al-Qaeda and other Islamic groups, traveling with—

A Russian national believed to be dead. Who certainly wasn't. Jesus.

Vladimir Zhukov.

And then Blythe saw his background and—

She opened a side drawer so hard that people around her craned their heads in her direction to see what was going on. In the drawer, sitting alone, was a thin folder, bound by a red paper ribbon. She lifted up the folder, broke the paper seal, and opened it. Her hands were shaking. She had never opened this type of folder before, except during training, so many innocent months ago.

Blythe flipped open the thin red cardboard cover. A single sheet was stapled inside with three instructions:

DENOTE DATE AND TIME OF WATCH LIST MATCH.

With a black Bic pen, she did just that.

CONTACT EXTENSION 4444.

She picked up the phone, dialed the four digits.

IDENTIFY YOURSELF AND REPORT STATUS TO OPERATOR.

A bored young man's voice: 'This is Operator Four-four-four-four.'

'This is Blythe Coonrod, Redmond Station. I have a Watch List match.'

'Your monitor identification?'

She peered at the letter and number sequence embossed on the sleek black plastic case.

'Four one two, B as in Bob, C as in Charlie.'

'Repeating, four one two, B as in Bob, C as in Charlie.'

'Correct.'

The man said, 'Remain at your station, please. You'll be contacted in sixty seconds or less for follow-up. Understood?'

'Understood.'

The man hung up. So did Blythe.

She folded her arms. She suddenly no longer had the urge to go to the bathroom.

CHAPTER TWENTY-FOUR

It was early morning in Memphis, and Brian Doyle sat alone, back in his room, sipping a cup of coffee, watching the hazy early-morning sunshine over the Mississippi River. He felt tired and flat and tangled up. What had happened last night with Adrianna had happened, and he didn't feel guilty about it. Not at all. It had been nice and delightful and tasty and all that good stuff. But what was pissing him off was what had happened about an hour ago. The woman had woken up in a panic, like she had realized that instead of bedding Mr Right she had bedded Mr My-God-I-Can't-Believe-What-I've-Done.

So Adrianna had bustled him out of her room, thoughts of having breakfast together put aside, thoughts about what he had said about his dad put aside, his demand to be sent back to New York put aside. All put aside. Hell, even what he had going on for today: put aside. As he had left Adrianna had called out, 'Take the day off, Brian. I've got other meetings with the General and his people . . . please, take some time.'

Which was a pretty clear message. Brian had fulfilled his duty earlier, with Adrianna using his father's death to score points with the General, and to get the General and his company to sign on for Final Winter.

Duty.

He went over to his luggage, picked up a carry-on case. It was locked and he put in the combination, popped it open, and from inside he took out a file folder. Presented to him a few days ago by the good colonel, the Director of the Tiger Teams. A peek into Adrianna Scott's life and background. Part of his job with the Tiger Team, part of his secret duty.

Brian held the file in his hand. He'd remembered earlier that he was going to review this file once Final Winter was done and over, and that had made sense at the time. But now . . . What the hell, if Adrianna had told him to take the day off, then what was he going to do today? Go to Graceland? Stay here and watch soaps and order room service?

He went over to a small round wooden table, sat down, opened the file and started to read.

In Maryland, Montgomery Zane was in the small kitchen area near the conference room, which was next to the offices for his fellow Tiger Team members. The damn place was empty, with the Princess, the cop and the doc out on a run to Memphis, and the code-puzzler not having shown up yet. Which was fine, since lots of times the Tiger Team members kept to their own lives and schedules and long ago, coming in, he had reserved the right to go on special missions without much oversight from the Princess. Like his recent adventures overseas, triggered only by pager and text messages from those who had the power. No big deal.

Monty poured himself coffee in a big mug that had Seal

Team Six and the trident-and-eagle insignia of the Navy Seals glazed onto it. He leaned against the counter, wondered about what to do next, which was a very big deal. In his old units, having something squirrelly come up just meant going to your CO about what was what. And what Bravo Tom had told him yesterday had kept him up for most of the night. If such a heavy shit-storm was heading their way in just a couple more weeks, then why was Bravo Tom going on leave? Why was his unit involved in nothing more arduous than the usual deployment and training schedule? What in hell was going on?

He took a swallow from his mug and looked up and saw that an answer to what was going on had just come into the kitchen.

Victor Palmer sat in his hotel room, staring at the locked case on the table. The cable was once more connected to his wrist. Adrianna was coming over to pick him up, to head over to the AirBox facilities to brief the General and his head machinist over what they were going to do with the dreamy little canisters that Victor's crew had thought up, and his stomach churned at what was going to happen in just a few short days. The whole idea of the terrorists slipping past the border with their little plastic containers of anthrax was still esoteric to Victor's mind. This, the canister in the metal case at his side, this was real. It was something that he could touch and feel. It was going to happen and what was going to happen sickened him.

It was easy enough to think of what was out there. Thousands upon thousands of innocents . . . slumbering in their beds, hanging on to some sort of life in hospital rooms or hostels, the very young, the very old, the very sick . . .

thousands for sure, and each one of them counted, each one of them was cared for and loved and had a life and history . . .

Thousands upon thousands.

All up until that night in the future, when the aircraft of their nation would take off in the middle of the night, and silently and secretly descend upon their cities and homes, spraying out something invisible to the eye. And in a matter of weeks they would all be dead.

Thousands upon thousands.

And Victor had helped it along.

My God, he thought, his stomach spasming and rolling: this is what it must have been like to have been a medical officer at Auschwitz or Birkenau or Bergen-Belsen . . . this is what it must have been like to have the fate of thousands in your hands, and to wash yourself of concern about it, to leave it alone, because it was your duty. It was what had to be done. The few sacrificed for the many. Work will make you free. The lies of the ages.

My God. How could he go through with this?

He picked up the case, headed for the door. He wouldn't, that was how. He would walk out and run away, and maybe the Final Winter project would go on, but it would go on without him, and wouldn't Doc Savage be proud of what he was doing, to face up to evil and to fight it and—

Victor's hand was on the doorknob. All right, let's be honest, now. We're not facing evil. We're not even fighting it. We're just running away, and that's all we can do and—

Victor opened the door. Adrianna was standing there, wearing a smart black business suit. A slight smile was on her face and she was carrying her leather briefcase.

'Very good, Victor,' she said. 'You beat me to it. Are you ready?'

He looked at that confident woman's face, took a breath, felt the quivering in his knees ease up.

'Yes, Adrianna, I'm ready,' he said.

Darren Coover went into the kitchen near the conference room, saw Monty Zane standing there, leaning against the counter. The counter probably had to be pretty strong to handle a weight like that, all muscle and bone and sinew. Monty nodded at him and Darren nodded back, and he was going to grab a cup of coffee when Monty said, 'Ask you a favor?'

Darren tried to hide his amazement. He had always enjoyed what little interaction he had with Monty, and he had always been thankful that the military man had treated him with respect. There was usually very little love lost between those in the field and those 'info pukes' in safe areas who sometimes determined when and how military options would be used. There were untold tales out there, of Special Forces groups being sent into harm's way on the basis of information gathered by people like Darren only to have those ops turn disastrous because of bad info or bad intel.

So Darren was always grateful for Monty's attitude, and when the question was asked Darren quickly said, 'Absolutely.'

He grabbed his own cup of coffee and followed Monty into his office, which was austere compared with those of the other Tiger Team members. Desk, chairs, bookcase, computer terminal, and only a few photos, and then only of Monty and his wife and two kids. Having visited a number of military officers over the years, one thing Darren always counted on was a display of plaques or certificates or some other memorabilia. But not for Monty.

Monty settled back in his chair, the chair creaking ominously from his weight, and he said, 'Just come back from a job.'

'All right.'

'What kind of job doesn't matter. It was a job. But it was the afterwards that freaked me out.'

'Go on.'

Darren held his coffee cup still in his hands. If something was freaking out this soldier in front of him, he wondered if he really wanted to know what was going on. But he had to. His damnable puzzle-curiosity would not allow anything else.

Monty said, 'Don't know if you're aware, but there are . . . places where guys who are on jobs go to unwind before being sent back to their home base. Allows them to let off steam, relax, get a good meal and a drink. That's where I was yesterday, unwinding.'

Darren just kept his mouth shut, knowing the story would come at Monty's own good pace. Monty took a swallow of coffee and said, 'Met a guy there. Friend of mine. Done some training together, one op. He works for the Hymen Squad. Heard of them?'

'Yes,' Darren said, feeling pleased that he could show Monty that he was in the loop. 'Deep black support group. Working the borders, north and south.'

Monty nodded. 'Yeah. Pretty secret. Thing is, this buddy of mine's been assigned to the Hymen Squad for over a year. We got to chatting. Tell me, Darren, you being a bright guy and all, with Final Winter coming down the pike like it's supposed to be, what do you think my buddy would be doing?'

Even though he had just poured coffee into it, the mug in

Darren's hands felt suddenly cold. He said, 'I know what he *should* be doing. But you tell me what's really going on, Monty, after you've let me guess. Nothing. Am I right?'

The skin around Monty's eyes tightened a bit. Darren felt that for a guy like Monty that was a good way for him to show a surge of emotion. 'How did you know?'

'I didn't. But there's something you should know.'

'What's that?'

Darren shifted his legs, which had started trembling. 'You and I have clearances for lots of things. Not sure if you have it but I've got one called "Gatekeeper". Lets me go into classified and compartmentalized bulletin boards, discussion areas, that sort of thing. One of the changes since 9/11 was breaking down the information barriers. If a guy in the field from the CIA needed to know the background of a Pashtun chieftain in some remote village in Baluchistan, it might take a week or two through normal channels. But by using Gatekeeper, he could hear from an FBI source who fingered this character as an opium smuggler. Or it could be a Defense Intelligence Agency analyst who helped this chieftain smuggle out some SA-7 missiles. Guy could get the answer he needed in minutes, not days or weeks.'

'Sounds good. What's your story, then?'

Darren said, 'Pretty damn simple. I wanted to do like you did. Check out what other people were doing about Final Winter.'

Monty grimaced. 'Let *me* guess this time. Nobody's doing a damn thing.'

Darren nodded. 'Just found one contemporary reference, from a week ago, when Adrianna got the clearance from the Colonel to proceed. Besides that . . . nothing.'

Monty raised his coffee cup and then, as if he'd changed

his mind, lowered it to the desk. 'Don't like this, don't like this at all.'

'Me neither.'

'What do you think's going on?'

Darren said, 'Maybe Adrianna's got bum info. Or maybe people higher up aren't taking her seriously. Or maybe this damn thing is so secret and need-to-know that nobody else, ah, needs to know. Could be a lot of things.'

Monty said, 'Lot of things, none of them good. Look, Adrianna should be back from Memphis tomorrow. I think it'd be time for a meeting, don't you think? I want to feel good about what we're doing and right now I don't feel good at all.'

'Sure . . . unless, well,' and Darren found himself laughing.

'What's so funny?'

'Unless Adrianna's working for them. The enemy. Then saying something tomorrow might be bad for our health. But she doesn't fit the profile.'

'And what profile is that?'

'Angry Muslim male.'

Monty nodded, 'Yeah. Thank God for that.'

'True,' Darren said, not sure if he even believed in God. But still, it wouldn't hurt. 'Thank God for that.'

Now Vladimir and Imad were in a rocky area of Wyoming, flat sand and scrub brush and sharp peaks and not a hell of a lot else. Along the way Imad had stopped for a few short naps, and the Russian was amazed at how these naps had re-energized the youth. Imad had also driven the truck and its cargo with ease, impressing even Vladimir with his skill. He had said something and Imad, almost shyly, had replied, 'You learn a lot, driving in Damascus and Yemen. My uncle, once he moved us away from Canada, he owned a trucking company. He taught you once, and he taught you again with the end of his belt if you failed him in any way.'

Despite everything else, Vladimir was impressed with the young man. It certainly took skill to drive such a big rig, and to drive it on such a poor road, just dirt and rocks, indicated a rare talent. They had gotten here with the aid of a detailed map provided along with the other documents and, as before, the map had been right to the point, indicating a turnoff from the interstate near a town called Dayton, and yet another turnoff that had led to this dirt road.

'Up ahead,' Imad said. 'We will have gone two point three miles. I see where we are supposed to go.'

Vladimir nodded, saw the spot. There was a large expanse of rocks and boulders that rose up to the left, in a sort of overhang. Imad maneuvered the truck underneath the overhang and switched off the engine. The sudden lack of noise made Vladimir's ears ring. Imad opened the driver's-side door and got out, and Vladimir followed from his own side. The dirt crunched underneath his boots. It was hot and the air was dry and still. He shaded his eyes from the sun and looked out. Nothing. He looked up at the overhang of rocks. Good choice. Hidden away from any prying eyes, whether it were a Cessna or a Predator or a Keyhole satellite thousands of miles up.

Vladimir said, 'Feel like home?'

'What?' Imad said, coming over next to him.

'The desert. Doesn't it feel like home?'

Imad laughed. 'What do you think, all Arabs are Bedouins, longing for the simple life of tents and camels and oases and the shits? No, thank you. I like the cities and I like electricity and flush toilets. And I'd like to get this job done before this damn air dries out my face.'

'All right, then. Let's get it done.'

They went to the rear of the truck, where Vladimir unlocked the sliding door. It clattered up and again he and Imad dumped the brightly colored boxes of Chinese toys onto the dirt. This would be the last time they would have to use these damn plastic trinkets. The black plastic cases came out and Imad unsnapped the lids, propping them open. Vladimir looked at the equipment nestled in the gray foam, and Imad said, 'Who are they?'

'What do you mean? Our paymasters? Our bosses?'

'Yes,' Imad said. 'Who do you think they are?'

Vladimir said, 'Does it really matter?'

'No, not really,' Imad said. 'It's just that . . . well, whoever they are they must hate America very much.'

Vladimir reached down to help the boy take the equipment out. 'Then they have plenty of company, don't they?'

Alexander Bocks was in his office with two members of the Tiger Team and Randy Tuthill, who was sprawled out in one of Bocks's chairs and who didn't look very impressed with what he had heard. Earlier, Adrianna had protested that she only wanted to make the presentation to the General and no one else, and he had not allowed that. He had said, 'Randy knows my aircraft better than I do, and there's no way I'm going to be able to pull this off without his say-so. Miss Scott, Randy stays or you can find yourself another airline.'

So Randy had stayed, right through a repeated briefing about the upcoming anthrax attack and the options the Tiger Team and the intelligence community had reviewed and rejected – save for one, the clandestine immunization of a large chunk of the American population. At that little gem of information, Randy had raised an eyebrow and looked over at Bocks.

'So because of anthrax, the union got dental?' he asked.

Bocks said, 'What use is anything if the anthrax gets through?'

Randy shook his head. 'What a cluster-fuck. All right, then, why am I here?'

Bocks looked to Adrianna, who looked over to Doctor Palmer, who was pale and seemed to be sweating. Palmer cleared his throat and said, 'A section of the Centers for Disease Control has been working on the airborne immunization system for some time. The canisters with the vaccine are almost completed. They look like this.'

He reached down to the floor, pulled up his small case, opened it up. He pulled out the green canister – about the size of a large thermos bottle – and passed it over to Randy. The mechanic turned it around in his big hands and said, 'The vaccine will be contained in this?'

'Yes.'

'Is it safe?'

Bocks felt uneasy, knowing that this was going to be a tough one.

No one answered.

Randy looked at each of them.

'I said, is it safe?'

Bocks said, 'Doctor Palmer? If you please?'

The doctor looked like he was in the dock of a courthouse. He said, 'Like any type of vaccine, there will be side effects. The vast majority of the population exposed won't suffer any ill effects, or if they do, it will be minimal. There will be others – statistically, only a few – that may suffer severe effects.'

Randy said sharply, 'Up to and including death, right?'

'Correct.'

Bocks said, 'It's tough, Randy. But there doesn't appear to be any other option.'

Randy sounded grim. 'Of course there's always another option.'

Adrianna said, 'And what do you suggest?'

The mechanic kept on turning the canister in his hands. 'Killing the fuckers over there, instead of waiting for them over here. That's a better option.'

Bocks felt his breathing relax. Randy was going to be okay. Sure enough, his chief mechanic changed the subject with the next question.

'How will it be controlled?'

Palmer said, 'Entirely automated. There will be a two-part radio-altimeter switch. When the aircraft rises to a certain altitude, the canister will be activated. When the aircraft descends to a certain altitude, the canister will cycle open, and the spraying will commence.'

Randy said, 'And where in hell do you expect this to go? Duct-taped on an outside wing?'

Back into the case the doctor went, and he came out with a bunch of documents. He leafed through them until he pulled one out. Doctor Palmer said, 'AirBox flies the Boeing MD-11 aircraft, configured to haul cargo. It has twin Pratt and Whitney engines, and associated with these engines you have two air-conditioning packs. One for each engine. Correct?'

Randy said, 'You're doing fine, doc. Go on.'

Palmer said, 'These air-conditioning packs take hot air from the engines, pass it through a heat exchanger, and it's then compressed and cooled. This air is used to pressurize the cabin and cool the air in it. With each air-conditioning pack, there is an exhaust system. We've examined the schematics. There is a way of installing the canisters such that they bleed into the exhaust system. Entirely automatic. Nothing to be controlled from the cockpit.'

Bocks looked at the expression on Randy's face, wasn't sure what was going on there. He said, 'Doctor, if you could, please pass over the schematics to Randy. I want him to have a look at it.'

The papers went over. Adrianna sat there, hands folded. She seemed tense, coiled. Bocks could not imagine the pressure the woman was under. Randy flipped through the pages, grunted a couple of times, and then flipped through the pages again, more slowly. Outside, the sound of a jet taking off made the windows rattle for a moment.

Randy said, 'General, it looks like it can be done . . . but where's the Supplement Type Certificate? You can't just add something to an aircraft without an STC from the FAA.'

Bocks said, 'Miss?'

Adrianna said, 'We'll take care of the FAA.'

Randy shook his head. 'Maybe so. But Jesus, somebody there's gonna raise hell about us doing something like this. I mean, doing this without—'

Adrianna interrupted. 'Like I said, we'll take care of the FAA. The question I have is, can security be maintained? We can't have scores of mechanics installing the canisters and then talking about it later. There has to be some way of keeping this confidential.'

Bocks said, 'Don't worry about my crews. My big question is the time-line. What are you looking for in terms of aircraft?'

Adrianna said, 'Forty. We determined that with forty of your aircraft, we can successfully complete the immunization of about seventy-five percent of the urban population. The intelligence information we have indicates a half-dozen of our largest cities are targeted, as well as Washington DC.'

'What the hell happens to the other twenty-five percent?' Randy asked. 'They get written off?'

Bocks was beginning to admire the woman, for she had a sure touch with answering the tough questions. He had served with similar women in the Air Force, especially with those women who ran maintenance squadrons and who had ready answers and a poor appreciation of bullshit.

Adrianna said, 'The anthrax attacks will take place in our major cities. It doesn't make sense for an attack to take place in rural areas, so those areas won't be treated with the immunization program. We also realize that we have a limited number of aircraft. A number will be tasked to one city. Five, for example, for the New York City metropolitan area alone.'

By now, Randy was scribbling on the back of one of the sheets of paper with a pen. Bocks waited patiently, knowing that the answer Randy was about to give was going to be the right one. It might not be an answer that the group was looking for, but it was going to be the only answer that counted.

Randy dropped his pen. 'When do you want to fly?'

'As soon as possible,' she said. 'We believe the attack will take place in just under three weeks, on May 29.'

'We can do forty aircraft in four days, if we're lucky, if the FAA isn't up our ass, and if you get the canisters to us. When can you get them here?'

'Day after tomorrow.'

'You sure?' Bocks asked.

Adrianna's voice was full of confidence. 'Guaranteed, gentlemen.'

CHAPTER TWENTY-FIVE

For a while, the silence in the Wyoming desert was interrupted by the low hum of machinery as Vladimir and Imad worked to change what they had been driving. All exposed areas that weren't part of the main body of the truck and the trailer – tires, mirrors, windshield, mudflaps, front bumper – had been covered by heavy-gauge brown paper and secured by equally heavy tape. It had been long, hot work, and both men had stripped off their shirts. When the paper had been secured and double-checked against guidelines from one of the black plastic cases that they had picked up in Idaho, they had continued their work. Portable spray-painting machinery and folding aluminum scaffolding had helped them to turn a bright yellow trailer with Seamarsk markings into something olive drab and military-looking.

Now Vladimir stood back, eyeing the truck and the trailer, matching it up with sample photos and schematics helpfully provided by their unseen bosses. Imad came up to him, clear plastic goggles pushed up over his head, respirator hanging around his neck. His chest was dark brown and scrawny, with a thick mat of black hair. Behind him was the scaffolding surrounding the truck, and the chugging air compressor that powered the spray gun, the compressor in turn powered by cables leading to the truck's battery.

'Well?' he demanded. 'Are we done with this darkie work?'

'Soon,' Vladimir said. 'Very soon. We let this coat dry and then we can put on the new license plates and serial numbers, and other identifying marks. Another two hours, then we'll be done.'

'Good, because I'm about—'

There came the sound of an engine, overpowering the noise of the compressor. Vladimir turned and so did Imad. Vladimir said something in his own language – 'Fuck your mother' would have been the best English translation he could have come up with – and Imad said something in his own language as well.

Coming down the dirt road was a dark brown Jeep Wrangler with oversized tires, bounding its way towards them.

'Don't say anything, don't do anything,' Vladimir said. 'If we're lucky, they will pass us by. There must be something in here they want. They don't want us.'

But God and luck were not with them. The Jeep Wrangler skidded to a halt about a dozen meters away. Hanging from the rear of the Jeep was a collection of sacks and ropes, and two young men and two young women got out, talking and laughing. They wore T-shirts and sunglasses and expensive-looking sport clothes and sport footwear. They talked among themselves for a moment, and then the two men started towards Vladimir and Imad, shaking their heads.

'Not good,' Imad said.

'You are correct,' Vladimir said. 'Not good.'

*

In his rental GMC Pontiac – and why in God's name were so many rental cars white? Was it a global rental-car rule somewhere? – Brian Doyle sat on a side street in the Mt Auburn neighborhood of Cincinnati, going over his notes for the day. The Princess had supposedly given him the day off, and he had taken the day off, but being the enterprising sort he had taken a commuter shuttle from Memphis to Cincinnati to see what he could find.

And so far, in the few hours he had been here, he had found a lot of nothing.

He scratched at the back of his head.

This part of Cincinnati was a large hill that years and years ago had been the home of the city's best and brightest, including President William Howard Taft. But the years hadn't played nice with Mt Auburn, and it had fallen into the urban cycle of poverty and decay. Now it appeared that it was coming back, as gentrification worked its magical market ways. The changeover in home ownership and such had no doubt led to Brian's problems, for Adrianna Scott's presence here was as thin as a piece of paper soaked in the rain. There had been almost nothing, nothing at all, save for two things. One came from a visit to her high school, known here as the Hughes Magnet School. The place had been a seemingly well-managed chaos of students and teachers and administrative staff, and a half-hour there had produced paper records that matched what had been in his file, save for one thing that he had been looking for. Adrianna had told him that she had come here after her parents had died, and neither the high school nor the earlier report had any record of her transfer. It was as if she had arrived out of nowhere and had slipped right into the classes without any problem.

And she had done well, scoring high honors in almost everything. But her previous life, before her parents had died in that car accident . . . gone.

And the other lead, slim as it was, had led to this address. Adrianna's apartment, which she had shared with her aunt – one Elyse Annanova – had been flipped so many times with new tenants that no one had any memories of an older woman and her young niece who had lived there. The few neighbors home this day that he approached also gave him blank stares. Him being a white man in a suit in this neighborhood, asking nosy questions, probably didn't help either, though a local grocery store had helped just a bit. The older man there, wearing a spotless white apron and well-shined black shoes, had said, 'No, sir, I don't remember anything about that woman and her aunt. But I have somebody who might know something. That'd be Mamma Garrity. She lives over on Prospect Street now, but she used to live here, and I don't like to speak ill of the elderly, but my God, that woman can talk a hole through a tin pot, and if that woman and her aunt lived here, she'd know, by God.'

So by way of thanking the helpful grocer, Brian had bought a couple of six-packs of Coors that he didn't want. Now he was on Prospect Street – a bit of punnish humor from the Big Guy Upstairs? – and he got out of his rental car and walked up to the small house, ready to ring the doorbell and keep on digging.

And why was that? he thought. Because it was his job, or because he was pissed at the cold treatment he had gotten this morning from Adrianna?

Who knew? Brian rang the bell.

*

The two young American men came over to Vladimir and
Imad, gave them quick nods. Then one of them took off his
sunglasses and said something. Vladimir couldn't understand
what he said, the boy talked so fast, and so he replied,
'Excuse me?'

'I said, man, what the fuck is up here?' the youngster said.
He had a goatee and there were earrings in both ears. His
companion kept his glasses on and nodded, arms folded.
There were tattoos on both forearms. His companion said,
'This place is protected, dude. You can't be painting your
truck here. Do you have a permit?'

Vladimir thought as quick as he could, but these two
young males in front of him seemed as foreign as if they had
stepped out of a spaceship from Mars. Imad said quietly,
'Why don't you mind your own business, then?' The young
man with the folded arms stepped forward and said, 'This
place *is* our business, dude. Earth is our business. Protecting
it is our business. And we don't know what the fuck you're
doing, but we came here for a day of rock climbing, and we
see this . . . this fucking mess here. What's up with that?'

The boy without the sunglasses said, 'Like I said, do you
have a permit? Do you? This is National Forest land, man.'

The young girls had been busy, taking the gear from the
rear of the Jeep, and one shouted out something and the guy
said, 'Jackie's right, man. You get your stuff cleared up and
out of here, and like now, or we report you to the rangers.
Got it? Get your shit clean and out of here. You don't belong
here.'

Imad stepped forward and Vladimir grabbed his arm.
'Please,' Vladimir said, 'We're almost done. We will be on
our way shortly.'

'Nope,' the tattooed guy said. 'Out now.'

Vladimir said, 'Perhaps a payment for your troubles, some compensation, and—'

And then the goateed one, the one with earrings, actually spat at Vladimir. Spat on the ground!

'That's what we think of your cash, man. Nothing. We can't be bought. So get the fuck out, or the rangers get the call.'

The two strolled away and Imad looked at Vladimir, eyes dark with fury. 'We can't let them call the police or the rangers or anyone else. You know that.'

'I know.'

'Then what do you plan to do about it?' he demanded.

'I . . . I . . . something must be done,' Vladimir said.

'Yes, but what?'

Vladimir stammered, then went silent.

He looked over at the Jeep where the four were still busy, though they kept on looking over at him and Imad.

Imad looked at Vladimir with contempt, and said, 'You. Brave man who plans to kill millions. Strike a blow. Smash. Be a barbarian and kill. All talk. All empty air unless you are safe, away from seeing what you are doing, what must be done. You don't want to get your fingers dirty, your precious fingers. Am I right? Am I?'

Vladimir felt the burning of humiliation in his cheeks as the young savage in front of him spoke the truth. He could not say a word. He just nodded.

Imad now looked satisfied. 'Good. I will do what has to be done, Russian, so you know. I will do what has to be done, and from you there will be no more dismissive words or gestures or insults. Understood?'

Another nod.

Imad said, 'I did not hear you, Russki.'

'Yes,' Vladimir said. 'Understood.'

'Good.' Imad strode to the truck and Vladimir stood there, just watching, an observer.

From the Jeep Wrangler, some more laughter, and a shout from one of the men: 'I don't see you moving, asshole. Get moving or you'll regret it!'

And so Vladimir stood.

The interior of the living room was dark, with the lights on low and the shades drawn. Mamma Garrity was an old woman, in her eighties or nineties, who moved slow and whose dark skin was wrinkled and lined, but whose tongue was sharp to go along with an equally sharp mind. She had invited Brian in after he had shown his identification, and now he was sipping a lukewarm glass of lemonade as she sat across from him in an overstuffed easy chair that looked like it was ready to swallow her whole. For about a half-hour she had talked to him about growing up in Cincinnati, about her youth and courting and marriage and two sons and three daughters and numerous grandchildren and great-grandchildren, about her hip-replacement surgery and her sore knees and cataracts, and using the listening skills that he had developed over the years at the NYPD Brian had nodded at all the right places, until finally Mamma Garrity had slowly used up her memories and stories, and had seemed to focus

'Mmm . . . Detective Doyle, you're asking me about that Scott woman . . . and her aunt – correct?' she said.

'That's right, ma'am,' Brian said, trying not to show any expression as he swallowed the warm, sour mixture. By his side was a fireplace, blocked off, with rows of photographs lined up on the mantelpiece, photos of families and young men and old women and serious-looking men in uniform, firefighter uniform, Navy uniform . . . a whole spectrum of an old woman's life, frozen forever with photo paper and chemicals.

The old woman said, 'Yes, I remember her now. Elyse Annanova . . . kept to herself. A well-dressed woman. Went to church every Sunday. A clean, quiet life . . . and then her niece moved in suddenly. There had been death in that young girl's family. So she came in and she kept to herself – the both of them. Just went to church every weekend, saw them in the local markets . . . kept to themselves. Quiet neighbors. Wish we had more of them.'

'Did you ever see if they had any visitors?'

'Not that I can recall . . . you see, it was different, back then. Before the money came in. Before those yuppies bought up buildings and such . . . not that I mind much, I mean, money is green and doesn't really care what color your skin is, am I right?'

Brian said, 'Yes, I believe you're right.'

Mamma Garrity smiled at him, like a retired teacher pleased at the progress of a long-ago student. 'Yes . . . yes, I do believe I'm right. So. Is there anything else I can help you with?'

He managed another sip of the sour lemonade. 'No, I'm afraid that's all. I'm very grateful for your time, Mrs Garrity.'

She smiled. 'It's so nice to have visitors . . . and this pains me to say this, detective, but . . . well, you said you're with the Federal government, am I right?'

'I'm attached to the Federal government, yes, in assisting them with inquiries about certain issues.'

'Like Miss Scott's life, right?'

'That's one of my roles, yes.'

She nodded, her smile in place. 'And this all confidential,

am I right? Everything I say to you is just as if I was talking to the government. Right?'

This was going in an odd direction. 'Yes, you're right. All confidential.'

Mamma Garrity seemed pleased as she nodded again. 'Good. I've been wondering for a very long time who I should complain to. You see, ever since I moved here, after my oldest son moved to Detroit and gave me this home, I haven't been getting my money. And I wonder if you can help me out.'

Brian said, 'You mean your Social Security?'

She laughed. 'Oh no, not that. My Social Security comes right as it's supposed to – one of the few things in God's world you can count on. No, it's the other money that I've missed, ever since I moved. The support money.'

Brian's head felt foggy, as if he had woken up from an unexpected afternoon nap. He had been seconds away from leaving this musty old house and tossing the Adrianna Scott file into his luggage, ready to ignore it for another few weeks. Until this.

'Mrs Garrity, I'm sorry that I don't understand about the support money, but if you let me know what it's about I'll see that you get it.'

Now she was a bit suspicious. 'Including the past months? I warn you, it's going to be a large number.'

'Sure. Whatever it is, I'll make sure.'

'Well . . . I hate to bring it up, but I was promised. And the others, we were promised, too, and we all got those checks, month after month. After a while, you got to depend on them. We surely did. And trust me, I think I might be the last one alive . . . but still, a deal is a deal, right?'

'Yes, you're absolutely right,' Brian said, looking at that

old, calm face. Mamma Garrity's words were making his fingertips tingle at the thought that something was going on.

He said, 'Tell me all about it, right from the beginning, and then I'll take care of it.'

Another sweet look. 'That's nice. I mean, we were told never to open our mouths, never to say anything. And we were told that if we did say something the money would stop, and the IRS would be called in, and we'd have to pay back taxes and penalties, and maybe even go to jail – for breaking our deal. So I'm not in trouble, am I? I mean, I've always kept my end of the deal. I've never said anything, until right now. It's her fault, you know, since the money's stopped. She broke the deal first.' The old woman's voice was now defiant, and he found himself liking her spirit.

'And who's "she", ma'am?'

The old woman seemed to struggle for a moment, and then said, her voice just above a whisper.

'Adrianna.'

Oh, Brian thought. Oh, shit. 'Go on,' he said. 'From the beginning, Mrs Garrity. Tell me what happened.'

She said, 'Oh, it was some years ago. Right after she had graduated from college. She came back and talked to me and talked to Mrs Grissom, from upstairs, and Mister Conklin, he served in the Navy, he was downstairs. Just the immediate neighbors, the three of us. She showed us some paperwork that said she was working for the government. For the CIA. It was a very important job that she was going to get, very important, but there was one thing she asked us to do, and it wasn't really a lie, it was part of the program, to get in. She said officers needed a . . . what did she call it? What do you put on a book? You know . . . a . . .'

The tingling in Brian's fingers was now up to his forearms. 'A cover. That's what she said. A cover. Am I right?'

A little series of nods, like an old bird dipping her beak into a water glass. 'That's right. A cover. She had to have a cover story in order to do her job well, and she asked the neighbors if they would help her out. And who wouldn't? Such a nice girl! And she promised us that we would be paid, every month, one hundred dollars, if we told the same story to anybody who came by and asked questions about her.'

Brian tried to pay attention to what he was hearing, but his mind was racing along on another path. He thought about a young Adrianna Scott who had graduated from college, who had gotten an interview with the Central Intelligence Agency, was going through the vetting process. Somehow, she has something in her past that must be hidden. Something that can't be uncovered by the background checkers in the employ of the CIA. She's fortunate in that her circle of neighbors are poor and are quite limited in number. So payments – all right, bribes – are made to present the perfect cover story. And what was the perfect cover story?

Brian said, 'Ma'am, I'll be able to pay some of your back payments today, and I promise that you'll get the rest by the end of this week. But can you tell me, what was the story that you were asked to provide?'

'Well! It was all kind of strange, you know . . . it was very simple. We were asked just to tell anyone who came by to ask questions that Adrianna had moved in with her aunt at a very young age. When that wasn't the truth at all.'

'I see. And when did Adrianna move in with her aunt?'

'Oh, I don't know the date . . . but I do know that she was

a teenager, a young girl. A very pretty young girl but a teenager nonetheless. And unlike the other girls of her time . . . she was different.'

'How was she different?'

And the old woman gave Brian a knowing look, one mature adult to another. 'Oh, come now, Mr Doyle. You know what I mean. Tight blouses, tight jeans, skirts up to here . . . wearing that awful jewelry . . . strutting their wares so the boys would notice. But not Adrianna. She spent two years here, I believe – before going off to college – and not once did I ever see her with a boy. She was very serious, too serious. Always seemed to be studying . . . like she had some big goal in front of her . . . and we respected her, yes, we did. Which was why we agreed to that odd request of hers.'

'And her aunt? What was her aunt like, during all of this?'

Mamma Garrity clasped her hands together. 'Oh, the poor dear. Do you know what happened to her? She died, just before Adrianna left for college.'

'She did, did she? And how did she die?'

The old woman made a cluck-cluck noise as she shook her head. 'Poor dear was murdered. Suffocated in her own bed by someone who held a pillow over her head. Can you imagine that? What an awful coincidence, just as Adrianna was getting ready to move out.'

Brian nodded slowly, feeling cold. 'Yes. What an awful coincidence.'

Vladimir saw the whole thing unfold in front of him, as if he was an extra in a stage production, destined to observe and stand still and watch all that happened.

Imad strolled over to the four young men and women, confidence in his step, one hand held out in a friendly greeting, the other behind his back, holding the automatic pistol. There was bile at the back of Vladimir's throat as he saw what was going on, and a part of him that he thought was civilized, a part that he had left behind in Mother Russia, that part of him wanted to warn the four rock climbers out there – children, really – of what was approaching them. For death was walking near, with a friendly smile and a hand held out in friendship. He wondered if this was what it was like in Palestine, when the suicide bombers approached a school bus or a nightclub or a pizza parlor with that same mystic confidence that they were doing God's work.

Vladimir did not believe in God, had never believed in God. But now, in this American desert, he was sure that he believed in the Devil.

One of the young men called out something and Imad replied in a friendly voice as he approached them. He said something else, and the four came to him. Vladimir thought, how sly, he got them to come to him and—

Imad's hidden hand whipped out, and Vladimir saw the confusion in the rock climbers' eyes. What could this mean? How was this happening? How had a safe day of rock climbing and adventure and a lunch eaten in the wilderness and a night ahead planned, perhaps a restaurant with a good meal and cold beer and lots of laughs and lovemaking later – how had it turned into this?

How?

They started to move but, like sheep before a wolf, they moved too slow and they moved separately. If they had been smarter and tougher – there were four of them against Imad – maybe something could have been done. But this was not a day for maybes and—

The first shot seemed to hit the tattooed man in the

chest. He fell to his knees. The next shot caught the other young man in the side as he was turning, his goateed face twisted in fear and horror.

Vladimir thought, the Arab boy's doing well, shooting the men, the obvious threats first, and now—

Now the women were screaming, turning to flee.

Imad shot each of them once in the back.

He paused.

All four young people were moving some. The tattooed man was on his knees, hands at his chest.

Imad stepped behind him, placed the muzzle of the pistol against the back of his skull, fired again. The tattooed man fell forward.

The goateed man was yelling, 'Please, Jesus, don't, please, don't . . .' as he tried to get up, one hand on the ground, the other hand against his side.

Imad moved again. Pistol barrel against the rear of the head.

Another shot.

Vladimir closed his eyes.

The girls were screaming and crying and then there were two more shots.

Then silence.

The Russian opened his eyes.

Imad strolled back, smiling, the pistol now tucked in his waistband.

'We have work to do,' he said.

Vladimir said, 'Yes, we do.'

He swallowed and followed Imad back to the Jeep Wrangler. It took a while. From the gear of the rock climbers, he and Imad took out ponchos and tarpaulins. Once the material was spread over the bodies, it was easier to work, for they didn't have to look at their victims' faces, didn't have to look at the blood and exposed bone and brain tissue. Vladimir worked with the Arab in wrapping up the bodies and tying them tight with bungee cords.

It took some work, but the bodies and the gear were eventually placed in the Wrangler. Vladimir was breathing hard and his legs and arms hurt when they were through. He said, 'It looks like you have experience with this, wrapping up bodies.'

Imad laughed. 'Yes. Bodies in the desert. Some experience. We don't have time to bury them, so to wrap them up like this is the next best thing. Keeps animals and vultures away for a while, so there are no curious people wanting to know why the animals are excited. Not good enough to last very long, but long enough for us to be on our way.'

Vladimir nodded, rubbed his shaking hands. Imad said, 'I will drive this Jeep away and be back in a few minutes. It shouldn't take long to get out of here.'

Another nod. Vladimir couldn't think what to say to the boy.

He walked back to the truck and started packing up gear they had used. He stripped away the heavy brown paper and then put on the new license plates. Using large decals, he followed the design schematics and made the truck into something else.

Imad came back after a bit, whistling, and they broke down the scaffolding, not saying anything except what had to be said to get the job done. Vladimir watched the boy work, wondering what was going on behind those calm brown eyes, those eyes that had seen what had to be done and whose owners had then done it. Killed four complete strangers, two young men and two young women, with hardly a moment of hesitation or guilt.

And he, the mighty doctor from the old, terrifying Soviet Union? He had almost pissed his pants like a Gorky Park drunk at the thought. But the barbarian youth, he had killed when necessary – and had done it with skill.

Now the truck, smelling of fresh paint, was loaded. Vladimir went up into the cab. Imad turned the key, the diesel engine grumbled into life and, once more singing some Arab tune, Imad maneuvered the tractor-trailer truck back out onto the dirt road. In a matter of minutes they were on the interstate highway, heading east. The air-conditioning had kicked in and Vladimir felt himself relaxing, just a bit. He said, 'Where did you put it?'

'Put what?'

'The Jeep. The bodies.'

Imad said, 'The Jeep went down a ravine. The bodies stayed inside. The Jeep may be found tomorrow, or next week, or next month. And by then, who cares?'

Vladimir looked in the rearview mirror. The sun was beginning to set. If all went well, they would be in Memphis in just under two days.

'You . . . you did well, back there,' he said.

Imad grinned. 'Thank you. And hold on, I have a souvenir for you.'

The boy steered with one hand as he put his free hand into his pants pocket. Out the hand came, stretched across the cab interior.

'Here,' Imad said. 'Evidence. Just for you.'

Something metallic tumbled into Vladimir's hand. He looked down. Empty shell casings. Imad said, 'Evidence. A good shooter picks up after himself. So this is my gift to you. Evidence of what I just did.'

Vladimir looked at the little bits of worked metal, wondered how things so small could be so deadly. And he thought of the canisters that rested comfortably behind his head, back there in the trailer, ready to kill millions. Also small and deadly.

He rolled the passenger's-side window down, stretched his arm out, and tossed the empty brass casings to the side of the road.

Imad laughed again. Vladimir rolled the window back up, and kept quiet for another hundred miles.

CHAPTER TWENTY-SIX

It was dusk as Brian Doyle finally emerged from Mamma Garrity's home in Cincinnati, trying to factor in what he had learned and what it might mean. He was thinking these things through as he got to his rental car, which was when they jumped him.

Brian's first thought as he heard the approaching fast footsteps and felt the hands grabbing him was, oh man, did we fuck up, and won't our partner laugh his ass off at what just happened. And then the punching and voices started.

'Get the motherfucker . . .'

'Grab 'em . . .'

'Shit ass, where's your fuckin' wallet . . .'

Brian was spun around and he threw a punch, caught someone a glancing blow on the side of the face. He took quick stock – four of them, four young 'uns, pukes, scrotes, yutes, whatever you wanted to call them – and he lashed out with a fist, catching one of them on the nose. A yelp and then something sharp sliced through his shirt and there were more punches, and his belt felt so light, so fucking light, because back home he'd be carrying his Motorola hand-held, a quick toggle of the panic switch or call for a 10-13, requesting back-up, but now there was nothing.

Save for one thing.

He reached around to his rear waistband, breathing hard and struggling, the young men clearer now in the glow from a nearby streetlight, more hands punching and slapping at him, something warm on his chest, and he got it, he got his 9mm Smith & Wesson out, out enough to slap one guy in the head with it, and the sight of the metal got everybody's attention. Like a sudden breeze they were gone, their sneakers slap-slapping on the sidewalk as they faded out.

Now Brian was tired, very tired, and he leaned back against the hood of his rental car, the pistol wavering in his grip. It was heavy, as heavy as he could ever remember it.

'Shit,' he said, his mouth dry. 'Damn.'

He touched the front of his shirt. It was wet. He touched it again. The cloth had been torn away. Now he felt light-headed. He put the pistol back in his waistband holster, touched his skin again.

It burned.

And it was very wet.

Brian held up his hands to the illumination from the street lights.

His hands were covered with blood.

From the Homeland Security building in Washington State that had first detected the border crossing of Vladimir Zhukov and Imad Yussef Hakim, the information was reviewed, enhanced and sent upstream to the Homeland Security office near Spokane that was responsible for the entire Northwest United States. A helicopter was dispatched to the Customs border crossing and by day's end two very tired and confused Customs officers were being debriefed by an ex-Air Force Special Operations Master Sergeant named Jason Janwick. This man loved his country, loved his service, hated terrorists, and would be out capping them with his crew had it not been for a bad heart that threatened every day to drop him like a gut-shot deer, and while he didn't particularly like his present job it was the best he could do.

Now he was talking to a bright Customs officer named Tanya Mead, who seemed almost relieved as she gave him her read on what had happened earlier in the week with Zhukov and Imad. Janwick kept his eye on her as she talked, gauging her response, seeing what kind of words she chose and how she said them. Janwick had a pretty good built-in bullshit detector – you had to, when you worked with guys who sometimes packed each other's parachutes – and he liked what he saw. He sure as hell hated the fucking message he was receiving, but he liked her.

With the two of them in this small meeting room were members of his staff, some of whom joined in with the questioning. When they were done, he stepped in.

'These two – they had valid travel documents and identification. Correct?'

'Yes, sir, that's correct,' Tanya said.

'Accents?'

'Yes – both very slight. Hard to pin down.'

Janwick said, 'You've given us some good information. What else can you tell us?'

'Sir?'

Janwick tried to be patient. 'Something that we've not asked you. Something that stuck in your mind. Anything else you can come up with.'

Tanya said, 'Well . . .'

'Go on.'

'I think they hated each other.'

'What?'

The young woman looked around the room for a moment and said, 'You see a lot of truckers crossing where I work. Part of the job. Most times it's single truckers . . . it's expensive for trucking companies to send out a two-man crew. And when you see a two-man crew, sometimes it's a man-and-woman crew. A married couple. And when you do get a two-man crew . . . they, well, they get along. They have to. Otherwise they'd end up killing each other or abandoning their partner at a rest stop somewhere. But not these two. It's like . . . it's like the older guy couldn't believe he got paired with that younger guy, and the younger guy, it was like it was all he could do to keep himself from cutting the older guy's throat. I think they really hated each other.'

Janwick saw his team taking notes. They were a good bunch. He said, 'You've done well, Officer Mead. If you like, we can get you back home tonight. Or you can spend the night here. We'll put you up in a nice place. Oh. And one more question.'

'Sure.'

He said, 'I know this is forward and all that, but would you like a new job?'

'Sir?'

Janwick liked the expression on the young woman's face. He also liked to surprise people. He said, 'Would you like something different? We could get you out of Customs, get you here in my group. Working for me. Hours would be longer, pay probably wouldn't be much better, but I can guarantee you it'd be a hell of a lot more interesting.'

That made Tanya Mead smile. He liked her smile. He liked intelligent young women – please, no sex involved, he was happily married and though he had a wandering eye he never once thought of cheating – and this one looked like a keeper.

She said, 'I think that'd be fine, sir. But my supervisor might have other ideas.'

Janwick looked at a notepad in front of him. 'Right. The gentleman who flew in with you. The one who wouldn't let you search the truck. Known as "Captain Commerce", right?'

Tanya tried to hide a smile and failed. 'That's right.'

'Don't worry about it. He's no longer working in the Customs Department.'

'Sir?'

'Gone. Out. If he's lucky, he'll be a night-shift stockboy at WalMart in a year or two. Officer Mead, thank you for your service.'

Tanya took the hint and left the conference room. Janwick's staff, a good mix of young men and women, looked at him expectantly. He took a deep breath, tried to ignore the tightness in his chest. He said, 'I need to make some phone calls. When I come back, I want a plan in place to get the photos of these two characters and a description of their truck out to every law-enforcement agency within . . . Paula, how long have they been in-country?'

'Forty-three hours.'

'Right. Forty-three hours. Work out how far they could get in that truck within forty-three hours. Postulate no overnight stops. Just occasional fuel stops. Write up a "be

on the lookout for" alert. Work a geographical arc, showing the territory they might have covered. Want to know
what possible targets might be in that arc. Nuclear power
plants, dams, shopping malls, airports, weapons facilities –
everything. And we want that BOLO in the hands of
every cop, customs, sheriff, game officer inside that arc.
Got it?'

No replies. Just nods. Janwick stood up.

'Good.' He left the room, thinking that his crew might
not be as tough or as smart as his Air Force buds but they
were good enough for what had to be done.

Adrianna Scott stood in Terminal B at the Memphis
International Airport, tapping her left foot, knowing that it
was a nervous gesture, knowing it was something that she
couldn't control. Their flight was leaving in under a half-
hour, and Victor Palmer stood with her at the gate, sweating
some in the cool air.

'He's late,' Victor said.

'I know.'

'And he hasn't answered his cellphone, or his pager.
What's going on?'

'I don't know, Victor, I just don't know.'

Which was only partially true. She knew that Brian was
gone, and had been gone for the day. He had been upset
with her earlier and who could blame him? A night of anger,
a night of arguments, a night of recriminations . . . followed
by a night of passion, a hot night for both of them, and then,
in the morning . . . the cold shoulder from her to him.

But what else could have happened?

Just days away from attainment, after years and years of all
this work and sacrifice, to complicate things even more with

a love affair with someone who was not only a co-worker but a cop with a cop's suspicious mind – she couldn't allow it.

So.

Where in hell was he?

Brian had been telling the truth yesterday: the only real reason for his presence on this trip was to sway the General's opinion, to appeal to that rock-solid and insane patriotism that most military types cherished, like a piece of the True Cross or something, and it had worked. And for that Adrianna felt no guilt.

So why the guilt now?

Victor said, 'We've got to start boarding, Adrianna. Even with our clearances, we've got to get to our seats. They won't hold the aircraft for us.'

'I know.'

Maybe Brian was done with it all, had taken a flight back to his beloved New York City, ready to take whatever heat the NYPD might deliver for backing out from his commitment to the Tiger Teams. Knowing Brian, maybe that's what he'd done. She wouldn't put it past him. She knew he was growing restless with the Tiger Teams, was getting ready to break out, and this little trip out Memphis way had probably tipped the scale.

Still . . .

Maybe he was hurt. Injured. Dead.

Jesus, she thought, that's morbid . . .

But easy. It would be easy.

She looked over at Victor. 'Let's get on.'

He said, 'Aren't you going to put out an alert? Maybe Brian's been in an accident. Or worse.'

Adrianna touched his arm – the one not carrying the canister, hooked up to his wrist – and said, 'Brian's a New York police detective. He can handle everything and anything that's thrown at him. If I put out an alert, that means a lot of involvement from a lot of agencies, looking for him. Suppose he's on a drunk? Or at a strip club? Having a Memphis police SWAT team raid a joint, looking for him . . . well, the embarrassment would be something else.'

'If I was missing, I sure as hell would hope you would take it more seriously, Adrianna.'

She started to the jetway, Victor trailing next to her. 'Victor, if you ever went missing I'd put out an alert within the half-hour. It's not your nature to be anything but predictable and punctual. Brian is neither predictable nor punctual. I'll give him one more day to report in before getting the world spun up.'

Adrianna strode down the gentle incline, thinking of what she had just said. And another thing, too, was that it would be easier for all concerned. Final Winter, just days from kicking off, and having Brian out of the picture . . . that would make it so much simpler.

For two reasons.

The first, of course, was that she didn't need to have his questioning mind at work, the closer they got to the day.

And the second . . .

A possibility that she found hard to believe, even in her most private thoughts.

She was falling in love with him.

And that could not be tolerated.

At the open door, leading to the cabin, a male flight attendant smiled and checked her boarding pass.

'Welcome aboard,' he said.

'Thank you,' Adrianna replied, thinking that those were probably the two most honest words she had uttered today.

*

Brian Doyle looked again at his hands. Soiled red, turning brown as the blood dried.

'Fuck,' he said.

He looked up at the street, saw headlights approach. A car passed. And then another.

A third car passed, then made a U-turn.

Could it be?

Blue lights started flashing from the radiator grille.

Luck, he thought, luck of the Irish . . .

The car stopped and a beam of light came out from a side searchlight, illuminating him and his rental car. He held out his hands and two Cincinnati cops came towards him, flanking him on either side, holding out their flashlights.

One called out, 'What's the problem?'

He said, 'The name's Doyle. I'm on the Job. I just got jumped and I think I've been knifed. Could you get some EMTs over here?'

One of the cops started talking into a portable radio as the other approached, cautious, one hand holding up the flashlight, the other hand on his service weapon. Smart. Don't trust anybody you don't know on the street. Anybody.

The second cop said, 'You got identification, Doyle?'

'I do. But just so you know, I'm carrying. Nine-millimeter, rear right of my waistband.'

'All right,' the second cop said. 'You just keep your hands where I can see them, and don't make any sudden moves.'

'You got it. All right if I bleed?'

'Bleed away,' the cop said. 'Just don't reach for anything.'

'Yeah.'

The second cop now joined the first one, and after a brief talk the first cop said, 'My partner's going over to see you, to check your weapon and ID. EMTs are on the way. You just stay still. All right?'

Brian said, 'It'd be easier for him if I stand.'

'Go ahead. Stand. But that's it.'

So he stood, feeling dizzy, and then the cop was there, pulling out Brian's gun and then his wallet and his other thin ID holder, and another confab was underway. Then the first cop whistled and said, 'You're with the Feds, then, huh?'

'On temporary duty.'

The cop's partner said, 'I guess. Says here you're a detective from New York City.'

The sound of an approaching siren grew louder. 'That's right.'

The first cop said, 'Man, you are so far the fuck away from home.'

Brian said, 'Truest thing you're going to say tonight.'

After getting home from Dulles Airport, Adrianna Scott collapsed on the living-room couch in her condo, stretched out her legs and closed her eyes, refusing to think about anything for a while. Anything at all. Just keep everything blank. It had been one long day in a series of very long days, and her feet were throbbing. She had them resting on a small pillow, elevated up on the end of the couch. More long days ahead, that was for damn sure . . . and right now there were decisions to be made, choices to be analyzed, and phone calls to complete.

She looked at her watch. Nearly midnight. Still . . . it would be nice to take care of this one chore. She went to her soft leather briefcase, pulled out her PDA, looked to the cellar door. She should go downstairs to her homemade bubble, make the phone call by using the stolen CIA laptop.

That would be the safest thing to do, to ensure that maximum security was maintained.

Still . . . damn it, she was so damn tired.

Back to the couch. She sat down, looked at the phone. Just one phone call. That was all. And what were the possibilities of something untoward happening?

Very, very slight.

And she was so tired. The thought of going down to the cellar, manhandling that huge piece of furniture away from the hiding place underneath the staircase, powering up the laptop, setting up the phone-calling software . . . ugh.

Adrianna keyed in her PDA, found the number she was looking for, grabbed her cellphone and dialed away.

It rang three times and a woman's voice answered. 'CDC, operator two, may I help you?'

Adrianna gave her a four-number extension. Waited.

'You have reached the Alpha Directory,' the automated voice said. 'Please enter the subsequent extension.'

Which she did, entering six more numerals. Then, with a practiced touch, she raised the cellphone slightly from her ear so that the low-pitched and then high-pitched squealing of the encryption devices coordinating their signals didn't burst an eardrum. The squealing stopped and then a man's voice answered.

'McCartney.'

She took a breath. 'This is Adrianna Scott calling. I'm the director of Foreign Operations and Intelligence Liaison Team Number Seven. Also known as Tiger Team Seven.'

'Yes.'

She looked to her PDA. 'You have a shipment ready to be made to the Memphis Airport, under a protocol called Final Winter.'

'Yes.'

'My authorization is Bravo Tango Zulu Zulu twelve.'

'Mark. Repeating, Bravo Tango Zulu Zulu twelve. Go ahead.'

'That shipment is to be canceled. Stand down and do not deliver. Please repeat.'

'Message repeat. Shipment is canceled. Stand down and do not deliver packages.'

'Very good. Scott signing off.'

She powered down her cellphone, felt a tingling in her chest. There. Nothing leaving from the CDC to Memphis. No, ma'am. But oh, there was going to be a delivery there, no doubt about it, and a very special delivery at that.

Adrianna yawned. Time to go to bed. Tomorrow was going to be another busy one.

Something woke up Vladimir Zhukov, and he wasn't sure what. It was night, somewhere in South Dakota. Or maybe Iowa. He rubbed at his eyes and looked over at Imad. From the glow of the dashboard dials he could see that the Arab boy's expression was concerned, and he knew what had awoken him. The Arab had the habit of muttering when something wasn't going right, and Vladimir was sure that was what his subconscious had heard.

'What's wrong?'

'There is a police cruiser following us.'

'So?'

'It's been following us for the last several kilometers.'

Vladimir rubbed at his eyes again. 'Are you speeding?'

'Just a little,' he said. 'Only a few miles over the limit. But not enough to— shit!'

Vladimir looked at the sideview mirror, saw what had

gotten Imad's attention. Blue flashing lights from the cruiser.
Damnation.

Imad started cursing under his breath, and Vladimir said,
'Pull over.'

'What?'

'Pull over, now! What do you think, that we can outrun
him in this rig? Pull over, and do it slow and polite.'

For once Imad did as he was told, switching on the turn
indicator, downshifting the engine and braking. Vladimir
looked around. A long, deserted stretch of highway. It was
three in the morning. What a dark hour.

Imad braked the truck to a stop, the cab shuddering
slightly as they halted. He reached under the seat and
Vladimir held back his arm.

'No,' he said sharply.

'We don't have much time!'

'No, I said! Listen, that patrol officer back there, he has
called in what he has done to his police unit. They will
know that a truck has been pulled over and they will have a
description and license plate number. What then, if you
shoot him dead?'

'We get away!'

'And for how long? Listen, that is a police officer back there.
Not some degenerate young people in a Jeep who won't be
missed for days. If that officer is killed and they believe we did
it, every police officer in this country will be looking for us.
This is not your country or my country. Here, they love their
men in uniform. Kill him and we won't make it to Memphis.'

Imad withdrew his arm. 'What, then? What do we do?'

Vladimir looked to the sideview mirror. Doors to the
cruiser were opening up. Just their luck, there were two of
them back there.

'We wait. We see what they want.'

Imad glanced over at his mirror. 'They're coming. You better know what you're doing.'

'I do,' Vladimir said, lying to the boy. 'I do.'

The phone call that Adrianna Scott had made to the secure CDC facility had been tapped and traced even before she hung up. The particulars of the call – her phone number, the CDC number, duration of the call and key words mentioned – was placed in a routine notification file and sent to a classified internal security mailing list. Among the recipients on the mailing list was one Durlane Foster, an overworked security analyst working for the National Security Agency, who was currently on one week's medical leave to take care of a prostate problem.

Unknown to Durlane Foster was the fact that as part of his e-mail address, an enhanced BCC – blind carbon copy – program sent a copy of the message to another NSA employee, who had been detached to a program called Foreign Operations and Intelligence Liaison, known by those in the know as Tiger Teams.

That NSA member was Darren Coover, member of Tiger Team Seven.

The phone rang and rang and rang and Alexander Bocks sat up in bed, wondering for a moment just where in hell he was when he realized he was in his big old bed in his big old empty home. He looked at the empty spot near him, which should have contained the sleeping and loving form of his wife, Amy. Poor, dear Amy, who had gone with him through all those stations and deployments, keeping things together with love and good wishes, hardly ever complaining, just wanting to share a life with her man, and upon his retirement, share him 24/7, never to share him with anyone else, just lots of travel and rest and catching up for all those missed meals and appointments because of some foul-up on the flight line . . .

Dear, sweet, patient Amy, who had been taken away from him just after his retirement, by a carcinoma that had no patience at all.

The phone was still ringing. He looked at the bedside clock, saw it was just past four in the morning, which meant—

Disaster. A crash somewhere. An AirBox jet down, crew dead, cargo destroyed, a major emotional and financial hit and, oh Christ, grab the damn thing.

He picked up the phone. 'Bocks.'

'First thing first, don't hang up.'

'Don't hang— Jesus fucking Christ, is that you, Frank?'

'Yeah, it is,' said Frank Woolsey, his CFO. 'Look, don't hang up.'

Bocks sat up against the headboard. 'Okay. I won't hang up. I'll just sit here and let you hang yourself.'

'Me? Hang myself? Look, first you don't answer my phone calls, you won't see me, you won't answer e-mail, you won't—'

'I've been busy.'

'Busy! I guess the hell you have been busy, settling the labor contract all on your own. Jesus Christ, General, you realize what you've done?'

'Yes.'

Bocks could make out the breathing on the other end of the line. Frank said, 'I've already heard from a number of board members. They are fucking shitting bricks. You've put the company in an untenable position.'

'It's my company.'

'Oh, sure, it's your company, but it also belongs to the stockholders, pal, and the board of directors are there, representing their interests, and if you think they're going to let you run the company into the ground because of some old concept of loyalty, why, you're off your rocker. It's not going to happen.'

'It's going to happen, Frank. Just wait and see.'

'No, it's not. It's a new world, General, one that won't allow you to run this company like your own private air force or something. I'm calling a meeting of the board, and if you're still running things by the end of the week, I'll be—'

Bocks hung up the phone. He picked up the base, found the phone wire that led into it from the wall, and pulled the plug. Shut off the light and lay back down, and gingerly, quietly, ran his hand across to the empty space beside him. Some nights, dear Amy would just lie there, listening to him bitch and moan about missing parts, missing personnel, missing directives, or whatever other nonsense he had to put up with, and despite the hour and time, never once had she seemed to mind.

A good woman. He could use her now, to talk to her about what he was doing for the next few days, for he was doing more than just opening the company up to financial ruin because of a dental plan for the union. Now it was much more than that: he was using his aircraft to save his country and his people from some terrible disaster that was approaching.

But now, would an eleven-member board still let him run AirBox? That was going to be the question. And what would happen if his fleet was grounded because of some court injunction, while those terrorists planned their anthrax attack? What then?

His hand stayed on the empty side of the bed as he waited for answers, as he waited to fall back asleep.

CHAPTER TWENTY-SEVEN

Vladimir Zhukov thought about those four young people back in Wyoming. Had somebody seen them approach the truck as it was being painted? Was it possible that they were being traced? What was going on—

By leaning over he could look into Imad's sideview mirror and see the approaching police officer come up on the driver's side. Imad rolled down the window and the officer called up, 'Your license and registration please.'

'Certainly,' Imad replied, and Vladimir was pleased at the boy's quiet tone. Imad passed over the paperwork through the window and said in a low voice, 'What now?'

'We wait.'

Imad snorted and Vladimir checked his own sideview mirror. The other officer was standing there at the side of the road, flashlight in one hand, his other hand resting on top of his service pistol in his holster. What were the options? What was to be done?

'Well?' Imad said. 'He's going back to his cruiser. What do we do now?'

Vladimir felt his palms moisten. 'We wait. Nothing has happened yet. We wait.'

So they waited.

Imad said, 'He's coming back.'

And Imad's hand reached down for his pistol.

'No, not for a moment,' Vladimir said. 'Leave it be.'

Imad said, 'I will give you your moment, but I will not end up in Guantánamo, or in any American jail. Understand?'

Vladimir looked over again. The second policeman was still standing there.

The first one approached the open window. Imad turned awkwardly, still holding his right hand at his side, ready to reach for his pistol.

'Here you go,' the policeman said. 'The reason I stopped you is that you have a taillight burned out on the right side.'

'Oh,' Imad said.

'Here's a chit, saying we stopped you. You've got twenty-four hours to get it fixed. All right?'

'Sure,' Imad said.

'Have a good trip.'

'Thank you.'

The policeman walked away. Vladimir closed his eyes and said, 'All right. Leave. Nice and slow. Don't give them any excuse to stop us again. All right?'

'Sure,' Imad said. 'Stupid fuckers. Didn't even ask to look in the trailer. What kind of country is this, when the police don't want a payoff or a cut?'

'Shut up and drive.'

Imad chuckled as he started shifting gears, and the truck lurched out onto the empty highway. He said, 'I never thought I'd say what I'm about to say.'

'Which is what?'

'That you were right back there.' Another laugh. 'If it were up to me, they would both be dead.'

Vladimir folded his arms, closed his eyes. 'Thankfully, it wasn't up to you.'

Late morning, Memphis International Airport. Brian Doyle sat in a waiting area near his gate, legs stretched out, resisting an urge to scratch at his chest. It had been one long goddamn night. When the EMTs had gotten to him outside Mamma Garrity's house, it had turned out to be not as bad as it had first looked. The two EMTs – professional young women who managed to ratchet down his tension with their soft voices – had wiped and cleaned the wound, which had only needed a few butterfly strips. No stitches necessary. They had suggested a trip to the ER but filled as he was with memories of how chaotic urban ERs could be on a busy night he had politely but firmly declined.

But Brian hadn't declined a ride to the local precinct house, where he had spent several hours going through mugshots of local perps – although mugshots was now an obsolete term, for the head-on photos of criminals were stored on a computer system, which meant just clicking the mouse and watching the grim faces parade by. The exercise had been useless, of course, but it had been a joy to be back in a real police station for a while. The phone calls, the parade of suspects into the precinct house, the foul and fun language of the cops and detectives – it had been bracing, like having your first real drink after a six-month dry period. One of the cops had lent him a clean shirt that actually fit, and all in all it had been a good night, after that tight spot he had gotten in.

One of the detectives in the precinct had shaken his head after learning what had happened. 'Goes to show you, man like you should always have a vest on, especially when traveling in strange places.'

Good advice. The detective – Joslynn had been his name – had also slipped him his business card and said he would dig up the report on the death of Adrianna's aunt. 'Strictly unofficially,' the detective had said. 'Paperwork is strangling us nowadays. I'll give you a ring in a day or two.'

And Brian had said that would be fine. After an early breakfast at a diner outside the airport in Cincinnati he caught a flight back to Memphis to fetch his luggage and here he was, waiting to go back to DC. But that faint taste of police work hours earlier made him want to change his flight to JFK or LaGuardia or even Newark. Anyplace but back to the Tiger Team.

His cellphone started vibrating. Brian picked it up, saw the incoming number, recognized it right away. The Princess, no doubt calling in to see what was wrong with one of her squires. He had ignored all her pagings and her phone calls from yesterday. Today was no doubt payback time, and he could give a shit. With one hand he answered the phone; with the other, he finally scratched at his chest.

'Yes?'

'This is Adrianna.'

'Yeah, I know.'

'Are you all right?'

Good question. Any answer would be a lengthy one, and Brian didn't have the energy or the inclination.

'I'm fine. And you?'

She said, 'I was asking because I was worried. You weren't answering your phone or your pager.'

'That's right, I wasn't.'

Adrianna started speaking faster. 'What we did the other night was special, Brian. It meant a lot to me but I don't have the time to handle something like that, not now. It may happen again. I hope it does. But the next few days . . . they are going to be crazy ones, Brian, and no offense to you, none at all, but I have all that I can handle right now. Do you understand?'

He scratched at the bandage again. 'Sure. I understand.'

He could hear her take a breath. 'I'm not sure that you do. But do know this . . . I do care for you. Care for you very much. And I hope you feel the same towards me.'

Another hell of a question. And he would like to ask her about her childhood: why did she bribe her neighbors to present a cover story, and what in hell really did happen to her aunt, all those years ago? But instead he said, 'I do, Adrianna. And I wanted to leave yesterday on better terms . . . I'm sorry we didn't.'

'I'm sorry, too.' Another deep breath.

'I have something important to say to you.'

'Go ahead.'

'What you can do for us in the Tiger Team over the next several days . . . will be minimal, at best. And I say that while admiring and appreciating all that you've done for us so far.'

'All right.'

'So I'm putting you on leave, Brian. Right now. Go back home, go see your boy, get caught up on things. I don't plan on seeing you for another week. All right?'

Talk about synchronicity. He'd just left the tender clutches of the Cincinnati Police Department, and now he was getting a Get Out of Jail Free card from the Princess. Part of Brian knew that he should talk to her, debate the issue, find out what in hell was going on with her and the Tiger Team . . . but he was tired and his chest itched and he didn't want to be in Memphis and he sure as hell didn't want to be in that concrete bunker in Maryland.

So he said, 'You got it,' hung up, and walked across the terminal to an American Airlines ticket counter, where he paid an outrageous amount of money to change his flight from Baltimore to JFK.

The day was certainly looking up.

Adrianna hung up the phone from her office in Maryland. Nicely done. One down, three more to go.

Victor Palmer was standing in his kitchen, staring at the counter, when the phone began to ring. He had been doing that a lot lately, losing himself in thoughts and dark fantasies. He would open up the refrigerator door to find something to eat and would imagine that he was looking at a hospital refrigerator, at little vials of medicines or vaccines, and that would lead into what was going to happen over the next few days, when the vaccine spraying would begin, when the old and the sick and the very young would choke on their own fluids and die . . . Sometimes he would stand in the shower and stare at the near wall, letting the water run down his back, thinking of the fake showers in Auschwitz and Bergen-Belsen and Birkenau, and how, in this world, he was now the one manning the showers for the innocents. But instead of being sprayed with Zyklon-B they were being sprayed with something from a different arsenal of evil and the spraying was going to be done in a spirit of idealism, the sacrifice of the needs of the few for the good of the many . . .

And the phone kept on ringing.

He felt a little snap as his head shook, as he came back to whatever terra firma he was standing on. He walked over to the counter, picked up the phone.

'Doctor Palmer.'

'Victor? Adrianna Scott here.'

'Oh.'

'Victor, I have some news for you.'

'Okay.'

His mouth felt thick, unwieldy. He was not sure what this bitch was calling about, but whatever it was he knew that some day he would probably have to testify in a secret Congressional hearing about how this whole disaster took place, and—

What?

Victor cleared his throat. 'I'm sorry, Adrianna. Could you tell me that one more time?'

'My pleasure, Victor. Final Winter. It's been canceled. No flights, no mass vaccinations. It's standing down.'

'But . . . but . . . I . . .'

Adrianna's voice was soothing. 'I just got word a few minutes ago. I wanted to make sure you were the first to hear it. Homeland Security got a break and they rolled up the Syrian squads that were in country. All of them. Double- and triple-checked, all taken in with their weaponized anthrax. There's one hundred percent confidence that they've been captured.'

'Oh . . . oh, please . . .' The phone receiver was slippery in his hand.

Adrianna said, 'I know you've been under a lot of pressure, Victor. We all have. But you most of all. I want you to turn off your pager, switch off your phone, and take a week off. All right? I don't want to see you in the office. Hell, I don't want you to even think about going into the office. You just take your time and enjoy yourself. Relax. Okay?'

It felt like the kitchen floor was gently quivering under his feet. Oh . . . how sweet, how sweet . . .

Adrianna said, 'Victor? Are you all right?'

He switched the phone receiver to his other hand. 'All right? I'm great . . . I'm . . . I . . . thank you, Adrianna. Thank you for calling. This is the best news . . . well, the best news I've ever received . . .'

She chuckled. 'Glad I could make your day. Now. You do what I told you, all right?'

'Yes. Yes, of course.'

'Good. See you in a week.'

And she hung up.

Victor hung up as well, turned – and the next thing he knew he was staring up at the kitchen ceiling. At first he thought he must have slipped, but as he sat up and checked the time he realized that he had fainted.

Which was fine. He got to his feet, swayed some, and pulled the phone jack free. He stumbled into the bedroom, found the pager, and not only switched it off but took the batteries out and threw them in a wicker wastebasket. Then he collapsed into bed and slept for almost twenty hours.

Adrianna looked at her watch. Two down, two more to go, and back home that little automated program that was running on the stolen CIA laptop should have uplinked the signal . . . now.

Good.

Montgomery Zane was in the parking lot in front of Callaghan Consulting, their Tiger Team home, when the page came in. He toggled the side switch of his pager and read the text message:

CODE CARLYLE
CODE CARLYLE

CODE CARLYLE
M. ZANE DETACHED & TRAVEL SOONEST FOR:
ANDREWS/LAKENHEATH/AVIANO/AL-UDEID
AWAIT ORDERS AL-UDEID
CODE CARLYLE
CODE CARLYLE
CODE CARLYLE

So there you go. This time of the month, any three-code group line that began with the letter C and ended with the letter E was legitimate. And the itinerary looked standard. From Andrews Air Force Base in Maryland to Lakenheath Royal Air Force Base in Great Britain, and from there to Aviano in Italy, and ending up in Al-Udeid in Qatar. Monty liked Qatar, had a number of friends there, and looked forward to that part of the trip at least.

And what waited for him in Qatar? Well, he would know when he got there. No time to get worried about that particular. All he knew was that he hoped the job was going to be brief and bloody, like that little whirlwind trip last week that had taken him to Britain, Bali and Pakistan. He hoped this trip was a one-fer – in and out with one little mission. These long missions were getting to be a bear . . .

And speaking of long missions, there was a good chance that he would be overseas when Final Winter started up in a few days. Not a problem, not with the wife and kids now safely tucked away in rural Georgia – and God, wasn't that a positive comment on the times, when the white wife of a black man and their mixed-race kids would find peace and security in rural Georgia, when just a couple of generations ago they would have been targeted for a beating or a lynching – but there was still a bit of business to attend to.

Monty looked at the pager readout again. 'Soonest' was what it said and 'Soonest' was what it meant. Which meant leaving here and driving hard-ass to Andrews. He was supposed to have met with Darren Coover this morning, to go over those funny bits of information that he and the NSA guy had gathered on Final Winter and what was – or wasn't – going down. But he was sure he could talk from Andrews to the little guy, find a secure phone there, and find out more about what was going on.

In the meantime, time to leave.

Monty backed out of the spot and left Callaghan Consulting.

Adrianna felt the little glow of good news starting to mellow through her. Brian was on his way back to his beloved New York. Victor was probably getting drunk or getting laid or just staying in bed, reading those pulp magazines he was so in love with. Monty was going to be on a plane shortly. And Darren . . . soon enough, she would meet with him and send him on some stupid assignment to Toronto or some such. Then the board would be clear and she would leave here and go back to Memphis, to oversee the installation of the canisters, and she wouldn't have any worries about what her Tiger Team members might be doing or learning or questioning while she was away.

She reached for the phone to make a call to Darren when there was knock on the door frame.

And wouldn't you know it, there he was.

Darren Coover stood in her doorway, face set, holding some papers in his hand.

'Adrianna,' he said. 'We need to talk.'

The little glow of triumph was gone.

'All right . . . well, my schedule is pretty tight this morning, but maybe we could—'

He shook his head, stepped in. 'You don't understand. We have to talk. Now.'

Complications, she always knew complications would come up, but at this very moment . . .

'Very good, Darren. Come in and close the door.'

He stepped in, closed the door, and then sat down.

Earlier Darren had been in his office, scratching at his chin, viewing and re-viewing the computer screen before him. Things weren't making sense, weren't making sense at all. After his talk yesterday with Monty he had gone back into GATEKEEPER, trying to find out more information about Final Winter. There had been a new reference, from an FBI operative working for AirBox. A routine report to his field office, stating that he had overheard a machinist supervisor talk about something called Final Winter that was going to be implemented at the airfreight company within the next few days. All right, then, that at least made sense. And the fact that he hadn't been seeing any other Final Winter references hadn't concerned him all that much, despite what he had told Monty. Lots of classified ops went under different names, depending on what groups were involved. Tiger Team Seven and its members might know the vaccination program as Final Winter, and other agencies involved could call it Ocean Foam or Mountain Breeze or some other damn thing.

Still . . . where was the urgency? Where were the alerts? Where was the heightened security within the major cities? Why in hell hadn't Homeland Security bumped up the Threat Level?

Then there was the other thing he had learned, just this morning . . .

The Princess had been a naughty girl, using her home phone to make a call that should have been secured. Adrianna had contacted a CDC facility in the wilds of northern Alabama that had been cooking up the experimental vaccine for the Final Winter project and she had told them that Final Winter had been canceled.

Fair enough.

But the FBI guy had stated – six hours after Adrianna had made the phone call – that Final Winter was proceeding and that a delivery associated with Final Winter was expected that day.

Hell, the government was slow. The government was always slow! But for something like Final Winter . . . there was no way any type of delivery was going to take place if the entire operation had been canceled.

And another thing. Monty Zane was supposed to have been here about a half-hour ago. They were going to match intelligence and then go into Adrianna's office to find out what the hell was going on, and now he wasn't here. And Victor wasn't here. And Brian wasn't here.

So it was up to him. And so off he went.

Now Darren looked over at the Princess. Even though she was well dressed and groomed and made-up she didn't seem quite right.

'Adrianna, something doesn't make sense.'

'Go on.'

Darren was surprised at how he didn't feel uncomfortable at what he said next. 'I have a slight confession to make. I've been performing some duties that are above and beyond what's been required of me.'

Adrianna seemed to try to smile. 'That sounds like you, Darren. What have you been up to?'

'I've been placing some rogue programs on some of the server systems, trying to enhance the information stream we've been able to play with. You know us NSA guys: there's no such thing as too much information.'

'True.'

'One program that I've used sends me copies of certain e-mails that have keywords flagged to a mail account I control. This program is called a BCC program. Stands for Blind Carbon Copy – funny, of course, since who in hell uses carbon-copy paper anymore?'

'Darren—'

'I'll get to the point. One e-mail I got in the system overnight was a report filed with the CIA Office of Security. You know what they do, am I right?'

Adrianna seemed to freeze right there in her chair. 'I do. What did the report state?'

'It seemed routine. It was . . . well, I'll just say it . . . Adrianna, it was a transcript of a phone call that you made to a CDC facility in Alabama. A facility that is preparing the vaccination canisters. The transcript said that you canceled Final Winter. You had all the proper authorizations and code phrases, and your command was accepted.'

Adrianna was quiet. Darren said, 'But I've got other information, from an FBI operative working undercover at AirBox in Memphis. This report said that something called Final Winter was taking place – he didn't have any details – and that a delivery associated with Final Winter would be made today. Adrianna . . . it doesn't make sense. And other things don't make sense either.'

'Like what?'

'I've talked to Monty Zane . . . and I've done other digging. Adrianna, there's nothing out there that shows any kind of preparedness in anticipation of Final Winter. Border security isn't on any type of alert. Monty told me that a friend of his, working in a classified border-security group . . . they're even allowing vacations and training sessions. I haven't found anything remotely associated with increased surveillance in any American cities – no one seems to be looking for those Syrian men who are going to attack us with anthrax.'

Adrianna nodded slowly, rolled her chair back from her desk. 'Who else have you told, besides Monty?'

'No one,' Darren said. Then, in a flash that seemed to last a long time, he realized that he should have lied, should have told her anything to protect himself, should have said that lots of other people knew that something wasn't right with Final Winter, that he had contacted his friends in the NSA and CIA and FBI, that a flying investigative squad was coming right now to check into her. He should have done that, should have done anything, he knew, as Adrianna came at him from around her desk. And punched him square in the throat.

In a small room at a terminal building at Andrews Air Force Base, Monty Zane tried one more time with his secure cellphone, and gave up after another long series of unanswered rings. Darren wasn't answering his phone or his pager, and calls to his apartment weren't being answered.

He looked at the cellphone, thought about calling Adrianna. To say what? For one thing, she'd probably want to know why in hell he had been detached again, and he didn't like going into those swamp arguments. He just did what he had to do. He stood up, clipped the cellphone back onto his belt, and picked up his tote bag. Time to fly.

Monty walked up to a senior airman who was standing by a wooden lectern, examining a clipboard full of papers. The senior airman – wearing camo BDUs – looked up as he approached and said, 'Help you, sir?'

'Yeah,' Monty said. 'You've got a C-20 transport leaving in ten for Lakenheath. I need to be on that aircraft.'

The senior airman shook his head. 'No can do. That's carrying a Congressional delegation, complete with wives, staffers, and luggage. Especially luggage. No room.'

Monty nodded, reached into a jacket pocket, pulled out a plastic-sealed embossed card that had his photo and lots of words around it. He silently passed the card over to the senior airman who glanced at the card, glanced again longer, and then – eyes widened – looked up at Monty.

'Man . . . you must have had to impress God Himself to get travel authorization like that.'

'Not God. Just one of his servants on earth.'

'Maybe so, but it's good enough.' The senior airman picked up a hand-held radio, motioned Monty to follow him as they went through an open doorway, out to the flight line. Military aircraft of all types were stationed on the tarmac, as far as the eye could see.

'Come with me, sir, we'll get you on that jet. There's a Congressional staffer there who kept on asking me for tea with honey this morning and pissed me off. I'll be glad to leave her sorry ass behind.'

Monty shouldered his tote bag. 'Won't she put up a fight?'

The senior airman laughed. 'Who can win a fight against God?'

*

Adrianna rubbed at her punching hand, glad that Darren had closed the door behind him. Darren was sprawled out on the floor, gurgling and wheezing, his face red. She knelt down next to him, lowered her head close to his.

'Sorry about that, Darren, but your larynx has been crushed. One of the many talents I learned at Camp Perry. Eventually you're going to choke to death. It will take a long time and be very painful.'

She leaned in further. 'My name is Aliyah Fulenz. I am an Iraqi Christian woman, and because your country killed my family many years ago I am going to kill many Americans in just a few days.'

The gurgling and wheezing grew louder. She said, 'I am doing all this for revenge. For hate.'

She reached out, gently touched his forehead. 'But Darren . . . I always liked you, always. And what I am about to do to you, I do out of friendship.'

And with her strong arms she clasped Darren's head close to her and broke his neck.

CHAPTER TWENTY-EIGHT

The BOLO alert that went out from the Northwest Homeland Security office was distributed, as ordered, to a variety of law-enforcement agencies that fell within the arc that showed how far the Freightliner tractor-trailer truck could have traveled after passing through the border checkpoint at Washington State.

At a South Dakota Highway Patrol substation off I-90, the incoming alert from the Homeland Security office was faxed to the on-duty dispatcher, who was a replacement officer filling in for a dispatcher who had had to go home sick that evening. This particular dispatcher was a fresh graduate from the South Dakota Highway Patrol Academy in Pierre, and in the hours he was on duty, because he was busy with fielding calls and trying to refamiliarize himself with on-air radio protocol, he did not notice that the fax machine near his elbow was out of paper.

The fax machine would not get refilled with paper until the next shift, several hours later and well after a Highway Patrol cruiser from this particular substation had stopped a Freightliner truck that had a missing taillight and was heading east.

For the last dozen or so kilometers, Vladimir Zhukov had kept his hands clasped tightly together as they at last got closer to the Memphis airport. It was amazing, really, to see how this country had changed so much in the thousands of kilometers they had traveled east. From the Pacific Ocean through the Rocky Mountains, across the deserts and plains and now, in this large city, on paved highways and bridges and overpasses. The traffic seemed heavy and he had a longing, for a moment, for the simplicity and purity that he had known in the wild emptiness of the steppes, working for a cause, nearly alone in the small city that he had grown up in. Such emptiness in which to support the Motherland, the Party, and all the greatness it represented.

He glanced over at Imad, who was driving with what looked like a bored expression on his young face and he said, 'Isn't the traffic heavy?'

Imad shook his head. 'This is nothing.'

'Nothing?' Vladimir looked again at the streams of traffic, recalling how seeing even two or three trucks a day back in Russia was a noteworthy event.

'Ah, nothing,' Imad said confidently. 'They may be un-believers, they may be infidels, and millions of them deserve to die, but they know how to build roads and make them work. To drive – you should drive in Damascus, Russki, then you'd know what bad and heavy traffic is . . . ah, here we go.'

Then it was up ahead. A magical sign that they had been waiting for, all these days on the road.

MEMPHIS AIRPORT NEXT TWO EXITS

Adrianna sat back on her heels on the floor, breathing hard. The cooling body of Darren Coover was on the floor next to her, starting to smell as the bladder and sphincter muscles let loose. Well, that was a fine way to start the morning, she thought. But what else could she have done? Short answer: nothing.

All right, she thought, getting up. Time to clean this mess up. She left her office, locked the door behind her. She made a quick reconnoiter of the other offices. Empty. Except for Stacy and a few support staff upstairs, she had the place – at least this level – to herself. She went down the hallway to the small kitchen, snooped around. There. The walk-in freezer. She undid the freezer door and looked in, suddenly shivering. Part of all that expensive planning to ensure that if they were stuck here for a week or so, at least they would have frozen peas and French fries to fall back on. She walked in, saw what she needed, and then went back to her office.

Unlocked the door, walked in. Darren Coover, staring sightlessly up at nothing. Poor American sodomite. Thought he was so very smart, and in a way he was. He was so very smart at sitting in a safe and secure room in a safe and secure city in a safe and secure country, pretending to be a warrior who was defending his nation against evil. Ah, but if evil is standing right in front of you, alive and breathing and ready to strike at you . . . then you are helpless. Just a helpless little boy.

She went around to her desk, brought out her office chair. Working quickly, she knelt down next to the body and undid his leather belt. She moved the chair closer to Darren's body, and lifted the corpse by the armpits. She had to grunt with effort as she managed to get the body to sit in the chair. Then, working with the belt, she strapped him in.

Adrianna stopped, breathing hard. She got behind the chair, put her hands against its back and started pushing it out the door. It was hard going at first, but once she got momentum in her favor she was out of her office and into the hallway.

In the hallway, gaining speed, she made it about a couple of yards when the sound of a chime caused her to look behind her.

The elevator door was beginning to open.

They took the airfreight exit and Vladimir felt again a grudging admiration for the skillful way the boy drove the truck. Imad maneuvered the tractor-trailer truck and its cargo with ease as they got closer to the support buildings. There was a constant roar of jets taking off from the airport, up into the blue Memphis sky. Vladimir followed the trails of some of the jets, thinking to himself that Elvis, one of the few Americans he admired, had once looked up at this very same sky.

'Where now?' Imad asked.

Vladimir looked back to the sheaf of papers in his lap, part of the package sent to him anonymously in Macao all those months ago. To think of all the work that their unseen employers had done to bring them here . . .

'Well?' the driver demanded.

'Up to the main gate,' Vladimir said. 'Once we get through the main gate, take your second left.'

'All right.'

The truck slowed as the traffic grew heavier. All of the vehicles ahead of them seemed to be just like their very own: trucks bringing freight and packages to be shipped elsewhere. Something caught in Vladimir's throat as he saw the busy traffic, the aircraft overhead, the quality of the roads and fencing and everything else. This was one of the smaller cities in this benighted nation, yet it seemed busier than Moscow had ever been. No wonder Russia had lost.

Imad braked and wiped at his brow. 'You know what I'm going to do, once we get paid off?'

'No, what?' Vladimir asked.

'I'm going to rent a hotel room and sleep for a day and a night. Take a long shower. Eat room-service food, good food, not that diner and McDonald's shit we put up with these days. And then go hire two whores. Two whores to entertain me, all day and all night . . . And you?'

'Almost the same. But a hotel in a small town. With good cable service, so I can watch all the news channels, when . . . when things begin.'

Imad said, 'Then maybe I'll do the whores first. Just in case.'

'That's a thought.'

Imad shifted into gear again. The truck moved forward. He said, 'What kind of security will they have?'

'We'll see, won't we?'

'Yeah.'

Another jolting shift, and then a gatehouse. An overweight black woman, wearing a dark blue uniform, carrying a clipboard. Imad rolled down the window, passed over a sheet of paper provided by Vladimir. The woman barely glanced at the truck as she matched the shipping number on the dispatch sheet to the daily printout and then passed the paper back up to Imad. She made a quick flicking motion with her wrist, already looking to the truck behind them.

Imad glanced over, grinned as he shifted into gear again and gave the accelerator a jolt.

They were in.

Vladimir said, 'Looks like security was great.'

'Are you joking? The security was nothing!'

It was Vladimir's turn to smile. 'The security was great. For us. Up ahead, the second left, like I said.'

When the elevator door started to open, Adrianna dug her heels into the carpeting and pushed the chair carrying Darren's body down the hallway. Don't look back, she thought, don't look back. Don't look back.

Ahead of her was the kitchen, and there was a jolt as the wheels of the chair passed from the hallway's carpeting to the tile floor.

Don't look back, don't look back.

To the right, the door to the walk-in freezer. She opened the freezer door, went back to the chair, the lolling form of Darren. Then the door started to close.

Damn it!

Adrianna propped the door open with one of the dining-table chairs, and then went back to her own chair. Into the chill air of the freezer. There. Some of the boxes of frozen food were piled so that there was a space a few feet wide at the rear. She undid the belt with cold fingers, jolted the chair forward, and the body of the NSA analyst tumbled to the floor with a loud noise.

Not too loud, she thought. Please, God, not too loud.

Another bit of maneuvering, and then she started to pull her chair behind her. Then she thought better of it.

Dining chair back out into the kitchen, freezer door closed. Adrianna walked to the sink just as—

Stacy Ruiz came in, heels clicking on the floor. She wore a tight yellow dress that emphasized her impressive chest and her auburn hair was down around her shoulders. She yawned, looked at Adrianna as she headed to the coffee maker.

'How's it going, Adrianna?' she asked.

Adrianna's heart was racing so hard she couldn't believe Stacy couldn't hear it. Stacy poured herself a mug of coffee, and Adrianna swallowed. 'It's going all right.'

'Good. Jesus, this place is practically empty. Just you and me and a couple of staff in the back rooms upstairs. Sure is quiet.'

'That it is,' Adrianna said.

Stacy took a swallow of coffee, looked over at the closed freezer door. 'Yeah. Quiet as a tomb.'

On the airfreight access road there was a small pylon, painted yellow and black. AIRBOX, it said, in large letters.

'What next?' Imad asked.

'Hangar one, bay four.'

Imad said, 'All right. Hangar four, bay one.'

'No, I said hangar—'

'Russki, you have no sense of humor. None. I heard you right the first time. Hah.'

Vladimir said, 'Just drive. No jokes.'

Imad laughed again.

An intersection, signs marking the hangar designations. Imad turned at the sign for hangar one. Other trucks followed them. The sun was starting to set and the sky was a deep reddish purple out to the west. The last day, Vladimir thought. The very last day of this hated place. Now a low, wide hangar was in front of them, a long row of truck bays leading off to the right.

Imad whistled a tune as he made a wide U-turn, and then started backing the truck up to bay four. Vladimir looked at the sideview mirror. It was only now that he realized his legs were trembling. So close. They were so very close. Men were now standing at the open roll-up door. With a hiss of the air brakes, Imad brought the truck to a stop. He left the diesel engine idling. Vladimir looked and noticed that the two truck bays flanking bay four were unattended. Security? Probably.

Vladimir said, 'Stay here. I'll take care of it.'

'Sure, whatever,' Imad replied.

Outside there was the smell of diesel and aviation fuel. Vladimir walked past the trailer as blue jumpsuited workers started working to unhook it from the truck. Up ahead was a set of concrete steps. He went up and two men stood in front of him. One was squat, muscular, wearing blue jeans and an AirBox sweatshirt. The other man was taller, held himself like a military officer. Vladimir recognized the man. The general who owned the company. Vladimir felt like laughing out loud. A proud member of the military forces who thought they had bested the USSR, forces who were about to be brought to their knees . . .

'Your papers,' the general said.

'Sir,' Vladimir said.

He passed over the dispatch and identification documents to the older man. He looked at the paperwork and said, 'How was your trip from Alabama?'

Just for a moment, the question confused Vladimir. Alabama? Why in the world would he think— Of course. The exhaustion of traveling across the country had muddled his mind. Of course this man would think that he had come up from Alabama.

'It was fine. Just fine.'

'Good.'

The general looked at the papers some more, said, 'Identification, please?'

Vladimir reached into his pants pocket, removed a thin leather folder, passed it over. The general opened it up, looked at the photo inside and at Vladimir, passed it over. 'Very well, Mr Komanski. Ready to open it up?'

'Yes, of course.'

Vladimir went to the rear of the trailer, to the electronic lock. Opened up the small plastic door, keyed the combination. There was an audible click as the lock released. One of the jumpsuited men came up and looked over at the general. The tall man nodded. The door rattled up and Vladimir felt his chest tighten. Here we go. The great deception continues.

By now floodlights had switched on. Insects were battering themselves to death against the bright clear glass of the lamps. The interior of the truck was illuminated, revealing rows and rows of black plastic cases, all held in a metal framework.

'Well?' the general asked.

Vladimir stepped forward, undid the nearest case. Nestled in the gray foam was a green canister, with input and output valves on each end, and a keyed switch on the side, halfway up the cylinder. The canisters carefully prepared in Asia, carefully painted to match the specifications e-mailed to him by his unknown employers. He walked back to the general and his companion, thinking to himself, death, I hold death in my hands. Death for tens of thousands of people.

He passed over the canister to the general, who took it and gave it to his companion. Vladmir said, 'Simplicity itself, gentlemen. Two canisters per aircraft. One for each of the two air-conditioning exhaust systems. Input and output valves pre-set to the aircraft's specifications. Here—'

Vladimir popped open the switch. 'See what I mean by simplicity? This is how it is activated. Pass this switch, left to right. Everything else is automatic. The radio altimeter arms the canister when the aircraft rises above three thousand feet in altitude. When the aircraft goes below three thousand feet, the canister releases its contents into the atmosphere. Aircrew has nothing to do except fly the aircraft.'

The general nodded, while his companion looked on, his expression grave. Vladimir thought, poor people, you have no idea, no idea at all . . .

'Very good,' the general said. 'I guess . . . I guess we're ready to begin, aren't we?'

'Yes,' Vladimir said. 'I guess you are.'

The general nodded, and did something that almost caused Vladimir to collapse in laughter. The general stuck out his hand, and Vladimir stared at it. Then he extended his own hand and shook the general's.

'You . . . you did good work,' the general said. 'You tell your people I said that, all right?'

'Yes. Yes, I will.'

Vladimir turned on his heel, went down the steps, and then back to the truck. He got up into the cab and Imad said, 'Everything fine?'

'Everything is great. '

'Amazing,' Imad said.

'The way of the world,' Vladimir said. 'If you have the right-colored vehicle, with the serial numbers and license plates, and the right identification, you can do anything in this country. Anything.'

'All right. What now?'

'How about you get us the hell out of here, all right?'

Imad said, 'You got it, Russki.'

Vladimir rubbed at his tired eyes as Imad drove out of the hangar parking area and then retraced their trip, back to the gate. There were two exits at the gate: TRUCKS WITH CARGO and TRUCKS WITH NO CARGO. Imad went to the second exit and they were waved through, without stopping.

'Made it,' Imad said. 'We made it.'

Vladimir kept on rubbing at his eyes. 'So we did, boy. So we did.'

Monty Zane stretched out on a chair in a waiting area in a small outbuilding at Lakenheath RAF base in Great Britain, feeling troubled. His hours of work trying to contact Darren had failed. The NSA guy hadn't answered his cellphone, his home phone, his office phone, or his pager. Monty had tried going through the on-duty NSA desk officer, trying somehow to get hold of Darren, and that approach had failed too.

And Adrianna. No Adrianna either. So what in the hell was going on?

He looked up at the digital clock. His flight to Aviano was due to leave in less than a half-hour. He was set to be on it, heading south, for another mission for his beloved land, another job for those like him who were on the shiny and pointy end of the spear.

But what of the Tiger Team? And what of Darren? The guy said he was going to contact him with additional information about Final Winter and all that, but then his own duty pager had gone off and had sent him across the Atlantic. And in a few minutes he was set to continue his journey south. All the while waiting and not knowing what was going on.

A female Air Force NCO came up to him, her nametag reading BOUCHARD. She said, 'You're on the Aviano flight, sir?'

'Yeah.'

'Time to board, then, sir.'

'Very well.'

Monty got up, slung his duffel bag over one shoulder, and looked back at the clock and at the flight desk.

He didn't like a damn thing that was going on.

Adrianna stood in her condo unit in Maryland, looking around it for the very last time. Her luggage was at her feet. She was traveling light: just a few changes of clothes, some books, and yes, just one more thing. She gazed at the mantelpiece where her framed photo of her parents rested, hidden behind that Sears portrait shot of her and her auntie.

Poor auntie. Another sacrifice made, when auntie began to ask too many questions about how Adrianna had gotten from Iraq to America, too many questions about what she intended to do once she was out of school. By then, she'd had a grand idea of what was ahead for her, and even at that young age she knew that auntie would never hold up against any background check from the FBI or CIA or NSA or wherever she intended to go to work.

So her auntie had to die. So be it.

Another glance around her condo. In the basement was her bubble and the stolen laptop. She had no use for it now. Archeologists from some future time could have an orgy of investigation, if they ever got here, to dig into the laptop and find the years of work that she had carefully documented and executed, all those years of clandestine work, to conceive Final Winter, to prepare for Final Winter, and now, just days away, to see Final Winter finally, finally happen.

One more thing to pack.

Adrianna reached up to the mantelpiece, to the photo, and perhaps she was nervous, or perhaps her hand was shaking, but instead of holding on to the photo she picked it up clumsily and it fell on the floor, the frame cracking.

Now they were on a rural road, about a half-hour out of Memphis, following another set of directions. Vladimir had a small flashlight, was calling out left or right or straight on to Imad. The truck felt odd without the heavy trailer behind it, like a draft horse suddenly free from its wagon.

'All right,' Vladimir said. 'Take a left at the dirt road, coming up.'

Imad did just that, and the headlights illuminated the narrow dirt lane. Branches whipped at the fenders and windows as they surged ahead. Then the dirt road widened into an empty space in the woods. A dark blue Ford Explorer was parked at the far side. Imad said, 'Once again, our secret bosses have pulled through.'

'Yes, they have. Let's hurry up.'

Imad pulled the truck up to the Ford, left the engine running and the lights on as Vladimir jumped out of the cab. He went over to the SUV, went to the rear tire and felt up against the fender. There. His hand emerged with a key, which he held up so that Imad could see it. Imad honked the horn in response. Vladimir went to the Ford, unlocked the door, climbed in and started up the engine. Their instructions were to wait for a day, possibly two, to ensure that all was in place and that the final payments to their bank accounts were made. He came out as Imad shut off the diesel engine and emerged from the Freightliner, carrying his belongings. Vladimir watched him carefully as he put his belongings into the Explorer. Vladimir followed shortly, carrying his own bags. Imad made to go into the Ford when Vladimir said, 'The truck. I forgot the paperwork. Could you get it? Please?'

Imad shrugged, went back to the Freightliner. As he did that, Vladimir ducked into the Explorer, looking, looking, looking, and there it was. The small leather case. He opened the case and grabbed what was in it, just as—

Imad was there, a folder of papers in his hand. He looked confused.

'What . . . what are you doing?'

'Showing you that I do know how to kill, boy,' Vladimir said. And he shot him three times in the chest with his own pistol.

Imad fell back, the paperwork flying from his hand.

Vladimir strolled over and, just to make sure, he placed the muzzle of the pistol against the boy's forehead and pulled the trigger again.

'And if you didn't hear me before, fuck you,' he said.

Vladimir picked up the papers, walked around and picked up the four empty cartridge shells, and then went to the Ford Explorer, ready to leave this place, this state, this country.

CHAPTER TWENTY-NINE

Two days after flying back from Memphis, in the laundry room of his small apartment building in Rockaway, Queens, Brian Doyle walked back and forth, listening to the comforting sound of his Highland bagpipes, echoing among the quiet washing machines and dryers. The sound was good in the basement, the drones echoing off the thick plaster walls, the keening sound of the chanter cutting through the steady tone of the drones.

He walked back and forth at a slow pace, going through some of his favorites, starting with the quick marches – 'Highland Laddie' and '42nd Black Watch Highlanders Crossing the Rhine' and 'Heroes of Vittoria' – and then a few slowsteps, like 'Skye Boat Song' and 'Blue Bells' and 'Sleep Dearie Sleep' – and as he was getting ready to start another round, there was someone there, standing by the doorway, a grin on his face, slowly clapping his hands.

Brian let the mouthpiece fall from his mouth, snapped the

bagpipes out from underneath his arm. Standing in front of him was his partner, Jimmy Carr.

Jimmy said, 'Welcome back to the world, partner.'

'Thanks.'

'Guess I missed you when you checked in at the house.'

'Guess you missed me 'cause I didn't show up,' Brian said.

'Hah. Goofing off?'

'Time I've had these past months, I deserve all the goofing off I can get. And then some.'

Jimmy went over to a low-slung dryer, sat up on it, folded his arms. 'So how come you're not back on the job?'

Brian shrugged. 'Like I said, I needed the time.'

'Time to heal? Heard you got cut in Cincinnati.'

'How in hell did you learn that?'

'I'm a detective. It's my job to detect, to learn things. Like my partner, who's been taken away by the Feds, found himself at the wrong end of a knife in Cincinnati. Jesus. Cincinnati. If you're going to die, that's a hell of a place to die in.'

'True.'

'Next time be more careful, huh?'

'Sure,' Brian said. 'Next time.'

'Seen your boy yet?'

Brian grinned. 'Last night. And later today. It's good to see him . . . But his mother, though . . .'

Jimmy laughed at that and said, 'So why in hell did you come back?'

Brian went over to an idle washer, gently placed his bag-pipes down. The bag collapsed a bit, making a sighing noise through the drones, sounding like an old dog trying to relax. Brian said, 'I guess I got tired. Guess I got fired.'

'So. What were you working on before you got fired?'

'Classified.'

'Boy, am I surprised to hear that. Did you like it?'

'Nope.'

'Then how come you're not back on the job? Hey, remember that car-chopping case we were working on, before you left? The Sanchez brothers?'

'Yeah.'

'Well, it's been to court and back. Their mother gave them up. Can you believe that? So much for maternal feelings.'

Brian leaned back against the washer, said nothing. Jimmy watched him. Jimmy said, 'All right. So you don't want to talk about the job. And you can't talk about your new job. Classified and all that crap. So what was going on with your Fed job that you *can* tell me, partner?'

Brian folded his arms. 'Thing is, on the job, you know that most of the people you meet out on the street, they've got an agenda, they're slinging bullshit, not telling you the truth, hiding stuff from you, all that. That's part of the job. But the Fed job . . . it's something when the people you're working with, they're the ones slinging bullshit, they're the ones you can't trust. Hell of a thing.'

'That why you left?'

Brian thought about what he had been doing in Cincinnati, unearthing all those questions about Adrianna, about her past, about the death of her aunt, about the payoffs to her neighbors . . . A lot of questions to be answered. But when he had been offered the chance to leave, he had jumped at it.

Like a tired and scared rookie, seeing his first body.

Running away.

'Good question.'

Jimmy said, 'Years with you, I think I can figure out what's going on.'

'Yeah?'

'Yeah. I think you've got unfinished business back there. I think you wanted to leave but something's back there, calling you. True enough?'

Brian looked at the cocky face of his partner, thought for a moment, and picked up his bagpipes. 'Request time. What do you want to hear?'

'"Amazing Grace",' Jimmy said, grinning.

'Fuck you,' Brian said.

'Didn't know that was a bagpipe tune.'

'Lots of things you don't know, for a detective.' And he started playing 'Teribus', trying, just for a moment, to ignore the truth that his detective partner had been slinging his way.

At 11:05 p.m. the night before the scheduled departure of the canister-loaded aircraft, on a catwalk above one of the three maintenance hangars that AirBox leased, Alexander Bocks stood with Randy Tuthill, looking down at the organized chaos below them. Off to the left and right, MD-11 cargo jets with the yellow and black AirBox markings – and, a secret to all in the company save for a few, it was dear Clara, his wife, who had come up with the colors and logos, back when the company was two old 707s, rescued from an Arizona boneyard – and people were hard at work underneath all of them. People. His people! Scaffolding had been set up mid-fuselage, to gain access to the air-conditioning packs, and it had been an amazing process to see. The big jets had been towed in with the small tractor carriers, and machinists and maintenance workers had swarmed around them like the proverbial ants on a sugar cube. And when it was finished, each jet was wheeled out the other side of the hangar, and another jet, parked outside on the tarmac, was wheeled in.

Bocks slapped Randy on the back. 'I've seen the work orders and routing sheets. Your folks are an hour ahead of schedule! An hour! Christ on a crutch, Randy, they're doing a hell of a job.'

Randy folded his big hands, leaned against the catwalk railing. 'Treat your people right, and give them an impossible job to do, and nine times out of ten they'll pull through for you, General.'

'Damn glad to hear it.' Bocks checked his watch. 'At this rate, we'll have the right amount of aircraft ready for the mission, and we'll be ready by the time for first flight. Two a.m. If nothing screws up.'

Randy didn't reply, so Bocks repeated himself. 'Like I said, if nothing screws up.'

His friend and machinist said, 'Sorry to tell you, General. Looks like a screw-up is approaching.'

Bocks turned and saw his CFO, Frank Woolsey, coming towards them, face red with anger, one hand tightly clenched around a business-sized manila envelope.

Bocks said, 'Hold onto your balls, Randy. This isn't going to be pretty.'

'Holding my balls don't sound too pretty, either, but I'll do what I have to do.'

In her hotel room at 11:10 p.m., Adrianna Scott put the picture of her family – still hidden behind the poorly repaired frame – on the small round table in her hotel room. She had spent just a few minutes looking at papa and mama, remembering. Her favorite collection of books was lined up next to the quiet television, on a low shelf next to a sliding glass door that led out to a waist-high balcony. For the past three days, while she hadn't been over at AirBox checking on the progress of the canister installation, she'd spent most of her free time on the balcony, looking over Memphis, seeing the aircraft take off and land at the airport. Watching the daily waltz of aircraft movements, feeling excited at the stage she had set for the wonderful event that was going to take place in just a few hours.

Now she looked at herself in the room's mirror. Presentable. That was all. Just presentable. She could not believe how tired she was. Ever since coming back to Memphis, after the death of Darren and the shunting aside of Victor, Monty and Brian – and truth be told, how often had she thought of that strong man's tender touch these past few nights? – she had hardly slept at all. The only reason she was coherent was because of a CIA-issued drug cocktail that allowed her to rev on for a few days at peak performance despite the exhaustion she was now experiencing.

But it was close. Oh so close. Just one more session with the AirBox boys and in just a few hours the jets would be taking off to bomb the heartland of this country, the very first time it had been bombed since a few futile efforts by the Japanese more than a half-century ago. And she purposely didn't count 9/11 and the few spastic attempts that had followed. She and the Japanese of the 1940s had one thing in common: an overwhelming desire to see the death and destruction of America.

Adrianna grabbed a light jacket, looked again in the mirror. The CIA cocktail was still working, but Jesus, there would be a price to pay once this was over. Two days of bed rest, if not more, while the body recovered . . . And then something struck her. One decision she had yet to make.

For where should she go after the aircraft took off? The continental United States was not going to be a particularly fun place to be within the next twenty-four hours, and she had no desire to be stuck here while Mexico and Canada – panicked about what was happening to their north and their south respectively – closed the borders. So where to go in the next few hours? Mexico or Canada? Canada had better government, better amenities, but in Mexico you could get things done quickly, especially certain illegal things, by the judicious passing of folding money to the right people.

Still, she would decide shortly. And she knew it would only be a temporary arrangement in any case, for she had no doubt that in a couple of weeks the entire North American landmass, from Acapulco to the Beaufort sea, wouldn't be a particularly fun place to be either. France, perhaps. Provence. Nice weather, great food, and even if the politics were self-centered and corrupt, well, at least France had never murdered her family.

She looked at her bag on the bed, ready to be packed when she got back from a meeting at the airport. Her very last meeting, ever.

Adrianna went out of her hotel room, shutting the light off behind her.

At his condo unit at 11:30 at night, Victor Palmer was playing music from the late 1930s, swing band stuff – he couldn't have identified who was playing what, for all he cared for were the sounds, not the composers or the bands – as he went through his *Doc Savage* collection, leafing through the brittle pages of the pulp magazines, trying to imagine himself alive and well during those magnificent times. Oh, he knew that the times weren't that special – the Great Depression was roaring along and the black clouds of fascism and communism were looming fast over the horizon – but there was just such an innocence highlighted in these pages. The diplomas by mail. The truss supports. The pamphlets that promised 'secrets of the ages'.

And, of course, the stories, the grand, brawling, pulse-pounding, improbable and wonderful stories of Doc Savage and his great adventures. Victor found himself sighing with pleasure as he turned the pages, saw the rough illustrations, and breathed in the unique scent of the old pulp paper. To have been alive back then, to have been innocent of the Bronze Warrior's exploits and to have seen them fresh, month after month.

Ah, it had been pure delight. A few days ago the Princess had given him a week off, and he was enjoying every single minute, and during all those hours the phone jack had stayed unplugged, and the batteries had remained removed from his pager and government-issued cellphone.

Victor Palmer was currently living in 1935, and he had no plan to leave it anytime soon.

Alexander Bocks felt himself draw up to his full height as his CFO roared up to him. Woolsey started speaking before the ambient noise died down so the first thing Bocks could hear was '. . . fuck you doing?!?'

Bocks leaned into Woolsey, saying, 'Say again, Frank?'

'I said, what the fuck are you doing?'

Bocks said, 'Working. And what are you doing, besides gumming up the works?'

'The works?!? You think I'm gumming up the works?

Besides what you did the other day with the labor contract . . . what the hell is going on now? I've checked the maintenance schedule. You had six aircraft scheduled all week for maintenance. Six! So how come you've had thirty-plus airplanes in there in the past three days? The overtime budget alone has been blown for the quarter. Already! And what the hell is so vital that you had to have thirty planes cycled through in three days?'

'Something important,' Bocks said.

'And what's that?'

'Important. That's all I'm going to say.'

'Fine,' Frank said. 'And this is all I'm going to say. I'm out of here and on the phone to a majority of the board of directors, and in a half-hour, you're out and the locks are put on everything. AirBox isn't going to be yours in an hour, and everything's grounded. Got it? Everything's grounded. I've got a fiduciary responsibility to the stockholders and the board, because you've lost it. Lost it big time.'

Frank spun around and stamped away so hard over the catwalk that the floor grille rattled. Bocks looked over at Randy, who was looking right back at him. Randy came over and said, 'Can he do it?'

'Yeah. He can. Hate to say it.'

Randy said, 'In less than two hours, you've got to start dispatching aircraft. You got any suggestions?'

'No. Do you?'

Randy said, 'Yeah. Let me and a couple of guys take care of him. Until the flights are gone.'

'There'll be hell to pay.'

Randy said, 'In a few days, we're going to be attacked by anthrax. And the only way to save this nation is to get those planes down on the floor out the door. Right?'

'That's right.'

'Then we'll do it,' Randy said.

'You sure?'

'I've flown this long with you, General. I'll see it through. Now, if you'll excuse me, I've got a CFO to catch.'

Bocks watched his former Chief Master Sergeant stroll purposefully off the catwalk, and then he shifted his gaze down to the hangar floor. His people. All of them. Working to defend what was right.

He checked his watch. Time was still slipping away.

It was near midnight when Brian Doyle looked out the window of the descending American Airlines aircraft over Memphis. His stomach felt sour and there was a sour taste in his mouth too. It had taken a while to get here, but he hoped it would be worth it. From New York to BWI and now to Memphis. He had spent a couple of hours at the Tiger Team installation in Maryland that was staffed only by a couple of support people, picking up a few things and trying to get to talk to the other team members. But Monty was gone and neither Darren nor Victor answered their phones or pagers. And the Princess was here, in Memphis.

So Memphis was where Brian went.

The ground seemed to rise to meet the plane, and there was just the quickest *thud-thud* as the aircraft landed. He made his way through the departing passengers, carrying a soft black duffel bag, remembering the last time he'd seen Adrianna, the time he'd spent in Cincinnati, and the touch and taste of her flesh . . .

He was angry at himself. Letting the little man overrule the big man.

Typical male.

Outside the terminal, Brian got a taxi, gave the cabbie the address, and sat back, the duffel bag across his lap.

At 12:05 a.m., Deputy Sheriff Kyle Thurgood of the Shelby County Sheriff's Department hesitated for a moment, sitting in front of a computer terminal at a substation where he worked. Before him on the screen was a digital photo of a dead man, found late yesterday afternoon in a turnoff from a country road about six miles from where he was sitting. The young guy – Arab, Jew, Mediterranean, Mexican, who the hell could tell – was a homicide victim, and even with Thurgood's minimal experience on the job that had been an easy call. Three to the chest and one to the forehead sure in hell hadn't been a suicide. Thurgood hadn't been the lead investigator on the case – he hadn't even been part of the investigating squad. He had been working perimeter security, just making sure that the media and the curious didn't trample in, destroying whatever traces of evidence might have been there. Of course, with a goddamn Freightliner parked there it sure didn't seem like it would take too long to figure out why this guy had been taken to that place and murdered.

But . . . there was one more thing. Before being relieved, Thurgood had snagged a photo of the dead guy with a small Olympus digital camera, something . . . well, 'souvenir' wasn't the right word, but he wanted to have some sort of memento from his very first homicide. And coming back to the station he had had another thought. The department two months ago had gotten a directive from Homeland Security, about some new security initiative or something. Called the Physical Characteristic Comparison Program – or Characteristic Physical Program for Comparison, who the hell could remember – it requested that all law-enforcement agencies submit digital headshots of certain 'individuals of interest' so that they could be compared with whatever files the Feds had on hand. There were a whole lot of definitions that made up an individual of interest, and one that Thurgood remembered was an open homicide of an individual with no accompanying identification or notable physical characteristics.

So. A dark-skinned guy with no ID, next to a vehicle whose license plates didn't match and had no paperwork or registration . . . that seemed to fit the profile pretty well. But when Thurgood had suggested to his shift commander that it should be followed up, the shift commander had looked at him and said, 'Son, our boss is up for re-election this fall, and you want to give his ACLU opponents ammunition like this? Screw that shit . . . we got enough to do.'

Which was true. Yet . . . Thurgood felt funny about what was back up there. Theft? Hijacking? What in hell had happened up there in that turnaround? He knew what he should do. Close the file and go home. Forget it. Not his case. Not his problem.

He got up from the desk, reached down, whispered, 'Ah, fuck it,' and sent an e-mail to a Homeland Security Office contact, complete with attached photo.

Thurgood left, went to the locker room, got into his civvies. Just as he was heading out the locker-room door to the station's parking lot, it seemed as though every phone in the building started to ring.

Adrianna came onto the floor of the maintenance hangar at AirBox. It was nearly one a.m. Past the entrance into the hangar there were three offices off to the left. The door to the first one was closed, and over the noise of the machinery and ventilation equipment she could hear people shouting. She couldn't make out the words, but she sure could make out the emotions. Somebody was extremely upset.

The door suddenly opened. She stepped back. The General stepped out, his face flushed. Adrianna could make out a tumble of bodies behind him, gathered in one corner of the office, and then the door was shut.

'Miss Scott,' he said.

'General,' she said. She gestured at the closed door. 'Is there a problem?'

'Nothing you should worry about.'

Something fell over in the office. 'Really?' she asked.

'Let's just say a few machinists are having a frank and open discussion with my chief financial officer. What can I do for you?'

Adrianna said, 'Just one last status check.'

'All right,' he said. 'From what I know, we're not going to make the schedule.'

Oh, God, no, she thought. Her feet seemed to merge with the cement floor.

Then the General smiled.

'We're *ahead* of schedule. First flight due to take off at two a.m., followed by thirty-nine others, at sixty-second intervals. Sound good to you?'

'Sounds . . . sounds great, General.'

'Good. If you'll excuse me, I've got to follow up on a few things.'

She shook the General's hand, idly thought of how long he would live when this was all over, and then she said, 'The same here. I'll be back east by the morning, monitoring your aircraft, monitoring the efforts to capture the terrorist teams before they strike. Thank you again for what you've done, General. You've done a great service to your nation.'

The General went back to the closed door. 'Service not done yet, Miss Scott. Have a good night.'

'You, too, sir.'

And when Adrianna left, she felt as light as a feather.

At the Northwest Homeland Security office, Jason Janwick looked over his people, looked down again at the printout on the conference-room desk. 'All right,' he said. 'Just to make sure we got this straight, the Yemeni boy who's been on our watch list has been found dead outside Memphis. Three to the ten circle, one in the forehead. Think somebody was pissed at him?'

Some smiles from his crew. Janwick said, 'What does this tell us?'

His new girl from Customs looked around, as if to see if anybody else was going to step up to the plate. Tanya Mead said, 'Silence.'

'Go on.'

'Somebody wanted the boy silent. Somebody wanted to make sure he didn't talk about what he was doing there, what he was up to, that sort of thing.'

'Suspects?'

Another voice from the other side of the table. 'His companion. The Russian.'

'Simple. But probably true.'

Janwick drew a hand through his thin hair. Another late night in a series of late nights. What had to be done to protect this country.

'Any word on the trailer that was supposed to have been attached to that Freightliner?'

'No, sir,' came the answer.

'Lots of things we still don't know,' he said. 'Don't know for certain why the Yemeni got whacked, though we do have our suspicions. Don't know where the Russian is. Don't know where the cargo went. Those are the unknowns.'

Those quiet, curious faces, looking at him for guidance. He took a breath. 'But this is what we *do* know. We know that the Yemeni – with links to al-Qaeda – crossed into this country illegally nearly a week ago. We know the Yemeni crossed the border in the company of a Russian scientist with biowarfare experience, whose past history includes working with unsavory types in Southwest Asia. We know they crossed the border with a trailer filled with something that they didn't want examined by Customs. We know the trailer is now missing. Conclusions?'

'Biowarfare attack,' came a voice from the other end of the table.

'Sure,' Janwick said. 'But where? Memphis? What does Memphis have besides Graceland?'

'Cargo,' came another voice. 'Lots and lots of cargo. Every major air freight company in the nation has its hub there. DHL, FedEx, AirBox . . . you name it.'

Then there was a buzz of voices, as scenarios were presented, argued, debated. One voice – Logan, an ex-Marine recon who had lost an arm in Baghdad some years back – said, 'Sounds like an attack on the airport, chief. Remember how DC was in such a cluster-fuck back in '01 when they thought a couple of post office centers and the Senate mail room was contaminated? What do you think would happen if all of the airfreight in the nation got contaminated somehow? Christ, the stock market would crash in a heartbeat.'

More discussion and Janwick raised his hand. 'All right. Our place isn't to find all the answers. Just the right one. And the right answer is that the evidence is showing that something is going to hit the airport in Memphis. Maybe tonight, maybe tomorrow, maybe next week. My recommendation is a priority contact to Memphis Airport. Ground and seal, until that missing tractor-trailer unit or the Russian is located. BOLO for the Russian dispatched a hundred-mile radius from Memphis. Any questions?'

No questions.

'Good. Let's start making the calls.'

Jason Janwick looked at the clock. It was 10:10 p.m. – 1:10 in the morning in Memphis.

CHAPTER THIRTY

At the AirBox dispatch center at the Memphis Airport, Carrie Floyd looked up from her early-morning paperwork to see her co-pilot approach. 'Looks like we're going to the Great Northeast today, lady.'

'Really? Where?'

'Boston, Massachusetts. It's not London, but it'll do.'

'Sure will,' she said with a smile. 'If we've got time, I'll buy you lunch at the waterfront. Fresh Maine lobster.'

He looked around the room, as if to see if they were being watched. They weren't.

'Is this a regular lunch, or I-plan-to-say-yes-to-your-offer lunch?'

She smiled, went back to her paperwork. 'You'll see when we get there.'

'Fine, Carrie. Looking forward to it.'

She checked the time. It was 1:25 a.m. Just over a half-hour to takeoff.

Adrianna unlocked the door of her hotel room, stepped inside, and froze.

Brian Doyle was sitting in a chair, arms folded across his chest.

'Hey,' he said

'Hey yourself,' she said. 'How did you get in?'

'Through the door.'

'Don't be funny, Brian.'

'Wasn't,' he said. 'It's amazing what you can do with an NYPD detective's shield, a Federal ID, and a convincing story.'

'What kind of story?'

'That you were my fiancée. And that I wanted to surprise you.'

Adrianna couldn't believe what she was hearing. 'That's a hell of a story.'

'Sure is,' he said, his face expressionless. 'And speaking of stories, Adrianna, why don't you tell me yours?'

'Excuse me?'

'Talk to me about Cincinnati. Why your school records are missing. Why your neighbors were paid off to help spread a cover story about you. And how your aunt was murdered.'

The phone call from the Homeland Security Office in Washington State to have the Memphis Airport shut down and to prevent any entry from outside traffic was routed to a communications office at the main Homeland Security Office in Washington DC. Due to the nature and classification of the phone call, it had to be approved by the overnight communications supervisor before being sent along to Memphis. The overnight communications supervisor had been on the job for three days. Uncertain of her authority for shutting down the Memphis Airport, she started making phone calls to numbers on her contact sheet, each phone call taking approximately five minutes.

Brian could tell that he had scored by the way Adrianna's eyes seemed to flinch. But she was good, the way she recovered so quickly. 'I don't understand what you mean.'

'I mean this,' he said. 'And I'm probably violating a half-dozen regulations by telling you this, but it has to be said. One of my roles within the Tiger Team was being a rat, Adrianna. Someone who investigates the squad. A duty assigned to me by the Director. "Who will guard the guardians?" was his motto for me, and my job was to look at the background of the members. I checked out Victor and I checked out Darren, and except for a few odds and ends they were clean. But not you, Adrianna. There are questions. Questions that bugged me so much I came back tonight to figure it out. Like Mamma Garrity. Your neighbor. Who claims she was paid a hundred dollars a month by you, to pass on a cover story to those doing background checks when you applied to the CIA. Care to explain that story, Adrianna?'

Adrianna's expression seemed shaky. She rubbed at her eyes with both hands and said, 'I'm sorry . . . this is coming at me so fast . . . I . . . I have to go to the bathroom, Brian.

Honest. Please wait for me. I'll ... I'll tell you everything when I get out.'

And she turned her back to him, and went into the room's bathroom, closing the door behind her.

Brian stood up, waited.

Once the permissions had been granted and accepted, the phone call from the Homeland Security Office in Virginia went out to the night-shift manager at the Memphis Airport. At the time the phone call was made, the night-shift manager was off on the flight line, overseeing an accident investigation that had begun an hour earlier when a United Airlines flight had clipped the top of a catering truck. He had left strict instructions with his administrative staff that he was not to be disturbed, 'even if the goddamn governor calls'.

The administrative aide who took the phone call wasn't sure if an urgent message from Homeland Security was as important as the governor's office, but he didn't want to face the wrath of the manager twice in one shift.

So the call was written up and placed on the manager's desk.

More minutes slipped away.

Adrianna looked at herself in the bathroom mirror. Her stomach felt as if it was filled with liquid cement. Her legs were shaking. She checked her watch. Not much time, but Brian ... he could not be allowed to ask her any more questions, could not be allowed to have any chance to make any phone calls or do anything.

She ran the faucet, splashed some cold water on her face, and then flushed the toilet.

Then she went to the door.

Carrie Floyd was now in the cockpit, doing a pre-flight check. So far, so good. Weather was wonderful, CAVU – ceiling and visibility unlimited – and she looked forward to a quick trip to Boston. Sean was at her side, saying, 'We're 107 today . . . AirBox 107. Got it?'

'Gotten.'

A touch from his hand to hers. She didn't look up. 'Later, tiger. Later.'

'Sure, chief, whatever you say.'

'Good.'

Brian waited for Adrianna, stood up and looked around the room. Some of her favorite books seemed to be there. He tilted his head, checked out the titles. *Art History of the Medieval World. Romanesque Architecture of the Twelfth Century. Gothic Cathedrals in Medieval France.* So on and so forth. Her very first love. He ran his fingers across the spines of the books, remembered looking at them back at her condo. Yet . . . there seemed to be something off. Something was missing.

What was it?

He looked at the framed photo of Adrianna and her aunt. A cute photo, the two of them wearing matching outfits. He picked up the frame, looked closer at the photo. Nice. But the death of her aunt . . .

Something was pressing against his finger.

He tilted the photo, saw something poking out between the thick frame and the matte on the back. The edge of a piece of paper. He tugged at it with his fingernail, heard the bathroom door start to open.

*

Adrianna went through the open bathroom door, saw Brian looking at the photo frame. She strode to her overnight bag where it lay on the floor.

The piece of paper was photo paper. It slid out and now Brian held it in his hand. There was movement as Adrianna came out of the bathroom. He didn't look at her. He looked at the photo. It showed a woman and a young girl, sitting in a formal pose on a couch, with a man behind them. The girl . . . a much younger Adrianna Scott. Standing behind the couch was a man, and the man was wearing a uniform, a uniform . . .

Brian recognized the uniform, recognized the flag patch on the shoulder.

Iraq.

The man was an Iraqi officer of some sort.

Adrianna was sitting in front of him.

Her father?

Supposedly dead in a car accident with her mother.

A young Adrianna, sitting with her Iraqi parents . . .

Her dead Iraqi parents.

And then it came to him.

The missing book.

The Army That Never Was.

About General George S. Patton and his hoax against the Germans.

A wartime hoax.

War.

Adrianna Scott, working for the CIA, head of Tiger Team Seven, head of the Final Winter project, was from Iraq.

Her dead parents.

Holy shit.

He looked back and Adrianna was standing near the bed, holding a pistol in a two-handed grip, looking right at him.

Adrianna said, 'I'm sorry it came to this.'

Brian moved away from the table, was now by the open door leading outside to the balcony.

She moved forward. He backed away, letting the photo of her and her parents drop to the floor. He said, 'Adrianna, look, this can be handled, I'm not sure what—'

Adrianna moved even closer. Brian was now on the balcony.

In all his years on the job, Brian had been in some tight places before. As a uniformed officer, he had been in a radio patrol car that had been broadsided by a drunk driver at two a.m. on East 87th Street. As an undercover narcotics officer, he had wrestled with a couple of drunk Columbia University students at a subway stop on 125th Street. And as a detective second class, he had fallen down a flight of stairs in a tenement building after a fight broke out over some guy who he and his partner were trying to serve a warrant on. Not to mention the little scuffle the other day in Cincinnati.

But he had never been in a position like this, the wet-pants option, facing down somebody holding a piece on him. Never.

He tried to catch his breath. 'Adrianna . . .'

She took another step toward him. 'You know those movies where the criminal spends fifteen minutes explaining to a cop why he or she is doing what they're doing? This isn't one of those movies. But I'll tell you this: my name is Aliyah Fulenz, I am an Iraqi Christian woman, and in a few short hours I will destroy your nation.'

Brian had opened his mouth to say something when there were flashes of light, something struck his chest twice with the force of a telephone pole swinging at him, and there was darkness and then nothing.

Adrianna was surprised at how easy it was. Two shots to his chest and Brian fell back, fell back, and then struck the railing, and—

Was gone. Just like that. Over the edge of the balcony – Brian was gone.

She lowered the pistol. Looked at the floor, picked up the spent shells, tossed her family photo into her bag, threw in the books, and then left the room.

She thought she heard sirens. She didn't care.

It was set in stone. Nothing could stop her tonight.

Nothing.

Carrie Floyd got a taste of the MD-11's power as she advanced the throttles slightly to taxi across the ramp, heading to the departure runway. In his co-pilot's seat, Sean said, 'Nice weather later today in Boston. Perfect for lunch. And other things.'

'And other things?'

'Like a yes,' Sean said. 'You *do* know how to say yes, don't you?'

Carrie smiled. 'Reminds me of a story I heard once.'

'What's that?'

'About President Calvin Coolidge. Old Silent Cal. Supposedly, at some state dinner or function, a society woman was sitting next to him. She said to him, "Mister President, I made a bet with a friend that I can get you to say more than three words." And you know what Cal said in reply?'

'No, I don't.'

'"You lose."'

Sean laughed, and Carrie said, 'Takeoff checklist, please.'

'Yes, ma'am.'

Something loud was screaming in his ears.

Something was poking him in his arms and shoulders.

Something . . . God, he hurt . . .

He opened his eyes.

Faces were looking down at him. There were lights, motion, more sound.

The faces . . . their lips were moving.

He opened his mouth. Grunted.

Blinked his eyes.

Focus. It was coming into focus.

One of the faces came closer and he heard '. . . luckiest man I've ever seen, by far . . .'

Brian Doyle closed his eyes, opened them again.

The screaming noise . . . a siren.

He was in the rear of an ambulance.

He looked again. An EMT and a police officer were there, sitting on each side of him.

'What?' was all he could say.

The Memphis cop – a young, tough-looking black man – said, 'Sir, could you tell us who shot you? Who was it?'

Brian closed his eyes again. The pain was now taking root in different parts of his body. His chest. His back. His shoulders.

'How?'

The EMT seemed to be checking Brian's pulse. 'You mean, how did you survive? First, you had a vest on, so those two rounds cracked a rib or two but didn't penetrate. Second, you fell three stories onto a cafe awning. I'm sure you've got some hellacious bruises on your back. Nice trick, pal. Remind me to stick with you next time you buy a lottery ticket.'

The cop came back to him, more insistent. 'Who shot you, sir? How did it happen?'

Adrianna. Iraqi father. Final Winter.

'Airport.'

'What?' the cop asked.

'Airport. You've got to get me to the airport . . . you've got to tell AirBox . . . no flights . . . there can't be any flights tonight . . .'

Brian saw the cop look over at the EMT, who looked back and shrugged.

They don't understand, Brian thought. They're not listening . . . they're not . . . Jesus, his back hurt . . .

'Airport!' he said above the siren noise. 'We've got to get to the airport! AirBox . . . it has to be grounded!'

The EMT took a wet cloth, wiped down Brian's forehead. 'Mister, you're ten minutes outbound from the ER, and that's the only place we're going tonight.'

The siren noise seemed to drill right into Brian's head.

Adrianna pulled her rental car over to the side, just a few minutes after leaving the Hyatt. Her chest hurt from her labored breathing, but she felt she was calming down. It was happening. Even at this moment. It was happening.

She just had two things to do before the night was perfect. The first she had planned to do when she had gotten back to the hotel room, but Brian's unexpected presence had taken care of that. But now seemed like a good time.

She opened her purse, dialed a certain number on her

cellphone, and pressed the send button. The phone rang once and that was that. Good.

Adrianna put the phone back in her purse, eased her car out into the traffic. She looked at the dashboard clock.

It was 1:47 a.m. Thirteen minutes until the first AirBox aircraft took off.

Twelve miles away from Adrianna Scott's rental GMC, a Ford Explorer on Interstate 40, heading northeast, suddenly exploded, sending flaming chunks of debris across three lanes of traffic. A tractor-trailer truck jackknifed in an attempt to dodge the debris, cutting off the final lane.

It would take the Tennessee State Police over an hour to remove the body of the driver from the Explorer, a body that was burned beyond recognition.

Next to her Sean said, 'Tower, AirBox one-oh-seven, will be ready for takeoff at the end.'

In her headphones, Carrie heard the airport's tower controller say, 'AirBox one-oh-seven, hold short runway three six center.'

'Airbox one-oh-seven, hold short three six center, roger,' Sean replied.

As always, the jet felt sluggish as it maneuvered toward the runway. Carrie flicked her gaze to the well-lit runway, to the final approach path. No one was landing. The night's clear weather made the lights of the airport and the surrounding area shimmer brilliantly. It was one of the few nice things about flying at night, the constellation of lights on the ground. She looked forward to the flight and going to Boston, and well . . . Sean was going to get his answer in Boston and she was sure he would be happy.

She started humming a tune, something garnered from an album collection hawked late at night on the cable channels, and then stopped herself. She didn't want to tip her hand.

The tune, of course, was 'North to Alaska'.

Instead, she just smiled as her jet approached the hold area.

Brian opened his eyes again. The pain had settled down some. His mouth was dry and he looked at his arms. An IV was running into the right arm, beside which the EMT was stationed. The cop was on his left side, still looking expectantly at him. Brian raised his arm, motioned with a finger. 'Here,' he whispered. 'Come here and I'll tell you who . . . who shot me . . .'

The cop leaned in and Brian raised himself up and the cop said, 'Sir, who did this to you? Can you tell me—'

Brian let his hand snap down to the cop's holster, grabbed his pistol, and pulled it away, and—

The EMT flinched and the cop struggled but Brian was quick, Brian was driven, and in a second he had muzzle end of the pistol jammed up against the cop's lower jaw. Brian said, 'Take it easy, now.'

The cop said, his voice strained, 'There's no round in the chamber. And the safety is on.'

'Maybe so,' Brian said. 'But maybe I've got the safety off, and maybe you're lying about having no round in the chamber. You don't want to have your jaw blown off, do you? Ready to gamble that, officer?'

The EMT said, 'What . . . what do you want?'

'Stop this ambulance. Now. I'm getting off.'

The EMT said, 'Sir, you're injured, you're not thinking right, you're—'

Brian said, 'This ambulance doesn't stop the next ten seconds, I'm splattering this cop's brains all over the ceiling. Understood?'

It seemed like the EMT got it. Edging past them so he didn't seem to get too close to Brian and the cop, he moved to a small sliding glass partition between the ambulance bed and the driver and pounded on the window. 'Emergency, Carol – you've got to pull over. Now!'

Some murmured words from up front, and the EMT said, 'No fucking around! Stop the goddamn bus!'

The 'goddamn bus' slowed down and halted. Brian sat up, gritting his teeth at the pain in his back, keeping his stare fixed on the cop, who had murderous hate in his eyes – and who could blame him? The EMT – showing some initiative – scrambled to the rear of the ambulance and opened the rear door. Brian tugged at his right arm, pulling the IV free. Blood spurted down his arm. He kept on moving, the cop moving with him. It was awkward, it was tough, but soon he was out on the pavement. The cop was standing there too and Brian nudged him and said, 'Back in the bus, pal. You get back in the bus and close the door and drive away.'

The cop stood still.

Brian said, 'Move away, or I start shooting civilians. Move away, and I run like hell, and nobody gets hurt.'

The cop said, 'You're a stupid fuck.'

'Probably. Move.'

The cop took a step back and Brian stepped away, still wincing from the pain. The cop went back into the ambulance, and Brian slammed the door shut and slapped his hand twice against it. The ambulance, lights still flashing, moved out.

Brian took in his surroundings. Apartment buildings, office buildings, small stores – he could waste precious seconds looking for a phone and the police would come down like a hammer on this area once the cop in the ambulance got on the horn. He put the cop's pistol in his coat pocket, and walked quickly down one block, then another, not running – running men always attract attention – and by God, luck must have been with him, for he caught a taxi and in a matter of moments was heading to the Memphis International Airport.

It was 1:51 a.m.

Carrie Floyd felt the subtle vibration of the MD-11 engines in the control yoke as they waited for takeoff at the end of the runway. Sean was there, just waiting, and she decided that she would tease him, all the way northeast, once they took off.

He was patient. And would have to be, to put up with her and her daughter.

Sean made a point of clearing his throat.

Carrie kept on ignoring him, though it was hard to do with a smile on her face.

In the rear of the taxi, Brian Doyle tried to work through the pain in his back, the pain in his chest, keeping his gaze straight on what was ahead of him, and what was ahead of him wasn't good. For some reason the traffic was backing up to the airport exits. He leaned forward and said to the cabbie, 'Why is it taking so goddamn long? What's the holdup?'

'Man, who the fuck knows?' the cabbie said, the lilt in his Jamaican voice pronounced. 'Maybe an accident. Maybe a drill. I dunno.'

Brian waited, hands folded, staring ahead, looking at the line of red taillights stretching in front of them. He said, 'You own a cellphone?'

'Yeah.'

'Can I use it? It's an emergency.'

'No, man, I'm 'fraid you can't use it.'

'Why?'

'Cuz I don't have it here. It's back at my place.'

Brian said, 'I thought you said you had a cellphone.'

The cabbie said, 'You didn't ask me if I *had* one, you just asked me if I *owned* one. Right?'

They still weren't moving. Screw this.

Brian opened the cab door, stepped out, and started running towards the fences on the other side of the highway. If the cabbie was screaming at him, Brian didn't hear it over the noise of the jets.

AirBox 107 sat at the end of the runway, its engines idling, the white lights of the runway stretching out ahead. Carrie kept switching her gaze from the displays to the runway. Sean waited next to her, then said, 'Something's up.'

'Why?'

'We've never waited this long before, that's why.'

Carrie said, 'Be patient, will you?'

Sean said, 'Some would say I've been too patient already.'

She thought of what to say, when the tower controller's voice came over their headsets.

'AirBox one-oh-seven, tower.'

'One-oh-seven, go ahead,' Sean replied.

'Stand by.'

'One-oh-seven.'

Carrie looked at Sean and he said, 'Look over there. By the freight hangars. Lots of lights.'

She did just that. He was right. A number of red and blue flashing lights.

'You're right,' she said.

'You should learn to listen to me more often.'

Carrie waited and said, 'Some people would say I already listen too much.'

'Which people?'

Carrie said nothing, waited.

Then the tower came back on.

'Airbox one-oh-seven.'

Adrianna Scott had scouted out this place months ago, and now she waited with anticipation, a pair of 7X50 binoculars in her hands. She was in a small park on a hillside, about a mile away from the airport. Among the picnic tables and swing sets, all empty, she waited. She looked around her, saw how empty the place was, and felt a wonderful sense of satisfaction. This place would never be used again by the people of this country and soon grass and saplings and trees would once more cover this cleared area.

She lifted up the binoculars, focused them on the runway. She could make out long lines of yellow and black AirBox jets, heading out for departure.

'Soon, papa, soon, mama,' she whispered.

Brian bent over, vomited, and then stood up, wiping spit from his chin. Before him was an access road, bordered by a chain-link fence that butted up against the runway. What the hell to do now? There was nothing before him except the fence. No phones, no guard shacks, nothing.

Damn!

He looked up and down the length of the fence. Noted the lampposts. Noted the power lines. And the cameras, of course, the—

Security cameras.

Only chance. The only real chance.

Brian took out the pistol he had lifted from the Memphis cop, started running the length of the fence, shooting the pistol into the air, raising as much hell as he could. If the airport security team was on the job, if these cameras were manned, they would see a crazy man with a gun at the end of this runway, apparently shooting at the soon-to-depart aircraft.

It was the only thing he could do.

Sean said, 'AirBox one-oh-seven, go ahead.'

'Tower, AirBox one-oh-seven, cleared for takeoff, runway three six center'

'AirBox one-oh-seven, cleared for takeoff runway three six center, we thank you.'

Carrie held onto the throttles tight, started pushing them forward. She felt the engine thrust push her back into the seat as the runway lights started accelerating past them. Sean started calling out the speed and then V-1, the speed at which take off was imminent: 'Sixty. Seventy. Eighty. Vee-one, rotate.'

Carrie pulled the control yoke back. 'Vee-two,' Sean said as she felt the jet break free from the ground, Sean now indicating that they were at their climbing speed in case they lost an engine. They were airborne.

She said quickly, 'Positive rate, gear up,' and Sean moved a wheel-shaped lever with his left hand. There was a clunking sensation as the nose wheel came home.

'Gear up,' Sean said.

As the speed increased, Carrie called out, 'Flaps five.'

The flaps moved to their position, and then she said, 'Flaps up.'

'Flaps up,' Sean said. 'We've got a clean aircraft.'

The tower controller's voice came over the radio. 'AirBox one-oh-seven, change to departure.'

Sean said, 'AirBox one-oh-seven' as he changed the radio's frequency. Then a different voice announced itself: 'AirBox one-oh-seven.'

'Departure, AirBox one-oh-seven, passing feet for five thousand,' Sean said.

'AirBox one-oh-seven, climb to one zero thousand, heading zero two zero, proceed to CENTRALIA when able, and proceed via your flight plan.'

Carrie loved this, loved the feeling of going up into the air, everything under control, everything nominal, clear night sky and nothing ahead but hours of blissful flying, heading to CENTRALIA, their first departure point – or fix – on their way to Boston.

'What do you say, Sean? Let's have a good flight.'

'You got it, Carrie.'

Brian looked up as one AirBox aircraft, and then another, and another, took off over him, deafening him with the noise of their engines. The pistol was out of bullets. He dropped the useless piece of metal on the ground.

He twisted his head to follow the aircrafts' flight, knowing that each of them was carrying something horrible, something deadly, and that he had failed to prevent them from taking off.

He clenched his fists, screamed up in frustration at the departing aircraft.

Adrianna lowered the binoculars, smiling widely with happiness. One after another, her gifts to America had taken off to spread across this wide and darkened land. She felt her heart swell with joy, thinking of what was in every one of those aircraft, thinking of what was going to be sprayed out over all those cities in just a matter of hours.

She went back to her car, binoculars in hand, ready to leave this soon-to-be-dead nation.

PART THREE

CHAPTER THIRTY-ONE

Alexander Bocks was in his office at 2:30 a.m. when the phone call came in.

'Mr Bocks?'

'You got him.'

'Sir, this is Carl Goodson, on-duty airport manager.'

'Go ahead.'

'Sir, we've got a threat report from Homeland Security. We're shutting down operations, sealing the grounds and aircraft.'

Bocks leaned forward in his chair, something nasty beginning to churn in his stomach. 'What's the basis of the threat?'

'Not known at this time, sir. We've been advised to close down. More information to follow.'

'Who's your contact with Homeland Security?'

Goodson said, 'Deputy Director Janwick. From the Northwest Office.'

'Give me his number.'

Goodson did just that. Bocks said, 'All right. I'm out of my office now. I'm going to my Operations Center. I'll be there in five minutes.'

He could hear Goodson sigh. 'Might be a while, sir. I've got other calls to make.'

Bocks stood, ready to hang up. 'I'm sure you have.'

By the time he reached his office door, he was running.

*

Something flickering and blue caught Brian's eye. He turned and saw a patrol car coming up the access road, blue lights flashing, headlights flickering left-right-left-right. About goddamn time.

A side spotlight nailed Brian as he stood there, still listening to the jets taking off. He raised his arms as the car stopped and two airport cops stepped out.

As they approached he held his palms flat out, showing that he wasn't carrying a thing.

One cop said, 'Freeze – don't even think of moving.'

'You got it.'

The other cop said, 'Kneel down.'

'Nope.'

The first cop said, 'Kneel down, or we'll—'

Another jet roared overhead.

Brian said, 'I'm Brian Doyle. Detective from the New York Police Department. Detached to the Federal Operational and Intelligence Liaison Agency. This is an emergency. I need to see Alexander Bocks, head of AirBox, right now.'

The second cop said, 'What the hell were you doing, shooting off your pistol like that?'

'Trying to get somebody's attention.'

'You sure the fuck achieved that,' the first cop said.

'You got ID?' the second cop asked.

'Wallet. Left rear pocket.'

The first cop said, 'Pull it out, using two fingers, toss it over here.'

Another jet went overhead. Brian did as he was told and said, 'Guys, no offense, but we're wasting time. This is a Homeland Security emergency. We've got to—'

'Hold it. And stand right there.'

The two cops huddled, looking at his wallet, and he was going to say something, something sharp, when he realized how quiet it was.

Quiet.

The aircraft had stopped taking off.

Brian looked over at the runway. Aircraft were there, sitting still. More flashing blue lights from other vehicles were racing along the runway, heading to the parked aircraft.

The cops came to him. 'Where do you need to go?'

'AirBox. I need to see General Bocks.'

The first cop said, 'We can get you there, but it's not up to us whether you get to see the General.'

'Got it.'

Monty Zane stifled a yawn, looked down at the lights of the runways and the city beneath him. It had been a long, long day, and an even longer night. The trick in flying so much was to catch as much sleep as you could, no matter which way you were traveling across the globe, no matter which time zone you ended up in. Earlier Monty had read stories about those 'business-class warriors' who traveled on behalf of their corporate masters and who tried to cope with jet lag. Everything from special diets to special exercises to special music CDs to listen to as you 'reorganized your inner energy' or some such shit. Hah. Just get as much sleep as you needed and try to store up some zees, 'cause in some of the places Monty had traveled to jet lag was for wimps.

He yawned again. Though, he thought, this particular wimp sure could use another few hours of sleep, in a real bed, not a red-webbed seat or some other airline chair.

The aircraft came down to the runway in the darkness. Monty folded his arms, idly thought of how many times he had been in aircraft before, and lost track just as the wheels touched down and there was a shudder as the plane settled in on the runway. There was the usual whine as the engines reverse-thrusted, and Monty looked around the interior of the well-lit cabin.

A woman's voice came over the intercom: 'Ladies and gentlemen, I'm pleased to report that we must be the luckiest flight in the world tonight. We've been informed that due to some unknown circumstance at this time, the airport has closed, and no other aircraft will be allowed to land. Or take off.'

Some of the passengers started talking. Monty sat still, listened. Lucky choice, he thought, to disobey his pager orders and come back here to find out what the hell was going on.

'In any event,' the flight attendant continued, 'thank you for choosing United, and welcome to Memphis.'

Soon enough, the aircraft reached the gate. There were plenty of blue lights flashing from vehicles on the runway, and then the flight attendant's voice came over the intercom again, a bit shakier than before.

'I'm sorry to say, ladies and gentlemen, we've been informed that all passengers are to remain seated. There . . . there appears to be a security concern. Thank you for your patience and understanding.'

Monty looked at the faces of the other passengers, didn't like at all what he was hearing. He unbuckled his seat belt and got up – always take an aisle seat, you don't have to wait for some grandma or grandpa to let you go – and went to the overhead bin. He retrieved one of his black duffel bags – a bigger one was in the luggage hold, and he doubted he would see it before tonight was over – and he strolled up the aisleway. Some of the passengers started talking and pointing him out, and he ignored them.

A flight attendant came toward him, saying, 'Sir, I'm going to have to ask you to sit back down. We're not allowed—'

He showed her his identification, waited a moment, and said, 'Ma'am, I've got to get off this aircraft. Now.'

She looked at the identification, looked at him, and back to the identification. 'We'll go see the captain.'

Monty followed her perky butt as they went forward, and a passenger in first class eyed him closely as he went by. The guy had close-cropped hair and had on a coat and tie, and Monty nailed him right away: sky marshal, just making sure things were copacetic.

At the forward area, the attendant went into the open cockpit, where the captain and first officer were still in their seats. She passed over Monty's identification, there was a quick confab, and the captain stood up and came to him as he stood by the closed cabin door.

'Hell of an identification card you're carrying there, Mister Zane,' he said.

'That it is.'

'Says here . . . well, you could probably requisition me and this aircraft to fly you to Peking if you wanted to.'

'Probably, but right now I just need to get off this aircraft.'

The captain handed Monty back his ID. He said, 'Nothing's moving out there. I can open the cabin door but you'll be on your own.'

Monty shrugged. 'I've been on my own in worse places.'

The captain said, 'I'm sure as shit you're right.' Then he said to the flight attendant, 'Louise, go ahead. Pop her open.'

Louise went to the red-colored door handle, swung it forward and there was a gentle whoosh as the door opened. The fresh air felt good. Monty went to the edge of the door, sat down, let his feet dangle over the side. He dropped the duffel bag to the runway below him, and then scooted out, grabbed onto the edge of the open door. He stretched out as far as he could, hanging there by his fingertips, and then he dropped. He let his body curl in a parachute fall, rolled onto his left side and shoulder, and then got up.

A spotlight got him before he reached his duffel bag. He raised his hands.

Two guys in black jumpsuits, body armor, helmets, and carrying automatic weapons with lit flashlight attachments under the stubby barrels approached at a fast trot. One guy shouted out, 'You got someplace fucking important to go to, pal?'

Monty said, 'That I do.'

'Unless you're the fucking president of the United States, I don't think you're going anywhere but a lock-up.'

Monty said, 'All right if I slide my ID over?'

The second guy said, 'Sure. Make it snappy.'

He dropped his identification wallet on the ground, gently tapped it with his foot so it slid over to the two guys. One of them picked it up and examined it with a small flashlight, while his partner kept his weapon trained on Monty. Good tradecraft.

'Sorry, Henry,' the guy examining the ID said.

'Huh?'

He tossed the ID back to Monty, who snatched it in mid-air. The guy said to his partner, 'Guess we had a presidential election and missed it. Mister Zane, where do you need to go?'

'AirBox,' he said.

'You got it.'

A half-mile and thirty feet underground from his corner office, Alexander Bocks exited an elevator into his company's Operations Center. Protected by steel-reinforced concrete and with its own independent power, water and air supply, the Operations Center kept track of every single AirBox aircraft in the air, from takeoff in Memphis to any of the scores of destinations in this part of the hemisphere.

Bocks walked into the dimly lit room, lined with desks and monitors. On the far wall was a large plasma screen depicting the continental United States, Mexico, the Caribbean, Canada and, in smaller subsets off to the left, Alaska and Hawaii. With a practiced eye, he looked up at the screen, saw the triangular icons marking those aircraft that were now airborne prior to the airport's shutdown.

The overnight manager – an ex-Air Force air traffic controller named Pam Kasnet – stood up from her desk, headset on, as he approached.

'What do we have up?'

'Nineteen aircraft, all on their paths, all on schedule.'

'Any word on a reopening?'

'None.'

In the room there was the soft murmur of the operations staff who were keeping an eye on the aircraft and also keeping an eye on the package-sorting and distribution center. Smaller screens on some of the terminals displayed the interior of the buildings where packages and envelopes were continuously sorted, bagged and tagged. Bocks spared them a quick glance and went back to his overnight manager. What a fuck-up. Besides hammering his company's schedule for the night, there was the more important Final Winter project, and he knew that very shortly he would need to let Adrianna Scott know what was going on.

'The word I got is that there's a threat against the airport, leading to the shutdown. You got anything more than that?'

Kasnet went to her desk. 'Got an info fax from Homeland Security about two minutes before you arrived, sir. Seems two men on the terrorist watch list crossed over into the United States through Washington State last week.'

Bocks said, 'Washington State? Hell of a thing to get us all spun up about.'

She said, 'True, sir, but the county sheriff's department found the body of one of those terror suspects about ten miles from here last night. They had information that he and his partner might have been in the area of the airport.'

'Let me see the fax.'

Kasnet picked up a sheet of paper from her desk, passed it over.

Bocks looked at the paper, and felt his left arm fly out to grab the back of a chair so that he could sit down without collapsing in front of his manager. He managed to get in the chair, managed to sit still, all the while staring at two faces, the faces of the two men who had been here just a few days ago.

Mother of God and all the Saints preserve us, he thought. He had never passed out in his life, but he was sure that he was damn close to collapsing right now. Oh God, he thought, oh God.

'Pam,' he said, hating how hoarse his voice sounded.

'Sir?'

'Get Homeland Security on the line. A Deputy Director

Janwick, from their Northwest Regional Office, in Spokane. Now. And— Hold on, wait.'

'Sir?'

Stared at the paper, stared at the paper, all Bocks wanted to do was stare at the paper, and he felt things slipping away, felt it all slip away, and he forced himself to take a long, deep breath, put the paper down, and then look at his concerned manager.

Took another deep breath.

'All right. Before you contact Homeland Security, listen to what I've got to say, and then do it. No questions. Understood?'

'Sir.' Kasnet had a small notebook and pen in her strong hands.

'Send this ACARS message to all airborne aircraft. "Positive threat to your aircraft. Threat altitude sensitive. Do not descend below three thousand MSL. Declare emergency with air traffic control. Hold present positions at maximum endurance. Contact dispatch upon receipt of message." Got that? Under no circumstances are they to descend. Make sure all nineteen aircraft acknowledge, and I want their confirmations passed on to me. All right?'

'Sir.'

'Good. Get going.'

Kasnet went back to her desk, started raising her voice, and there was a quick huddle of her staff. Bocks let her be. She knew what she was doing. In a matter of seconds that message would be going out on ACARS – Aircraft Communications Addressing and Reporting System – to those nineteen aircraft. He could count on her. She had a job to do and, right now, so did he.

He found an empty desk, unlatched his Blackberry PDA

from his belt, checked something, and then started dialing a cellphone number. It rang and rang and rang, but there was no answer.

Adrianna Scott was gone.

He knew it was odd, but Randy Tuthill had never been woken up by a telephone in his life. He was always half-awake, laying in bed or a bunk over the years, whenever a phone rang. He claimed to Marla that he was psychic, and she would say, 'Psycho, maybe,' and that was that. So when the phone rang at 2:40 a.m. this morning, he got it before the second ring.

'Tuthill.'

'Randy?'

'Yes, who is it?'

'It's the General.'

Randy sat up in bed, as wide awake as if he had drunk a gallon of coffee. He had never heard such despair in the General's voice before. Aircraft down, that was what it had to be, aircraft down and it was time to go rooting through maintenance records, to see if it had been one of his guys or girls who was responsible for sending a multimillion dollar piece of fine machinery and two human beings slamming into the ground . . .

'Sir, what is it?'

The General said, 'I need you at the Operations Center ASAP. I can't say over the phone, but . . . the project you completed so successfully – it's about to bite us in the ass, big time. Get over here. Now.'

'You've got it, General,' Randy replied. But by then he was speaking into a dead telephone.

*

In Washington State, Homeland Security Deputy Director Jason Janwick answered the phone in his conference room, with his people there. The advance word was that the guy on the other end of the line had information about the Russian and Arab who had slipped across the border last week.

His people looked at him with concern as he said, 'Is this General Bocks, from AirBox?'

The strained voice on the other end said, 'Yes, it is. Director Janwick?'

'That's right. What do you have for me?'

The caller said, 'Vladimir Zhukov and the Arab boy that was with him. Imad. What can you tell me about them?'

'Why do you want to know?'

'Because the two of them were at my airfreight company a few days ago, that's why.'

Shit, Janwick thought. 'Hold on. I want my staff to hear this.'

He set the phone up to speakerphone, put the receiver down, and said, his voice louder, 'Go ahead, General Bocks. Tell me again what you just said.'

The general said, 'Those two men on your watch list. They were at my airfreight company less than four days ago.'

'Doing what?'

'Making a delivery. And it's my time for answers. What can you tell me about those two?'

Janwick said, 'The Arab kid is a truck driver, spent time in Canada, Yemen, Saudi Arabia, Lebanon. Has family contacts to groups associated with al-Qaeda. Zhukov . . . a tricky, slippery bastard. One of the brightest biowarfare scientists the Soviet Union ever produced. Disappeared and was thought to have gone rogue after the breakup of the USSR. Might have spent some time in Iraq, Iran, any place that didn't like us and that would pay good money for his talents. And from what I've been told, his biggest talent is weaponized airborne anthrax.'

The only sound from the speakerphone was the hiss of static. Janwick looked at the attentive faces of his staff and said, 'General, you said they made a delivery. We need to know. What kind of delivery? Packages? And if so, where did they go?'

Bocks sounded even more strained. 'Canisters . . . they were delivering canisters that supposedly contained anthrax vaccine . . . but now . . .'

Murmurs from Janwick's staff. 'General, where are those canisters now? Are they being delivered? Or are they still at your facility?'

Bocks cleared his throat. 'Director Janwick, those canisters are on nineteen of my aircraft. That's where they are. And they're set to disperse their contents if the planes descend below three thousand feet.'

Janwick had to sit down. Then he looked at the speakerphone in fury as a clicking sound indicated that the man on the other end had hung up. He was going to have one of his staffers get hold of Bocks, but thought better of it.

There were other things that had to be done.

'Tess?'

'Sir?'

'Memphis. Whatever biowarfare resources we have near the airport, get them the hell over to AirBox.'

'Yes, sir.'

Bocks watched his people at work in the Operations Center, knowing that they would do almost anything and everything he would ask of them. He wondered just how far they would go tonight, because . . . well, because they were going into uncharted territory. *Terra* very fucking *incognita*.

He looked at the telephone on the desk before him, flanked by framed pictures of some family. Three little girls and mom and dad. He wondered if it was mom or dad who worked for him, who sat at this desk, and whose lives he was quite sure he had put in jeopardy tonight.

The telephone. He was sure that Homeland Security guy was severely pissed at being hung up on, but time was slipping away. Other calls had to be made, he dreaded every single one of them, but there was no choice. He looked at the Blackberry and started dialing.

The phone rang once.

'Night desk, FOIL,' came the young man's voice.

'This is General Alexander Bocks, of AirBox. I need to speak to the Director, right away. Authorization is Bennington. I repeat, authorization is Bennington.'

'Hold on.'

No clicks, no hum, no buzzes. Top-of-the-line comm gear.

The colonel came on the line. 'General. What's going on?'

Bocks squeezed the phone receiver quite hard. 'I know this isn't a secure line. But this is an emergency. I need information, and I need it fast.'

'Go ahead.'

'Adrianna Scott. The project I was performing for her. Does it . . . did it . . . did it involve a vaccination protocol at all?'

He waited only seconds, he knew they were seconds, but God, in those seconds hope lived, it lived bravely and forthrightly, and at the end of those seconds hope died.

'General . . . what the hell are you saying? There's nothing involving vaccination connected with Final Winter. Nothing! Final Winter is supposed to be a test release of non-toxic bacteria, to measure wind patterns and dispersal records. Talk to me, General Bocks. Talk to me.'

Bocks knew the Operations Center was kept climate-controlled, but his shirt was soaked. 'Colonel . . . we've got a hell of a situation over here. We've got nineteen aircraft airborne, containing canisters that we believed to be an emergency airborne anthrax vaccine. These canisters were installed under the direction of your Adrianna Scott. In the past half-hour, I've been unable to contact Adrianna Scott. And there's one more thing . . .'

'Go on.'

Another deep breath. 'Homeland Security has closed down Memphis Airport. They received information that two individuals on the terrorist watch list were in the area this past week. One was an Arab youth, with connections to a Yemeni branch of al-Qaeda. The other was a virologist from the former Soviet Union. A Vladimir Zhukov. Colonel, four days ago these two individuals delivered the canisters that we believed contained an airborne anthrax vaccine. Adrianna Scott supervised the installation of those canisters aboard my aircraft. Whatever's in them, I'm sure as hell convinced it's not vaccine.'

The colonel swore once, very loudly. 'Are you sure they made the delivery?'

'I'm positive. Colonel, I was there. I saw the bastards myself.'

The colonel swore once more, and then hung up.

Bocks followed suit and then picked up the phone and started dialing some more.

*

Within ninety seconds of the colonel hanging up on Bocks, a message was transmitted worldwide on a secure Department of Defense information network called DEFNET. The message said:

FLASH PRIORITY ALPHA
ALL STATIONS
COMMENCE CASE SUMTER
COMMENCE CASE SUMTER
COMMENCE CASE SUMTER
ALL STATIONS ACKNOWLEDGE

Within sixty seconds of the Flash Priority message being sent across DEFNET, certain pre-planned events began to occur.

The President of the United States was at a resort hotel in Sun Valley, looking forward to a day of fly fishing on the Snake River, when armed Secret Service agents came into his hotel room and bundled him out to a waiting armored Chevrolet Suburban. Before he could ask what in hell was going on, agents had placed him in a biowarfare protective suit, complete with respirator, and he found that he could only make himself heard by yelling.

So he kept quiet until he was in Air Force One, which went airborne in twenty minutes and headed north to Canada. By the time it reached cruising altitude, it was joined by four F-16 fighters of the 119th Fighter Wing of the North Dakota Air National Guard out of Fargo, ND, and the President was receiving the first of many briefings that were to be conducted over the next several hours.

*

The Vice President was at his official residence at the US Naval Observatory outside Washington DC when his Secret Service detail grabbed him and placed him in a specially modified Humvee with its own air-control and filtration system. Within a half-hour he was in a secure location that as yet had not been disclosed by those enterprising members of the Fourth Estate.

The Speaker of the House was taken by Blackhawk helicopter from his apartment at the Watergate in Washington DC and was flown north to a rural area in West Virginia. Approximately fifteen minutes away from landing at another government retreat facility, the pilot of the Blackhawk misjudged his altitude and the tail rotor of the helicopter struck a high-tension power line belonging to the Appalachian Power Company. The subsequent crash of the helicopter killed the crew, three members of the Secret Service, and the Speaker the House, the second-in-line in the presidential succession.

All across the United States, as the wreckage of the Blackhawk helicopter in West Virginia continued to burn, members of the Cabinet, members of the US Senate and US House leadership and other government officials were brought – sometimes forcibly – to retreat areas that were designed to withstand not only nuclear attack but airborne biological and chemical attack too. As this retreat took place, US embassies across the globe went on Threat Condition Delta, as did the armed forces of the United States. Very soon the major news organizations in the United States became aware that something terrible was underway.

*

Two minutes after the President was awoken in Sun Valley, Idaho, a phone call was made to the Northern Command of the US Air Force stationed at Peterson Air Force Base in Colorado Springs, Colorado. The on-duty commander who received the call – Lt General Mike McKenna – said one thing when the call came in and he was briefed on the situation: 'This is real world, correct? Not a drill?'

'That's correct, general, not a drill,' said the male voice. 'This is real-world.'

'Understood,' General McKenna said as he hung up the phone. His office was a glass-enclosed cube overlooking the rows of terminals, desks and overhead display screens that observed the airborne space over Canada and the United Stations. His adjutant, Colonel Madeline Anson, looked on from a nearby chair.

'Sir?' she asked.

The general said, 'We have nineteen aircraft airborne over CONUS,' he said, referring to the continental United States. 'It's believed they may be carrying an airborne agent of some kind. Sarin, plague, anthrax – not sure at this time.'

'Shit,' said the colonel. 'Where did they come from?'

The general grimaced. 'Memphis. They're aircraft from AirBox.'

'General Bocks's company?'

'The same,' he said. 'Madeline, execute Strike Angel. Now. I want those nineteen to have company within the next thirty minutes and we'll need to brief our FAA rep.'

'Sir,' she said, getting up from her chair.

'And one more thing. I need to talk to Bocks. ASAP.'

'Yes, sir.'

When his adjutant left McKenna waited, his hands folded. Thoughts were racing through his mind, were pressing against him, and he was pleased that so far he was keeping on top of things. He looked up at the clock. A few hours from now his shift would have ended and another general officer would be at this desk, with this responsibility.

McKenna looked at his empty coffee cup. He would need some caffeine, and soon, and he refused to feel sorry for himself. Shift change or not, this was his job, his duty, and right now his duty meant that—

The phone on his desk rang. He picked it up. Colonel Anson said, 'Hold for a second, sir, for General Bocks.'

'Thank you, Madeline.'

A very long second indeed, McKenna mused, and the concept of his duty came back to him as he finished the thought.

Duty meant a lot of things, and at this very moment it meant explaining to the head of a company why it was necessary to shoot down his nineteen aircraft and kill their crews.

CHAPTER THIRTY-TWO

Brian Doyle was in an empty terminal, looking for somebody, anybody, when he saw a man approach him from around a ticket counter, whistling. The man had on a dark blue janitor's uniform and a bundle of keys at his side and was pushing a wheeled bucket with the handle of a mop. Brian strode over to him and showed him his ID.

The older man whistled. 'NYPD. You're far from home, pal.'

'That I am.'

The man asked eagerly, 'You ever been on *NYPD Blue*? That's my favorite show. Even though it's off the air, I do love it so. I see all the repeats.'

Brian looked at the man's eyes, and sensed the intelligence back there was that of a teenage boy. He hated to lie but he had no time. 'Sure. A couple of times. As an extra. You know, just part of the crowd.'

The man laughed, showing bad teeth. 'That's wonderful. That's truly wonderful. What can I do you for?'

'AirBox.'

The janitor nodded. 'Know it well.'

'That's good. Because I need to see the people who run it. Not the office types, the guys who keep track of the aircraft.'

The janitor said, 'Lots of police and troopers out there tonight. There's some sort of emergency. They're not letting people through from one terminal to another.'

'That so?'

The janitor grinned again. 'But for a real true NYPD Blue, I can get you there real quick. Skip the places where the blockades are. That sound good?'

Brian said, 'Best news I've heard all night.'

Alexander Bocks heard a click on the other end of the phone. He said, 'Bocks here.'

'Sir, this is Lt General Mike McKenna, Northern Command.'

'Yes.'

'I understand you have nineteen aircraft outbound from

Memphis, carrying canisters that may contain airborne pathogens. Correct?'

'That's correct.'

'Are the crews aware of this situation?'

Bocks said, 'Not yet.'

'Do you intend to notify them?'

'Of course. The crews . . . they have a right to know what's going on.'

General McKenna said, 'Are they still heading to their destinations?'

'No,' Bocks said. 'They're holding at altitude along their routes at maximum fuel conservation. They've all declared an in-flight emergency for a positive threat against their aircraft.'

'Good. General Bocks . . . I've also been notified that those canisters are designed to release their contents if the aircraft descend below three thousand feet.'

Bocks's eyes felt as though they were burning. He rubbed at them. 'That's right.'

'Sir, you need to ensure your pilots understand that they are to maintain altitude and stand by to divert. Understood? In a matter of minutes each of your aircraft is going to have an Air Force or Air National Guard escort. They have orders to respond if any of your aircraft begin an unauthorized descent. Do you understand what I'm saying?'

Bocks said, 'That I do. You intend to shoot down any of my aircraft that start descending without authorization.'

'Correct. Sorry to have to tell you this, sir.'

Bocks said, 'Not as fucking sorry as I am to hear it.'

The airport was a cluster-fuck early this morning, and Randy Tuthill had to use guile, arguments, and his old Air Force ID to gain entry to his maintenance hangars. After parking his Jeep Cherokee, he was about to trot down to the Operations Center when one of his senior machinists, a guy named Clarke, grabbed his arm.

'Randy, you've got to see what's going on over here.'

'Shit, Gary, I'm overdue to see the General.'

'Trust me, the General's gonna want to know what's going on up here.'

He followed Clarke to one of the open bay doors and stopped. Yellow tape had been strung across the entrance to the bay, and men in black jumpsuits, Kevlar helmets and automatic weapons strapped to their chest kept a quiet vigil from inside the hangar.

'Holy Christ,' Randy said. But it wasn't the men with guns that had caused the outburst. Before him, about twenty yards away, was one of his MD-11s, parked quietly, but looking like some giant science experiment. A huge translucent plastic bag of some sort had been draped over the fuselage, and small air generators were keeping it inflated. Two dark green trailers had been backed up to the covered airplane, and Randy could make out shapes working just below the aircraft.

Randy rubbed at his chest. It felt like it was about to tear itself open. He knew what was going on, but he had to ask.

'What do you know, Gary?'

'All the fuck I know is that these guys took over both maintenance hangars, kicked us out, and they've started working on this first piece of equipment. I think they're going into the air-conditioning packs.'

'All right.'

'Oh. And one more thing. Just before you got here, I saw one of the guys – wearing an EPA suit or something – go into the trailer, carrying something. And a while after that, one of those guys started yelling something.'

'What was he yelling?'

'Positive,' Gary said. 'He was yelling that whatever it was, it had tested positive.'

Randy nodded, his chest even more tight. 'I'll make sure to tell the General.'

Carrie Floyd was thinking of what to say when she and Sean had their little conversation in Boston when a blinking light caught her eye. She looked down at the control pedestal between her seat and Sean's, and saw a flashing yellow light in the corner of a small square box that was starting to spit out a piece of printed paper.

'Sean, message coming in from ACARS.'

Sean reached down, tore off the slip of paper as it came out of the top of the ACARS unit. ACARS was a data link system to their Operations Center and allowed them to send text messages back and forth. Most airlines in the world used a type of ACARS and AirBox was no different.

Sean said, 'What kind of bullshit is this?'

He passed the message slip over to her. She read:

AB 107
POSITIVE THREAT TO YOUR AIRCRAFT
THREAT ALTITUDE SENSITIVE
DO NOT DESCEND BELOW 3000 MSL
DECLARE EMERGENCY WITH ATC.
HOLD PRESENT POSITION AT MAX FUEL
ENDURANCE
ACKNOWLEDGE WITH DISPATCH
MORE TO FOLLOW

It felt like a jet of cold air was playing against the back of her neck. ACARS was usually used to inform aircraft about changes in weather or advise about conditions at destination airports. Nothing as ... nothing as terrifying as this one. Had to be a bomb of some sort. Something that would be triggered in a change in altitude ... a barometric device of some sort.

Carrie said, 'You've got to be shitting me ... Sean?'

'Yeah?'

'Contact ATC. Declare an emergency and ask them where we can hold. Tell them we want to stay at altitude.'

She started to throttle back the engines and said, 'All right, I'm slowing to max conserve speed ... and in fact, I've changed my mind. You take the aircraft. I'm going to contact ATC.'

'Roger, I've got it.'

She toggled the microphone switch on the yoke handle as the aircraft slowed down, allowing the minimum amount of fuel flow to the engines to keep them airborne for the longest period of time.

Big question, of course, was how much time?

Carrie said, 'Memphis Center, AirBox one-oh-seven.'

'AirBox one-oh-seven, go ahead.'

'Ah, we've been advised by our dispatch that there is a positive threat against our aircraft. We're declaring an emergency and need to hold at altitude for the present time.'

The woman's voice from Memphis Center said, 'Roger, one-oh-seven, we just got advised same over the landline as well. Hold present position, leg length your discretion, maintain flight level three three zero.'

'Roger, present position, three three zero and we'll use twenty-minute legs,' Carrie said, indicating the length of time they would fly while maintaining their current position at 33,000 feet.

'One-oh-seven, approved and we need souls on board and fuel remaining when you get a chance.'

Carrie said, 'Two souls and let's call it four hours of fuel.'

'Roger, one-oh-seven. Do you need any further assistance?'

'Not at this time, but we'll get back to you if necessary. One-oh-seven out.'

She looked to her co-pilot, who was not happy. 'They knew,' he said. 'They were advised before you called in. They know what's happening to us and why we were declaring an emergency.'

'That they do,' she said. 'And I intend to find out, too.'

Sean nodded. 'Glad to hear that.'

'All right,' Carrie said. 'I've got the aircraft back, Sean. Let's see if you can get a phone patch set up. I want to talk to Dispatch, and soonest. Something screwy is happening here and I'll be goddamned if I'm going to let the Ops Center and ATC know what's happening before we do.'

Eddie Mitchell liked to get in early for work, which meant emptying the trash bins, cleaning the bathrooms, and vacuuming the carpeted offices before most of the workers got there. Sometimes people were working in the building and its offices when he got there, even at such an ungodly hour, but usually they treated him nice, and he knew not to bother them if they seemed to be working hard and having meetings. Then he wouldn't vacuum but would work around them.

Eddie was retired US Navy, with a clear security-clearance record, and he did this work because he liked to get out of the house, and also liked to think that he was doing his part – tiny as it was – with the war on terror.

So when, last month, his duties had been expanded to do an inventory check he didn't mind. He liked to think that what he did here made a clean and cheerful work environment, and might give these people a bit of an edge to do important work.

He was now in the kitchen and thinking about getting his second cup of coffee of the morning, but only after checking the inventory list. There was a clipboard hanging on the wall, near the light switches, and he pulled it off. He walked to the walk-in freezer, and started checking off the number of boxes of frozen French Fries, fish sticks, juice drinks, and—

Something smelled odd. Odd indeed.

Eddie pushed a box out of the way, to get a better look, and—

Shit.

His very first thought was that he hoped he hadn't screwed up a crime scene, for he had no doubt that this was a crime scene. The dead man – Darren, that had been in his name – had been murdered and stuffed in here. Now Eddie felt angry that someone here with a security clearance and working for the Feds had committed murder, for no one else could have gotten access here.

He stepped back out of the freezer, gently closed the door, and made a phone call.

More than eight hours would pass before he got that second cup of coffee.

Monty Zane stepped out into the Operations Center of AirBox as a uniformed security officer came up to him, looking serious and holding a clipboard, though the poor fellow couldn't have been more than eighteen or nineteen.

'Sir, you don't belong here. You need to have a—'

Monty held out his ID card. He said, 'Pal, some heavy kind of shit is going down around here, and it's all coming this way. I certainly need to belong here, and I need to see your boss. Your boss of bosses, that is. General Bocks.'

The young man handed back the card, seemed to swallow hard. 'Yeah, there *is* some heavy shit going on around here. Come on, I'll see what I can do.'

Bocks was in a small conference room off the main floor of the Operations Center as Randy Tuthill came in. Randy said, 'We're seriously fucked, aren't we?'

'That we are.'

Randy said, 'There's a hazmat crew up top, at maintenance hangar two. They're working on one of our MD-11s. They took out the canisters that we installed and—'

Bocks said, 'I know. They don't contain anthrax vaccine. They contain anthrax itself. A vicious airborne strain. Supplied by that CIA woman, Adrianna Scott. Like you said, we've been seriously fucked over.'

Randy stumbled a bit as he spoke. 'What . . . what . . . how are we going to . . .'

'That's why I need you here, Randy. We've got to figure out a way of disarming those canisters, or immobilizing them, or doing something so our aircraft can land. We've got to . . . Randy, why in hell are you shaking your head?'

Randy's face was the color of snow. 'General, I've been thinking about this ever since I left the maintenance hangar. We can't get to those canisters. We simply can't. And the moment those jets go below three thousand feet . . . sir, what are we going to do?'

Bocks couldn't think of a thing to say.

Adrianna Scott checked her watch, saw that it was now four a.m. She clicked on the car's radio, found an FM station that carried a CNN radio news feed at the top of the hour, and caught the latest newscast. The woman announcer's voice was shaky and listening to the news made Adrianna smile.

From the car's speakers, she heard, 'CNN has learned that the Department of Homeland Security will shortly increase the threat level color to red – meaning that a terrorist attack is either underway or imminent. CNN has also learned that . . . that evacuation procedures for the President, Vice-President and Congressional leaders are also taking place at this moment. Military threat levels have also been raised at American military installations here and overseas. CNN has not received any official notification of these events. Stay tuned to CNN radio news for the latest—'

Adrianna shut the radio off with just a tinge of regret. Somehow word had gotten out, and it was too late to care about it. All she was sure of was that a number of AirBox jets were in the air. One would have been a success – tens of thousands of deaths from one just aircraft. Everything else was just, as was said, gravy.

She continued driving, a smile sometimes playing across her face.

Randy Tuthill hated the look on the General's face, knew his boss was looking to him for some sort of answer, some sort of miracle. But he couldn't provide one. There was a knock at the door, and then a large black man with a scarred face was there.

'General Bocks?'

'Yes?' he said, looking up from the conference-room table.

'The name is Montgomery Zane. I'm the military representative for the FOIL team that's been working with you, the one that—'

Tuthill watched in amazement as his boss lost it. Bocks stood up, the tendons in his neck standing out in whiplike fury as he said, 'I guess the fuck you are! I guess the fuck you are the ones working with us, the ones who've used us and fucked us over! Tiger fucking Team Seven! Where in hell is your boss, Adrianna Scott?'

The black guy seemed to be a cool customer, for he didn't flinch one bit as that acid stream poured out in his direction. Zane said to the General, 'I don't know where Adrianna is. I've been trying to contact her for nearly a day. No answer.'

Papers in the General's hands were being shredded. 'Sure. Why not? Do you have any fucking idea what in hell you people have done? Do you? Do you?'

Zane, his voice low and even, said, 'No, I don't.'

Bocks tossed the papers at him. 'And I don't have time to tell you shit, pal. I don't. So why don't you get the fuck out of my building before I have your ass in jail and—'

Another voice from another man, entering the office. 'General, if you'd like, I'll tell him. If you'd let me.'

Randy didn't know who the tired-looking guy with a torn and dirty shirt and jacket was, but Bocks seemed to recognize him. But even the flash of recognition didn't seem to turn down the anger.

'And why the fuck should I do that?' Bocks demanded.

'Because,' the other guy said, 'I know more than anybody else here does, and we don't have much time.'

Brian Doyle looked at Zane, the General, and the other guy, who seemed to be working with the General. His chest still hurt like hell and he was bleeding some from where he had torn out the IV from his arm. The General said, 'Yeah? And what the hell do you know that's so important?'

Brian said, 'Those canisters in your jets, they don't contain a vaccine.'

'Already knew that, pal. They contain anthrax.'

Zane swore once, very loud. Brian said, 'Far as I know, it was Adrianna's play, start to finish, though she certainly had help. Somebody to create the vaccine, somebody to deliver it and—'

Bocks raised his hand, dismissing him. 'Sorry, pal, you're batting oh-for-two and I don't got time to fuck around. Homeland Security's on it. Your bitch boss was working with a virologist from the Soviet Union, and some al-Qaeda punk who knows how to drive trucks. They made the delivery a few days ago. Truck and license plate matched what was sent to us, their identification was all in order, and—'

'Iraqi,' Brian said.

'What?' Zane said. The General stayed quiet.

'Her real name isn't Adrianna Scott. It's Aliyah Fulenz, or something like that. She's an Iraqi Christian woman. She made sure to tell me that. And everything tonight . . . it's revenge for what was done to her parents. I'd guess they died during the first Iraq war.'

Zane started asking him questions but Bocks was louder, saying, 'And why should we believe that story, detective? Why's that?'

Brian thought, well, dad, you're going to do more now for me than any time ever in your whole drunken life, and he said, 'You've met me before, General. You know why I joined the Tiger Team, why I did what I did. Because of my dad and 9/11. That's why. And that's why you're going to trust me. You know that.'

Silence. Lots of raised voices and phone calls from outside the office, from the floor of the Operations Center. Then Brian's pager and Monty's started going off, but the two of them ignored the noise.

Monty said, 'All this about Adrianna . . . Aliyah. How did you find that out?'

'She told me.'

Bocks was incredulous. 'She told you? When? How? And why in God's name would she tell you?'

Brian said, 'She told me a couple of hours ago. And I think she told me because she wanted to brag, wanted to tell somebody before it was too late. And she told me in her hotel room, just before she shot me.'

The fourth guy in the room said, 'She shot you? The hell you say.'

Brian opened up his shirt, displayed the bruise marks that were going to be an ugly green and yellow in a few days. 'I was wearing a Kevlar vest. She tapped me twice in the chest and I fell off a balcony – landed like some freak circus performer on an awning. And now I'm here to tell you what happened . . . Monty?'

'Yeah?' Monty was looking at his Blackberry pager with a grim look, toggling through whatever text message had been sent to him.

'We've got to get the rest of the team here. Victor and Darren.'

'Going to be hard to do that, Brian,' he said.

'Why?'

Monty shook his head. 'Check your pager. Darren's been found dead, back in Maryland: broken neck and stuffed in our food freezer.'

Brian said, 'Jesus Christ.'

Monty looked at the three men in the office, knew it was starting to slide away, knew he had to step in before things got lost and more time vanished.

Keeping his voice cool and level, he said, 'All right. We got hosed. Adrianna did a spectacular job. When the Congressional hearings and special commissions are done with this one, we'll all probably be doing jail time, especially me.'

And it came to him in a flash. Those missions over the past months – hell, years – meeting those characters in London, Bali, Jenin, and Lahore. A setup. A goddamn set-up. All that chatter that had been discussed earlier – shit, he had helped get that chatter going! The type of planning and pure malevolence that had gone into what she had done . . . Amazing.

Monty sighed. 'Yeah. Especially me. To quote a famous mayor, "the bitch set me up." I've gone places and killed people, all apparently on her behalf, all to help her sell the idea of an anthrax attack to us and the higher-ups. Goddamn.'

And he slapped a hand on the table. 'All right. That's my *mea* fucking *culpa*, and I'm done with it. We've got to move on. First,' he said, looking to the stranger sitting with Bocks and Brian, 'sir, I'm afraid I don't know who you are. Would you . . .?'

The man stuck his hand out. 'Randy Tuthill. Head of the machinists' union local. And probably an unindicted co-conspirator when this hits the papers.'

The man's grip was strong. Monty liked that, showed he wasn't going to pussyfoot around. 'General, before we proceed, I'm going to need another member of our team to be here.'

Bocks said, 'The doctor who came here with Alyiah – Adrianna – and the detective?'

'Yep. He knows this stuff, and I don't want to be dealing with somebody that doesn't have the background. It'll take too long to get up to speed. Brian, any idea where he is?'

Brian said, 'Probably at home, in Maryland. Might take a while to get him out here. Can you do it?'

Monty said, 'Man, get me to a phone, you'll be surprised at how fast things can happen.'

Carrie didn't like the expression on Sean's face. He turned to her and said, 'Carrie, you're not going to believe this but the line is busy – I can't get through to Dispatch.'

'Busy? You sure you got the right number?'

'Christ, of course I'm sure. Dispatch's number is busy – shit, I've never heard that happening before. Either things are seriously fucked-up on the ground or there's a whole bunch of AirBox flights trying to talk to the ground.'

She wiped her moist hands across her uniform pants leg, checked the autopilot again to make sure it was still keeping them on their holding pattern. 'See if you can't get a text message to the ground using ACARS. Tell them to get off the damn phone. Then try setting up that phone patch again.'

'You got it.'

Sean leaned to the left, started working the ACARS terminal, laboriously typing in a message using a single finger, one letter at a time. Carrie went back to the instrumentation, back to the windscreen, and—

Something caught her eye.

A flash of light.

She looked off to the left, tried to swallow.

'Sean.'

'Yeah?'

'We got company.'

'Huh? Where do you— Oh, shit.'

Off to port, flying about two hundred feet out and a bit below and forward, was an F-16 single-seat fighter jet. Its flashing red anti-collision strobe lights were on and the cockpit was illuminated, so Carrie could make out the shape of its pilot.

Sean said, 'Got another one, to starboard.'

'Yeah.'

They flew on for long moments, neither one saying anything, until Sean said, 'You know what this means, don't you?'

'That I do,' she said. 'They're not here for their health. They're here because of what we've got in the cargo hold, I'm sure.'

'What do you think? Chemical? Bio? A dirty bomb?'

Carrie said, 'Whatever it is, the powers that be certainly don't want us to land, and they certainly want to keep close eye on us.'

'Fuck. Those lousy ground-pounding sons of bitches, not telling us a goddamn thing about what we're carrying—'

Carrie said, 'Sean.'

He stopped talking.

'Try to raise those fine boys on the Guard radio channel, find out what their orders are. And then let's try Dispatch again. Jesus.'

Sean went to work and Carrie briefly regretted her sharpness towards him. But there was work to be done, answers to be sought, and the thought of her daughter Susan, slumbering safely at home while her mommy was just seconds away from being blasted out of the sky . . . Christ.

She returned to her flying.

CHAPTER THIRTY-THREE

Monty had no idea how the phone call would go. In the event, he was stunned at how quickly matters developed.

'Colonel,' he said to the Tiger Team Director, 'this is Montgomery Zane, Tiger Team Seven.'

'Go ahead.'

'I'm at the AirBox Operations Center. Have you been advised of what's going on?'

The colonel's voice was flat, unemotional. 'That I have. Nineteen aircraft, airborne and carrying anthrax, and in a situation to release that anthrax unless something can be done in the next few hours.'

'Sir, it appears that Adrianna Scott was an Iraqi citizen. We've been played, and played bad. I'm now the senior officer for Tiger Team Seven.'

'All right,' the colonel said. 'And I have a team working on Adrianna Scott and what she's done, but right now, that's only going to be of interest down the road. What matters now are those nineteen aircraft . . . and Zane?'

'Sir?'

'As of now, it's yours. I'm not in a position to second-guess you. But you've got lots of resources at your fingertips. Use them, and use them well, and keep me informed.'

'That I will, sir.'

He had been dreaming, no doubt about it, and my God, how that dream had slipped into this horrible nightmare. Men were there, men with lights and uniforms and loud voices, and this was one hell of a dream and—

Victor Palmer sat up in bed, chest heaving, looking at his suddenly crowded bedroom. There were three men in there, two of them wearing black uniforms and carrying stubby automatic weapons. The third man, the one with the large flashlight, said, 'Sir, you're Doctor Palmer, correct?'

Victor held a hand up to his eyes, to block the light. 'Yes . . . yes . . . who are you? What the hell is going on here?'

The man said, 'Sir, I'm afraid you're in our custody, under direction of the National Command Authority. You need to join your Tiger Team members in Memphis, right away. What do you need?'

'Um . . . ah, well, my laptop, of course, in my office, and—'

One of the men with automatic rifles quickly left the bedroom, and Victor said, 'And . . . uh, what's going on? Why do they need me so quickly?'

'Sir,' the man said, pulling away the bed coverings, 'all I know is that there is an emergency, and your presence is required, now.'

Victor wiped at his face. 'I . . . I need to shower. And get dressed . . . and—'

The man with the flashlight stepped forward. 'Sir. There's no time.'

And so Victor started protesting. But, quickly enough, other men came forward and literally picked him up, and he was taken out of his condo and down the central stairs, and now there was a loud noise coming from outside, and he was trying to say something, ask what in hell was going on, and the men were behind him, one of them carrying his laptop, another carrying a bundle of his clothes, shoving the clothes into a small leather bag.

Outside it was chaos. They propelled Victor along a paved walkway, to the common area of the condominium. The noise beat at his ears. Before him were the tennis courts for the condo units and other men were there as well, cutting and pulling down the chain-link fences, tearing up the netting. Overhead was a helicopter, a military helicopter with a belly-mounted searchlight that illuminated the whole area. Other residents of the condo units were now coming out their own homes, staring up in awe at what was going on around them.

The helicopter began to land and again Victor was picked up. His knees suddenly felt like the tendons and muscles had turned to mush, for he realized that this – all this! – was being done for him!

A mouth close to his right ear. 'Keep your head down, doctor!'

Dirt and pebbles were being flung into his face as he went forward, hunched over. Men in the helicopter grabbed him and strapped him down, and he looked and saw that his clothes and laptop had joined him. He shouted out questions but the crewmen just tapped the side of their helmets and shook their heads.

Victor thought that he would throw up as the helicopter swooped and dove, and it was a short hop indeed, for now they were flying into an airbase, it looked like, military aircraft. The helicopter landed. Other uniformed men nearly dragged him off it and he tried to ask more questions, but no one would talk to him, nobody at all, as two or three of them dressed him in a flight suit of some sort and a helmet was jammed over his head, and then in front of him was a jet, a fighter aircraft of some sort, and his bags were placed into a small storage bin on the side of the fuselage and good Christ, he was actually hauled up into the open cockpit, put into the seat, straps and hoses were connected and he blinked his eyes very hard as the jet started moving down the runway, and the cockpit canopy started lowering over his head.

'You okay back there, sir?' came a crackling voice through the headphones in his helmet.

'I . . . I guess so. What in hell is going on?'

'The name's Major Hanratty. Sir, my job is to get you to Memphis as soon as possible.'

'Why?'

'Don't know, sir. All I can tell you is to hold on back there. Once we're wheels up, we're going supersonic for a bit.'

Victor tried to swallow. Tried to swallow three times before he could produce saliva.

'But . . . but I thought supersonic wasn't allowed over civilian areas.'

The major said, 'Usually you're right, sir. But not this morning. Word I got is to break as many windows as I wanted, just as long as I got you to Memphis quick, like. You must be some big-ass VIP.'

Victor heard the tremor in his voice. 'I'm . . . I'm just a doctor. That's all.'

The major said quietly, 'Must be a hell of a medical emergency out there in Memphis, then.'

Victor said nothing, tears springing to his eyes, nausea swelling in his guts, as he knew right then and there that it had all gone wrong.

Final Winter.

May God have mercy on me, he thought.

And as the jet took off, he had a sudden wish that something mechanical would happen, something bad so that this would all end now, in a clean and quick fireball, rather than ending up in Memphis.

But God wasn't listening to him.

The aircraft took off safely.

Just his luck.

Brian looked to Monty who had just hung up the phone, arranging for Victor to come southwest. It had been a hell of a performance, and Brian wished that some of his commanders back at the NYPD had Monty's presence and authority. But there was one more thing. Brian said, 'You better be good, the next few hours.'

'Only way I can be, son. Why did you say that?'

'Because the higher-ups are going to want to have their say, have their input, have their command. You and me and Victor and the General, we know what's happened, what can happen. We don't have time to bring half the government up to speed on this fuck-up, much as they're eager to know.'

Monty said, 'You've been reading my mind, pal. Time for another phone call.'

*

Air Force General Mike McKenna had just received a status report from his adjutant on the deployment of F-16s and F-15s to track the AirBox aircraft when his phone rang. He picked it up, heard from the senior airman who served as his admin aide, and said, 'All right, put him through.'

There was a click and he said, 'General McKenna, Northern Command.'

'Sir, this is Montgomery Zane. Department of Defense representative with Foreign Operations and Liaison Team Seven. Sir, I'm at the Memphis Airport, at the Operations Center for AirBox.'

'So?'

'General, please check your standing orders. Especially the Presidential Directive 61-10, issued on September 12, 2001. Sir, I'm the command lead for this incident. You're not to take any hostile action against those nineteen AirBox aircraft without my authorization. And for purposes of identification my ID code for today is Bravo Bravo Zulu Twelve. I'm lead.'

'The hell you are.'

'The hell I'm not, general. Check your standing orders. This baby is mine. You'll be informed at all times about what's going on, and I may need you to take action against those aircraft, but right now it's in my lap.'

General McKenna said, 'I don't have time to argue with you, Zane.'

'Good. Neither do I. Look, we've got a situation here: I don't want to be a hard ass, but check your standing orders.'

McKenna shifted the phone to another ear, scribbled a note, writing down BBZ12. 'I intend to do just that. And to get those orders changed.'

Zane said, 'Your prerogative, sir. But I think you'll find

that to change that means going through the White House, and I think the President is kinda busy right now.'

Alexander Bocks felt the iron band of tension around the base of his skull start to ease, just a bit. He looked to Zane and said, 'Can I ask you a question?'

'Sure.'

'What branch of the service did you serve in?'

Monty smiled, started making notes on a legal pad in front of him. 'All of them.'

The police detective interrupted. 'All of them?'

'Sure. Special program, set up after 9/11. Besides intelligence communities not talking to one another, there were also problems with branches of the military not talking to each other. Each branch had its own bit of turf, guarded quite jealously. Bunch of us were recruited to spend time with each branch, make contacts, know deep down how each side ticks. Help break down barriers. So I've trained and deployed with Army Special Ops, Air Force Special Ops, Navy SEALs . . . so forth and so on.'

'And what branch did you start with?'

Zane said, 'Coast Guard.'

The detective looked incredulous. 'No shit?'

'No shit. But as my mama used to say, let's look to the future. General Bocks, how much time do we have with your aircraft before they have to land?'

Bocks said, 'Depending on how far they got before we told them to hold and orbit – four, maybe five hours.'

'Know this is a wild question, but I've got to ask it. Any airborne-refueling capability for your aircraft?'

Bocks shook his head. 'No. They're MD-11s, converted to cargo carriers. Pilot and co-pilot for a crew. That's it. When they get low on fuel, they're going to have to come down. No choice about it.'

Monty turned to Randy and said, 'These canisters – is there any way for the crew to get to them? Any access hatch, inspection plate – any way they can get their hands on them?'

'No,' Randy said.

'Can they be disabled? Power shut off to them – circuit-breaker popped – anything like that?'

A violent shake of the head. 'No, damn it . . . these canisters – they were designed to operate automatically. The radio-altimeter switch arms the canisters when they go above a certain altitude – and when the aircraft descends to the critical altitude they open up and start spraying. There's no way to stop it. No fucking way. Guys, let's face up to it. In a few hours, no matter what we do, those canisters are going to start spraying airborne anthrax over the United States, and there's not a goddamn thing we can do to stop it.'

Carrie heard Sean work the communications through her earphones. 'Ah, this is AirBox 107, broadcasting to our F-16 neighbors to port and starboard. How's it going, guys?'

A male voice, coming through, loud and clear. 'This is Lance One, lead aircraft here, good morning.'

'And good morning to you. Where you from, guys?'

'Ohio ANG, out of Toledo.'

'What's up?'

'Sorry, repeat.'

Sean said, 'Lance One, what's up? What's going on?' His voice rose some. 'Come on, Lance One. What's your mission?'

A pause, another hiss of static. 'AirBox one-oh-seven, we've been told to escort. That's all.'

'Escort us where?' Sean demanded.

'Don't know yet, AirBox.'

Sean said, 'Are your weapons hot? Are you? What's going on with us? Is there a bomb on board? A nuke? A chem weapon?'

'Ahh . . . AirBox one-oh-seven, be advised, we've been ordered to escort. And that's all I can say. Lance One, out.'

Sean swore and Carrie looked at him, raised an eyebrow. 'Goddamn Air Force, eh?'

He said, 'Days like this, I cheer for the fucking Navy.'

Brian saw the General glare at his machinist guy and heard him say, 'We've got a few hours. And in those few hours, we'll come up with something.'

Monty said, 'You got any ideas?'

'Not a one,' the General said, suddenly scribbling on his notepad. 'But there is one thing I've got to do.'

'What's that?' Brian asked.

The General stood up, and Brian saw that he was holding a sheet of paper, and that his hand was shaking. 'Time to be straight with my crews. Time to tell them what's going on.'

Brian said, 'Sir, are you sure that—'

Bocks looked pissed. 'They don't know because me and you and your goddamn Adrianna thought they didn't have a right to know. But they sure as hell do have a right to know now. And I'm going to take care of it, right now.'

He went out of the room, striking a chair with his hip as he went out to the main Operations Center. Monty said to Randy, 'Your boss is one hard charger.'

Randy toyed with a pencil on the conference-room table.

'The general's doing just fine. Over a week ago, his biggest worry was whether my union was going to strike his ass over dental care. Now he's worried about nineteen aircraft and thirty-eight people that work for him, plus the fact that his equipment is getting ready to kill hundreds of thousands of his fellow citizens. So cut the General some fucking slack, all right?'

'Sure,' Monty said.

'Sure,' Brian said.

The flashing light from the control pedestal caught her eye again, and Sean said, 'Incoming message, Carrie.'

'All right, then.'

The ACARS communication coming out was one long goddamn message. The strip of paper came out and came out and came out, and Carrie sighed as Sean reached down and tore it off. She held it up to the light and read:

AB 107

    YOUR AIRCRAFT AND EIGHTEEN OTHER AIRBOXES CARRYING TWO CANISTERS IN AIR CONDITIONING PACK EXHAUSTS THAT CONTAIN AIRBORNE ANTHRAX.

    REPEAT, YOUR AIRCRAFT CARRYING TWO CANISTERS IN AIR CONDITIONING EXHAUST PACKS THAT CONTAIN AIRBORNE ANTHRAX.

    CANISTERS SET TO RELEASE ANTHRAX UPON DESCENT BELOW THREE THOUSAND FEET. SORRY TO SAY NO METHOD CURRENTLY AVAILABLE TO ALLOW YOU TO DISABLE OR REMOVE CANISTERS.

CONTINUE TO HOLD CURRENT
ALTITUDE. AVOID ICING CONDITIONS,
MAXIMIZE FLIGHT ENDURANCE.
    WE ARE WORKING TO RESOLVE ISSUE,
GET YOU AND AIRCRAFT SAFELY TO
GROUND WITHOUT RELEASING ANTHRAX.
    MORE TO FOLLOW.
    BOCKS.

Sean read the message and said, 'Well, the General is there.'

'Hurray for the General,' Carrie said, crumpling up the message sheet and letting it fall to the cockpit floor. 'Notice what he left out?'

'Huh?'

She pointed out the windscreen, to their quiet escorts. Lance One and Lance Two.

'He didn't tell us what we already know. That those fine pilots out there, if they start seeing us descend, are going to blow us out of the sky. That's what he left out. That if they don't figure out something, something quick, we and the eighteen others are going to be shot down.'

Ahead of them dawn was breaking.

Brian listened to Monty and Randy debate options, plans, possibilities, and Brian yawned and rubbed at his sore chest and hoped that in the next few hours the Memphis police wouldn't figure out where he was and come arrest his ass for assaulting that cop and the EMT. And for stealing the cop's service weapon, one of the worst crimes to commit against a cop.

Monty said, 'Look, isn't there any way to get fuel in those wing tanks? Get a guy lowered down from a helicopter or something . . . get the cap off . . . get some fuel in. Anything to buy us some time.'

Randy said, 'No. Shit, man, this isn't like one of those *Airport* movies, where you're going to get somebody dangling from a cable, ten thousand feet up, and ask him to unscrew a fuel cap about seven inches in diameter while the outside air temp is twenty below. Not going to happen. And even if you were able to get those fuel caps off, where is the fuel coming from? Air Force and Air National Guard are the only outfits that have airborne-refueling capability, and only with aircraft that have the refueling ports designed to receive a refueling hose. Otherwise you'd be trying to dangle something like a garden hose into a small hole while traveling at two hundred knots in mid-air. Can't happen. Trust me, I know. I was in the Air Force long enough and my own son is a pilot for a refueling jet, the KC-135.'

Brian said, 'Okay. Let's agree that airborne refueling is off the table. We already know that the crew can't reach the canisters from where they are. Is there any way to block those air-conditioning exhaust vents from the outside?'

'Oh, sure,' Randy said, his voice sharp. 'We'll just ask for volunteers from my machinists. We'll go up in an open-cockpit aircraft, like a Sopwith Camel, a two-seater, maybe, and my guy will reach up and plug the vents with chewing gum. Is that what you want?'

Monty leaned forward. 'No. What I fucking want are some goddamn ideas, that's what, some suggestions on how to fix this goddamn problem.'

Randy shouted back, 'It wasn't our goddamn problem to begin with! We listened to you, we trusted you, and look what the fuck happened! We're hours away from killing hundreds of thousands of people, and I'm telling you, we can't get to those canisters! We can't! And it's your fucking fault!'

And in the silence following this outburst, a new voice was heard in the room:

'Excuse me, could somebody tell me what all the screaming is about?'

Somehow, somewhere, the word got out to the news media, and as usual the first stories were a mix of truth and supposition, seasoned with ill-informed speculation. With the story breaking of the color change to red in the Homeland Security threat level – coupled with the story of the evacuation of the President, his Cabinet and Congressional leaders off to secure areas – there was a media frenzy as reporters, assignment editors and network and newspaper executives, some of them awake for less than a hour, worked the phones.

MSNBC was first, followed by Fox and then CNN, reporting that the government was responding to a threat involving AirBox aircraft and airborne anthrax. In addition to this bit of truthful news, the story was also broadcast that the aircraft had been hijacked and were now heading for major metropolitan centers.

And in these same major metropolitan centers, within less than an hour, outbound highways were clogged with American citizens desperate to get away from what they thought was going to be a new Ground Zero. As a result of this unofficial evacuation the very first civilian deaths associated with Final Winter began to occur as traffic accidents happened, the elderly and the ill succumbed to the fear and, in a few cases, police shot looters taking advantage of the chaos.

The unplanned and unanticipated evacuation also meant

that instead of being concentrated in target cities the exposed population was now spreading out to the suburbs and countryside, increasing the possible target areas for the still-airborne AirBox aircraft.

Victor Palmer came into the conference room, groggy and confused about what was going on, still feeling weak from the rigors of the flight that had picked him up in Maryland and brought him to Memphis. He went into the room, laptop under his arm, and took a seat. He looked at the faces, recognized them all, and turned to Brian, the only one he felt truly comfortable with. He knew bad news was just seconds away from hitting him, and for some reason he wanted it to come from the police detective. They were experts at passing on bad news.

'Brian?' he asked. 'What went wrong?'

'Lots, doc. I'm not sure where to begin.'

Victor said, 'I don't understand. Adrianna told me two days ago that Final Winter was canceled. That the vaccine wasn't going to be distributed. What happened?'

Monty sat up at that. 'Tell us, doc. Tell us what she said.'

Victor looked again at the other men, thinking of his residency, thinking of all the times that groups of men and women had asked and poked and prodded. He hated all those questions, all those demands. He just wanted to be left alone.

God, did he want to be left alone.

'She . . . she called me at home. She said Final Winter had been canceled, the Syrian cells had been rolled up, that I should take some time off. Which is what I was doing when . . . Brian, what's going on?'

And damn that man if his voice didn't change, like he

was doing his old job, telling a husband or mother or grandmother that someone they loved and cherished dearly had been killed by a bullet, a knife, or a drug overdose.

'Doc, what happened is this . . . it's something that makes Pearl Harbor and 9/11 look like overwhelming victories . . . Adrianna Scott.'

Brian paused, and Victor said, 'Yes? What about her? How come she isn't here?'

Monty made to speak but Brian raised a hand. 'Doc, she's on the run. Her real name isn't Adrianna Scott. It's Aliyah Fulenz. She's an Iraqi. She's been here since she was a teenager . . . I think her parents were killed in the first Gulf War. And she's been plotting for years.'

A feeling returned to him, only an hour or so old, of what it had been like, going up in the air in that Air Force fighter jet, his guts squishy, his limbs tingly, like he was on the edge of something magnificent and terrifying.

'Final Winter . . .'

Brian said, 'It's a reality. It's happening now. Adrianna lied to all of us. There are canisters aboard nineteen AirBox aircraft, nineteen aircraft that are airborne. And those canisters are carrying airborne anthrax. All of them.'

Somehow Victor got the words out. 'But . . . but the canisters . . . they have the automatic radio altimeters. If those jets descend, they're going to release the anthrax . . .'

Monty said, 'That's right.'

Victor tried to speak. Tried to gather the words. He . . .

It . . .

Everything slid into darkness.

Emptiness.

And a voice:

'I think the poor son-of-a-bitch has fainted.'

CHAPTER THIRTY-FOUR

Randy Tuthill saw the cop and the military guy gather around the doctor, sprawled out on the floor. Randy looked out through the window. He had been in the Operations Center off and on over the years, usually trying to solve some last-minute mechanical problem that was bedeviling an air-craft, either in the air or on the ground. At those times the Center had been a low-key place, murmurs of conversation, men and women at the terminals, the low ring of telephones. But now . . . men and women were racing from desk to ter-minal, the ringing phones were now a roar, and the chatter of the people out there in the Operations Center almost drowned out the conversations of the Tiger Team guys.

'General,' he said.

'Yeah, Randy,' the General replied, joining him by the window.

'You've . . . you've got to keep tight control here, sir.'

No reply.

'Every politician, every nut, every reporter, is going to be calling here and pressuring you and trying to grab a chunk, trying to solve the problem, trying to assign blame, trying to do a lot of shit.'

Randy gestured to the three men in the corner. The doctor was now sitting up. Randy said, 'Like it or not, if we're going to take care of this shit-mess it's going to happen in this room.'

The General turned to him, and Randy felt a little some-thing in him die away. The General looked like he had aged a decade in the last ten minutes.

'All my years, all the years of my life . . . I've dedicated to protecting this nation and its people. I've sacrificed my health, my happiness . . . I've been stationed in places with no running water, with heat so hot it could melt your brain at noon on the flight line, and I've been in places so cold that lubricants turned into jelly. I . . .'

He couldn't go on. Randy reached over, grabbed his shoulder. 'General, please.'

The General shook off Randy's hand. 'And now I'm about to kill millions of my countrymen . . .'

There was motion at the other end of the room. It looked like the doctor was now back on his feet. Randy again squeezed the shoulder of the man who'd been his superior officer for all these years.

'Don't give up now, General. Don't give up now.'

The General nodded briskly. 'I'll do my best. You can count on that.'

'Of course.'

At the Peterson Air Force Base Lt General McKenna was on a conference call with his boss of bosses, the Chairman of the Joint Chiefs, and the Chairman's boss, a former governor who was now orbiting a patch of Albertan prairie land, hundreds of miles away.

'McKenna,' the Chairman said. 'Are your flights in place?'

'Affirmative,' he said.

'All right. What then?'

'Awaiting developments, sir, from AirBox and the Tiger Team that's running the show.'

The Chairman said, 'Are you comfortable with what they're doing?'

A hell of a question. McKenna glanced out his office window to the terminals and display screens that were designed to protect this nation and its borders, from the time of the Soviet empire to now, when the threat had been changed to hijacked aircraft being flown into office and government buildings. Now? Nineteen aircraft, airborne biological bombs, and so far, the only defense he and his staff could devise was to blow them out of the sky.

'No, sir,' he said finally. 'No, I'm not. But I'm afraid I don't have any better ideas.'

The Chairman grunted. 'Yeah. Who does? All right. We're trying to work the problem on our end as well. But remember one thing. Those aircraft are not going to fly low enough to release their payloads. Understood?'

'Understood.'

'Very good.' Then, the Chairman's voice changed, and he was talking to the other man on the line. 'Sir? Any questions for General McKenna?'

'No, not right now,' the third voice said. 'Appreciate all you're doing. Both of you.'

'Thank you, sir,' the Chairman said.

'Thank you, sir,' General McKenna said, though he couldn't imagine that he would be in this job at the same time tomorrow.

When news was released about the supposed hijacked aircraft in the United States that were carrying anthrax, Mexico, quickly followed by Canada, closed its airspace to United States-flagged aircraft. Japan followed, then the Caribbean nations, France, and lastly, reluctantly, Great Britain.

Victor was helped to his seat. He rubbed his hands together and then rubbed at his face. He was tired and he felt humiliated by what he had done, and he despised the look of pity from the other men in the conference room.

'I'll be fine. Honest. Jesus.'

Again, the face, staring at him, waiting for information, waiting for a miracle. It brought back bad memories of his residency, working in the ER during the night shifts, looking at the same expressions from moms who wanted to know if their young boys were going to live, even with the tops of their heads blown off by nine-millimeter bullets. He said, 'Nineteen aircraft. Where are they?'

The General said, 'Orbiting at various locations in the southeast, over areas with the least amount of population.'

'How long can they stay up there?'

'Another three, four hours. Tops,' the General said.

Victor said, 'Can't they get refueled up there? The Air Force or something?'

Monty shook his head. 'No. Civilian aircraft. They don't have aerial-refueling capability.'

Three or four hours . . . Christ on a crutch . . .

'And what happens at the end of the three or four hours?'

Bocks said, 'They start to descend. And before they get to three thousand feet . . . the Air Force will shoot them down. They can't be allowed to let those canisters release the anthrax.'

'No,' Victor said.

'No, what?' Bocks said.

'The aircraft. They can't be shot down.'

The machinist guy, Tuthill, said, 'Well, yeah, we don't *want* them to be shot down. I mean, they're our guys and—'

Victor said, 'Excuse me, am I speaking in fucking Latin or something?'

Tuthill's face reddened. Everyone else kept their stare on

him. Monty said, 'I'm afraid we don't understand, Victor. Tell us what you mean.'

'The aircraft. They can't be shot down.'

'Tell us more,' Monty said.

Victor couldn't believe that they didn't realize what was going on. He said, 'Monty. You're our military whiz, Right?'

Monty said calmly, 'Yes, I'm the military rep for this Tiger Team. Go ahead.'

'When the jet tries to shoot down a cargo aircraft like this, how does it happen? Do they have laser beams? Anti-matter disintegrators? When they shoot it down, does everything turn to dust?'

'No,' Monty said. 'You know that.'

'Maybe I do, but I think you've all forgotten. Tell me how the aircraft would be shot down.'

Monty said, 'There are F-15 Eagles or F-16 Falcons up there, with air-to-air missiles. Probably AIM-9 Sidewinders. If they get the order, they drop back, fire one, maybe two missiles. Heat-seekers. Go right into the engines, explode . . . aircraft spirals down, breaks up.'

Victor slapped the table for emphasis. 'Exactly! You damn fools, don't you see what this means? The fuselage remains intact. It spirals in. Even if the fuselage does start to break up, the canister is in there, self-contained, with its own radio-altimeter-triggered switch, and as it's spiraling into the ground, sure as shit, gentlemen, that anthrax will be released, no matter how many missiles get fired at those aircraft.'

AirBox personnel might wear the same uniforms and have the same pension plan, and most had the same military back-ground. But in the air that early morning were thirty-eight scared and angry men and women whose company loyalty was under a severe strain.

Among them was Helen Torrinson, the co-pilot aboard AirBox 10, which was currently orbiting a patch of Mississippi sky about twenty thousand feet above Biloxi. With her, in the captain's seat, was Hank Harmon, also known as 'Hammerin' Hank', not only for his checkered flying past with the Marines but also because of his habit of heading straight to one of Memphis's nightspots whenever he got back from a flight. Helen – who had flown C-130 transport aircraft in the Air Force Reserve – knew that in most other carrier companies Hank might have been grounded months ago for his drinking.

But AirBox, as the advertisements liked to point out, wasn't like any other carrier.

And ever since that ACARS message had come through, Hank had remained pretty quiet for Hank, though Helen had noticed that his face had been turning grayer, with trickles of perspiration dripping down his cheeks and neck. Her own attempts at conversation had been met with an occasional 'yeah' or a grunt as they continued to fly on autopilot.

But it had been the arrival of the F-15s – calling themselves Sword One and Sword Two – that finally triggered something.

Hank had whipped his head back and forth, leaning forward in his seat to get a better view of the escorting fighter jets, and he had started murmuring something, about plots, about death, and Helen had sat there, almost frozen with indecision.

What to do?

And then Hank made the decision for her.

He turned and said, 'You know we're dead, don't you?'

'No,' she said, 'I didn't know that.'

'Christ, yes,' he said. 'We both know this fucking aircraft. You can't get to those air-conditioning packs, you can't unplug 'em, you can't block 'em. If there's anthrax down there, the only solution is to give those guys flanking us the shoot-down orders.'

'Hank, we should just give them the time to—'

'Fuck that. We need to act before they realize that a shoot-down is the only solution. Put on your oxygen mask.'

Helen put on her mask and switched on her microphone, and there was a *click-click* sound as Hank disconnected the aircraft's autopilot and associated autothrottles.

Hank turned to her and said, 'We're going to get this piece of shit on the deck *now!*'

His right hand pulled the throttles to idle and extended the aircraft's speed brakes. As Hank pushed the control yoke forward and lowered the nose, the aircraft's rate of descent quickly increased.

Over the cockpit's speaker, Helen heard the voice of one of their escorts: 'Ah, AirBox Ten, this is Sword One, level off and halt your descent, please.'

Hank keyed the microphone. 'Houston Center, AirBox Ten, we're an emergency aircraft and we are now descending for immediate landing at Keesler Air Force Base.'

Helen felt herself being pressed back in the seat as the jet quickly descended. Declaring an in-flight emergency meant that for most intents and purposes Hank was the closest thing to an air god. He and she and this aircraft now had priority for everything, including an immediate clearance to land at any airfield in the vicinity. Hank could pretty much do anything he wanted to get the aircraft on the ground, and it was a hell of a gamble, because once they had landed there would be some serious hell to pay, from the FAA to the military to the General himself.

But they would be on the ground. That was what counted. Yeah, most times it would work.

But this wasn't most times.

An urgent voice in the earphones: 'AirBox 10, AirBox 10, this is Sword One, Sword One, immediately resume your previous altitude. Immediately. Please acknowledge.'

Hank said nothing. The ground was approaching. Helen swallowed.

'Hank?'

Not a word.

The earphones. 'AirBox 10, AirBox 10, acknowledge. This is Sword One.'

'Hank . . .'

'Fuck them all . . .' he said.

Suddenly bright lights flared in front of them . . . flanking them, reaching out ahead of them.

Tracer fire, from the F-15s' cannon.

'AirBox 10, this is Sword One. You will level off immediately. You will climb back to altitude. You will continue to hold.'

'Or what!' Hank shouted.

'Sir, we are authorized to engage. Don't force us to shoot you down!'

'Fuck you! You don't have the balls to shoot down a civilian aircraft! Go ahead, Air Force!'

Helen watched in horror as the altimeter unwound as the jet descended. Twelve thousand feet and lowering . . . She thought of the anthrax in the belly of her jet. She thought of her husband Tony, her two kids, thought about the Air Force pilots back there, knowing what they had to do . . . knowing that after 9/11 so many of the rules had been rewritten or tossed out.

'Hank, pull up! C'mon, they're going to shoot us down!'

Hank yelled back. 'Shut up! They don't have the balls. They're not gonna do it!'

'How do you know that? Hank! Pull up.'

'Shut up!'

Ten thousand feet.

'AirBox 10, Sword One. Your last warning. We are weapons hot, repeat, we are weapons hot.'

Eight thousand.

What to do, what to do – a fight in the cockpit? Helen remembered that Egypt Air flight years back, when the co-pilot flew the jet right into the ocean, even with the pilot struggling with him and the controls . . . Hank was taller than her, stronger, and thirty pounds heavier . . . it wouldn't work.

Seven thousand.

'AirBox 10! Last warning!'

Six thousand feet.

'AirBox 10!'

Five thousand, five hundred.

Helen rotated in her seat, reached up back against her seat restraints . . . reached out, fingertips barely touching, Hank busy with flying . . .

There. Grabbed it.

'Sweet Jesus, forgive me,' she breathed. Then she bashed in the back of Hank's head with the emergency crash ax.

And bashed him again.

And again.

She dropped the ax, grabbed the controls so she was now in command of the aircraft, started pulling back on the control yoke and adding power.

Helen keyed the microphone switch, saying, breathing heavily, 'This is AirBox 10 . . . AirBox 10 . . . we're climbing . . . we're climbing back to altitude . . .'

There seemed to be relief in the F-15 pilot's voice. 'Roger, AirBox 10. Good job. We'll get through this together. This is Sword One.'

She looked over, at the slumped figure of Hank, at the blood on his shirt, blood on the panel, blood on the windscreen.

'Sword One – to hell with you. I've just killed my pilot – and you're going to land and be alive today . . . which is more than I can be sure of for myself.'

Sword One didn't answer.

Monty looked at the flushed face of Victor, at the other faces of Brian and the General and Randy, the machinist. He said, 'General, what will those pilots do when they get low on fuel?'

Bocks said, 'What do you think they'll do? What any one of us would do in the same spot. They're going to try to land. They're going to try to dodge their fighter escorts, fruitless as that'll be.'

Land . . . of course they'll try to land, Monty thought. What else would they do?

Land.

At an airbase.

Lots of airbases he'd been at over the years, busy ones like Offut and Eglin and Wright-Patterson. And, of course, lots of empty and quiet ones like—

Shit.

Empty ones.

Lots of empty ones.

'Doc!'

'Yes, Monty?'

'The anthrax – how long does it stay in the atmosphere?'

'A few hours – maybe four or five.'

'And where does it go after that?'

Victor said, 'Then it comes to rest on the ground.'

'Still dangerous on the ground?'

'Sure,' the doctor said. 'But in the air is where it's most dangerous. When it's on the ground you can protect yourself through normal decontamination efforts.'

'How far can the anthrax spores travel when it's airborne?'

'All depends on the wind. Several miles . . . less, if there's no breeze.'

Monty felt a little flicker of excitement kindle inside him. Maybe. Just fucking maybe.

'C'mon,' he said. 'We're going for a quick walk.'

He stood up and opened the conference-room door, stepped outside to the Operations Center. There was a low roar made up of phones ringing, people talking, keyboards being tapped, men and women, delivering and picking up messages as they moved back and forth. Monty gestured to the large display screen, depicting North America and parts of the Caribbean. Up on the screen, the triangular icons marking the orbiting AirBox flights were highlighted.

'Look, I see at least two AirBox flights out in northern Texas. Am I right.'

The General said, 'Yeah, you're right. So what?'

'General, the so-what is where those two aircraft can go. They fly an hour west, they can hit a base I've trained at when I was detached to Air Force Special Ops. Tyler, used to be an Army Air Corps base back in the 1940s. Nothing there now except tumbleweed, coyotes, and a runway.'

In the span of those few seconds, Victor's color improved and it looked like he was standing taller.

'Good Christ – they could land there, let the anthrax get released . . .'

Monty slapped the sweating doctor on the back. 'Sure as hell, and there's nobody out there. Nobody.'

Victor turned to him, eyes bright. 'There must be other bases. Am I right?'

'Shit yes, if there's something this country is full of it's military bases. Get me a phone and I'll starting making calls to that Northern Command general. If we're lucky, doc, we'll start getting these aircraft on the ground, no fuss, no muss, and no civilian casualties.'

Randy and Brian and the General looked like they were family members at an ER ward, suddenly being told that the body in the morgue wasn't their dad but somebody else.

Monty looked back up at the screen, looked at the icons, and then saw one little triangular light that was orbiting over a part of Georgia.

His hands seemed frozen. In front of him a serious-looking young man was tapping at a terminal that had a miniature display of the wall screen. Monty bent down to him and said, 'Son?'

'Yeah?'

'You know where those jets are, the ones shown up on the screen?'

'Sure.'

'The one in Georgia. Can you tell me – is it anywhere near a town called Miller's Crossing?' Where his aunt lived. Where Charlene and the two girls were staying.

The guy worked the keyboard, shook his head. 'Nope, it's not near it.'

'Oh.' The relief going through him made Monty feel giddy.

And the feeling lasted only a moment.

The guy said, 'The damn jet's nearly orbiting on top of it.'

CHAPTER THIRTY-FIVE

General McKenna of Northern Command hung up the phone and looked across to his adjutant, Colonel Madeline Anson. 'We might have a solution.'

'Sir?'

'Cross-check with the information we're getting from Air Traffic Control and AirBox. Get the locations of those aircraft, their fuel states, and see what airbases we have within flight range of the aircraft. I want a listing of airbases in abandoned areas, old airstrips, anything and everything that can handle those aircraft types. Hell, even if it's a stretch of highway in a remote part of Texas or Oklahoma or South Dakota . . .'

Colonel Anson got up. 'I see. If we can land those aircraft in unpopulated areas . . .'

'Then we're good to go. The anthrax gets sprayed out and nobody gets hurt.'

'Some of these places, our personnel might have to get into MOP suits. And the decontamination process afterwards . . .'

McKenna said, 'A hell of a challenge, I know. But a better challenge than trying to explain to NBC or CBS or ABC how we came to shoot down civilian aircraft when we had a better option. Get to it, colonel.'

'Yes, sir.'

Victor Palmer pulled General Bocks aside and said, 'Your crews. To protect themselves, they need to wear their oxygen masks as they land.'

'Got it.'

'Oh. One more thing. How good are your pilots?'

'Most of them are ex-military. Lot of hours flying fighters or transport aircraft. Why?'

'I'm not familiar with the language of the flying . . . but it's important that they land in a way that minimizes the release of the anthrax.'

'In what way?'

Victor said, 'I'm not the flying expert, General. All I know is that if you can get them to land . . . well, in a way that they wouldn't normally do. I mean, they usually land straight on, right? That means the anthrax is spread out in a wide stream. But if they can land . . . well, tight, like a corkscrew . . . it means the footprint of the anthrax contamination will be that much smaller.'

Bocks said, 'It's tough flying. Most of them haven't maneuvered a jet like that in years. And never in a transport aircraft.'

Victor said, 'I know, General. But it could mean a better chance of reducing the area of contamination. Can it be done?'

The General rubbed at his face, and Victor felt a sudden burst of sympathy for the poor man, whose aircraft and entire company had been hijacked by a cruel fate.

'Yes, it can be done,' he said.

*

Aboard AirBox 101, which had been orbiting south of Imperial, Texas, Pete Renzi, a former Navy pilot, saw that his co-pilot, Jack Shaefer, already had his oxygen mask on. Pete said, 'Ready to land?'

Jack was sweating. 'Shit, yes, let's put this damn piece of metal on the ground.'

Pete donned his own oxygen mask and glanced once more at the ACARS message that had come across a half-hour ago. Proceed along such and such a course, arrive near abandoned Army Air Corps base, and land this lumbering cargo jet like a stunt pilot flying an acrobatic machine. He hadn't flown like that for more than ten years . . . it was going to be a hell of a thing.

'All right,' Pete said. 'All right, we're over the field. Let's get ready to start this abortion.'

'You got it.'

'Very good.'

Pete pulled the engine throttles to idle and rolled into a banking maneuver, letting the nose of the aircraft fall below the horizon in one smooth move. Breathing the cold and rubbery-tasting air, he saw the airspeed increase to 250 knots and he extended the plane's speed brakes. The trick, he thought, was to keep the spiral tight but not to exceed the two-and-a-half-G limit for aircraft like theirs. Anything under two and a half times the force of gravity was fine . . . anything more than that, well, he thought, they'd see just how damn good the maintenance crews were in keeping routine repairs updated.

But there were no G-meters in this aircraft; Pete would have to bring her in on experience and instinct alone, keeping the banking motion of the turn at a constant sixty-degree angle; anything too much higher than that and he and Jack and several tons of debris would be scattered over this desert floor . . .

Pete watched the airspeed and attitude gyro indicator as he dove the aircraft to the left. The desert landscape below them appeared to tilt up as they moved in a corkscrew, descending to the ground. The G-forces pushed both of them back into their seats. Thank God it was just him and Jack on this baby. A passenger flight would have had the passengers gripping their armrests and screaming in terror. Jack kept up the chatter as Pete kept the downward spiral as tight as possible, Jack's voice sounding muffled through the oxygen mask as he read out their altitude and rate of descent.

'Ten thousand feet,' Jack called out. 'Six thousand feet per minute down.'

The land continued to spin around. Pete forced himself to scan outside and then back inside to the instruments. Ignore everything else.

At four thousand feet it was time . . . time to descend as rapidly as possible and then pull out at the last minute to attempt a type of landing that was so crazy they didn't even bother to train for it in the simulators.

His co-pilot said, 'Gear's down, flaps thirty, landing checklist complete.'

Pete said, 'Let's do it.'

He pulled the throttles to idle, lowered the nose and extended the speed brakes. The aircraft, as one of his old instructors would have said, started to come down like a ton of shit.

Jack called out, 'Three thousand feet!'

'Roger,' Pete said, as he retracted the speed brakes and started the turn to the final approach.

There you go, he thought. Below three thousand feet and somewhere in the belly of his aircraft – his responsibility! – anthrax was now spraying out. A few hours ago their original destination had been Los Angeles; he refused to think of how many would have ended up dead because of him if they hadn't been stopped in time.

The aircraft seemed to vibrate more as they quickly lost altitude. Ahead of them was the narrow runway, and at five hundred feet they were now on final approach. Pete lined up the aircraft with the fast-approaching runway and increased throttle speed, to reduce their descent speed.

Jack was murmuring something, over and over, and Pete realized that the poor guy was praying . . .

A hard shudder, a screech.

Touchdown.

Things moved very quickly then. As the spoilers were deployed, Pete engaged full reverse on the engines, and pushed his feet down on the brake pedals for maximum braking. These old military fields were so damn short.

The plane vibrated some more as it started to roll to a halt. It was a bright, sunny day in the desert, and as they slowed and finally stopped Pete started breathing in the oxygen harder, thinking that he had never tasted anything so fine. The airstrip was deserted. Not even a single building. Well, so what? They were alive

As the engines whined down there was a *thud-roar* and another *thud-roar*, and he looked up. Two F-15s were rolling up and out above them, after giving them a close flyby.

'What the hell was that?' Jack asked.

'Victory roll,' Pete said.

'Victory? Victory for what?'

Pete picked up a checklist, let it fall. For later.

'Victory for not having to shoot us down,' he said.

As they descended into their approach, Karen Hollister of AirBox 88 said to her co-pilot Mark LaMontagne, 'We get through this, want to go to unemployment together tomorrow?'

His voice sounded odd through the oxygen mask: 'What do you mean?'

She couldn't believe that she laughed, but what else was there to do? 'You think AirBox is going to be in business this time next week?'

'Huh?'

'Mark, old boy, a bunch of AirBox aircraft have been carrying anthrax for the past few hours. Do you think that's a keen strategy for keeping our market share?'

Mark coughed. 'Shit. Hadn't thought about that.'

'Plenty of time to do that later. Let's go.'

And though this was going to be a landing for the record books and news magazines, it ended up being pretty routine. The touchdown was just a tad rough but when they were done, the plane at a halt, the landscape flat and pretty much abandoned, Karen sat back, breathing hard.

'Not bad, eh?' she asked.

Mark looked out the side windscreen. 'Got to hand it to you, Karen. You put us down like you've done this before.'

'Not hardly. Look. Company coming.'

Flashing blue lights ahead of them. Getting closer. Vehicles, of course.

In a couple of minutes, the lights were close enough to make them out.

South Dakota Highway Patrol.

Which made sense, for right now AirBox 88 was smack dab in the middle of a stretch of Interstate 90.

'Hope you got your license with you,' she said to her co-pilot as the state troopers came up to them. 'Hate to be arrested for landing without a license.'

Mark didn't laugh – which made some sense, for the troopers below them looked odd.

All of them were wearing gas masks.

Air Force Major Terrence Walker was standing out on the flight line, moving clumsily in full MOP gear, gas mask and gas suit, as he and his small staff – all of them wearing the same gear – waited near a Humvee. There was one small building next to the long runway, with satellite dishes and radio antennas on its roof.

Captain Cooper leaned toward him, his voice muffled through the gas mask. 'Still can't believe they're ending up here.'

'Good a place as any. Look. Here they come.'

Walker looked up as the aircraft – AirBox 12 – started its descent, coming down like a goddamn brick. He hoped they could pull this off because there was nothing here to help them – this small base in Colorado tested weather-monitoring equipment for the Air Force, and didn't even have a control tower or crash equipment – but it was going to have to work.

Somebody said, 'C'mon, hoss, ease her on down,' and so they waited.

Eugene Williams was the co-pilot of AirBox 12, and earlier he had said to his pilot, 'Alex, I really think I should take her in. I've had the experience. You haven't.'

And AirBox 12's pilot Alex Hinz had replied in his

clipped, accented voice: 'No more talk, please. Prepare for landing.'

Stupid moron, Eugene thought, as he started reading out the altitude, rate of descent and airspeed of AirBox 12. He had flown F-16s before being RIFed out from the Air Force three years ago, and knew how to put an aircraft thought its paces. But Alex had flown some in the German Air Force and for Lufthansa, before ending up in the States and AirBox. He was a typical European pilot: follow all the rules and procedures, even if it meant killing you. Like the SwissAir flight that had gone down near Nova Scotia some years ago. Bastards had indication of fire somewhere in the plane, and they wasted time getting the passengers ready for landing, picking up meal trays, trying to troubleshoot the problem, following everything nice and procedure-like instead of landing the damn thing, until they—

'Alex, we're at five hundred, sinking 1500 and 10 knots slow.'

No reply. Just a grunt.

'Alex, we're at four hundred, sinking 1500 and 15 slow!'

No reply

'We need power!' Eugene shouted.

From the Humvee, an alarm started going *Whoop! Whoop! Whoop!*, causing Major Cooper to jump. He shouted out, 'What the hell is that alarm?'

'Bio alarm,' came the voice. 'It's detecting anthrax.'

'Shit, of course it is. We knew that. Shut the damn thing down.'

And he turned back to the approaching aircraft and saw the disaster unfold.

*

Eugene shouted, 'Alex, we need power, we need power now!'

He reached over and pushed the throttles full forward to the stops and—

— And the last thing that was heard on the cockpit recording system – the infamous black box – reconstructed months later by the National Transportation Safety Board: 'Oh, you stupid cocksucker, I told you—'

Major Cooper thought to himself, if I live another hundred years, please don't let me see anything like this, ever again, as AirBox 12 started to pull out late from its descent at the end of the runway. For a moment it looked like it was going to make it, and then the aircraft's right wing dropped suddenly, smacked the ground, crumpled, and in a flash, the jet and its crew and its cargo disappeared in a billowing black greasy cloud of smoke and orange flames.

Cooper and his crew ducked behind the Humvee as the roar of the explosion reached them, the ground shaking from the impact. It took long minutes afterwards before anyone was calm enough to use their communications gear and contact Northern Command about what had happened.

Adrianna Scott looked in the mirror of the restroom at the highway rest stop somewhere in Michigan, liked what she saw. She had spent some long minutes in a stall, listening to the nervous chatter of other traveling women and girls. She'd worked quietly and efficiently, doing everything that she had planned to do, all those years ago, all those long years that started in Baghdad when she had gathered up some belongings and valuables and had gone to Jordan. A journey of walking, hitching rides, and fending off the advances of the noble Arab men who had wanted to fuck her as she made her way west.

And from Jordan into Israel, where she had portrayed herself – rightfully! – as a Christian refugee. A small Christian community in Bethlehem had helped her fly to the United States, to Cincinnati, and in those hours and days and weeks of travel she had planned her revenge so carefully that she had somehow known, even back then, that it would end like this.

Before her in the mirror, through her own talents and the help of the nice people at the CIA's Technical Services Division, a blonde-haired, blue-eyed, fair-skinned woman gazed out confidently. The hair she had trimmed and colored herself. The eye color was from contacts. The skin color was a dye job, and even her fingerprints were no longer hers, through a temporary skin graft job with artificial skin that made her into somebody else.

That somebody else, according to a Michigan driver's license, was one Dolores Benjamin. Adrianna Scott no longer existed.

And as she walked out of the restroom she knew that somehow, in the next few months, in her new home, Aliyah Fulenz would finally be allowed to live again.

Randy Tuthill was standing next to the General when there seemed to be a sudden intake of breath and a sigh, as one of the AirBox icons, set over Colorado, began flashing red. The ringing of phones reached a crescendo and the General was passed one. He took the message. Randy couldn't make out the General's words, but what he saw was enough: Bocks closed his eyes and nodded and seemed to shrink four or five inches in size, right before Randy's eyes.

The General let the phone fall back into the cradle as Randy went to him and said, 'Colorado?'

'Yeah. AirBox 12. Augered right into the end of the runway at an Air Force installation.'

Randy gripped his friend's shoulder. Bocks shook it off. Randy said, 'If you want, sir, I can start making the calls and—'

'Not your place, Randy, not at all,' Bocks said, straightening himself up. 'It's my call. My company. My fault they're dead.'

'General, if it's anybody fault, it's—'

'Randy, I'll make the calls. But later.' The General turned his head to the display board and said, his voice bleak, 'I'm afraid there're going to be more calls later. Look up there, Randy. Look at the board. Those planes aren't getting to the ground quick enough.'

Brian Doyle sat next to Monty Zane as Monty worked the phones and keyboards with a vengeance, cursing, plotting and planning. Brian's chest ached and he'd just realized his underwear was damp – he'd probably pissed himself falling off that balcony and wasn't embarrassed by it, for who wouldn't have pissed themselves in such a situation? – but he didn't want to move. He had hardly anything to do now but he liked being in Monty's company. He thought if the NYPD had a half-dozen guys like Monty working for them the crime level would go so low that it would even impress old Giuliani and his crew.

'Fuck,' Monty said, slamming down the phone. Then he leaned back in his chair, stretching out his arms.

'What you got?' Brian asked.

'What I got, my friend, is the problem of fuel versus geography, and fucking geography is winning.'

'Go on.'

Monty raised a hand toward the display screen. 'We've been putting these aircraft down where we can, at deserted airfields, remote strips without many people around, and even a couple of stretches of Interstate. But we still have a fair amount in the southeast and middle Atlantic seaboard. It's pretty crowded out there, Brian. Not many places to put down, and man, we are running out of time and fuel.'

Brian looked at the board, looked at the triangles that represented the airborne cargo planes. There were fewer up there than before, but Monty was right. There were still too many. He recalled seeing other display boards in the past, during the COMSTAT precinct meetings, another bit of Giuliani history. Precincts could no longer make do simply with shuffling paper and ignoring statistics. COMSTAT put up your history against everybody else's and there was no hiding, no excuses. Brian remembered one of the first times his precinct chief came back, cursing, saying it wasn't fair that he was up against another precinct, because that other precinct had a shitload of vacant lots, and of course they'd have a better burglary rate, because what the hell was there to burgle in an empty lot?

He looked again at the map, at the southern and eastern states, at the icons marking the AirBox aircraft. A little flashing light, carrying all that death, all over the crowded United States, no place to run to, no place to go, no place . . .

Empty.

Not a place.

Monty was on the phone again and Brian reached over, pressed the receiver button down, disconnecting Monty. The big man's eyes flashed with anger and he said, 'Brian, what the fuck was that?'

'The ocean,' Brian said.

'The fuck you mean, the ocean?'

'The jets . . . why can't they go over the ocean and let the anthrax dump out there?'

'Case you haven't learned, there's not many landing strips out in the middle of the Atlantic or Gulf of Mexico.'

'But they wouldn't have to land, would they? Shit, Monty, all they'd have to do is fly in circles over a patch of water, let the anthrax spray out, and then head to land when the canisters were empty. Right?'

Monty stared at Brian for what seemed like a long time. Then he yelled out, 'Doc Palmer! Get your ass over here! Now!'

Carrie Floyd looked at the ground below her, several thousand feet and a lifetime away. Pennsylvania. Definitely not Boston and definitely not home. She raised her head, saw the patient escorts out there, the proud F-16s that were ready to blow her and Sean out of the sky.

She said, 'Find anything out?'

Sean said, 'Dispatch is quiet. I've been trying to pick up some of the local radio stations. Getting a CNN feed every now and then.'

'What's up?'

'Well, we and the eighteen others are the lead story. Funny about that. Foreign airspace's been closed to all American flights. Stock market will be closed today, people are bailing out of cities, it's being called the biggest terrorist attack since 9/11.'

'Should have kept my mouth shut.'

Sean said, 'Well, there is a bit of good news. Some of the AirBox flights, the ones headed to Seattle or LA or Salt Lake City, they've been able to divert them to empty airstrips out in the desert. Landing with no problem.'

'Lucky bastards.'

'You got that,' he said.

Carrie tilted the aircraft, just a bit. Farmland and towns and highways, as far as the eye could see. 'Not much desert down there. Or emptiness.'

'Alaska,' Sean said.

'What?'

Sean said, lips tight. 'Lots of empty places in Alaska. Lots.'

She reached over, grabbed a hand, squeezed. 'Let's say we quit this gig later today and go to Alaska tomorrow. The three of us. You and me and Susan.'

Sean just nodded. Carrie thought she saw that his eyes were filling up. She released his hand and went back to the day's flying, boring holes in the sky, waiting for instructions, waiting for rescue, waiting for those F-16s to drop back and do their jobs.

Victor Palmer listened to Monty and said, 'Yes . . . I think it'd work.'

'How much time before the canisters empty out?'

'Twenty minutes, to be on the safe side. But you need to make sure that stretch of ocean is empty. Ah, the Coast Guard or Navy will have to be contacted. Get shipping out of the area.'

Monty went back to the desk he had taken over, picked up some handwritten notes. 'Tight. Christ, it'll be tight.'

Victor said, 'Do it. Just do it.'

Monty started making a call. 'It'll be done.'

At Northern Command, Lt General McKenna was on the phone with the Chairman of the Joint Chiefs. He said, 'Sir, we're making progress. We've got just over half the planes on the ground. And I've been advised that the Tiger Team is working on a way to handle the other aircraft by vectoring them out to the ocean. Apparently the anthrax will be dumped over the water. Hell of a better place than downtown DC or Philadelphia.'

The Chairman said, 'All right, Mike. I've got a briefing with the Man in five minutes. I'll tell him about the progress . . . but Mike, those aircraft have got to be out of the air within two hours. Or you'll be taking them out for us before those pilots try to land them someplace populated. Understood?'

'Absolutely, sir.'

Aboard AirBox 10, Helen Torrinson flew south, lowering the aircraft towards the warm waters of the Gulf of Mexico. Off to starboard she could make out oil-drilling rigs, but she didn't care about them, not at all. She had gotten the instructions from ACARS and from Houston Air Traffic Control on where to go and how to do it, and she knew that back there were two F-15s, making sure that she went where she was told.

Part of her – a part no doubt corrupted by her captain – thought that this was probably all just a ruse. The DoD probably wanted her and the other AirBox planes to head out over the ocean so they could be shot down without any problems, without any witnesses.

Beside her, the body of Hammerin' Hank lay still, slumped back in his shoulder straps. She was grateful that at least his bloodied head was turned to the left so she didn't have to look at his face.

Helen checked the altimeter. She was dropping below one thousand, was now at nine hundred, and when she got to five hundred feet, she leveled off the aircraft. Twenty minutes. She was to fly for twenty minutes.

Which was what she did. She checked the time, watched as each minute slipped by, wondering if this was going to be the minute when an air-to-air missile ripped through her aircraft's engines.

But the minutes still slipped away, and when the twenty-minute mark had been reached her earphones crackled with a message.

'AirBox Ten, this is Houston Center. You're cleared directly to Hutchinson Field, Louisiana. Initial heading zero-one-zero, climb to one-five thousand.'

'Roger, direct Hutchinson Field, and fifteen thousand,' Helen said, keeping her voice curt and proper. She'd be goddamned if she was going to be grateful to somebody who was ready to help the Air Force drop her plane and kill her without warning.

She went to her kit bag and pulled out the approach charts that would help guide her into Hutchinson Field, wherever the hell that was. Then she turned her head to the left.

'Oh, you stupid bastard,' Helen said to the body of her pilot. 'Why did you have to be so goddamn impatient?'

Aboard the shrimp boat *Flanagan*, out of Metairie, Louisiana, Georges Bouchard stepped out of the pilot house as the jet aircraft roared nearby, almost passing right over their heads. His two boys, Henri and Louis, were at the stern, and they looked up as well as the jet circled around, and kept on circling around, at a low altitude.

'What's up with that plane, eh, papa?' Henri called up to him. Henri and his younger brother were shirtless, tanned, and Georges felt such pride, seeing those boys who would carry on the family name and business for years to come.

'Not sure,' he said, shading his eyes with his hand. 'It doesn't seem to be in trouble ... look ... it's going away now.'

The jet flew off to the north, and Georges noticed two things: the first was that it looked like two fighter jets were flying with the larger jet as well, something he hadn't noticed earlier.

The second was that something was tickling his throat. He swallowed, and then went into the pilot house to drink from a plastic jug of water and clear his throat. The water was kept on a wooden shelf underneath the radio, which had been acting up since they had left port nearly a week ago. The water went down well enough, but something still tickled back there.

By that night, Georges and his boys were ill, very ill, breathing hard, coughing. And by the next morning the *Flanagan*, named after his wife's family, was wallowing in the Gulf Stream, crewed only by corpses.

The shrimper was boarded some time later by the Coast Guard. It was burned down to the waterline and sunk, along with its dead crew, as soon as night fell.

CHAPTER THIRTY-SIX

Homeland Security Deputy Director Jason Janwick hung the phone up, saw the expectant faces of his crew, sitting there, looking at him for answers. He said, 'That was the Secretary. Due to time constraints, this emergency is still ours to manage.'

'Sir?' one of his people asked.

'It's like this,' he explained. 'Like the Secretary said, there isn't time for him or for anybody else to catch up on what's happening. One way or another, this sick puppy is going to be done with in an hour or so. So it's ours to solve, or it's ours to fuck up. Let's make the right choice. Sam? Status.'

Sam Pope, his IT guy, said, 'It looks like the AirBox guys and that Tiger Team have taken care of the majority of the AirBox flights. Either they've been able to land at airstrips with minimal population density, or some have flown out over the Atlantic or the Gulf of Mexico. But there's still a handful up in the air.'

'Where?'

'Pennsylvania. Missouri. Kentucky. They're conserving fuel and holding in orbits but . . . soon enough, they're going to be running out of fuel. That means they're going to come back to earth, and there's not much unpopulated land where they are. The choice is . . . the choice is not a good one.'

'Explain.'

'Sir, when the fuel is at a certain limit those pilots are going to descend and pick the nearest airfield. There aren't that many airfields in those areas that don't have some populated areas around them. The choice, then, is to direct them to those airfields or . . . or direct them someplace else, where the population density is low, thereby reducing anthrax exposure. Like a federal park or wilderness area. A mountain range, for example.'

Janwick said, 'And what then, after they're over a minimally populated area?'

Pope's voice was just a touched strained. 'Then, sir, they would have to be shot down. I doubt the pilots will crash into the side of a mountain on anyone's say-so.'

Janwick nodded. 'Yeah. I figured that out a while ago. Just wanted to see if anybody else had any better answers. Well, the shoot-down order is out of our hands. But we'll still be making a recommendation. In the meantime . . . Gail?'

'Sir?' answered Gail Crayson, his Public Health adviser.

'Two things,' he said. 'First, we need to get Public Health resources into those states as of yesterday. Hazmat teams, medical assistance to area hospitals, Cipro stocks moving in . . . everything and anything that's needed to nip this anthrax exposure in the bud once it gets sprayed. If we can keep the exposure areas to those three states, we'll be lucky indeed.'

'You got it, sir,' she said. 'And your second request?'

'Time is running out,' he added. 'Determine the locations of those remaining airborne aircraft, see what areas they're orbiting, and for those areas I want a seal-and-remain advisory going out, as soon as possible.'

She said, 'We'll lose some people, you know. They'll seal up their rooms too tight with plastic wrap and duct tape. They will suffocate.'

'Yeah. But if that anthrax gets sprayed out in the next hour or so, we could save thousands. Which is what we're going to do. Get those advisories out now, Gail.'

'Yes, sir.'

*

In her vehicle, still heading north and thankfully away from the chaos unfolding in some parts of this cursed country, Adrianna Scott made it a point to listen to the news at the top of the hour, usually getting a CNN or AP news feed. She knew that she was tired and still had hours of driving ahead of her, but oh, was she pleased at what she was hearing.

She looked at the dashboard clock. It was seven a.m. Pretty soon those AirBox aircraft out there would be falling from the sky, no matter what, and there was no way that this day wouldn't end with thousands, perhaps hundreds of thousands, exposed and later dying.

Time for the news. On went the radio, on went the woman announcer from CNN, who seemed like she wanted to cry: '. . . Homeland Security has issued an advisory to a number of counties in the states of Kentucky, Missouri and Pennsylvania. Residents in these counties are advised to remain indoors and close all doors and windows. Close dampers and flues to fireplaces. If possible, go into a room or basement with no windows. If you do not have a room or basement without windows, remain in a room and tape the windows closed. In any event, the advisory states that people in these counties need to be in a place with no openings to the outside. The counties affected are—'

Adrianna turned off the radio, sighed with satisfaction, and continued driving.

Monty put the pen down, raised his head and rubbed at his eyes. It was done, as much as could be done. He looked to the display board and all that was written up there was failure.

AirBox 15, over Missouri.

AirBox 107, over Pennsylvania.

AirBox 22, over Kentucky.

'Doc,' he said quietly.

'Yes, Monty.'

'Worst-case scenario, how many deaths we got flying up there?'

And for once in his life, Monty thought, the good doctor didn't dance around or try to rewrite the question. 'Each canister has enough to infect about fifteen to twenty thousand people, if properly dispersed. Let's say about a hundred thousand, in total.'

Monty heard the machinist guy whisper in awe, 'A hundred fucking thousand . . .'

Yet the doctor wasn't finished.

'But that's not the problem. The problem is what happens afterwards. You can't expect people, once they get sick, to sit still at home. They'll be heading out to hospitals, clinics, their mama's house. Even with roads cut off by the National Guard and police forces, people will still get through, unless there's a shoot-on-sight order, which I doubt this or any other President will issue. Which means more and more infections, more spread of the disease. By the end of a week, we could have a half-million infected, with more to come.'

Monty kept his eye on the display screen. Just three aircraft. And he had a brief bout of nausea, thinking what might have happened if all the AirBox aircraft had taken off, and if this damn thing hadn't been uncovered. Scores of aircraft would be descending over major cities right now, infecting millions upon millions . . .

'Mister Zane.'

He turned as General Bocks rolled his own chair over to him. 'Our crews have less than an hour's flight time. Pretty soon, unless we tell them otherwise, those aircraft are coming down. What is to be done?'

Monty felt that nausea return. He swallowed, nodded, knew the harsh advice he had gotten from Homeland Security was the only thing left to do. 'Sir . . . there is no choice . . . we have to vector those aircraft away from populated areas, to send them to mountain ranges or state or federal parks . . . and then I'm going to order those three aircraft shot down.'

'You are, are you?' Bocks said. 'You're going to kill six of my people, just like that?'

'No, sir, not just like that,' Monty said. 'I'm going to kill those six people after a lot of agonizing thoughts, and I'm going to kill those six people so that six thousand or six hundred thousand aren't dead this time next week. That's what I'm going to do.'

'The hell you will,' Bocks said.

'The hell I won't,' Monty said.

Bocks picked up a phone. 'You're not listening to me, Mister Zane. Those are my people, my aircraft up there. I'm the one who's going to give the order. Not you.'

Steve Jayson of AirBox 15 couldn't believe who he was hearing in his earphones so he said, 'Ah, Dispatch, this is AirBox 15, repeat last, over.'

His pilot, Trent Mueller, glanced over at him with a questioning look, and then the voice came again. 'Guys, this is General Bocks calling in. Can the both of you hear me?'

Steve toggled the microphone switch on the control yoke. 'Sir, you've got us both. Go ahead.'

The General cleared his throat. 'Guys, I'm not going to sugarcoat a damn thing. You're in a hell of a spot. A hell of a spot due to decisions I made, bad decisions based on . . . well, that sounds like an excuse, and this isn't the time for excuses.'

Fucking understatement of the year, Steve thought to himself. The General said, 'We've gotten most of you safely on the ground. But there's you and two other flights. Guys, we're running out of time, and you're running out of fuel. Those are hard facts. I'm sorry. But we've got to send you . . . we've got to send you over the remotest area that's nearby. We're going to have you head out to the Ozarks . . . we're still trying to come to an answer, we haven't given up yet, but if we don't have that answer . . . we're going to need you to be over the mountains. Do you understand?'

It was Trent's turn to reply. 'Sir, we understand. And I need to know something . . . sir.'

'Go ahead, son.'

'Our families. We need to know that our families will be taken care of. Get everything they need. No bullshit or stalling.'

Bocks said, 'You got it. No bullshit or stalling. My personal guarantee.'

Trent said, 'Then you'll see us over the Ozarks, General. AirBox 15, out.'

Hugh Glynn was the captain of AirBox 22, and when the general signed off the air, his co-pilot, Stacy Moore, said, 'I'm sorry, I don't understand that. What the hell was that all about?'

Hugh said, 'We're heading for the Smoky Mountains, Stacy. What else do you need to know?'

'And what are we going to do when we get there?'

Hugh liked Stacy, had flown with her for several months,

admired her skill as a co-pilot and her eye for details, but when it came to the big picture . . . Jesus. Sometimes she was as thick as a plank. He rubbed at his chest. Damned indigestion was coming back again . . . he was going to visit his doctor later this week but his schedule looked pretty damn full over the next seventy or so minutes.

'What do you think?'

'Our fuel is . . . oh . . . oh, no . . . please . . .'

'Stacy, we're heading to the Smokies. Get the charts out, all right?'

No answer.

Hugh looked over. Tears were in her eyes. 'Stacy, we need those charts.'

He waited. Wondered what she was going to do. Wondered how this was going to end.

And then Stacy went to her chart pack, and for some reason Hugh felt good, even with the discomfort in his chest. They would go out as professionals. Not in a panicked frenzy.

Something to be happy about, at least.

Carrie Floyd of AirBox 107 sat in silence as they continued to go around in circles. For once Sean was silent as well. They had just gotten off the horn with General Bocks himself, and the brief conversation had just laid it out there. Nowhere to go, nowhere to land. But in a while it would be done. No doubt about that.

She looked at the fuel gauges. Less than an hour to go. Some decisions could be put off, some decisions could be put off forever. But the gauges didn't lie. They were now outbound to the Poconos, and there was a sort of grim sense of humor there, about her and Sean ending up in that honeymoon paradise, no doubt to be spread over a few mountain peaks in a tumble of wreckage and scorched protein.

And all because of fuel. Ah, the gift of fuel. If there had been some way of getting more fuel into their aircraft, they could stay up another six, eight, twelve hours, with no problem. Oh, shit, they'd be cramped and hungry, but at least they'd be alive. Give the folks on the ground more time to figure out what in hell to do with the little canisters of death they were carrying back there. She recalled all the times back in the Navy, flying the S-3 Viking, and the comfort of knowing that there were usually airborne fueling stations out there, other Vikings modified to carry fuel, Air Force KC-135s and KC-10s, all ready to lower a boom and give you all the fuel you needed.

Fuel. A lifesaver.

God, such a lifesaver.

Carrie rubbed at her tired eyes, stopped. Looked out the windscreen. Thought for a moment. Thought again.

Well, she said to herself.

'Hey,' she said to her co-pilot.

'Hey yourself,' he said.

'Sean, did I ever tell you about my grandfather, my dad's dad?'

'No, Carrie,' he said, his voice soft. 'I don't think you ever did.'

'Let me tell you about him,' she said.

Sean shook his head. 'Sure. Why the hell not? I could use a good story about now.'

'Sure,' she said. 'Name was Frank Floyd. Double-F, they called him, when he flew in the Navy. He was in World War Two. Flew Grumman TBMs. Know what TBMs were?'

'Nope.'

'Torpedo aircraft. Flew off aircraft carriers, went against Japanese ships. Especially Japanese aircraft carriers. They carried a single torpedo and their job was to fly low, slow and level, heading towards a target. All the while, they're being shot at by anti-aircraft fire from Japanese ships. Machine-gun fire, anti-aircraft artillery, exploding shells, shrapnel, all being tossed up in front of them. And if that wasn't enough, Japanese fighter aircraft – Zeroes – were strafing them as they flew in. They made nice fat targets, because they had to be low and slow to drop their torpedoes, and they couldn't fly evasively. It was the nearest damn thing to a planned suicide mission that the US Navy ever created.'

'Carrie, this is all just fascinating stuff, but—'

'One time,' she pressed on, 'right after I joined the Navy, I had a nice long talk with him, just before he died. I had done some reading about the torpedo squadrons and found that on an average mission the pilot and gunner had about a twenty percent chance of coming back alive. Can you believe that? Twenty fucking percent. And they still went out, mission after mission. So I asked him. I said, "Grandpa, how in God's name did you get in that torpedo bomber each time, knowing what was out there for you?" Know what he said?'

'No, but I guess you're going to tell me.'

'He said a twenty percent chance was better than no chance at all, and that a good pilot would do everything and anything to survive. That's what he said.'

By now Sean was staring at her, his eyes moist with tears. 'Carrie, what's the point? What's going on?'

She said sharply, 'The point is, my dear heart, is that we still have time, I'm still a good pilot, and we're not calling it quits at all. Get Dispatch back up. I want to talk to General Bocks. Right away.'

He said, 'You think he'll talk to you?'

'Sure he will,' Carrie said.

'Why?'

'Because the poor bastard is feeling guilty, and that's half the battle, right there.'

He said, 'You're not going to start—'

'Sean, hurry up. Please. Trust me on this. I've got to talk to him. Now.'

He kept on staring at her, and she knew that he wanted answers, but she didn't want to start discussing, arguing, or debating. She just wanted the damn general on the line.

Sean pressed the radio switch. 'Ah, Dispatch, this is AirBox one-oh-seven. I have an unusual request for you . . .'

Now the four of them were in a conference room, away from the low roar of the Operations Center. Brian sat on one side of the table, looking at the three other men. It was coming to an end, and he was exhausted by it all. He knew what was ahead for him, at least. Possible arrest, probably Congressional investigations, blah blah blah. Maybe he'd get back on the job. Maybe not. But at least he wouldn't be in a small room, waiting for tens of thousands of Americans to die over the next few days. So much for being a guard for the guardians.

Monty was slumped in a chair, looking out the windows to the display board, and Doctor Palmer sat next to him, staring at his laptop, not moving. General Bocks seemed to be talking to himself, as he said, 'Bankruptcy. As soon as we can, we'll declare bankruptcy . . . sell the assets, try to get some settlement with the lawsuits . . . set up a trust fund for the families of the crews . . . Pay for the medical care of those who get sick . . .'

The doctor shifted slightly in his seat. 'Monty.'

'Yeah.'

'Homeland Security is going to have to be advised where those planes go down. If we're lucky, we can get a perimeter set up around the crash areas and the anthrax dispersal footprint. We can keep the outbreak to within reasonable limits.'

'How reasonable?'

'A thousand, maybe less. If we're lucky.'

Monty said, 'Fuck, doc, with luck like that—'

The phone on the conference-room table rang. Bocks picked it up and said, 'Who? Are you sure?'

He put a hand to his face. 'Sure. Put her on.'

Brian saw some agony in the General's eyes, and with something cold starting to spread in his gut he realized that the man was talking to one of his flight crews, one of the doomed flight crews who would be dead within an hour.

'Yes . . . Carrie . . . I'm sure I've met you before . . . thank you for all you've done . . . I understand . . . but there's . . . hold on . . .'

Then something changed in the General's expression. Brian leaned forward. The General sat up and said, his voice now entirely changed, 'Hold on, Carrie. I'm in a conference room with some other people, including a DoD representative and a doctor from the CDC. Hold on.'

The General looked down at the phone and said, 'Shit, there's a speakerphone here somewhere . . . but I sure as hell don't want to disconnect her . . . Christ, here we go.'

A button or two were pressed, the handset was replaced, and a hiss of static burst from the speaker. Bocks said, 'Carrie, can you hear us?'

'AirBox one-oh-seven is here, General.'

'Carrie – repeat what you said to me. Please.'

'All right. Look – we know the score up here. We know there's not much time. But we're not ready to roll over and play dead for you or anybody else. Got it?'

'Yes, Carrie,' the General said. 'We got it.'

'Good. The way I see it, everything comes back to making sure that the anthrax doesn't reach the ground. Right?'

'That's right,' Bocks said.

'I know that sounds simple to you guys, but I've been thinking. We can't get to those damn canisters, we can't turn them off, we can't plug them up. So that anthrax is coming out, one way or another. Thing I see is, how do you stop the anthrax from getting to the ground? I think I've come up with something . . . shit, I know I've come up with something, and sorry, Mr FAA, for that little slip back there . . .'

Now Monty and Victor were staring at the speakerphone, and Brian thought they looked like religious pilgrims, staring at a holy relic that was going to save them and their family.

His voice louder, Bocks said, 'Carrie . . . please . . . tell us what you've got.'

A burst of static, and her voice came back, '. . . kill the little bastards. Right? We've got to kill the anthrax before it reaches the ground. Why not use jet fuel?'

Monty turned to Victor and said, 'Is she right? Can jet fuel kill anthrax?'

Victor said, 'I . . . I don't see why not – jet fuel is petroleum-based, quite harsh to anthrax. But how do you get the fuel from their fuel tanks to the canisters?'

Carrie's voice seemed to carry through the entire room. 'Not fuel from *our* jet. Fuel from another jet. A refueling jet, like the Air Force KC-10 or KC-135. They have booms they lower to refuel aircraft. But instead of trying to fuel us up, they'd fly ahead of us while we're descending to below three thousand feet. And when we cross that mark, they start dumping fuel. I've seen it before. The fuel makes a big cloud of vapor, and we and the anthrax will fly right through it. Very precise flying, but if it works . . . we can dump that anthrax into a big cloud of JP-4 aviation fuel. Kill it before it reaches the ground.'

Brian could not believe what he was hearing. Could it? Would it?

Monty said, 'Victor – tell me it'll work.'

Victor swallowed. 'It's . . . it's possible . . . I mean, you won't have a hundred percent . . . but hell, it's a lot better than a shoot-down and having the anthrax spray out as the fuselage descends. Question is, can you get those refueling aircraft to those three AirBox planes in time?'

Monty got up and started running out to the Operations Center.

Lt Gen. Mike McKenna said, 'Mister Zane, we're working, working it right now . . . hold on, all right.'

'All right,' came the voice on the other end of the line. McKenna put the phone down. He waited in his office. Waited. Looked at the phone, knew that one of these days he'd have to meet this guy, face to face, and find out how in hell he did what he was doing without cracking. Right now, he could use some tips. Outside on the floor his adjutant, Colonel Anson, was huddled with other officers, talking, gesturing with her hand, and then she looked around at the other officers, nodded, and ran back up to his office.

She was out of breath. 'General . . . with so many overseas on deployment . . . it's . . . it's . . .'

'Go on.'

'Two. We have just two KC-135s that can reach them, once we configure the refueling booms so they can dump the necessary fuel.'

'Which ones?'

'The flights in Missouri and Kentucky. We don't have anything in the area that can reach the one in Pennsylvania in time.'

'I see. All right, get on it, get those jets to the AirBoxes in Missouri and Kentucky.'

McKenna picked up the phone and said, 'Mister Zane, got a mix of news for you . . .'

CHAPTER THIRTY-SEVEN

Monty said, 'Could you repeat that, general?'

McKenna said, 'We will have two KC-135s airborne shortly that can reach the AirBox aircraft in Missouri and Kentucky. The KC-135 heading to Missouri just came back from a refueling mission over Nebraska. They'll have enough fuel to do the job. The Kentucky KC-135 is fully topped off and is on its way. But your AirBox flight in Pennsylvania, one-oh-seven . . . it's going to be tricky.'

'Define tricky.'

'If we can get the KC-135 in Kentucky to your AirBox flight in time – and if they can disperse the fuel in record time – and if your AirBox flight in Pennsylvania flies on an intercept mission to them . . . they might have enough time and fuel to pull off a rendezvous.'

'That's a lot of ifs,' Monty said.

'Like I said, tricky. But your one-oh-seven flight – if it doesn't get pulled off . . .'

'I know. A one-way trip.'

'Hell of a thing,' McKenna said.

'On that we agree, general.'

Aboard AirBox 15 over the Ozark Mountains, Steve Jayson said to his captain, Trent Mueller, 'Tell me again you've had experiences with KC-135s.'

'That I surely have, son,' Trent said. 'Back in my days, humping C-141s, I refueled from them a number of times. But today it's going to be some tough flying. We're breaking all the rules, you know.'

'No, I don't know,' Steve said. 'Enlighten me.'

'KC-135s are converted Boeing 707s, flying fuel tanks. Carries about 120,000 pounds of JP-4 aviation fuel. You've got your pilot, co-pilot, navigator and an NCO in the rear who operates the refueling boom. The boom is an extendable piece of equipment, deploys from the rear. Job of the other aircraft is to fly tight formation directly behind and below the KC-135. The guy at the rear, the "boomer", maneuvers the boom into the second aircraft's refueling port. Airborne refueling at its best.'

'And what rules are we breaking?'

Steve heard his captain laugh. 'Thing is, the receiving aircraft – us – is supposed to be below and behind the KC-135. Flying constant altitude and speed. But according to the ACARS message, we're going to be flying just above the KC-135 as it's dumping its fuel, and we're both going to descend at the same rate. So that fucking anthrax flies into the fuel cloud. And, by the by, we'll be flying into the fuel as well. Might screw up our instrumentation. Might cloud up our windscreens. Might cause the engines to choke up and cause a crash. Nice stuff like that.'

'Holy shit,' Steve said.

'Nothing holy about it, pal.'

A message crackled in Steve's earphones from the regional ATC: 'Ah, AirBox one-five, your tanker, Cheyenne Six, is 270 for fifteen miles, heading three-six-zero at flight level two-two-zero.'

Steve toggled the radio microphone, 'This is AirBox one-five, flying heading three-five-zero for rendezvous.'

'Maintain flight level two-one-zero and two hundred and fifty knots. Contact Cheyenne Six on second radio on frequency one thirty-two point five.'

Trent said, 'Steve, I'll talk to the tanker. You keep talking to ATC.'

Steve saw Trent dial in the radio frequency and key his own radio microphone. 'Ah, Cheyenne Six, this is AirBox one-five.'

'AirBox one-five, this is Cheyenne Six. Air National Guard, at your service.'

Trent replied. 'Glad to see you, guys. You got the brief, right?'

The pilot said, 'Got it. Let's do it.'

Trent swallowed. Just beyond a range of mountains, the gray form of the KC-135 came into view.

'All right,' Steve said. 'We're visual. We'll be coming up behind you shortly.'

'Roger, AirBox one-five. You're cleared in.'

Steve said to his pilot, 'Air National Guard. Christ.'

Trent said, 'What's the problem?'

'Weekend warriors.'

Trent was silent and Steve thought his captain hadn't heard him. Then Trent corrected him.

'Steve, most of these weekend warriors have ten or twenty years' flying under their belt. They have a hell of a lot more experience then some active-duty guys. And these weekend warriors are putting their asses on the line to make sure that you and I don't end the day as smoking pieces of charcoal – try not to forget that, all right?'

His face burning, Steve said, 'I won't.'

In an Air Force KC-135 designated as Pegasus Four – the aircraft was almost ten years older than the oldest member of its four-person crew – the navigator, Lt Jeannette Smith, tapped the pilot on his shoulder and said, 'Sir, incoming flash message.'

The co-pilot and pilot both read the message, then looked up at each other. The co-pilot, Lt Travis Wood, said, 'Can you believe this?'

'These times, I can believe almost anything. Travis, get the rendezvous going with ATC. Looks like we don't got much time.'

'Roger, sir.'

'All right, let's do it,' the pilot said. He toggled the intercom and said, 'Pilot to boomer.'

'Sergeant Hiller, sir.'

'Come forward, will you? We've just been assigned a mission. Two missions if we can handle the first one well – and it's screwy as all hell.'

'Bless the Air Force, sir. I'll be right up.'

The navigator looked at the message again. 'AirBox . . . your dad works for AirBox, doesn't he?'

Captain Thomas Tuthill said, 'Yes. He's head of the machinists' union.'

'What a coincidence,' she said.

'Yeah,' Captain Tuthill said, seeing the Kentucky landscape unfold beneath them. 'Hell of a coincidence.'

Aboard AirBox 107, Carrie Floyd maneuvered the jet to the intercept heading that had been sent to them by Air Traffic Control, and said, 'Sean, Alaska is sounding better and better.'

Sean said, 'So now you tell me . . . Carrie, check the fuel gauge, all right?'

She gave it a glance. 'I see it.'

'We'll be right at the edge. If it doesn't go right we'll be sucking fumes . . .'

'Then it has to go right, doesn't it?'

'Love your attitude.'

Carrie said, 'Glad it was that and not my tits that attracted you.'

'Among other things.'

'Co-pilot, do me a favor, start looking for the Air Force, all right?'

'Sure.'

Aboard AirBox 22, Captain Hugh Glynn rubbed at his chest again as the indigestion burned and burned at him. But the pain was forgotten when his co-pilot, Stacy Moore, said, 'There. I've got it at eleven o'clock!'

He saw the familiar shape of the KC-135 out there on the horizon, felt his chest tighten with excitement – a welcome change from indigestion. Stacy was excited and who could blame her? Less than a half-hour ago, they were looking forward to becoming one of the first civilian aircraft to be blown out of the sky since 9/11 – a hell of an achievement that he could cheerfully have skipped.

Now, now there was a chance. A chance to make it through this day alive.

In his earphones, he heard Stacy say, 'Pegasus Four, AirBox 22, we're visual . . .'

The strong voice came back. 'Roger, AirBox 22, you're cleared in. Time is short, ma'am, so let's get going.'

'A pleasure, Pegasus Four,' Hugh sent back. 'A real pleasure.'

Steve Jayson of AirBox 15 had flown on some serious asspuckering missions, including one in a sandstorm over Kuwait, and another time, coming into Gander when he was flying FedEx, with one engine and then two quitting on him just before landing. But nothing had prepared him for this particular mission, with his asshole crawling up to his mouth.

Ahead of them was the steel-gray KC-135, flying slightly below them, and behind the jet, trailing out, was the refueling boom, with a tiny wing on each side, spraying out fuel, a pinkish cloud that spread out wide. Trent was flying so tough and hard, chatting it up with Cheyenne Six, and Steve's job was to monitor the instruments, especially the altitude, engine performance and time.

'AirBox one-five, maintain two thousand feet.'

'Roger that, Cheyenne Six. Maintaining two thousand feet.'

The KC-135 was so close that it seemed to fill the sky in front of them. In a bubble just above the refueling boom, a man was visible, maneuvering the boom. The boomer, he was called, and Steve was praying that the older man knew what in hell he was doing.

'Looking good, AirBox 15.'

'Thank you, Cheyenne Six.'

Another look at the gauges. Everything looked normal and level at two thousand feet. That was for sure. And down there, in the belly – the belly of the beast – that damnable anthrax was being sprayed. If the guys on the ground knew what they were doing, the vile stuff was being killed before it could reach the ground.

Steve kept his mouth shut, knowing that Trent was so fucking busy, keeping everything in place. Just a few minutes more and—

Jesus!

A bump of turbulence or something and the damn refueling boom was closer and closer and—

THUD!

The top of the boom struck the hull, right near the windscreen, and Jayson didn't know what to say, when—

Trent tweaked the yoke, just tweaked it, and the KC-135 was where it should be, back in position. Steve swallowed and the radio crackled. 'Nice job, AirBox one-five.'

'Thanks,' Trent replied

Steve tried to swallow again. He couldn't. His throat was too dry.

Hugh Glynn on AirBox 22 got to where he had to be, his chest burning again, and saw the fuel boom extend from the rear of the Air Force jet. His co-pilot said, 'All right, just twenty minutes of flying, Hugh. That's all. We can get on the ground nice and safe. Twenty minutes of flying and we're done.'

'Yeah,' he said. 'That's all.'

The jet seemed to grow larger in the windscreen as they approached.

*

In his earphones, Captain Thomas Tuthill heard his boomer Master Sergeant Bobby Hiller say, 'AirBox flight is in place, captain.'

'All right. Start the dump. When you reach fifty thousand pounds, shut her down. We've got another AirBox flight depending on us.'

'Yes, sir.'

He switched from intercom to radio, called out, 'AirBox 22, Pegasus Four.'

'Pegasus Four, good day.'

'Good day, sir. We're dumping fuel now. Maintain altitude and speed.'

'Roger, Pegasus Four.'

Thomas Tuthill looked over to his co-pilot, Lt Travis Wood. 'Hey, Trav.'

'Sir?'

'What a job, huh?'

'Sure.'

'Well, at least you're getting what you want.'

'What the hell is that . . . sir?'

He punched his co-pilot lightly on the arm. 'You said you wanted to do more in the war on terror – so here's your chance.'

'Shit. Lucky me.'

'Nope,' Tuthill said. 'Lucky us.'

The pink cloud in front of AirBox 15 suddenly slowed and disappeared. Steve Jayson said, 'Trent, what the fuck is going—'

And then the interruption: 'AirBox 15, this is Cheyenne Six. Gas station is empty, we're heading home – suggest you do the same.'

Trent Mueller said, 'Cheyenne Six, nearest piece of flat concrete you got, that's where you'll find us. Thank you and good day.'

'Good day to you, AirBox 15.'

Steve checked the fuel gauge. Less than twenty minutes' worth of flying. He was going to say something but what was the point?

'Trent?'

'Yeah?'

The jet was now descending and turning, and off there in the distance was a beautiful, beautiful county airfield that was probably too small but was going have to do.

'Trent, whatever happens, a brilliant piece of flying. Beautiful.'

'Hey, that's very nice of you. Want to do something for me?'

'Sure.'

'Shut the fuck up so we can get this piece of metal on the ground.'

'You got it, Trent.'

Back in the Operations Center the low roar of phone calls, keyboards being tapped and people talking was starting to subside. Monty sat back, feet up on a desk, looking at the display board and the three icons marking the last of the AirBox flights. Brian Doyle sat next to him, hands folded across his lap. Tuthill and the General were confabbing about something, and Victor being Victor, the doc was keeping to himself.

Monty said, 'Ever hear the expression "hoist on your own petard"?'

'Yeah.'

'Know what it means?'

'Not sure. I think it means something about getting fucked-up because of something you yourself did. Am I right?'

Monty kept his gaze on the display screen. 'Yep. Came from a line in Shakespeare, from *Hamlet*. A petard was a crude explosive device, used to breach gates. But they were tricky to use. Sometimes the fuse burned too quick and blew up the guy setting the bomb, as well as the gate. Hence, to be hoist on one's own petard.'

Brian said, 'When this is all done with, I guess the Tiger Teams will be one huge petard.'

'Yeah. Lots of books and TV scripts will be written about this fuck-up when we're through – but they'll miss the essential story.'

'Which is what?'

'Which is that we had to do something after 9/11. The Tiger Teams were a great idea. It was the staffing of them that caused this disaster. Always goes back to the people factor. Not the technical factor. It's the people that make it work, and in this case, it was the people – Adrianna and those CIA people, years ago, who did a shit-ass job of checking out her background – who failed us.'

'Nice essential story, but I don't feel too essential. I feel like we came within minutes of killing several million people. Not the kind of way I'd like to spend my days.'

Monty reached over and slapped Brian on the leg. 'True enough, my friend. And I'll make you two predictions. By the end of this week, the Tiger Teams will be done. And a week after that, they'll be planning something else to replace them. For something like the teams are always needed. No matter what we and others did, the main essential truth still remains: there are many, many people who want to do us harm, and the old ways of protection don't work.'

Brian looked like he was going to say something when a nearby phone rang, and the guy picking it up gave a little whoop of joy.

'AirBox 15 is on the ground, safe and sound!'

Monty looked up at the display screen. Two icons remained.

He turned to Brian. 'See? Day's getting better already.'

Captain Tuthill said, 'How much longer, boomer?'

'Another five, six minutes, sir.'

'Very good.'

He turned in his seat, said to his co-pilot, 'Travis, minute we're done dumping fuel, tell ATC we'll want a rendezvous heading to that last AirBox flight immediately. Got it?'

'Roger that, sir.'

'All right.'

The navigator said, 'Bet your dad will have a story to tell you when this is through.'

Tuthill said, 'More than one story, I'm sure.'

Good point, he thought. Dad loved to tell stories about all the places he had been, all the aircraft he had repaired, all the pilots whose butts he had saved. God, the hours he had spent in the backyard, those damn tiki torches burning, Dad talking about—

His boomer's voice, shouting, 'Captain! Pull up, pull up, pull up!'

So close, Hugh thought, so close, just a few more minutes, and Stacy Moore confirmed it, saying, 'Hugh, we're going to make it, just a few minutes more, and we've got enough fuel to—'

The KC-135 was there, right in front of him, a huge

construct of steel and fabrication and the fuel was dumping out and—

Oh, damn, oh damn—

Hugh's chest felt like it was exploding, like it was swelling up and he fell forward, choking, and the last thing he heard was his co-pilot, screaming . . .

An amateur filmmaker from Hobson, Kentucky, caught it on tape, the moment when the AirBox flight sped up and descended, its nose colliding with the tail of the KC-135, the AirBox shuddering and breaking up in flight, the KC-135 catching fire, turning over, and then exploding in mid-air, fuel burning, debris raining down, falling to earth, yet—

Yet not that day, nor ever, did a single spore of anthrax from that aircraft make it to the ground.

General Bocks saw the display screen, heard the reports, sat down. For a moment it seemed as though the phones had stopped ringing, the voices had stopped talking, the keyboards had stopped clacking. All that he saw in his world was the blinking icon of that one single aircraft up there that belonged to him, yet which had been stolen such a very long time ago.

'One-oh-seven, am I right?' he asked no one in particular.

'Yes, sir. One-oh-seven, airborne over southeastern Pennsylvania.'

'Fuel status?'

'About twenty minutes.'

He looked at the faces, saw that the night manager, Pam Kasnet, was still there. 'Pam?'

'Yes?'

'Get a phone patch set up. I need to talk to one-oh-seven.'

CHAPTER THIRTY-EIGHT

Carrie Floyd's eyes hurt from the strain, looking and looking out there for that damn KC-135, but the sky was blank. She checked the fuel gauge and the time on her watch. About twenty minutes of flying left, if they were lucky, and luck would mean having that damn Stratotanker pop over the horizon and shag ass to their position. Because if that particular Air Force aircraft didn't show up, she was sure that the two Air Force fighters still shadowing them would take care of business.

Sean whispered something and said aloud, 'Carrie, the General's on comm two.'

She felt everything just fade away. Sean's face looked ashen. 'Not good news, is it?'

'Seeing a Stratotanker out there would be good news,' she said. 'Hearing from the General is not good news. All right, let's hear what he has to say.'

And in the space of those few seconds when she made the comm switch so that she could hear the General's voice, she also hoped against hope that her worst fears weren't about to come true. She said a quick prayer, too quick to reach God, she thought, for the General came on and said what had to be said.

'Carrie . . . Sean . . . I'm sorry to say we're unable to get a KC-135 to your position.'

A feeling came to Carrie, that horrible empty feeling she had felt once before, back on the *Enterprise*, when the Viking S-3 that she had been piloting had fallen off the end of the flight deck, knowing that she was seconds away from her and her co-pilot's death.

'What happened?' she finally asked. 'I thought we had one in-bound from Kentucky, after it had met up with AirBox 22.'

Bocks said, 'Mid-air collision. I'm sorry, we lost both aircraft. There are no other refueling aircraft available in the area.'

Sean whispered something again. For the briefest of moments, she closed her eyes. So close. Her own idea . . . and so close.

She triggered the microphone, and the voice that came out wasn't her own, it wasn't someone panicking over what was about to happen, no, it was her old Navy voice, old Smash, come to life. The voice said, 'We understand. Thanks for trying. General, you need to make it right for our families. Understood?'

Bocks said, 'Of course. Is there . . . is there anybody you'd like to talk to . . . Carrie? Sean?'

She looked to Sean. He shook his head. Carrie thought about her Susan . . . Susan, safe and secure in school. To talk to her, at this last moment? To have her hauled out of class and taken to the principal's office, to have a phone shoved at her and be told that . . . well, mommy wants to say goodbye?

'No,' she said. 'No. There's nobody we want to talk to. But I have a request, General. And you better make it happen.'

'All right,' Bocks said. 'I'll make it happen.'

She made her request, and when Bocks signed off she said to Sean, remembering her service aboard the *Enterprise*, 'Sorry, my dear. I have a rotten record of taking care of my co-pilots.'

'Maybe I'll complain to the union, when I get a chance.'

'Yeah,' Carrie said, looking out to the empty sky, no last-minute reprieve out there. 'When you get the chance.'

Grayson Carter worked in one of the maintenance shops for AirBox, and he was trying to catch up on some paperwork when the door to the offices blasted open and General Bocks and Randy Tuthill were there, staring at him.

'Sir . . . what can I—'

Bocks said, 'Grayson. You're a minister, aren't you? At a church in the city?'

'Yes – yes, I am. Fourth Street Baptist. I minister there on weekends and—'

His upper left arm was grabbed hard by the General. 'Grayson, we need you to come with us, right now. We need you, and we need you bad.'

'What . . . what for?'

Randy said, opening the door and waving the two of them on through, 'We'll explain on the way, and by God, Grayson, please tell us you'll do it. Please.'

Carrie no longer wanted to look at her watch or the fuel gauges. She just wanted to look at her Sean and at the Pennsylvania landscape beneath them, small cities and towns, tens of thousands of innocents alive down there, and here she was, with the unintended and unwanted power to sicken and kill them all. Sean was doing all right, though his hands trembled some and it looked like his eyes were filling up. She took a deep breath as her earphones came alive.

'Carrie – I think we're all set,' Bocks said.

'Thank you, General . . . and one more thing.'

'What's that?'

Carrie said, 'Thanks for hiring me, when I got out of the

Navy. I had . . . had some troubles, before I left. Some thought I wasn't tough enough or hard enough to be a pilot. But you took a chance on me. Thank you.'

Bocks said, 'No, thank you, Carrie. Thanks for everything . . . and I need to ask you something, if you will.'

'Go ahead.'

'I . . . I . . .' It seemed like the poor guy's voice was breaking up, and then he went on. 'I was responsible for putting those canisters in your air-conditioning system. I thought I was taking part in a confidential emergency immunization program – those canisters were supposed to be carrying anthrax vaccine, not anthrax spores. It was my call, my decision to install those canisters – and for that . . . I ask you for your forgiveness . . .'

Sean said 'Fuck. Fuck me, so that's how it happened . . . shit . . .'

Carrie said, 'General, consider yourself forgiven. It's all a moot point now . . . all right? Were you able . . . were you able to—'

'Yes, Carrie. Hold on . . .'

She reached over, took Sean's hand, squeezed it hard. A man's voice came over the headphones, a strong, deep voice, and she squeezed Sean's hand as he started. 'Carrie . . . Sean . . . my name is Grayson Carter. I'm a minister with the Fourth Avenue Baptist Church – are you ready?'

'Yes, reverend, we're ready,' Carrie said, as Sean squeezed her hand back.

'Very good,' he said. 'Dearly beloved, we are gathered here in troubled times, under the eyes of God, to perform sacred matrimony upon your servants, Carrie Ann Floyd and Sean Barnes Callaghan . . .'

*

By now the broadcasts between AirBox 107 and the company's Operations Center had been monitored by the news media. So it was that millions of Americans, most of them frightened, others angry, some stuck in cars and SUVs attempting to flee major cities, others in basements or sealed rooms in their homes, listened as a pilot and a co-pilot shared their wedding vows.

'I, Carrie Ann Floyd, do take thee, Sean Barnes Callaghan . . .'

'I, Sean Barnes Callaghan, do take thee, Carrie Ann Floyd . . .'

'. . . for better or worse . . .'

'. . . in sickness and in health . . .'

'. . . til death do us part . . .'

And most were amazed that the last phrase was proclaimed with such strength, conviction, and obvious love.

Bocks stood there, hands folded in front of him, in the nearly silent Operations Center. Several times he wiped at his eyes as the familiar refrains were uttered, and he looked to his people, his AirBox staff, and realized that there was not a dry eye to be seen. Save for Grayson Carter, his maintenance worker and minister, who was keeping it under control as he performed God's work this late morning.

Grayson's voice rose at the end, saying, 'And by the power vested in me, through God and the State of Tennessee, I now pronounce you man and wife. Praise the Lord.'

And faintly, through the speakers, both Carrie and Sean repeated the phrase.

'Praise the Lord.'

*

Carrie tried to keep a smile on her face as she looked to her husband. 'What? You're not going to kiss the bride?'

Tears were streaming down the cheeks of her strong man and he bent over, kissed her softly and quickly on her lips, and she kissed him back, still holding his hand. 'Carrie . . . God, I wanted so much for us . . . I wanted . . .'

She kissed him again. 'Shhh . . . my love, it's almost over. We're . . . we're going together. You and me. I love you so.'

'And I love you, too . . .'

She turned to the windscreen, saw something out there on the horizon, and a sort of peace came over her. There. That would work.

'My love . . . that's a lake over there, isn't it?'

Sean glanced at a chart. 'Yeah – Lake Douglas.'

'Okay. That's where we're going . . .'

'Carrie – it's not wide enough.'

She said, 'Width isn't what counts,' and she explained to him what was going to happen, and all he could do was nod in agreement.

Bock's Operations Manager said, 'General?'

'Yes, Pam.'

'AirBox one-oh-seven wants you again.'

'All right.'

He picked up a headset, placed it over his head, no longer seeing anything around him. It was a blur now, just a gray blur. 'Carrie, this is Bocks, go ahead.'

'General . . . I don't know if you can do this for us . . . but we know we have company up here. Two F-16s. Have them pull away. All right? We're . . . we're going to do this right . . . you don't have to worry about a thing . . .'

'Carrie, I don't know if I—'

'Sir, we don't have time to argue. Pull them away. We figure if we go down because of those F-16s lots of innocents can still die. We've got a better way.'

'Carrie, I'll—'

'AirBox one-oh-seven, out.'

Monty was now at Bocks's side. The General said, 'Did you hear that?'

'Yeah, I did.'

'Call off those planes. Now.'

'General, I can't see how—'

'Just try, all right? Just try, damn it.'

Monty said, 'You got that.'

Lieutenant General McKenna of Northern Command listened to the man in Memphis, said very little, and hung up the phone. He waited just a few seconds, long seconds during which he knew that he was being asked the impossible. Procedures and plans and operations took precedence over everything, and he was being asked to toss it all aside.

Over the promise of a woman he had never met.

A woman who . . . God, what she had ahead of her . . .

'Sir?'

His adjutant, Colonel Anson, stood in front of him. She looked at him expectantly.

He clenched his fists, released them. 'Colonel, contact the two F-16s escorting AirBox 107.'

'Sir.'

'Tell them . . . tell them . . .'

A pause, and then, 'Sir?'

He looked away. 'Tell them to break off. Tell them to break off and not do a damn thing.'

Anson was a good adjutant. She just nodded. 'At once, sir.'

So now this lake was beneath her, a beautiful lake it looked like, and she said to Sean, 'Guess it's too late to suggest to AirBox that they put parachutes for their aircrews in these things.'

'Guess so.'

'Funny thing, this . . .'

'What's that?'

'You and I swore when we joined the service to defend the Constitution and our countrymen, our civilians. Never thought I'd be doing that today.'

'Me neither,' he said.

She grabbed his hand again. 'Be of good cheer, my love. It'll be quick.'

'Carrie..'

'Yes, Sean.'

'The Navy was fucked-up. You're the best and toughest woman I've ever known. And I'm so happy you're my wife.'

'And I'm so happy you're my husband.'

The low-fuel warning light had been on now for what seemed like a month. Fuel status was way past critical. Only minutes were left to them . . . just a grouping of seconds, that was all.

'Here we go, my love.'

No answer. Just another squeeze of the hand.

Carrie took a breath, thought, forgive me, Susan, and she pushed the yoke forward with a slight roll. The nose of the aircraft dropped like an elevator, and now they were both weightless in their seats as the jet fell from the sky, bits of metal and crumbs and paper scraps flying past her, Sean still holding tight to her hand on the control yoke, the only thing now visible in the windscreen the rapidly approaching waters of the lake.

While the F-16s were ordered to break off, they still kept view of the AirBox aircraft as it approached the lake. In a matter of seconds the lead pilot could not believe what he was seeing as the plane suddenly pitched over and headed down to the lake.

'Chris . . .' said Lance One's wingman. Lance One said, 'Yeah, I see it . . .'

The jet moved quickly, so quickly, and the wingman choked a bit as he realized what the flight crew had done. Whatever anthrax was in that aircraft was designed to be released when the jet went below three thousand feet but at the speed they were traveling it would be just a second or two and—

Something was said over his earphones. Not Chris. Had to be AirBox and—

'Jesus God,' he whispered as the plane disintegrated and crashed in a huge geyser of water and metal debris and flying papers and packages –

Oh, Christ.

'Ah . . . Center, this is Lance One,'

'Go ahead, Lance One.'

'Ah . . . AirBox one-oh-seven has crashed into a lake at this location . . . advise you send Public Health officials to the area . . .'

'Lance One, we acknowledge . . .'

Another voice, his wingman again. 'Chris, did you ever see anything like that . . .'

'No, and I never want to, ever again. Hold on, Ed.'

He looked to the lake, at the widening circle of water,

debris, wreckage . . . obliterated. Absolutely and totally obliterated.

'Center, Lance One.'

'Lance One, go ahead.'

'Also advise that we monitored last transmission from AirBox one-oh-seven as it descended.'

Nothing. No answer.

'You copy, Center?'

An embarrassed voice. 'Ah, go ahead, Lance One. What was AirBox message, over?'

'Message follows: "This is Smash, signing off."'

'Understood. Smash, signing off.'

The pilot known as Lance One didn't acknowledge. He just kept on circling the waters of the lake that had become a grave.

CHAPTER THIRTY-NINE

Bocks looked at the display board. It was empty. No more AirBox flights were airborne. It was over – at least, this part was over. Ahead there would be hearings and charges and TV documentaries and court battles, and no doubt bankruptcy and some jail time.

But it was over. The country would survive. His duty was done. And so was Carrie's.

Smash had completed her last mission, successfully.

He sat down, exhausted, put his head in his hands, and wept.

*

Victor Palmer knew that he should be following up with the crash of the AirBox in Pennsylvania, knew that he should be making recommendations to minimize whatever possible exposure was out there, but he was just too damn tired. He was sure that Doc Savage could put up with almost anything, but he doubted that even the Man of Bronze could have handled this.

Did this make him better than Doc Savage?

A treasonous thought. He lowered his head, closed his eyes, and for the second time that night passed out.

But this time, he was left alone.

Grayson Carter closed his eyes in repose, praying for the souls of Carrie Floyd and Sean Callaghan. There was a touch at his elbow. 'Yes?'

'Grayson . . .' the woman said. 'I'm Pam Kasnet, night Operations Manager . . . I'm sorry, but . . . well, we have a situation.'

He saw the troubled look on her face, and said, 'Well, what is it?'

She told him. He nodded. God was putting him to work tonight, and that was fine. It was his calling. He would bear the burden as best he could.

'Yes,' he said. 'I'll help you.'

Brian Doyle saw Randy Tuthill being taken to the conference room, Bocks and the minister joining him and the woman Operations Manager. There was a loud, bellowing, 'No!' from Randy before the door closed.

Monty came up to him, held out his hand, which Brian shook.

'What was that about?' Brian asked.

'Randy Tuthill. The machinist guy.'

'Yeah?'

'His son was the pilot of the KC-135 that collided with the Kentucky AirBox flight.'

Brian nodded. 'That sucks.'

'Yeah.'

Brian took in the ordered chaos of the Operations Center, the terminal displays, the phones and the host of people who worked for AirBox, who had done their best to manage a disaster that would have made 9/11 look like a parking-lot fender-bender if it had succeeded, and he just closed his eyes. Couldn't take it anymore.

'Good job, Brian. A real good job.'

'No, not really. It was a fuck-up. A while ago I knew something was hinky with Adrianna. I should have done more, done better, done it sooner. That's all.'

Monty slapped him on the back of his neck. 'Brian, you fret too much. You did all right. For a cop.'

Brian said, 'I'm supposed to take that as a compliment?'

'Take it any way you like it.'

He rubbed at the back of his neck. 'Somehow, I don't think I'm gonna be a cop this time next week.'

Monty said, 'Don't worry. Anything happens, I'll set you up somehow. You've got balls and brains – and a couple of gunshot bruises to the chest. A hell of a combination.'

'Thanks.'

Monty yawned and said, 'Speaking of Adrianna, I wonder where that little minx is right now.'

'Out there, I'm sure.'

'Yeah . . . man, if she ever gets caught, I just want ten minutes with her. Ten minutes.'

'What do you mean, if?'

Monty laughed. 'Man, that was one smart bitch. You

telling me she didn't have a bag of plans, ready to get her ass out of here?'

Brian said, 'Maybe so. But she's still going to get caught.'

'Hell of a large country. Hell of a large world, Brian.'

Brian shook his head. 'She's going to get caught. Guaranteed. But one thing.'

'What's that?'

'You don't get first crack at her. I do.'

Monty shrugged. 'Considering the bitch shot you and all, yeah, I'll give you that.'

'Good,' Brian said. 'Glad to win one once in a while.'

With less than an hour to go to the Canadian border, Adrianna Scott felt a burning sense of frustration at the news coming from her radio, for it seemed like things weren't going her way, not at all. As she tried to find a different channel to listen to, there was a roaring noise that made her head snap back and—

A black Kiowa helicopter, landing in the road in front of her, men coming out and—

BANG!

Somehow, they had something that shattered the windshield and side windows and—

The engine died. She scrambled around, trying to get out, trying to move and—

Black-jumpsuited men were on her, spraying something in her face, something that confused her and made her eyes burn, and now she was on the side of the road, coughing and hacking.

One of the men removed his face mask, knelt down beside her.

'Adrianna Scott, in the name of the United States of America, I place you under arrest.'

'But . . . but . . . this is a mistake. Look at my driver's license. My name is Dolores Benjamin. There's been a mistake!'

Another man came into view, dropped one of her bags on the ground. He poked around in the bag, took out a little pin with a thick metal head on one end.

She instantly recognized it. A Mark 10 tracking device. She looked back at her bag, and—

Now she remembered.

Back at the hotel room, with Brian. When she went into the bathroom the bag had been on the bed.

When she had come out of the bathroom the bag had been on the floor.

Brian had bugged her. The bastard.

The man said, 'Adrianna Scott, you have the right to—'

'The name isn't Adrianna Scott!' she spat at him. 'My name is Aliyah Fulenz.'

The man grinned at her as she was helped up and shackles were placed about her ankles and handcuffs on her wrists.

'Adrianna, Dolores, Aliyah, I don't give a shit – all I know is that your ass now belongs to us.'

And as she was brought to her feet, the man leaned in and said, 'You're ours, princess.'

CHAPTER FORTY

The room had no air-conditioning, and it was stifling hot. Brian Doyle walked in and there she was, sitting in front of

him, her hands cuffed to a metal ring centered in the middle
of a table. She had on an orange jumpsuit, her hair had been
cut short, and her skin was rough. No make-up or beauty
products allowed, he thought, as he pulled up a chair and sat
across from her.

'Well,' he said. 'Was I that lousy in bed that you had to
shoot me afterwards?'

She looked tired, sullen. 'How long have you been thinking of that little joke?'

'A while,' Brian admitted. 'Thought you'd smile, at least.'

'You thought wrong.'

'I guess I did. About a lot of things.'

She moved her hands, the chain clanking some. 'Why are
you here?'

'To see you, face to face. To ask you why. The usual.'

'Hah. The usual.' She leaned forward and said, 'They
showed us a movie the other night. A rare treat, I am told.
So what kind of movie did they show us? *Ben-Hur*. Can you
imagine that, with the population they have here, that they
would show such a movie?'

'I can imagine almost anything. But to get back to my
original—'

'No, don't you see? I am answering your question, Brian.
There is a scene in that movie, early on, when Judah Ben-
Hur meets an old Roman friend. They talk politics. Ben-Hur
talks about his hatred of Rome, and he says, "The day Rome
falls, there will be such a shout of freedom across the
world . . ." That's why I did what I did, Brian. The day
America falls, there will be such a shout across this globe,
from Pakistan to Russia to France to Vietnam, so on and so
on. You have no idea of the hate, the deep and unabiding
hatred that so many have for you. Your trade policies destroy

small farmers in Kenya and Malaysia. Your chemical companies pollute in countries like India and Zimbabwe. Your media companies turn women around the world into whores. Brian, your America is a large elephant, blundering its way through history, caring not whom you trample, whom you kill, as you pillage and rampage. The world hates you, Brian. The entire world. Don't you see that?'

Brian looked at that sharp face, wondered how he had ever been attracted to her. 'I don't care,' he said. 'I don't come from the world. I come from New York City. And if it wasn't for us, the world would—'

She tried to raise a hand but the chain stopped her. 'Yes, I know. You are so generous. You are a beacon for the world, the shining example, the shining light of freedom. You defeated fascism, communism, and you fool yourself that you are on your way to defeating radical Islam. But you are so alone . . . your so-called friends laugh at you, your so-called allies work to make deals with your enemies, all to isolate you, to keep you confused . . . you are in the throes of destruction, Brian. Like a wounded elephant that is too stupid to know that it's about to die.'

Brian said, 'Pretty bold talk for a woman in your position, whatever your name is. We're an odd country, with even odder people, but we're resilient. Most of the time we're underestimated. Ask the Germans. Ask the Japanese. Ask the Russians.'

'Ah, but look what I did.'

'And what was that? You gave Wall Street a jolt, bankrupted one company, destroyed four aircraft, directly or indirectly caused the deaths of scores of people . . . not much return on such a long investment, from when you were a Baghdad teenager. '

She smiled. 'Ah, but enough.'

'Really?'

'Truly. Here's a secret, my friend. You and yours have to be lucky, all the time. All the time. Those who follow me, wherever they are, they just have to be lucky once. And, trust me, they *will* keep trying. And, trust me, they *will* be lucky.'

Brian said, 'Someone once said that God looks out for fools, drunks, and the United States of America. I like that saying better. And that's what I'm going to leave you with, Adrianna. Or Aliyah, whichever you prefer.'

He got up, made to leave, and then he turned and said, 'For what it's worth, that night we had . . .'

She shook her head. 'Spare me, Brian. It was nothing to me. Nothing.'

He said, 'You know, I almost pity you, Adrianna. You let all that hate eat you up, year after year, crippling you, changing you . . . You could have done so much with all that strength, all those smarts, if it wasn't for the hate. Yeah, I almost pity you, Adrianna.'

Brian Doyle leaned forward, over the desk, looking down at her. 'Almost.'

Then he left.

She waited for the Marine guards to come in and take her back to her cell, and she felt her legs and arms quivering with emotion. The talk with Brian had disturbed her more than she had let on, for she had felt something when she had seen him.

Utter and total defeat.

And as she was finally led back to her cell by the large and unsmiling Marine guards, she tried to apologize again to mama and papa, for letting them down. But strange music distracted her, strange music caused her to stop everything and look up at the small hill above the prison.

It had been a favor, but once the news had been sent around to the right people Brian could have done pretty much anything he wanted to do, which was why he was here at Camp Delta, Guantánamo Bay, Cuba, playing his bagpipes. The tune this time seemed to make his hair rise straight up as he stood there, playing for Adrianna, playing for the other prisoners down there, playing for the Marine guards, some of whom stood in a respectful half-circle, watching him.

The sound of the pipes seemed to carry out in the tropical air, the keening and whining cutting right through him, and he played the tune twice, conscious only at the end that he was weeping, which upset him, for he had never cried, not once, while playing the pipes at all those funerals that had haunted that fateful September.

Then he was done. The pipes fell silent. He stood there, sweating, looking at the camp buildings and the cell blocks where the enemies of America awaited their fate.

'Sir?' came a voice.

Brian turned. A young Marine stood there, ramrod-straight, and he said, 'Sir . . . if you don't mind, what was that tune you were playing? I've never heard it before.'

Brian tucked the silent bagpipes under his arm and said, 'In the original Gaelic, it's called "Cogadh no Sith." It was made famous by a piper named Kenneth MacKay, who served with the 79th Cameron Highlanders during the Battle of Waterloo in 1815.'

'No shit. Really?'

'Really. The Highlanders were set up in a square, waiting for the French forces to counterattack. It was a desperate time. Nerves were on edge. Men were gripping their muskets, waiting for the charge. And Piper MacKay, he stepped out beyond the square of soldiers, beyond his comrades, and stood out there on the battlefield. Alone. And he marched around the square, playing "Cogadh no Sith". Taunting the enemy to come out and fight. Which was what they did. And when the day was over, the French were defeated.'

The Marine nodded. 'Some story. The tune . . . what's it called again?'

'"Cogadh no Sith."'

'What does that mean?'

Brian said, 'It means "War or Peace."'

'"War or Peace." Hell of a choice.'

Brian looked at the confident face of the Marine, at his comrades lined up behind him, at the base here and everywhere else, out there in the big wide world that was more than New York City, much more.

War or peace.

'Yeah,' he said to the young Marine. 'Hell of a choice. Only one we got.'

CHAPTER FORTY-ONE

Days later and miles away, a man was admitted to a waiting area at an embassy in Ottawa. As he sat down he crossed his legs, relaxed. He examined the magazines on the counter before him, tossed a couple aside. There was just one thing he wanted to read.

He reached into his coat pocket, took out the tiny clipping, something taken from a *USA Today* last week. With all the news these past few days, he was surprised that the story had gotten any play. But he was glad to see it. Always nice to see a loose end tied up.

The door to the office opened up. A man with a closely-trimmed beard, white shirt buttoned at the collar with no necktie, and a black suitcoat came out.

'I am ready for you,' the man said.

'Very well,' he said, standing up and putting the clipping away, the story of a mysterious accident outside Memphis the night the AirBox flights had taken off, an accident involving a Ford Explorer that had blown up, the body of its driver burned beyond recognition.

Ah yes, the driver, whoever he had been, had no doubt thought he had been so lucky to find a brand-new Ford SUV with the keys in it and a full tank of gas.

Luck. It was where you found it, it was where you made it. He had gotten this far and survived for so long not by trusting in others, especially unseen others, no matter how generous their pay had been.

Inside the office he noted the flag behind the man's desk, the flag of the Islamic Republic of Iran.

'My name is Vladimir Zhukov,' he announced, 'and I have a business proposition for you.'

'Very good,' the man said. 'We are eager to hear it.'

6 DAYS

Brendan DuBois

A week is a long time in politics but six days can
destroy democracy.

It should be the happiest of days for former special forces
agent Drew Connor. Out walking in New Hampshire's
White Mountain range with his girlfriend Sheila Cass, he
has butterflies in his stomach and an engagement ring in
his pocket. Then a thunderstorm hits, and they take
shelter in what Sheila thinks is a relay station for a state
utility. But when Drew enters the building, he realises they
have stepped into something far more sinister.

Bullet-proof checkpoints. Telephone hotlines. A sign by a
map that reads 'INTERNMENT CENTRES'. Drew's
instinct is to get Sheila out as quickly as possible, and
when they stop at a general store, and the police open fire
without asking questions, his worst fears are confirmed.

Someone wants them dead for what they have seen . . .

'This is a fascinating addition to the world of
"what if?" fiction'
The Times

ISBN 978-0-7515-4806-8

BETRAYED

Brendan DuBois

When Jason Harper's doorbell rings late at night, he can scarcely believe who is standing on his porch: Roy, his elder brother, who three decades earlier went to Vietnam as a pilot, and never returned, presumed 'missing in action'.

Where has he been? Why hasn't he contacted them? When Roy is insistent that no one should know he is there, Jason suspects that something strange is going on. And then two further visitors arrive – the sort that don't bother to knock – and his worst possible fears are realised . . .

Jason may be a successful local newspaper editor, but nothing can prepare him for the astonishing story his brother reveals. It is a scandal as explosive as Watergate, and one that powerful and sinister forces will stop at nothing to keep secret. Jason soon realises that by helping Roy he is putting his own life in terrible danger, but after all these years he can't let his brother down . . .

ISBN 978-0-7515-3418-4

GIDEON

Russell Andrews

When they asked him to be a ghost writer, he didn't realise that they wanted him dead.

Struggling writer Carl Granville is hired to turn an old diary, articles and letters – in which all names and locations have been blanked out – into compelling fiction. But Carl soon realises that the book is more than just a potential bestseller. It is a revelation of chilling evil and a decades-long cover up by someone with far-reaching power. He begins to wonder how the book will be used, and just who is the true storyteller.

Then – suddenly, brutally – two people close to Carl are murdered, his apartment is ransacked, his computer stolen, and he himself is the chief suspect. With no alibi and no proof of his shadowy assignment, Carl becomes a man on the run. He knows too much – but not enough to save himself . . .

'A fast-moving thriller in the Grisham genre'
Sunday Telegraph

ISBN 978-0-7515-4585-2